The Cambridge Diaries
A Tale of Friendship, Love and Economics

The Cambridge Diaries
A Tale of Friendship, Love and Economics

C N Barton

JANUS PUBLISHING COMPANY
London, England

First Published in Great Britain 2006
by Janus Publishing Company Ltd,
105-107 Gloucester Place,
London W1U 6BY

www.januspublishing.co.uk

Copyright © 2006 by C. N. Barton
The author has asserted his moral rights

British Library Cataloguing-in-Publication Data
A catalogue record for this book
is available from the British Library

ISBN 1 85756 666 1

Cover Design: Michael Hopson
Printed and bound in Great Britain

This book is dedicated to Mum for years of love, support and cups of tea, and to Claire for changing my life in more ways than she will ever know. I love you both so much.

First Term – September 2000

It was the sound of her voice and the harsh smell of freshly brewed coffee that awakened him from his familiar dream about falling. He swore quietly to himself, not because he was annoyed at anything in particular, but because swearing had become an integral part of his early morning ritual; as necessary to get the day up and running as breathing and opening his eyes. Body and mind would have gladly welcomed at least another two hours peaceful slumber, and normally he would have been powerless to resist. On this late summer morning, however, as the sun crept into the room through the rose-coloured curtains, some other force drew back the duvet and coaxed his heavy, sleep-laden body out of the cosy, warm bed. Movement was a chore, but through his weariness he was grateful, for after today he did not know when he would see her again.

Chapter 1

A lot of people said a lot of different things when I told them I was thinking about it. My teachers at school said it would be a wonderful and enlightening experience for me. My Mum said it would hopefully lead to a ridiculously high-paid job so she could retire and go and live somewhere a little hotter than Preston. My friends said it would turn me posh and gay. I wasn't sure what to think. In the end, I applied.

Chapter 2

I'd love to say that the journey down had been fun, but if the truth had been told, it hadn't. Long car journeys with my Mum rarely were. One of the problems was our differing taste in music. Basically, mine was good, and hers was nothing short of awful. John's car had one of those six-CD multi-changer things, and Mum and I were permitted to load three CDs each. And "load" was definitely the operative term, because some of Mum's CDs were certainly lethal weapons. Whereas I had selected a broad range of beautiful music from The Beatles to Coldplay, calling in at Bob Dylan and Badly Drawn Boy along the way, Mum had opted for (*The Love Album – 40 Love Songs Straight From The Heart,*) and its two equally painful sequels. The CD player was set to random mode, and I felt like I was playing a game of Russian roulette as I watched the digits spin round and round. I found myself unable to enjoy any of my songs, as I knew that, by the law of averages, Lionel Richie, and a subsequently slow and excruciating death, was only moments away. When Ronan Keating started going on about a roller coaster, I nearly opened up the car door and jumped out.

The second problem was the system that decided who sat where. Now, as John was driving, he had a pretty legitimate claim on one of the front seats. However, seeing I was a good eight inches taller than my Mum, I reckoned my case for the extra leg-room in the front was significantly stronger than hers. But, of course, Mum feels sick when she sits in the back of cars, and Mum is boss, and so it was I that was forced to endure 240 cramped-up minutes spent sharing the back seat of a Vauxhall Astra with two large suitcases, a duvet and a desk lamp. To make matters worse (I can hear the violins playing) the desk lamp was precariously perched on top of one of the suitcases, and chose to constantly remind me of its presence by thrusting its base into my head every time we turned a corner. My only respite was the time it took us each to eat a greasy, but nevertheless very tasty, bacon-double-cheeseburger in a service station just past Birmingham. And so, when we eventually turned into the car park of St. Catharine's College, Cambridge, on an otherwise unremarkable Saturday afternoon in the late September of 2000, I had no blood left in my legs, permanently scarred ear drums and a couple of butterflies tumbling around in my stomach.

A Tale of Friendship, Love and Economics

There was no time to attempt to cure any of the above ailments, as no sooner had the car stopped, than Mum leapt into action.

"Come on Josh, stop being so lazy!"

This was an all too familiar phrase. Variety would be found in the command that followed, selected by my Mum from a list of about fifteen, including such gems as: don't leave your dirty washing in your room, put it in the machine, don't leave your mug on the table, put it in the sink, and (who could forget) don't leave the newspaper on the floor, put it in its proper place. Music to my ears, from a sound-track that seemed to play all day, every day. Today's command was a new release, chosen to fit our new surroundings.

"Quickly go and find out where we, or should I say you and John, have to carry all your stuff to."

"Yes, Mother, anything you say, Mother."

Mum hated being called Mother.

I heaved my aching limbs out of the car, breathed in a gulp of fresh Cambridge air and headed towards the narrow stone archway that stood at the end of the car park. I felt like a lost little child who doesn't want to be found just yet as I wandered around, hands in my pockets, and head swinging loosely at the end of my neck. I had been here once before for my interview, but I had been too nervous to notice anything back then. Now my eyes were wide open, trying to take in every detail of this new world I found myself in. Having ventured through the archway, I followed the little path around, being careful not to trample on any precious flowers or trip over my own feet and make an idiot of myself.

My eyes soon fell upon what would later come to be known to me as Sherlock Court. Cambridge was very keen on its courts, and most colleges housed a family of at least two or three. In the family of St. Catharine's College, Sherlock Court was the shy little sister of Main Court, preferring to spend her days hidden out of sight, as opposed to flaunting her wares in front of the gazing public. The dominant feature of the Sherlock Court was the grass, neatly cut, and laid in an L-shape across the ground. This smooth carpet of green was bordered by a combination of paths, plants, soil and bushes, and was shut off from the rest of the world by the surrounding buildings. Some of these buildings looked old, some looked new, some were a nice sandy colour and some were a dirty white. I was about to avert my eyes from the surrounding buildings when I found myself pausing for thought.

Any two-year old who wasn't blind could have come up with that last remark. Surely I could do better. After all, I was at Cambridge now, and it was about time I started producing profound observations on such matters. I stared at the buildings again. Most of them had doors, but that wasn't much better. I was no architect, but the buildings had a few too many windows for my liking. Yes, too many windows. Maybe that was symbolic of the importance of an open mind, or clear thinking, or something deep like that. Great point, Josh. I wondered if it was too late to transfer to a philosophy degree.

Sufficiently satisfied at my own brilliance, I made my way around the court towards the Porter's Lodge. I had been in this building twice before; once to ask where my interview was, and then a few minutes later to ask where the toilet was. The Porter's Lodge (or "plodge" as people in Cambridge liked to call it) played an extremely important role in college life. It was the heart of the college and – according to the porters anyway – the brains as well. Whether you wanted a gym pin, to report something lost, to book a squash court, to report a disturbance, or if you had lost your keys, then the Plodge was the place you came. If you wanted to pick up your mail from the pigeon holes (a few of us referred to these as the "p-holes", but sadly that never really took off in the way "Plodge" did), you would have to go through the Plodge. And, of course, the Plodge housed the Porters – "college gatekeepers and guardians of good behaviour," if you want the official definition, "a strange breed of men with the ability to sense fun within a thirty-mile radius and extinguish it within a second," if you want the truth. I reckoned that a Porter would be just the man to inform me as to the location of my room and present me with a key, and so I tentatively approached the office.

"Hello, I'm Josh Bailey."

"Really?"

"Erm... yes... and I'd like to sign in please... so I can get my room key."

The Porter sighed as if I'd just asked him the run a marathon with an elephant on his back. He was an elderly man, tall and skinny, with a thin mop of grey hair and silver glasses that sat at the very end of his nose. The few porters I had seen on the telly all had bowler hats. This one seemingly possessed neither a hat, nor the ability to smile. After a few moments of frowning he begrudgingly stood up and slowly made his way over to a shelf containing a set of large, heavy-looking books.

A Tale of Friendship, Love and Economics

"What name was it?"

"Bailey, Josh Bailey."

I'd always liked the way I had the same initials as James Bond, and was always glad of the opportunity to announce my name in that way. My new friend, the Porter, didn't seem all that impressed, and so I quickly shelved plans to ask for my room key shaken, not stirred. He slowly made his way back across the office to his chair and thudded down upon his desk a book labelled "A–C". After pausing for either breath or effect, he opened up the book and impatiently leafed through the pages looking for my name, going too far one way and then too far the other. Browns, Brooms, Braithwaites, Badleys, Bagguelys, were all rapidly by-passed until the book rested open on a page headed "Bailey, Joshua." The Porter slapped down a dated stamp in one of the squares on the page and instructed me to place my signature on it. This was a simple enough task, so as I did it I tried my hand at some small talk.

"You must be busy this time of year," I offered as an opener.

"We're busy all year," he replied dryly.

I produced a sound that was part giggle, part snort. I sounded like a pig with a cold, and quickly followed this up with a cough to try and cover it up. The Porter carried on like a well-drilled machine operating on auto-pilot.

"Here are your two keys. This one opens your room. This one is a 242 key. It opens the other doors that you will need, especially the front and the back doors to get into and out of college at night. If you lose either key, but especially the 242 key we will have to change a hell of a lot of locks, and you will have to pay a hell of a lot of money. Your room is M14, which is out of this door, across Sherlock Court, and through the door with marked 'M'. Is that clear… Mr Bailey?"

"M14. Isn't that some type of gun?"

Nice one, Josh. The question displays knowledge, quick thinking, a willingness to participate in pleasant conversation, and, most importantly, the fact that you have posed it as a question and not a statement acts as a gesture that you look upon this Porter as a fountain of knowledge. Moreover, I had heard that a lot of these Porters were ex-Army, and thus would love any talk of guns. Yeah, nice one, Josh, I smiled in anticipation of his response.

The reply came not in the form of words, but in a disdainful raising of the eyebrows. Before I could say thank you, or think of a better question to ask, the Porter had moved on to dealing with the girl standing behind me, a girl with ribbons in her hair who was dressed the same as her mother and had the nose of her father. I never found out why the second key in my hand was called a 242 key, but the popular rumour that if you lost it, all the locks in college were changed and you had to pay £3000 (a hell of a lot of money indeed) was proved to be, thankfully, a scare story.

With keys gripped firmly in hand, I returned to the car park to pick up Mum and John, and some of my stuff. Bags and adults collected, I made my way to the room that would be my new home for the whole of the year.

Access to my room involved mounting two flights of stairs in M-block; easy enough carrying nothing, or even with the two pillows Mum had generously burdened herself with, but not so straightforward with a heavy suitcase tugging away at the end of each arm and a couple of jumpers wrapped around my neck. By the time I reached my door – the first door I came across after weaving like a snake through the narrow corridors and reaching the summit of the second flight of stairs – I was sweating and completely knackered.

There were two black stickers that stood out prominently on the outside of the white door. "14" and "Bailey J" they read.

It was with a slight trembling of the hand that I placed my newly acquired key into the lock and turned it. If this room turned out to be a hovel the size of a shoe box, I knew I would be faced with the awkward situation of Mum rushing to bring to my attention its good points ("Isn't this nice and cosy? I mean, you wouldn't want it too big, would you Josh? You might lose things"), and I would be forced to dutifully play along with the game of self-deception. Thankfully, the room was far more spacious than I could have imagined. Indeed, if you wanted a word to describe it, then look no further than "big". It was a rectangular room with the door tucked away in the corner, and the room opened up both in front of me and to the right. It had a sink just by the door, two big windows, a large wooden desk, two wooden wardrobes, and a single bed. What more could you want? The most pleasing feature for me was the gap under the wooden desk, between the left-most edge and the three draws on the right. It was obviously designed to fit a chair in, but more importantly it formed a perfectly sized mini football goal for me to practice free-kicks and re-create classic goals to my heart's content (in private, of course). For as long as I had possessed the ability to walk and swing my foot I had, perhaps understandably, been banned from kicking my mini football around the house. However, whenever my house-proud Mum was at out at work, the lounge was quickly transformed into Wembley Stadium, with the door as the goal, and a few vases as defenders. Now I had my very own pitch to play on.

A combination of a slight stuffiness in the room, my dangerously increased body temperature from the exertion of a few moments ago and a wish to subtly convey that this was my room and I made the decisions compelled me to open up one of the two large windows. A couple of minutes later I was still trying to get it open. We didn't have windows like this back in Preston. It was a window divided into two parts, and had to be opened by sliding the heavy wooden frame of the bottom half up and behind the wooden frame of the top half. The verb "slide" makes the process sound smooth and simple. It was not. By the time I had summoned up all my remaining strength to force up the stupid wooden frame, I was twice as hot as before with a heart that appeared to believe it was providing the beat for a speed-garage track. At least I had finally got it open. All on my own.

As I lay dying on the floor, I noticed that Mum and John seemed quite impressed with the room. Mum was stretching her arms out like she was pretending to be an aeroplane, and John was walking around the room, tapping walls and nodding his head. During the summer I had been sent a form, which asked me to select the price band I wanted my room to be in. I had gone for the "medium" option of £350 to £410, and it later transpired that at £410 a term, I had got a good deal with my not-so-little M14. The *en suites* were about £100 a term more expensive, but I knew I could put the saved money to better use. Anyway, sharing a shower was not such a big deal. It sounded like a good way to meet people. Also, as much as I kidded myself at the time, deep down I knew that if push came to shove, and I really really needed to go, I would quite happily, for want of a better expression, take a piss in my sink.

The next couple of hours were spent bringing the rest of my stuff up from the car and unpacking. Despite being caught up in my imminent independence, I was sensible enough to follow my Mum's advice concerning the optimum location for boxer shorts, socks and T-shirts. I put myself in charge of setting up my TV, video and CD player, and arranging all my CDs. I even put on a nice little Beatles number to provide the soundtrack to our unpacking experience.

At about 7 pm we were finished. I took a moment to look around my room. Whenever I fixed my eyes on my books and files, or my TV and CDs, I was reminded of my bedroom at home. Whenever I stared at the sink, the blank white walls, and most importantly, the little bed in the corner, I felt like I could have been standing in the room of a complete stranger.

"You'll get used to it, Josh."

"I know I will, Mum."

And with that I picked up my mobile and my wallet, with the two new keys swinging and clinking merrily on its inside, closed the door of M14, and led the way down the stairs of M-block, my new home.

Mum and John asked me if I wanted to go out and get some food with them, but I politely declined, partly because I had arranged to meet an old school friend that night, and partly because I did not want to prolong the goodbye any longer than was necessary. I joked that with the fridge stocked up with food and all my clothes unpacked, Mum had served her purpose. Under normal circumstances my misplaced humour would have gone down well, and at worst had a neutral affect, but Mum was clearly feeling high levels of emotion at leaving her only son all alone for the first time. The tears started coming, and I gave her a big hug and a kiss.

"Call me to let me know you've got home, okay?" I whispered to Mum. I couldn't quite make out her exact reply, but I got the gist of it. "I'll be fine, Mum. Please don't worry."

After a minute or so I offloaded her onto John, and after shaking his hand and thanking him for driving me down here, I watched and waved as they made their way across the car park to the car and drove away. Next time I would see them would be Christmas

Chapter 3

Time for a bit of a history lesson. Cambridge University is made up of thirty-one colleges, of which St. Catharine's is but one. Residents of M-block tended to be pretty well informed about the history of their college, and could readily be relied upon to produce a date, fact, or anecdote to impress or bore any visitors. This was because in the summer months, and on the few bright winter weekends, the open-top tour bus would drive under our windows on the streets below, with various pre-recorded facts and figures

A Tale of Friendship, Love and Economics

leaking out from the loud-speaker into our rooms and into our ears. St. Catharine's is Cambridge's ninth-oldest college, having been founded by Robert Woodlark, third Provost of King's, in 1473 (Peterhouse College is the oldest, having been around since 1284). The reason it is spelt with an A instead of the traditional E is that the college is named after Catharine of Alexandria, and that's how she spelt her name. Now, there is a good story about old Catharine. She was condemned to be crucified on a wheel – undoubtedly a very painful death indeed – but when she touched it on the day of her execution, it miraculously broke. It was not all smiles for our Catharine with an A however, as they decided to behead her soon after, and unfortunately her strange ability did not appear to stretch to breaking axes and guillotines. Anyway, for her apparent power over wheels they named after her both the Catharine wheel firework, as well as our little college, with our crest proudly displaying a yellow eight-spoke wheel on a red background.

In terms of numbers of students, St. Catharine's College features pretty high up on the list, with around 120 in each year. However, in terms of the area of its grounds it is pretty tiny. This means that at its best the atmosphere is cosy, and at worst claustrophobic. But at least you are forced to get to know everyone in each year, whereas in some of the more spacious colleges, you could easily go through your three years and not once bump into half of your fellow students. Also, across the university, by students and fellows alike, my little college is commonly referred to as simply 'Catz'.

Famous names that studied at St. Catharine's include the actor Sir Ian McKellen (he of *X-Men* and *Lord of the Rings* fame), the novelist Joanne Harris (she wrote *Chocolat*), the big name theatre guy Sir Peter Hall, and the *Newsnight* and *University Challenge* presenter Jeremy Paxman. St. Catharine's can also claim one of the youngest ever undergraduates. A little lad called William Wotton, who was born in 1666, apparently knew Latin, Greek and Hebrew when he was six, and came to study at St. Catharine's at age nine. I bet the smart arse was no good at football, though.

Chapter 4

The old friend in question was Kevin, a Chinese guy from my old school who happened to be a black-belt in one of the martial arts. Meeting him served the dual purpose of providing both company and protection for my first night alone on the mean streets of Cambridge. Kevin had been in my Further Maths class at school and was one of the cleverest people I knew. He specialised in science-based, technical subjects like Physics and Mechanics, whereas I preferred the descriptive (chatty/wishy-washy), less-technical (easier) subjects such as Psychology and Economics. He had chosen to go to Christ's College, like myself, on the strength of a teacher's recommendation, where he was to read Engineering over a course of four years. We agreed to meet outside the front of my college because he knew where it was, whereas I had no clue at all where Christ's was.

It was nice to see a familiar face in such unfamiliar surroundings. Moreover, it was nice to be with someone who had a few contacts and seemed to know what was going on in our new home. Kevin's sister was just starting her second year at Robinson College, and she had told her little brother just the place to eat on your first night in Cambridge. Gardi's was the name of the establishment, happily just a couple of minutes' walk from my college. It was a Greek fast-food joint that did all sorts of burgers and kebabs and Greek things that I couldn't pronounce. Thankfully, for my sake, they also did pizzas.

Before coming to university, the only meat that had crossed my lips in living memory were one McDonald's cheeseburger on a drunken night in Tenerife, and a bacon and mushroom sandwich made by Mum one morning that just smelt too good for any would-be vegetarian to resist, especially when compared to the bowl of Weetabix without sugar that I was about to tuck into. Since then I regularly ate burgers and bacon, and I had recently progressed onto sausages, so long as they didn't have any funny sauce on them (ketchup was fine, mayonnaise was the worst crime of all), but I had not dabbled, nor felt any strong inclination to, in any of the other wide variety of meats or fish that Preston's supermarkets offered. I didn't trust the grinning man behind the counter at Gardi's to resist slopping a giant dollop of white, mayonnaise-looking, sauce on any burger I should order, so I played it safe and went for a Funghi pizza (just mushrooms) and a portion of chips. I was starving. It was truly delicious.

A Tale of Friendship, Love and Economics

We consumed our food sat on a wall outside King's College, facing a row of shops, one of which had a giant teddy bear keeping guard on the pavement outside. King's College is huge, and is my lovely St. Catharine's next-door neighbour along Kings Parade. Its front stretches for well over 100 metres, and its monumental, ancient walls, and radically left-wing reputation (I would later be informed that King's only admits lesbians and members of the Communist Party) made it a favourite spot for the tourists' cameras. My college had neither the size nor reputation to rival King's. Indeed, I'm sure many tourists missed it by blinking as they strolled along Kings Parade, no doubt still mesmerised by the awe-inspiring college they had just passed. It was something of a blessing that we never had hoards of Japanese and American tourists frantically snapping at us through our large front gate armed to the teeth with their lenses and tripods as we tried to relax on the benches of Main Court. At the same time it is a great pity that you cannot capture on any photograph just what a wonderful place St. Catharine's College is.

With pizza and chips well acquainted with my stomach I needed a drink, and luckily Kevin felt them same. We tossed a coin to see whose college bar we would have a pint in. Tails rarely fails, and thus we were off back to Catz in search of the bar. Due to the size of my college and the amount of people flocking towards it, the bar was not hard to locate, and I even managed to find it on my own. Through the Plodge, take a right along Main Court, through a stone archway, bear left, go through the glass door following the sounds of the jukebox, and you are there.

Catz bar was one large room, and tonight it was bustling and busy. There were no hidden corners, and as such its entire contents could be observed within a second of entering. It appeared well-equipped, containing a pool table, arcade and quiz machines, a table-football table, a jukebox, about ten round metal tables that could comfortably fit five chairs around but any more than seven would be a tight squeeze, and of course the bar area, which took up one of the far sides of the room. A tiger also caught my eye, quietly perched above the centre of the bar, eyeing up the new cohort of students that were busy sampling their first drink in Cambridge. Again, I was later informed that this was in fact a large papier-mâché cat, the mascot of Catz. As tradition had it, whenever it was someone's birthday they had to mount the bar, heave themselves up to the level of the cat, and give it a big kiss. The birthday boy or girl usually had more than a couple of drinks on board at this stage of the night, and as such few found the sizeable climb too daunting to take on, a few lucky souls even appearing to enjoy the twelve-foot unbroken fall to the floor afterwards. I ordered a couple of pints of lager from the barman, who introduced himself as Jim; a small, balding, friendly Londoner who referred to every boy as "mate" and every girl as "darling." Pints in hand, I stood with Kevin, casually leaning against a wall, watching the wide variety of people chatting and mingling in the bar. My bar.

It was during a conversation about Blackburn Rovers that I had my first encounter with someone from my college. Just as I was politely explaining to Kevin that regardless of the amount of money they had spent in the summer they would still be shite this season, my flow was interrupted by a theatrical cough designed to attract our attention produced by a figure who was slowly coming into view through the corner of my right eye. I stopped mid-sentence, took half a step back, and turned to face him. He spoke first, as Kevin also readjusted his position to allow this character a corner of our triangle.

"Are you guys Freshers?"

"Yep," we replied, nodding simultaneously as if rehearsed.

"You don't do Maths do you?"

"I'm afraid not, mate. I do economics, and Kevin here is taking on a bit of engineering," I replied. I expected my response to dampen his spirits as I presumed he was searching for fellow mathematicians to talk about numbers and symbols with over a pint. In fact it had quite the opposite effect.

"Thank fuck for that. I've just been stuck in a conversation with a load of Maths geeks over there" he pointed, with all the subtlety of a brick in the face, but I did not look. "I was about to kill myself," he added.

An instinctive response did not spring to mind. Kevin and I both produced awkward smiles and, hoping that a suitable reply had been brewed in with the hops and barley, quickly lowered our eyes and took long slow sips of our drinks. "Sorry, I'm Adam. Adam Sylvester. Nice to meet you."

Adam Sylvester offered forward his hand and with Kevin's eyes still focusing on the beer that he had been continuously sipping on since our new friend's arrival, I took the lead and met his outstretched hand with a firm northern shake.

A Tale of Friendship, Love and Economics

"Hi, I'm Josh. Nice to meet you. Can I get you a drink?"

"Cheers, mate. I'll take a pint of lager. You're from the North, aren't you?"

"Aye. So is Kevin."

And with that I scurried off to the bar smiling, and with only the tiniest bit of guilt at the thought of leaving poor Kevin to make small talk with Mr Sylvester.

I know it is probably not wise to place so much emphasis on first impressions of people, especially in a place where I didn't know anyone. Indeed, I should have been grateful for any kind of conversation at all. However, by the time I reached the bar I had decided 100 per cent that I didn't like Adam Sylvester. I wondered what kind of person slags off someone they had just met to another person they had just met. Moreover, being seen in public with him, and thus inevitably acquiring the title of "Maths Geeks Hater Number 2" as a big brush fell from the sky and covered me in tar from head to toe, would not, I believed, be in my best interests when meeting so many people for the first time in the coming days. I returned to the conversation, pints in hand, with a degree of enthusiasm normally reserved for visiting the dentist.

From the standard pleasantries of first-time conversation it transpired that Adam Sylvester had Sri-Lankan parents, lived in Croydon – a town in south London (which to me and Kevin simply meant he was a southerner) – and was studying History. He was a stocky lad, standing a couple of inches under six feet but probably weighing as much as me, and he wore clothes far cooler than anything Kevin and I had on. He liked cricket, rugby, and DJs who I had never heard of. He was not at all posh, with his Croydon accent evident in each of his words, but he was very well spoken, and confidently maintained eye-contact throughout our conversation. I didn't like him.

For the next hour, Adam Sylvester talked, and we listened. His outstretched arm slowly rotated full-circle around the bar like the second hand on a watch as the historian of Sri Lankan origin pointed out other people he didn't like. One lad had committed the crime of having ginger hair, and another had funny ears. Throughout it all, I tried to hide behind my pint. Having apparently exhausted that little game, he asked Kevin what college he was at, and when my good friend replied "Christ's," Mr Sylvester succinctly explained that he'd heard it was shit. In what felt like a gift from the gods, Adam Sylvester's bladder finally gave way, and he went off to the toilet.

Adam Sylvester had burst my bubble somewhat, and, judging by Kevin's deflated face, he felt the same. The moment had gone. I no longer wanted to meet any more new people tonight, for fear that they might turn out to be like our friend, the Sri Lankan from Croydon. I suggested that whilst we had the chance, we could run away to his college, but Kevin announced that rather unfortunately, Christ's college bar closed each night at 8.30 pm. I asked my good friend if he was taking the piss, but his solemn expression suggested he wasn't. Apparently Christ's was very academically orientated, even for a Cambridge College, and a philosophy of "early to bed, early to rise, and don't dare have fun at any time" had been successful in keeping them right up at the top of the all-important league tables for some time now. With a simultaneous sigh, Kevin and I shuffled towards the bar, bought a couple of pints, and scurried over to a corner to drink them. It was fairly easy to be inconspicuous in a room of so many people, and thankfully Adam Sylvester failed to spot us on his return from the toilet. He was soon talking to a bulky brown-haired lad, no doubt opening up his conversation with, "You don't do economics, do you?"

As we reached the end of our drinks, I looked at Kevin, and saw that there was no need to ask the question. Lost in the middle of a sea of unfamiliar faces, and with a papier-mâché cat staring down upon us, we were all dressed up, and with nowhere to go but bed. I followed Kevin out of the bar, across Main Court, and towards the Plodge. There I shook his hand, apologised for the rather shit end to the evening, and loosely pencilled in a get-together sometime next week.

With Kevin on his way back to Christ's, I walked round the deserted Sherlock Court and marched up the stairs of M-block. Several of the rooms I passed on my way to M14 had their door on the latch, with the sound of music and voices leaking out into the corridor. A combination of shyness and tiredness stopped me from knocking on any of them. Instead, I pressed onwards to my room, stopping only to grab my bulky four-pint bottle of semi-skimmed milk, bought from my local supermarket the previous night, from the shared fridge in the shared kitchen (that lay to the immediate left out of my door if you were coming out of my room.) I was not yet sure of the personalities or numbers of the people I would be sharing this little kitchen with. As a precaution, and following the advice of my wise mother,

A Tale of Friendship, Love and Economics

I had clearly marked my precious milk and economy orange juice in thick, black felt-tip with the word: "Josh". I wrote in the unfriendliest and most intimidating writing I could muster to further deter any would-be thieves that hung out in this intellectual ghetto. I wouldn't normally be so fussy and protective over such possessions but through the years I had become so dependent upon a pint of milk before bed and four Weetabix and two glasses of nice, cold orange juice in the morning, that I dared not risk going without them. I let myself into my room, turned on the light, filled the pint glass I had brought from home right up to the top with the delicious white liquid, popped the remaining milk back into the fridge, and closed my door to the outside world. With a suitable tune on, the windows shut (happily shutting them proved to be a far easier task than opening them) and the curtains drawn, I got ready for bed.

Sporting my standard T-shirt and boxer-short bed-wear, I snuggled under the covers. With my eyes closed and pointing up to the ceiling, I stretched out my left arm, allowing my hand to manoeuvre itself around the small bedside table, generously provided by college, until it fell upon the desk lamp that had become all too acquainted with my head throughout the car journey that afternoon. My index finger pushed the plastic switch a little more firmly than normal to remind the lamp that I was still not happy with its behaviour today, and, like a naughty child sent to his room, the light abruptly disappeared leaving M14 in complete darkness save the green flashing digits on the video player whose time I had not yet got around to setting. I was alone, free from distraction, with only the occasional hum of passing traffic from the street outside my window to remind my ears of their role in my body. It was the end of my first day in Cambridge, surely a perfect time to collect my thoughts, and reflect upon what I had learnt so far.

Unfortunately, I found I had nothing really to reflect about. St. Catharine's College and Cambridge itself seemed nice enough, but I hadn't had sufficient time to find things about them I really liked or disliked. As for the people, well I had only come into contact with a few. The Porter didn't really seem to have taken a shine to me, but I had plenty of time to sort that out. Kevin was a nice guy, but I already knew him, and Adam Sylvester wasn't, and I never wanted to see him again. I would not say I was worried about meeting a load of new people tomorrow. Most of the time, I like meeting new people. All the things my friends at high school said about the people at Cambridge were exactly the same as what my friends at primary school had said my friends at high school were going to be like when I went to a different one to everyone else. And they turned out to be okay. At the same time, I wouldn't say I was really excited by the prospect. I almost wished I could fast-forward my life about four weeks. ("You should never wish your life away, Josh," I could hear my Mum say,) when I would know people well enough to have proper conversations and not the *Blind Date* classic: "So, what's your name, and where do you come from?" that I would inevitably be forced to endure over and over again in the coming weeks. I thought briefly about my friends back home, but then realised that I had seen most of them this morning so not enough time had yet elapsed for me to miss them. I hunted around for my mobile and re-read the text message Mum had sent me about an hour ago letting me know she and John had got back safely, but even that failed to trigger off any kind of feelings (apart from a tiny chuckle that "modern" Mum had again tried to use predictive text messaging but once more had not checked what was on the screen, such that the intended: ("call me soon. love Mum") came out: ("call of room. love nun") Out of desperation I tried forcing a voice inside my head to begin questioning whether I had made a huge mistake coming to Cambridge, but another voice simply replied, "I don't know, leave me alone." In the end I resigned myself to the fact that I just couldn't instigate a moment of deep reflection. It was time to sleep.

To my dismay, I discovered that I was now wide-awake. For some reason my lack of reflection had stimulated my mind. Moreover, the pint of milk had worked its way quickly through my system and I now needed the toilet. Once again I searched for the desk lamp. As quickly as there was darkness, there was light, and after blinking a few times, I rolled myself out of bed. The heavy wooden door of M14, shut and locked itself automatically, and if I had have been a bit more sleepy I would have definitely forgotten to pick up my keys and take them with me, thus locking myself out, and the obligatory trip to see my friends the porters would have ensued. This was a prospect I certainly did not fancy, not on the first night, and especially not when dressed in boxers and an old yellow T-shirt with a hole in the left armpit.

The toilet itself, located just to the right of my room, was not exactly of five-star quality. It was a room no more than six feet long and three feet wide. There was a sink with no towel or hand-dryer, which meant that the door-handle was either constantly wet or worryingly dry. The toilet itself

A Tale of Friendship, Love and Economics

probably started life being white, but in the centuries that had passed since its construction, its outer skin had metamorphosed into a multi-shaded, multi-stained, dirty colour. The toilet seat was plastic and black, and should have come fitted with a seatbelt and been marked on tourist maps as Cambridge's only white-knuckle ride. As soon as you sat down you were swaying and sliding from left to right, frantically pressing your palms firmly against both sidewalls to keep yourself from toppling over. In the room next to the toilet was a bathroom containing a bath, shower and sink. At first glance the bath appeared to come with a fitted carpet, but experience soon told that this was merely clumps of hairs that failed to make their way down the blocked plug hole. Throughout the year the M-block residents often participated, either privately or as a group, in the game 'Guess Who Owns the Hair'. However, the game soon lost its appeal, and we began taking showers on the floors above and below, when we discovered a few short grey stands nestling within the collage of hairs. Suddenly, the £100-a-term-extra *en suite* didn't look too bad an option.

Having relieved myself, I went back into my room. Sleep still seemed at least an hour away, so I decided to keep myself occupied by tuning in my telly. For a brief moment whilst we were packing up my stuff back in Preston I contemplated leaving my TV at home. This ridiculous thought was soon banished into exile when I considered being parted from soaps, football, reality TV shows and Teletext. So, from the comfort of my bed, with remote control in hand and my head rested against the elevated pillow, I set about tuning in the TV. To my horror, no matter how much I tried, the picture for BBC1 and Channel 4 were completely unwatchable. My brain immediately began running through exactly which shows this tragic occurrence, should it prove permanent, would deprive me of: *Eastenders, Neighbours, Friends, South Park, Brookside, Hollyoaks, Match of the Day,* any new series of *Big Brother.* The list was endless. Life would not be worth living.

Whilst fighting back the tears, I flicked around the remaining three channels to find something to watch. Channel 5 had breasts, ITV had adverts, but fortunately, BBC2 had *Lennon Night.* Jo Whiley was presenting interviews and live performances from a load of big-name musicians who were fans of the late great Beatle. I happily watched and listened to the Stereophonics, a few members of the Rolling Stones and then, thank the Lord, my childhood hero Liam Gallagher. The lovely Ms Whiley asked Liam what Lennon meant to him. The great twentieth century philosopher, and

17

my idol for many a year, replied something along the lines of, "You know, man, he's like the fucking alphabet. I mean, he's me A, and me B, and me C. He's the reason me feet move. D'you know what I mean?" Ms Whiley pretended she did and moved swiftly on.

Fortunately, as *Lennon Night* drew to a close with the last few bars of *All You Need Is Love*, tiredness fell upon me, and I turned my little portable telly off. I had just about enough consciousness left to say my prayers, and then as I sunk into my pillow, pulled the cover up tight, and turned to face the wall that the right-hand side of the bed was pressed firmly against, I drifted off into a deep, deep sleep. One day down, three years to go.

Chapter 5

I had set no alarm. There was no need. When I finally awoke I had no real indication of what time of the day my mobile phone would be displaying on its screen. I reckoned on 9am, maybe 9.45 am at the absolute latest. I scrambled around for my phone, hindered by the fact that my left eye was refusing all orders to open, and my right eye was functioning at about 42 per cent. 11.47 announced my mobile. Shit. After I swore, it still said the same.

Getting up late when I know I've got loads of stuff to do really annoys me. I've absolutely no problem with rolling out of the scratcher post-noon on a holiday or a lazy Sunday, but when there are things to be done, I need an early start if I'm to have any hope at all at doing them. According to the *Freshers' Handbook* that had found its way through my letterbox over the summer, at 3 pm today I was meeting my Nanny, but I had a fair bit to do before that. I sighed, and looked again at my phone. Getting up at 11.47 am was as good as getting up at twelve, so I decided to pull up the covers and snuggle up in my warm bed for thirteen more precious, peaceful minutes. Yes, just thirteen little, tiny minutes, and then I'd get up. Definitely. The sound of humming traffic and chattering voices on the street outside seemed to aid my return journey to the land of nod. Thirteen minutes soon became twenty-five. I wearily looked again at my mobile. 12.12 pm, seemed like a bit of a funny time to be getting up at. Nobody ever gets up at twelve-

A Tale of Friendship, Love and Economics

past-twelve. And so it was half-past twelve before I finally got my first day at university up and running.

First things first, I needed a shower. I wasn't really in the mood for meeting anyone new just yet with my hair looking the way it always does in the morning (like it had been subject to the combined efforts of an electric shock and a blind stylist), so I was relieved to find no queue for the bathroom. There were only a few hairs lining the base of the bath, all seemed too long to be considered pubic, and the shower was hot and powerful. Water and shampoo successfully flattened my hair, and my trusted Sanex shower gel removed all remaining Preston grime from my body.

Fully dried and dressed in my favourite blue jeans and a T-shirt that had once been described by a girl as cool, I set about getting my breakfast. I had brought my cereal bowl from home down to Cambridge with me as it was one of the few I had come across in my short life that could adequately satisfy the demands of housing my daily requirement of four Weetabix. I had my breakfast sat at my new desk. I munched happily on soggy Weetabix and slurped down big mouthfuls of economy orange juice whilst tapping my foot to the sound of Bob Dylan and flicking through the football news on Teletext. Already I felt at home.

Reality soon struck when the lack of a dishwasher or a Mum meant that if I wanted to eat Weetabix tomorrow without the dried reminisces of today's batch still clinging to the sides of the bowl, I would have to wash it now. I ventured into the kitchen immediately to the left of my room, armed with the mild, green Fairy Liquid that my Mum had kindly packed for me. Whilst in the process of washing and scrubbing bowl and spoon (a quick rinse was all I was prepared to give my orange juice glass) I heard the sound of approaching voices with accompanying footsteps getting louder and louder, closer and closer.

"Right then, here's M14, so where the bloody hell is M13?"

"Its here, Dad. Next door to it."

I reckoned the voices were from the *EastEnders* part of London, wherever that was, although this was more noticeable in father than daughter. I continued washing my bowl, waiting in anticipation for the meeting that would inevitably follow.

She walked past the kitchen and glanced in my direction. I sensed her presence, and coolly removed my gaze from the murky waters towards the doorway. She was a tall, pretty girl, with strawberry blonde hair and a few

Chapter 6

The music from the bar could be heard from Main Court. It was not a great song. On the way into the bar, on the wall beside the door, a large sheet of paper had been fastened containing the passport photos, names, and subjects of all the Freshers. I had wondered why we needed to send them in over the summer, and here was my answer. I stopped and quickly scanned across the vast collection of names and faces. One boy had sent in a black and white photo of himself, taken side on, with his long, wavy hair blowing in the wind. He looked like a prick. There weren't as many double-barrelled names as I'd imagined, no Lords or Ladies, or His Royal Highnesses. There didn't appear to be any Percivals, Cuthberts or Marthas either. I managed to count up ten first-year economists, most of whom I recognised from the afternoon at the pub. Low and behold, there was even a girl economist called Leila. She looked a little bit scary. I also noticed Adam Sylvester's face staring menacing up at me. After a couple of minutes I moved on. Briefly glancing back, his eyes seemed to follow me into the bar.

The college bar was busier and louder than on the previous night. I didn't know where to start. I armed myself with a drink, and went looking for familiar faces. I found a few of the economists chatting to some people that I didn't recognise over by the pool table. I greeted them by their names that I had made a mental note of from the picture board, and threw in another handshake for good measure. I saved them the embarrassment of having forgotten mine by quickly introducing myself to the mystery members of this little group. Thankfully they were still discussing football and, seeing as I was feeling better, I took this second opportunity to make my views known. From this the conversation moved onto the recent Sydney Olympics and *Big Brother*. With regard to the latter, I was something of an expert, easily able to recite the order that the contestants were evicted. This throw away boast was challenged by the Malaysian economist, and its successful performance went down well with fellow fans in the group.

I stayed by the pool table for an hour or so, occasionally popping to the bar to get a drink, still trying to force my fussy palate to enjoy the taste of lager. People came and went, and pretty soon I had met at least one person from nearly every subject. Once you got past the initial formalities of name, subject and town of residence, the conversations were surprisingly varied and interesting, and thankfully the people, on the whole, appeared pretty freckles. As I raised my hand in a soap-sudded gesture of welcome, she rolled her eyes and walked away. Bitch, I thought, and I promptly returned to my bowl. Right, that's two fellow students I've seen and two I've taken an immediate disliking to.

"Hello. Where do you live?"

A lady who I rightly assumed was the bitch's mother now stood in the doorway recently vacated by daughter. I hadn't notice her arrival whilst I'd been silently abusing her offspring. She reminded me of a primary school teacher; quite small, with short hair and glasses.

"Erm... erm," I replied, thrown off-guard by this unexpected question. "Erm... Preston... I mean, here... I mean there... I mean M14."

Jesus Christ, Josh, I'm sure you used to be able to speak.

"Oh, that's lovely. My daughter, Mary Jane, lives in M13. You're going to be next-door neighbours," replied the Mum.

After a minute or so of small talk, where I clarified that I did come from Preston and that I could in fact speak English, and she informed me that Mary Jane came from Croydon, she returned to her unpacking, and I to my washing up. Croydon? The same place, what's-his-name, comes from. Adam Sylvester. Maybe it was just people from Croydon I should avoid in this place.

The rest of the early afternoon was spent settling in and doing a bit of boring but necessary admin. I made my way across Sherlock Court through the Porters Lodge, and down to the pigeon holes, where I found my name among hundreds of others. J. C. Bailey. I placed my hand inside the narrow, post-box-sized wooden hole, and scooped up the bundle of mail that lay waiting inside. On the way out I stopped to look at the freshers notice board just to confirm that it was at 3 pm that I was due to be picked up by my Nanny. Back in my room I examined the mail. First there was the college bill. A grand total of £643 for accommodation, kitchen fixed charge, electricity, and a 50p charity donation, that had to be paid by cheque within a fortnight (or be subject to a £25 administration charge, I was sternly informed in bold type). I put it to one side and searched for something more interesting. Next came the hefty *Student Survival Guide*, containing booklets and leaflets about the various societies, help-lines and sexually transmitted diseases that were available in Cambridge. It also contained two condoms, one of which was apparently suitable for anal sex. Other mail included appointments to meet both my tutor and Director of Studies tomorrow afternoon, pamphlets advertising various college film Societies, and a nice-looking letter addressed to a "Clare Bagley," which I begrudgingly returned to the correct pigeon hole.

3 pm came. As did 3.15 and 3.30. Finally, just before four, a knock rattled against my door. I opened it, and was faced by Trevor Starkey. My Nanny.

I feel some explaining is necessary. My Nanny, Mr Starkey, wasn't in fact a transsexual childminder, or a notorious London gangster. He was a plump, scruffy-looking lad from Newcastle. Cambridge is very keen on ensuring all first years have a senior student to look after them. Someone who can give them the kind of advice that isn't readily available from books or senior staff, someone to help them settle down as quickly as possible. Nearly all colleges practised this system in one form or another. Some had "family systems" with Mothers and Fathers (a female and male from the second year) who, by means of an immaculate conception, found themselves at the end of September with a grown-up Son and Daughter (a couple of first years) to take care of. We had Nannies and Nannettes. Trevor Starkey was my Nanny, and I was his Nannette. Nice idea. Terrible name."Hi. I'm Trevor," announced Trevor in a mumbling Geordie accent that was barely comprehensible.

"Hi, Trevor. I'm Josh, but I guess you already knew that," I replied, shaking the hand of my guardian.

Trevor Starkey had sent me a nice letter over the summer explaining that he was my Nanny, and giving me his home number in case I needed to call him about anything. He also told me a bit about himself. He was a mad keen Newcastle United supporter, and a stand-up comedian. He didn't really know why he was at Cambridge studying Economics, the letter continued, but he was aiming for a third in his finals, and then doing the comedy circuit until he made it big. My Mum thought it was was one of my friends from home taking the piss. I had replied, thanking Trevor for his letter, offering up a few boring facts about myself, and asking if it was a good idea to bring my bike down with me to Uni (I couldn't think of any good questions). Trevor then phoned me at home, at which point I embarrassingly mistook him for my mate Trevor ("Big Trev") and asked him if we were still going into town that night. My Nanny informed me that he probably wouldn't be able to make it out to Preston that night as it was a three-hour drive away, and that he had never felt the need for a bike at any stage during the last year. I took his advice and arrived in Cambridge bikeless.

"Sorry I'm a bit late, I've just got up," announced Trevor. I wasn't sure if this was a joke or the truth, he certainly looked like he might just have gotten up, but then he may have been one of those people that always looked like that. To be on the safe side I emitted a sound that was neither a laugh nor a cough, but could be passed off as either. "How've you settled... Shit. You've got a big room."

"Yeah, I'm pretty chuffed," I replied. "Hey, can I get you a drink of anything? I've got fresh orange or milk. Semi-skimmed."

"No, ta. We best get going, like. We were supposed to be at the pub with the other economists an hour or so ago."

And with that we set off to the pub, taking the back entrance out of college through the car park onto Queens Lane, and then turning right onto Silver Street.

Our first port of call was The Anchor, conveniently located only a couple of minutes away from college. It lay on the banks of the River Cam, and was sandwiched between the colleges of St. Catharine's and Queen's. The pub had a few wooden tables and benches outside that were positioned right up to the water's edge. On this reasonably sunny Sunday, the river was full of ducks and punts, and The Anchor was jammed full with Nannies and Nannettes. We forced our way through the crowds and made it in one piece to the bar area. Trevor kindly bought me a pint of lager (at this time on a Sunday, what would Mum think...) and got himself a bitter lemon, explaining that he was on a diet. Again I wondered whether this purchase was part of a sketch, and that I was once more missing the joke. You were never sure with Trevor. I followed him, sipping my pint quickly to stop it spilling, as he nudged and barged his way around the pub. Eventually Trevor found someone he knew and they informed him that the rest of the economists had already rolled on to the next pub, The Granta. Trevor quickly saw away his remaining bitter lemon in two gulps and indicated that I should do the same with my pint. Within five painful gulps my drink was gone and we were off on the road again.

If the truth be told, I was not a big drinker, and I didn't particularly like the taste of lager. I hated the smell of it on my skin and on my clothes, and I detested the stale taste it left in my mouth. I was a bigger fan of the so-called alco-pops, like Smirnoff Ice and Reef. They didn't taste like alcohol, and even tasted quite pleasant. However, I didn't think it would do my as yet un-built reputation any good to meet and greet pint-holding people with a

A Tale of Friendship, Love and Economics

colourful bottle of bright liquid – a drink usually consumed by girls and thirteen-year-old lads on park benches. No, it was about time I got a taste for lager and became a real man.

Trevor and I left the overcrowded Anchor via the back door, escaping into the Cambridge sunshine. The River Cam was still congested with punts, and its banks were packed with young men and women in waistcoats and straw hats sweet-talking out-of-town visitors into taking a guided river tour. The good weather seemed to be helping their cause as the queues began to fill up outside the little wooden punting office. The guides helped their passengers on board; the arm of an elderly lady in one hand, and a ten-foot wooden pole in the other. As we crossed the little bridge sandwiched between the back of The Anchor and another pub, The Mill, I felt as much of a visitor to this strange place as the hoards of tourists did.

The walk to The Granta was short and picturesque. The little bridge led us onto a pathway bordered on the left by a quieter section of the Cam, and on the right by a large grassy area littered with groups of people sprawled out on the grass drinking wine and pints of beer from plastic glasses, and happily smoking in the sun. Trevor, my personal guide, informed me that this was called "Beer Island." It wasn't technically an island (the river did surround it on two sides), but the "beer" part of the name seemed completely justified. As I tried to take in all that lay around me, a stream of bikes thundered passed at ferocious speed, almost as if they were fleeing the anti-bike related obscenities that followed from Trevor's mouth. He had no time for bikes. Too much exercise. Too much of a hurry. Too clever a use of physics. I smiled politely.

The Granta was equally jammed, and equally difficult to get close enough to the bar to stand any chance of getting served. I asked Trevor what he wanted to drink, and he opted to ditch the bitter lemon in favour of a pint. His diet was temporarily put on hold. I offered the stressed-looking lady behind the bar a fiver in return for the couple of carefully poured pints she had laid before me. She kindly explained that the amount due was in fact £5.60. £2.80 a pint!? Bloody southern prices. Bloody Trevor upgrading his drink as soon as it's my turn to buy. I lost a few pounds as he gained some.

There wasn't room to breathe in The Granta, so we moved outside into its courtyard. Here I was introduced to "The Economists", a group of fifteen or so all huddled around a table, with none of them electing to sit down.

The first thing that caught my eye was that there was a distinct lack of female presence. There was one girl, but she was chatting away to the rest of the group with a degree of familiarity that suggested she was a second or a third year. My college was supposed to have one of the most reasonable female – male ratios, and economics as a subject is not too low down the list of female participation. Alas, the combination of economics and Catz did not appear to attract the women. The testosterone-fuelled group that lay before me were a funny-looking bunch, but then I suppose I was pretty funny-looking too. One lad was sporting a black bowler hat. He looked like cross between the Godfather and Charlie Chaplin, with an Eastern European complexion thrown in for good measure. Another lad had a circular piece of cloth on his head, attached to his hair with a safety pin. I guessed he was Jewish, but as for the significance of his strange headgear, I was clueless. There was a Chinese-looking guy, a tall black guy, a short black guy, a nerdy-looking guy and a Craig David-looking guy. The latter was a classicist, but was hanging around with the economists as he had lost the rest of his gang. Trevor explained that not all the economists were here as there had been some "fuck-up" in the arrangements.

The second years encouraged the freshers to bond. Nannies left their little Nannettes to play alone. For the first few minutes I alternated between smiling, shaking hands, introducing myself and sipping my pint slowly (at £2.80 a pint I was in no hurry to buy another). After exchanging names and handshakes, the conversations naturally progressed to where we all came from. Every one of them was from London, apart from the Chinese-looking guy, who was from Malaysia, but had a flat in London. As a result, most of them seemed to know someone who went to one of the others' schools, or at least could pass a reasonable comment about where they lived. I had nothing really to say on the matter, and so I didn't say much. I just smiled and sipped.

By the time the conversation moved onto football, I felt I had failed to lay sufficient foundations to justify my contribution. I briefly comforted myself with the thought that I had been let down by geography. I knew this was just an excuse. I suddenly felt nervous and out of place. I felt that if I did offer some remark, however funny or insightful, I would be looked upon as a stranger, maybe acknowledged by a fleeting glance, before the group turned their attention back towards those who belonged. Of course, I was being stupid, ridiculously paranoid. These people seemed nice, and

A Tale of Friendship, Love and Economics

even if they weren't, they were certainly too polite to act in such a way at this stage. I needed a slap in the face or a kick up the arse. The problem was it was all too easy to just keep sipping my drink, keeping my mouth closed, occasionally nodding at a remark I didn't even agree with, waiting for my membership of this group to expire. I wanted to be alone. I wanted to start it all again.

I was saved by hunger. As the time rolled on to six o'clock, stomachs started rumbling, and the second years returned with talk of food back at college. We left our empty glasses and conversations in the pub, and made our way back to Catz just as the sun was thinking of calling it a day. Trevor asked me how I got on with the economists. I said fine, and that they seemed like a nice bunch. They were a nice bunch.

Back at college, everyone went off to eat food in hall. I made some excuse to Trevor about needing the toilet and scurried off to my room, explaining that I'd meet him in there later. In the safety of M14, I slumped on my bed. I did not cry. I tried to force the tears out of my eyes, thinking that such a release would make everything alright. I had not cried for years. Maybe this was not a crying situation, or maybe I had forgotten how to.

I am not a shy person. I am not a sad person. I have lots of friends. I love meeting new people. I love being in big groups, talking for hours about any old shite that pops into our heads. Most of the time. I didn't know exactly what happened back in the pub that afternoon, or why I felt so bad now, but it was certainly not the first time. Sometimes I didn't want to talk, I just wanted to be on my own. I could feel a cloud coming over me. I could see myself stood there, fully aware of what was happening. Fully aware of the consequences. Bubbling and bursting with things to say, but with no desire to say them. Sometimes I'm the loudest person in the world. Sometimes I may as well be dumb. I didn't want people here to see that side of me. Not yet, anyway.

I made myself some toast and a big cup of tea. I felt much better. In fact, I felt really good. Ready to meet and greet the whole world. When all visible signs of sadness were removed from my face, hidden away somewhere else, I made my way out of my room and headed off to the college bar.

A Tale of Friendship, Love and Economics

down to earth. I was told so many names that in the end I gave up trying to remember them. I had not yet met anyone from Lancashire, or indeed anyone who had ever been to Preston (only about 40 per cent had even heard of it). Maybe it was just my imagination, but apart from London, the second most popular place of origin appeared to be Yorkshire. I had been brought up to hate the Yorkshires, and did not expect to surrounded by so many when I was away down south, especially as I was having to defend the honour of the red rose all on my own. Some of these "fellow northerners" were surprisingly alright, although I would inevitably tell my friends back home that they were typical Yorkshire nobs. Some had apparently lived all their lives in Leeds, but had accents posher than the Queen's.

At 10.30 pm a couple of porters entered the bar and flashed the lights on and off three times. The jukebox stopped abruptly, and I wondered whether they were two DJs about to launch into their set. They weren't. They were here to shut the bar, as it was a Sunday, and the bar shut at 10.30 pm on a Sunday. People quickly finished off their drinks and their games of pool, and the metal shutters crashed down closing off the serving area. The crowd shuffled out through the door and along the corridor passed the freshers picture board. I wasn't really tired enough to go to bed yet, and I was still feeling bad about my little glitch that afternoon, so I followed a couple of people into the JCR.

"JCR" stands for "Junior Combination Room", and basically is the name of the common room for undergraduates. There is also an SCR for postgraduate members of the college, with the "S" standing for "Senior". I was never sure why the "C" in both cases did not stand for "common" instead of "combination", as that would have made more sense to me, but then this was the place that called maids "bedders", and where May Week was in June, so I shouldn't really have been surprised. Anyway, the JCR was pretty bog standard as far as common rooms go. It had a load of comfy chairs, a TV and a video. Just outside in the corridor were a couple of vending machines with the usual assortment of chocolate and fizzy drinks. There was a notice board upon which posters were attached advertising things like Christian Aid Week, the University Quiz Society and a Used Textbook Sale. The dominant colour of the JCR was blue.

There were several groups sat in the JCR when I made my entrance. There were not enough chairs to go around, so many were slumped against the side walls or the backs of chairs. I couldn't see any one I already knew, apart from this girl who I had shook hands with briefly but now couldn't remember a single thing about her. I figured that if she had been really nice I would have recalled some detail, so on the basis of that dodgy assumption I opted to try my luck with a new group and plonked myself down by the side of a pretty girl with strawberry blonde hair.

"Hi, I'm Josh. Do you mind if I sit here?" She did not appear to be locked into conversation with anyone at that particular moment, so I felt comfortable addressing my introduction just to her. I didn't, however, mean it to sound like a bad chat-up line.

"Well, Josh, be my guest." She smiled as she replied, and tucked some hair behind her left ear, "I'm Mary Jane."

Bloody hell, I thought, you're the bitch from next door.

"You're the... erm... you live next door to me." She looked confused. "I mean, we live next door to each other. You know, in M-block? I'm number 14, you're number 13. I met your Mum this morning. We're neighbours."

"Well, hello neighbour!" she replied as a smile thankfully replaced the confusion on her freckled face. "Everybody, I'd like you to meet... erm... ("Josh," I whispered. After all, I could only remember her name because I'd taken an immediate disliking to her)... Josh. Yes, Josh! He's my neighbour!" and then she gave me a big hug and a kiss on the cheek. I quickly concluded she had taken more than a few drinks on board that night.

I did my little piece for the rest of the group and nearly pulled a muscle stretching across to shake everyone's hands. This bunch had had far more to drink than the economists, and as a smiley girl with a ponytail produced a bottle of red wine from behind her chair, I figured that they had no immediate plans to stop. The conversations followed the usual format, but this time I was really enjoying them. I had decided to vary my responses due to a combination drink and a desire for variety.

"So, let me guess, you're from London?" I asked the next in line for a handshake, a lad who looked like a squashed version of my cousin.

"Well, not really," he replied, "I live in a suburb to the north of the city called..."

"Sounds like London to me," I replied. He looked a little offended.

"Well, Mr Funny Accent," began Mary Jane, hanging her arm around my shoulder, as much for support as for affection. She sensed I was flogging a dead horse with my compressed relative, "I bet you're from the north." She screwed up her face as she said these last two words and attempted some sort of accent.

"In no place on earth do people speak like that" I replied. It got a better laugh than it deserved. The alcohol was flowing. "Yes, I am from "the North", but it's actually quite a big place you know?"

"Really, I thought there was just one town called 'North' where all you funny people live."

"Well, we've actually evolved quite a bit recently, and now we've got lots of different towns and counties. We've even got TVs."

"Shit."

"I know. My Mum still talks to it, thinking it's the neighbours looking through the window."

Mary Jane seemed to think about this for quite a while.

"I like you, Northern Josh. I think we're going to get on just fine as neighbours" she gave me another hug, and spilt a bit of wine on my jeans.

"I like you too, Ms Mary Jane."

After a while, people were starting to get sleepy. All the wine was gone, and the JCR was slowly emptying, leaving MTV playing away to a dwindling audience, and free comfy seats that I was too tired to crawl over and occupy.

"Will you walk me back to M-block, Mr Josh?" slurred Mary Jane. She had not spoken for twenty minutes or so. While I chatted about The Beatles to a girl who knew far more about them than me, she had been sleeping and dribbling.

"Of course. I'm knackered too."

With half-open eyes she dangled her hand in front of her like a floppy spout on a teapot. I took this as my cue to pull her up out of her chair. She was surprisingly heavy, and thus this was not an easy task. Successfully out of the JCR we walked arm in arm across Main Court and up the two flights of stairs to our rooms. Mary Jane stumbled a few times. She was not embarrassed. She laughed, hauled herself up, and carried on. I sensed she had been drunk in the presence of others a few times before.

I stood by and watched as she tried to get into her room. Her keys jangled and fell to the floor, and Mary Jane fell after them. She refused to let me help. On the fourth try she was in, and as the door swung open, Mary Jane swung with it. She invited me in for a cup of tea, but I knew the chances were that I would fall asleep as soon as I sat down. We hugged again and wished each other sweet dreams. I poured myself a big glass of milk and began the closing ceremony that would bring this eventful day to an end. I'd met a hundred faces, and remembered one. Mary Jane. I sensed that living next door to her was going to prove eventful.

Chapter 7

In the folklore of my school, Freshers' Week at uni is known was known as "bed-hopping" week. Apparently, everyone sleeps with everyone. I had only been in Cambridge a couple of days, but I was beginning to realise that things worked a little differently down here. Firstly, Freshers' Week at Cambridge could have been taken to court under the Trade Descriptions Act. It actually ran from Sunday to Thursday. More importantly, on the Monday, we were set not one, but two lovely essays.

It was our Director of Studies (shortened to "DOS"– ironically pronounced "doss," as in to mess around, take it easy, generally not do any work) that was the propagator of these essays. He was a young-looking man, although he could have been over forty as I was never too good at guessing ages. I had met him once before when he was interviewing me at the end of the previous year. I took an immediate liking to him. He didn't give me too hard a time, and only really screwed me with one set of questions at the end of the interview, just as I made the mistake of relaxing a bit.

"So, Josh, are you looking to do anything else apart from economics if you are offered a place at St. Catharine's?"

"Oh, yes. I love playing sport. I am going to play football, tennis, cricket and basketball. I might even try rowing, I hear it's the thing to do down here, although I'm not too keen on the early starts."

"And anything else?"

"Well, I was Chairman of the Sixth Form Committee at my school, which I really enjoyed, you know, acting as a link between staff and pupils, and all that, so I might try and get involved with something like that here."

"And anything else?"

"Well, I might try my hand at some university-wide things like Uni Radio, or even a bit of debating."

"Anything else!"

"Well, I suppose I've not ruled out improving my French at the Language Centre."
"Josh."
"Yes."
"Are you going to actually do some work whilst you are here?" Bastard.

But apart from that he seemed alright, and in my mind I had built up images of Cambridge fellows who were a lot worse. He liked football and supported Spurs. He had two young children and liked wearing smart shirts with cufflinks. He spoke a bit like a farmer from Devon or Somerset, and I think he came from somewhere around there. His job was to co-ordinate our studies in economics. He arranged our supervisions and even gave some himself. He was who we went to if we had a work-related problem, and likewise if one of our supervisors had a work-related problem with one of us (like if we weren't doing any), then it was out DOS who we would be summoned to see. His name was Mr Stevens. He did not like being called Doctor.

We thought Mr Stevens might be joking when he told us we had two essays to do and that they were due to be handed in, in a week's time. He wasn't. One was a macroeconomic essay on the differences between Keynes and the neo-classical economists, and the other was a set of microeconomic questions about consumer behaviour.

First year economic students at Cambridge, whatever college they were from, did what was known as Part 1 Economics, which involved five papers that all students in all colleges had to sit. One was Macro (the economy as a whole, including stuff like unemployment and inflation), one was Micro (individual parts of the economy like the labour market or firm and consumer behaviour), one was Statistics (the boring bits of A-level maths), one was Political Economy (politics with an economic spin) and the last was Economic History (involving such classics as the Victorian era, the industrial revolution and the interwar period). In addition, we were to sit a maths paper called EQEM (standing for – although not entirely, with one too many Es for my liking – Economics Qualifying Examination in Elementary Mathematics), which was designed to make sure everyone was at a reasonable level of mathematical ability. We had one supervision in each part every fortnight, apart from the maths one, which we were supposed to teach ourselves from the lectures. Each piece of work normally required a couple of days' reading and then half a day's writing. On top of this, we had about three one-hour lectures a day. If we had a bit of spare time, we were also allowed to enjoy ourselves.

No, that's a bit harsh. It was a lot of work, but with a bit of planning it was easily manageable. It was nowhere near as much work as the medics or the vets had to do, but it was about 230 times the workload of the geographers. In the end we were all here primarily to do work to get a degree, but I didn't really want to hit the library in the middle of Freshers' Week.

All the economists were gathered together in Mr Stevens' room for the first time. I did a quick count and, as the freshers notice board had suggested, there were indeed ten of us, one of whom was a girl. There were two Irish lads whom I had not yet met. One looked like he belonged in a boy band, the other like he belonged in the 1970s. I was reassured that I was in a good group when Mr Stevens' announcement of the two pieces of work was met with a naive snigger and then a universal groan of realisation. Thankfully, there were no "Yippees!" as I had feared. With pieces of work in hand, the group moved on to our next port of call, a meeting with our tutor.

Dr Harris differed from Mr Stevens in that she was a woman and she didn't seem to mind being called Doctor. She was a plump lady, probably somewhere in her fifties, who wore big round glasses and old-fashioned dresses. Her room was littered with books being kept open at specific pages by various makeshift bookmarks. She was also a lesbian, and possibly an MI5 spy. The first of these was definitely true as Dr Harris lived in college with her partner, a woman who looked just like Dr Harris. The latter of these was naturally unconfirmed, but our tutor was often spotted lurking behind corners and in alleyways around town, her face wrapped up and concealed by her disguise of a woolly hat and a tartan scarf. Moreover, I don't think I've ever met anyone least likely to be a spy. She looked petrified to be talking to another human being, her voice was barely audible, and she had a terrible memory for names and faces. All of which, of course, made it easy for her to track down and eliminate unsuspecting Russian agents, thus making her perfect spy material. No, Dr Harris was definitely a spy, no doubt about it, and I enjoyed the idea of having a lesbian secret agent as a tutor. It was far cooler than having a heterosexual professor of Biochemistry, or something like that.

As our tutor, Dr Harris' role was to make sure that we were all getting on alright in both the academic and non-academic elements of life at Cambridge. This meant that we should go to see her, along with Mr Stevens, if we were not happy with some aspect of our degree (if that aspect happened to be Mr Stevens himself, then it was probably best to just go and see Dr Harris), but also if we ran into financial difficulty, or had problems at home, or something along those lines. Seeing as we were all new to this strange town, I found it quite reassuring in these early days to know that we already had a couple of people whose job it was to make sure all was going well for us, and to help us out wherever they could. I liked this idea, and I liked the whispering, almost scared, manner of our tutor. It made you feel that she was as nervous and bemused by this whole experience as you were.

The meeting today was simply for Dr Harris to introduce herself and tell us what her job was (not her real job, of course). There weren't enough chairs to go around, but thankfully the meeting only took a couple of minutes. We all had to sign in to say what date we arrived in Cambridge, even though we had already done this with the Porters. Signing in with your tutor at the start of each term was called *redeat* and signing out was called *exeat*. Dr Harris told us that our degree was in jeopardy if we did not *redeat* and *exeat* at the start and end of each term. We did not believe her. After we were dismissed, I had a quick chat with the economists I'd met yesterday, and then headed off for my next rendezvous – the doctors. This day was just non-stop fun, fun, fun.

The doctor was friendly enough, although you could tell he'd seen more than a few new students today at the office. I successfully provided a urine sample, only missing the container with a couple of splashes. The doctor told me I looked tired, but I was the right weight for my height, which was a bonus. On the downside, I apparently had high blood pressure, which the doctor, with his years of experience and medical degree, suggested was a result of the anxiety caused by starting a new chapter of my life at uni, and which my mother, via the phone later that day, armed with years of experience of forming uniformed medical opinions, speculated was due to me putting too much salt on my food at meal times, something she'd always warned me about. The doctor told me to come back in a week or two so he could keep an eye on my blood.

With high spirits and high blood pressure, I made my way back to college. I had left myself sufficient time to sing along to a couple of songs, check the showbiz gossip pages of Teletext, and have a leisurely shower, and still be ready for pre-dinner drinks at 6.45 pm in Mr Stevens' room as a warm-up for the scary-sounding Matriculation Dinner, which kicked off at

7.30 pm. The first two of these tasks were completed successfully, and I left my room naked but for my pale blue towel and a bottle of Sanex, my mind full of thoughts about Britney and Justin's plans to buy a house together after her latest tour.

Then, problems started. The shower was busy. Of course it was busy. It was Matriculation Dinner night, all the freshers in college were going, and most of them probably wanted to be clean for it. I should have seen this coming. I thought it was a bit rude to knock, and I had left my shampoo in the bathroom this morning, so unless Sanex could give my hair its natural shine and volume, I couldn't really wander around M-block looking for a free shower, not that any would be free anyway. All I could do was hang around outside the shower, and wait for whoever was in there, happily getting clean, to get out and let me in. I decided to pass the time by whistling.

Within a few minutes, I was joined in the queue for the bathroom by a small girl in a red dressing gown. She had short brown hair and a few freckles on her face. In her hands lay a towel of the same colour and a couple of bottles of girls' shower stuff. I altered the position of my mouth from a whistling shape to a smiling shape.

"I guess your waiting for the shower as well?" I began, already hazarding a guess at her answer.

"Aye, I am indeedy." She was Scottish.

"You're Scottish, aren't you?"

"Aye, how can you tell?" I reckoned she was probably being sarcastic. "Let me guess, you're from the North. Probably Lancashire or Yorkshire?".

"Definitely Lancashire. No probably about it. Anyway, hello, I'm Josh. I would shake your hand, but I don't want to run the risk of dropping my towel and flashing you. Also, I've got Sanex in my other hand.' On reflection, I probably should have saved a line like this for later on in our friendship. At least until I knew her name. I was surprised she didn't phone the police. Instead, she laughed, and smiled back.

"No problem. My Mum uses Sanex. I'm Faye. Very pleased to meet you."

No sooner had we met than the shower door opened, and out stepped a scantily clad girl in a white dressing gown. Her hair was concealed by a wrapped yellow towel that looked like some brightly coloured Indian head gear.

"Hi Josh. Hi Faye. Oooh, me and my two neighbours together for the first time! How are you both? No, on second thoughts, no time for that. I've got to be at pre-Matric drinks in fifteen minutes. Must dash. See you at the dinner. Bye" And with that, Mary Jane elegantly jogged round the corner and into her room.

"Jesus Christ, is that the bloody time?" squealed Faye, in an accent that I was already beginning to like, "I've got those stupid bloody drink things to get too as well. Ooh no"

"Me too. Look, I'll be five minutes max in the shower. I'm really fast if I don't sing".

I bombed in and out of the shower in record time. I decided not to wash my legs, as I couldn't see how they would have got dirty from this morning. Once again I rejoiced the fact that I had been blessed with minimal facial hair, meaning I could put off the time consuming act of shaving at least until a week on Tuesday. Like a relay runner who had been caught in the rain, I tagged and flew past my waiting Scottish neighbour, and ran dripping into my room.

I put my new suit on for the first time, and chose my favourite blue shirt and a not too bad stripy tie to go with it. I was at a time in my life when I couldn't be arsed with hair products, so a quick comb through with the fingers sufficed and saved me a few more minutes. I cleaned my teeth, straightened my collar, and paused to think if I had forgotten anything. Of course I had. My gown. I grabbed my gown from its home inside the wardrobe and scurried though the door. I was just in time to see a figure in a red dressing gown, her short brown hair looking like it had been subject to an electric shock, shuffling down the corridor, mumbling the words, "Ooh no, ooh no!" over and over again.

The gown in question was my college gown. I had seen my teachers at school bombing around in fancy gowns whenever we had a prize-giving night, or if someone special was coming to visit. My teachers' gowns were good. They had big hoods of all different colours, and made the wearer appear elegant and sophisticated. When I forked out £65 for my college gown, I expected something similar. This was Cambridge, after all. I was to be disappointed. My gown was crap. It was just black. No fancy pattern, no fancy hood, nothing. It looked like the cloak of a cheap Batman costume. All Cambridge colleges had their own unique gowns, and the thing that was supposed to make ours different from the rest was the way the folds were arranged down the side, or something. What a rip-off. Anyway, we had to wear our gowns any time we went to a formal hall or a big dinner like tonight. Also, you had to put them on if you ever got into serious enough trouble to warrant a trip to see the Dean, who was in charge of discipline in the college, and if you wanted to graduate. I often felt a bit of a prat bombing around in my gown, but like everything in that place, you soon got used to it.

Despite the fact that I had been in Mr Stevens room earlier that day I still managed to get lost en route, taking a wrong turn down some stairs and inadvertently discovering the location of the laundry. Luckily I made it to the correct destination with a couple of minutes to spare. All the economists from my year were there, dressed in suits and clutching tightly onto their gowns like they were some kind of strange pet that could escape at any minute. The economists from the two years above were also there, dressed more normally for this time of the day as Matriculation Dinner was only for Freshers. I smiled and nodded at my Nanny, Trevor, who was sipping away at a glass of orange juice. Also present were a strange breed of people called "Land Economists".

I had seen the subject of Land Economy whilst flicking through the Cambridge prospectus, but dismissed it as some kind of farming studies. Apparently, it wasn't. Apparently, it was a dynamic subject, comprising of elements of law, economics and geography, a subject of the future. Unfortunately, it had acquired an almost universal reputation within Cambridge as being a bit of a joke. It seemed to steal the easy bits of the courses of most subjects, leaving its students with a wide-ranging knowledge of not a lot. Moreover, the Land Economy students were hardly stretched to breaking point in the workload department, rivalling only the geographers in the competition of who could avoid picking up a pen the longest. Anyway, the bottom line was that in St. Catharine's College, the land economists always tagged along with us (proper) economists to such formal occasions, largely because of the influence of the silvered-haired Brummie, and college Dean, Dr Tinsley. Dr Tinsley would not hear a bad word said against his beloved subject, and always referred to the college Economics Society as the "Economics and Land Economy Society", whilst everyone else tried not to laugh.

As my eyes continued to work their way around the room I was greeted by a glass of champagne, courtesy of Mr Stevens. To the best of my memory I had never tried champagne before, and to be honest, I was not that impressed. I found it too fizzy, and quite painful to drink. I sipped it slowly and winced each time I swallowed. It even made me sneeze. Many of life's delicacies are wasted on me. I had a brief chat to Trevor, a brief chat to some of the economists from my year, a couple of glasses of champagne, a couple of sneezing fits, and then, before I knew it, we were off down the stairs to dinner.

The hall where Matriculation Dinner was held was the same place where we ate lunch and dinner every day (and breakfast if you were up early enough). It was a huge room, full of long wooden tables, easily able to seat twenty at a time. At the end of the hall was the so-called High Table, which was, as you might expect, raised by a stage to be a good foot above the rest of the tables. Fellows of the college dined at this high table each day, whilst us lowly students tucked into our grub down on the deck below. On occasions like tonight, the hall was transformed from a simple canteen into a banqueting hall fit for a king. The tables were adorned with white tablecloths, candelabras and more cutlery than I had ever seen before. Each place setting contained five glasses and five sets of cutlery, and I immediately felt sorry for whoever was doing the washing up. Mum had told me to just start from the outside, but I decided I would hold fire picking up the cutlery until I saw what everyone else was doing. The room was dimly lit, the wall covered with past Masters of the college, and any floor space not taken up by tables was filled by kitchen staff smartly dressed in waistcoats and ties.

We were all given designated seats, marked by our names, and grouped together with members of our subject. I sat myself down and took a moment to look around. Hoards of gowned young men and women flooded into the hall, smiling, matching their names with the ones on the tables. The majority of faces were new to me, and as countless strangers drifted by my eyes I wondered which of these would become my close friends, my sworn enemies, occasional acquaintances, my loves, and those who would break my heart. Whilst lost in my thoughts, the two empty seats beside me, and the empty seat opposite me found themselves in employment. A skinny lad with short brown hair sat to my left, the Irish lad from the 1970's sat to my right, and Mr Stevens slid in opposite me. I was surrounded on all sides by economists, and I didn't know whether to feel safe or scared. I smiled and nodded, and whilst all three were busy smiling and nodding at other people, I took the opportunity to peruse the menu that was laid out beside each place.

It was an A4 sheet of thin card, folded over once to make a booklet. The front read: "St. Catharine's College, Cambridge, Matriculation Dinner, Monday 2nd October 2000," in fancy writing, together with a drawing of the college made looking through the front gates into Main Court, and the college crest containing our lovely Catharine wheel. On the inside left page was the wine list; four wines that I had never heard of, nor could ever hope of pronouncing, from the years 1994 to 1997, which I could only presume were good years for these particular wines. On the opposite page was the menu itself. We were opening up with Tomato and Basil Soup. No problem. We were then moving onto Poached Breast of Chicken with Lemongrass and Coriander Sauce, complemented by Parisienne Potatoes and Saute Vegetables. Bloody hell. I had never had chicken before, and the only sauce I was a fan of was ketchup. As for what Parisienne Potatoes were, I didn't have a clue. Pudding was Steamed Mexican Chocolate Pudding with Chocolate Sauce, which sounded good, and I began wishing we were up to that bit now. Then there was Cheese and Biscuits and a Fresh Fruit Desert Bowl, followed by Coffee and Mints. I carefully put the menu back down, and quickly exhaled a mouthful of air. The bottom line was that at that particular moment in time, I was scared. I had promised myself that I had to try new things at uni, especially in the food department, and now that I was faced with the chance, I wished I could have some of my Mum's sausage, mash and beans. However, I didn't want to be labelled too much of a freak at this early stage, so I resigned myself to an evening of sampling funny foods, and trying not to be sick.

Just as everyone had sat down, the thud of a gong resounded around the room and everyone rose to their feet. Then, the Master of the college, a tall, lanky, dignified-looking gentleman with a healthy head of silver hair, from his standing position in the centre of the head table, began reciting grace in Latin. Thankfully, all we had to do was chip in with an "Amen" at the end. He then told us in English to "enjoy the feastings", and we took this as our cue to sit down and tuck in. Mum was right; people did start from the outside.

Since I had arrived, I hadn't yet had a chance to speak to the Irish guy who was sitting to my right. He had been on the end of a few of my smile-nod combos, but that was about it. He had very long, wavy brown hair that easily covered his ears and formed two wings at the side of his head that were in danger of propelling him into the skies if the wind picked up, or

A Tale of Friendship, Love and Economics

catching fire if he got too close to that candle. I had also noticed that he dressed strangely, having worn in the first couple of days a blue Adidas top that I thought had come off the production line thirty years ago, and brown flares, that were only available in Preston in fancy dress shops. I had overheard him talking to various people, and he seemed to be proving hard to understand. He was also prone to laughing a lot, with his laugh resembling a pneumatic drill. He looked an interesting character, and as one of the kitchen staff scooped some red soup into my bowl, I realised that I was looking forward to chatting to him.

He had just finished talking to the lad opposite him – Simon, the Jewish economist with the funny little hat on his head – when I caught his eye.

"Hi, I don't think we've met. I'm Josh." I presented forward my hand for him to shake, which he took with a smile.

"I'm Usheen. Howerudoin?"

What?

"Hi... erm... look... I'm really sorry, I didn't catch your name." I left out the bit that I didn't catch anything else that he said. His accent was incredibly strong, and he talked so fast.

"No bother, I have to learn to speak slower over here, or whatever." He laughed as he spoke, probably partly because of the confused look on my face and partly because he laughed at everything. In time I would also learn that he also ended most sentences with "or whatever," not because there were more options forthcoming, but because this was just how he spoke.

"My name is Ush-een. Here, this is how it's spelt, or whatever," and with this, my first ever Irish acquaintance pointed to his name on the card in front of him. "Oisin Kerrigan", it read. I was confused. I was sure he said his name was Usheen, or something along those lines, but now he was showing me Oisin. Sure, I didn't know exactly how to pronounce Oisin, but I knew it couldn't be "Usheen." No way.

"Oh," I said, increasingly sceptical of the honesty of the shaggy haired-Irishman, "is Usheen your nickname, and... excuse me, I'm not sure how to say it... Oisin yes Oisin, is that your real name?" He laughed, and then laughed some more.

"No. That is my name, or whatever. It's spelt O-i-s-i-n, but it's pronounced Ush-een."

"Bollocks" my thoughts were immediately translated into words without my permission. "Erm... I mean, really... honestly, you're not taking the piss?"

"I promise. Cross my heart and hope to die."

Something about him made me trust him, even though there was a very large chance I was being made to look a right prick. I mean, I could just about live with the "in" bit at the end of "Oisin" being pronounced "een," but where did the U and the H come from, and where the hell did the O go? In the interests of not falling out with someone I didn't know at all and someone that I would inevitably have to spend a lot of time with over the next three years, I did the only thing I could in the circumstances.

"Look mate, I'm really sorry. I didn't mean to be rude. It's just that I don't think I've ever met an Irish person before, and I've certainly never come across a name like that... not that there's anything wrong with it... Oh, God, I think I'll just shut up now. Please forgive me."

"Like I say, no bother. It's my fault for having a stupid name, or whatever." We shook hands again, and I decided there and then that I liked Usheen or Oisin, or whatever he said his name was.

Throughout the rest of the meal I chatted away to Oisin. I found out that he came from Derry in Northern Ireland, a city on the border with the South and the location of the Bloody Sunday tragedy. He was an Arsenal fan, he played football but he didn't think he was very good, and he had three younger sisters, all of who had names that weren't spelt like they should be. This information took about an hour to extract, partly because I often couldn't understand him, and partly because his stories would often fly off on tangents and take a while to get back on track. I also discovered that, incredibly, he had never had a drop of alcohol in his life. Apparently, in Ireland a lot of Catholic children take a pledge at school not to have any alcohol until they are eighteen. Oisin had stuck to his pledge and decided to carry it on a few years. He was planning to have alcohol at some stage, but not tonight. I explained that I too was Catholic, a former alter boy no less, but I had very few morals.

Feeling quite proud of myself for conquering the two feats of trying chicken for the first time (not bad, not bad at all) and having a conversation with someone I couldn't understand, I decided to take a stab at chatting to the skinny lad to the left of me.

"Hi, sorry, I don't think we've met properly, I'm Josh."

A Tale of Friendship, Love and Economics

I had met him before at the pub, but I couldn't remember his name, and I didn't want to admit it.

"Hi, I'm Mark."

"And how do you spell that?"

"Erm... M-A-R-K... you know, like rhymes with bark."

I smiled, whilst my new friend looked at me like I was a strange species of animal with three heads and forty-three noses. Then the proverbial penny dropped.

"Oh, I take it you've met Oisin."

"I certainly have. Hey, is he taking the piss?"

"Don't think so, but then I suppose he could be. I don't know. Anyway, I'm just plain and simple Mark. Mark Novak."

"Well, nice to meet you Mark. The food's pretty good, isn't it?"

And from there we talked for a while about the usual things strangers talk about, things I was growing increasingly good at talking about through the intensive practice of the last couple of days. Mr Mark Novak was from a place called East Sheen, which was, unsurprisingly, in London. He had a younger brother, supported Spurs, and had done Maths, Further Maths, Economics, Physics and Chemistry for A-level (straight As, of course). He was also not happy that Mr Stevens had set us a couple of essays so early on. I took an immediate liking to him. He appeared a little shy, but was very friendly. Like Oisin he laughed at the things I said that I intended to be funny – a characteristic that always endeared me to people – but unlike Oisin, he didn't laugh at everything. Also contrary to Oisin Kerrigan, on the evidence of the night, he certainly had not taken a no-alcohol pledge.

I didn't talk to many other people during the meal, which was a good job as I had my hands full chatting to Mark Novak and trying to understand Oisin Kerrigan. Mr Stevens was happily chatting away to Simon, the Jewish lad, whom I had ashamedly refrained from making a great effort to talk to, put off as I was by my ignorance and irrational fear of the tiny piece of circular cloth that was safety-pinned to his hair. The other economists were all locked in conversation, and I had chatted to most of them over the last couple of days. All apart from the other Irish lad who still, even in a gown and suit, looked like he belonged in a boy band. Oisin had told me his name was Caolan, Caolan O'Donnell, but this was a bit easy to grasp as you said it Kee-lan or Kay-lawn. I opted for Kee-lan, as I thought it sounded better. Oisin also informed me that he and Caolan lived on the same road in Derry, but amazingly had never properly met until they found themselves attending interview on the same day to get into St. Catharine's. Caolan was also an Irish Catholic who had taken the no-alcohol pledge, but was very much a drinker in these post-eighteen days. Finally, Oisin told me that I would find Caolan a lot easier to understand as his Mum was from down south (of Ireland, that is) and this had softened his accent a little. I knew I would meet him at some stage and thus was in no real rush to do so now.

Having moved on to the coffee part of this lavish meal, the Master of the college stood up again to make a speech. This time we were allowed to remain sitting. He began by encouraging us to thank the kitchen staff by means of applause for preparing such a lovely meal, which was a fair point as it was very tasty indeed. He then welcomed us to the "family of St. Catharine's college," a place where you would always have a home. He spoke powerfully and elegantly, and the hairs on the back of my neck stood to attention for the first time since Steve Redgrave had won his fifth Olympic Gold earlier that summer. I'm a sucker for grand occasions and corny words.

We moved from the hall into the college bar, leaving the fellows to go back home. I was feeling a little bit giddy, but the wine was served in sufficiently low quantities and with a sufficient interval between top-ups to ensure that no-one was completely hammered. That is, until over a hundred suits and gowns and their owners hit the bar and started ordering drinks in bulk. Events were a little hazy, but somehow, through Oisin I think, I got talking to a new group. As the shutters fell and the porters began their flashing light show, I found myself carried along in the wave of this new group and washed up in a room in E-block.

Chapter 8

This was my first visit to E-block, and I was not impressed. For a start, the stairs were never-ending, and once you finally reached the summit of the never-ending stairs, you were faced with a never-ending corridor, that seemed to twist and turn its way around the whole city. By the time we reached a dark-haired girl's room (I presumed it was her room as she had the key) I was ready for bed, and the only thing stopping me going was that

A Tale of Friendship, Love and Economics

I knew I wouldn't be able to find my way out of E-block on my own. The room itself was pretty nice, but happily smaller than mine, and the space on the bed that I had fought hard to acquire was adequately comfy. As for the group itself, my impressions were mixed. The dark-haired girl, whose room it probably was seemed to act coldly towards me, and her small friend was rather loud and had a tendency to say weird stuff. There was also an Asian lad who I took an immediate disliking to. Within a couple of minutes I had decided he was arrogant, obnoxious and, for want of a better expression, a big bullshitter. He often managed to talk shite and down to me in the same breath, and clearly thought his role in life was enlighten us all with his countless pearls of wisdom and clichéd soundbites as to how we could improve our meagre existence. He claimed he was born and bred in Bradford (the wrong side of the Pennines, but I was fast learning to be tolerant so I didn't hold this particular blip against him) but spoke as if he was born and bred in Buckingham Palace. He pronounced his family's country of origin as Parky-starn. He had ridiculous facial hair, and blew his nose on hankies. Worst of all, everyone else in the room loved him.

There was another girl in the room who I reckoned looked a little bit like the popular actress Kirsten Dunst (her of *Spiderman* fame). I fancied Kirsten Dunst, and I fancied her look-alike from Leeds. She didn't seem all that keen on me, however, and appeared happy and humbled to be in the presence of the great philosophising Bradford prophet. My fellow economists Caolan and Oisin were also there and equally engrossed.

After an hour or so I was tired of listening, tired of the smoke-filled room, and tired of The Group as a whole, and so I quietly excused myself. Oisin had had enough as well, and thankfully his sense of direction was significantly better than mine. We successfully navigated our way out of E-block, across Main Court, and into my beloved M-block. Oisin, as it turned out, was also a resident of the M-block Massive, living in M8 on the floor below me. He offered me a drink of tea with sufficiently little enthusiasm in his voice for me to politely decline, safe in the knowledge that I wasn't causing offence. I was asleep moments after my head hit the pillow, transported off to a land where prophets from Yorkshire listened but did not speak, and girls who looked like movie stars fell in love with me.

Chapter 9

The rest of Freshers' Week flew by. The days were fresh and varied, the nights painfully the same.
It started off with a headache. My alarm rudely beeped me awake at 8am. My body was at least five hours and three litres of water off being ready to be exposed to the world, but today I had to get up. The college authorities, in their infinite wisdom, had chosen this ungodly hour, on the day after the alcohol-soaked Matriculation Dinner, to have the Matriculation Photograph. The whole year had to be dressed smartly in last night's suits and gowns and in the hall for 8.30 am sharp. In my drunken state last night I had calculated that half an hour would be sufficient time to shower, get dressed, eat and make myself look lively. The mirror suggested I would never look lively again.
Thankfully there was no queue for the M-block showers. Mary Jane was dressed and ready to go, and Scottish Faye was running even later than me. I just about made it to the hall on time, the only signs of my thirty-minute rush-job being the splodge of Weetabix on the upper-left part of my gown. This morning the hall lay cleared of all fanciness, with not even a red wine stain or a stray Parisienne potato to remind this morning's guests of the previous night's feasting. Many pairs of red eyes and several red faces sat on the wooden benches or leant against the walls for support. A fellow of the college had the unenviable task of convincing this weary tribe of young adults to align themselves in alphabetical order in preparation for the photo. He stood in the middle of the hall and called out surnames in reverse order, starting with the Ws (there were no Zebras or Yoghurts).
An alphabetised snake of one hundred and twenty three parts slithered its way slowly out of the hall and towards the metal frames that had been erected at the far side of Main Court. The As, Bs and Cs, a group of which I belonged, got a raw deal, having to wait the longest to be positioned, and then being led up to the very top of the shaky scaffolding to take up our precarious position balanced at the back. I found myself stood next to a tiny pretty girl with blonde hair and a medium-sized boy with short brown hair, which still contained the remnants of last night's gel. I was slap bang in the middle of the back row, and a quick glance left and right suggested I was the tallest. Behind me was a ten-foot drop. It was windy, and I felt a bit worse for wear. The chances were I would fall, but if I survived, at least Mum would

A Tale of Friendship, Love and Economics

be able to see me in the photo. Just as the photographer was happy with our positions and our smiles, our row was joined by a new member. His surname started with "S," but he was made an honourary "A" today after missing his slot, having been sick last night and subsequently sleeping in.

Having officially matriculated and thus become full members of both St. Catharine's College and Cambridge University, the rest of Tuesday day was spent feeling rough and having cups of tea and toast in the company of my new neighbours, Scottish Faye and London-based Mary Jane. We spent an hour in each of our rooms, and did this circuit twice. I had six cups of tea, nine unbuttered slices of toast, and a really good time. We were a good match; Mary Jane liked to talk, I liked to listen and Faye liked to laugh. We thankfully breezed by the usual formalities in a couple of minutes. Mary Jane was a vet, which meant she would be here in Cambridge for six years. Faye was a geographer, which meant she would be here for three very easy years. Mary Jane liked to sing and play the flute. Faye liked to watch *Neighbours*. Mary Jane had a younger sister and an older brother. Faye was an only child. Mary Jane fancied her Nanny. Faye didn't, largely because hers was a girl. We then, through a process of trial and error, laid a few ground rules for conversations in the future. I wouldn't talk about football if they didn't talk about funny girls' stuff like menstruation and periods. I wouldn't make Mary Jane listen to any of my so-called "heavy" music if she didn't force me to listen to crappy Enya. Faye and I would refrain from calling Mary Jane a posh southerner if she left our proud northern routes alone. We then chatted about people we'd met so far and what we'd done over the summer. We took a break to watch *Neighbours* in my room (thankfully, all five channels were now tuned in and up and running, although Channel 5 was a bit fuzzy), and then started discussing and speculating as to who could have stolen a considerable amount of Faye's mature cheddar from our fridge.

Conversation was easy with Faye and Mary Jane. I could relax and be myself. I could say what I wanted, and though Mary Jane tended to ramble on a bit, she would always stop and listen whenever Faye or I wanted to speak. They reminded me of my mates back home, and I felt very much at home with them. Which is more than could be said for the additional time I spent with The Group that I had met the previous night.

I was a little worse for wear after the subject pub-crawl earlier that evening. Thirty-two crazy economists from St. Catharine's College

Cambridge, created carnage across the city's pubs. Oisin, despite my best efforts at engaging in some good old fashioned peer pressure, refused to break his nineteen-year-old pledge and wasn't drinking. Poor Mark Novak was trying his hardest to drink, but was deemed too young looking to be served alcohol in a pub called The Hog's Head. Thankfully, the ever mature-looking Caolan got him a pint.

This was the first time I had chance to talk to Caolan properly, the boy-band-looking second Irish economist. I say properly, but you could never really talk to Caolan O'Donnell properly unless you tied him up in a room with just you and him and no distractions. He was always on the move, easily distracted, always trying to get everyone involved in the conversation and get himself involved in every conversation. He was very much a "people person." He had dark brown hair that clearly took a lot of time to prepare. It was spiky, quiffed at the front, and complemented on either side by two impressive sideburns. He was a good-looking lad, and was always going to be popular. He didn't tell you much about himself unless you asked, and he didn't ask much about you. He had a poor memory and a Catholic background, sober high morals and a drunken weak will. He would happily engage in a conversation about anything, so long as it didn't get emotional. He wasn't afraid to be different; not afraid to admit that he enjoyed the music of Westlife, that his favourite male solo "artist" was Ronan Keating, and that he couldn't stand football. He seemed to be doing his best to alienate himself from every male member of the group, but still everyone liked him. Caolan O'Donnell was friendly, bubbly, funny and easy to talk to. I too liked him a lot, but I had the feeling we would never be that close.

The pub-crawl consisted of about five pubs, which were all busy. We lost a few economists along the way, but picked up members of other subjects to replace them. The medics had come dressed in lab coats with token stethoscopes draped around their necks, and the geographers had split into teams of red, yellow and green. Us crazy economists had gone absolutely mental and opted for trousers and a shirt, although my Nanny Trevor was sporting jeans and a black Guinness T-shirt. The crawl that had began a walk soon turned into a stumble and culminated in a final stop at Cambridge's branch of Wetherspoons, called The Regal. The pub used to be a cinema and was now the home of cheap drinks and meals all week long. Apparently it was also the largest pub in England, but its impressive size came at the price of a loss in atmosphere. Tonight, all subjects from Catz were gathered as one big happy family, and I found myself temporarily separated from the economists, and chatting away to people I had met briefly on previous nights. In our present state, names were surplus to requirements. Last orders were called at 11 pm, and the remaining economists joined the contingent in search of a nightclub. We tried to get into one called Cindies, which was apparently the place to go on a Tuesday night, but the queue was deemed too long, so we headed back to college. Again, with every intention of finding someone else to talk to, I found myself swept up and dumped in the dark-haired girl's room in E-block.

There, I was preached to for hours on end by our resident prophet. Tonight he was tackling the issue of crime in Britain. He explained to his captive audience that his area of Bradford had a crime rate of 60 per cent: 60 per cent he repeated for emphasis. What did that mean, I wondered? Sixty per cent of people in Bradford committed crime? Sixty per cent of crime in Bradford was committed in his area? Sixty per cent of crime in the UK was committed in Bradford? More like 60% of the words that left his mouth were complete shite, and the validity of the remaining 40 per cent was very much open to question. I bit my tongue and didn't challenge him for fear of being alienated from the group. They were lapping up his words like a bunch of cats after the richest cream. They all thought he was wonderful, even Caolan and Oisin who I had hoped for more from. Moreover, I still fancied the Kirsten Dunst look-alike, so I didn't want to be kicked out just yet. I wasn't really having a good time at all. I found the conversations pretentious and pompous, with most things said for effect and not driven by true feelings. It was everything I feared Cambridge could be. I knew it wasn't me and I knew I needed to get out of it.

Chapter 10

Thankfully, the days continued to free me from The Group.

Wednesday was a day for getting things done. In the morning I took myself off shopping with the intention of making M14 feel more like a home; more like my home. The town was buzzing with new students. You could tell they were new by the way they walked; either heads swinging around trying to take everything in, or heads hanging down, trying to look cool. Sainsbury's was teaming with young adults stocking up on the essential items for their new homes such as milk, bread and beer. The queues were long, so I decided to take the opportunity to fill out an application for a loyalty card.

The entrepreneurs of Cambridge had clearly responded to the new influx of students just like me. Everywhere in the city there were signs for poster sales, huge discounts on books for Freshers, great deals on music for Freshers, and alternative clothing sales for anyone who fancied them. I opted for the poster sale advertised in the church that lay on my way back to college. After much careful deliberation, flicking through racks and looking at posters sprawled out on the floor, I went for two large back and white head shots of Martin Luther King and John Lennon.

Back in M14 I carefully positioned the posters with Blu-Tack (even though this was banned by the college authorities – I liked to think of myself as a bit of a rebel) on the wall next to my bed in such a way that the two great twentieth-century icons looked like they were staring deep into the eyes of each other. This effect was achieved more by accident than design, but once I noticed it, I spent the next twenty minutes or so lining the pair's eyes up better. The ex-Beatle looked concerned, and King looked defiant. This was not meant as some deep symbolic statement, I just thought it looked quite good, but some visitors to my room happily read a bit more into it than I had intended: "Yeah, Josh man, I see what you're trying to say. Nice one." I also stuck up pictures of my pals from back home, hung my Beatles calendar above the TV, and had a general tidy up. After a couple of hours of work, I invited Faye and Mary Jane in for a cup of tea, and they seemed suitably impressed with my new-look room. Seeing as they were complimentary, I also offered them some swiss roll I had snapped up at a reduced price from Sainsbury's. I smiled as I looked round my M14, still with one ear open to Faye's protests about the bloody price of drinks in this bloody stupid country. Things were coming together nicely. My friends at uni seemed a good bunch, and my friends from Preston looked surprisingly at home on the wall in the company of messrs Lennon and King.

That Wednesday afternoon brought with it the Fresher Sports Squash. I didn't know what this was going to be, but went along, as instructed by the informative freshers Notice Board, to the Hall at 3 pm. I was greeted by a room full of noise and stalls. All of St. Catharine's College's various clubs and societies had been invited into the Hall on this windy Wednesday to try and sign up as many naive Freshers as possible. Their task was aided somewhat by the fruity cocktail that was on offer for free from the middle table. A few glasses of this and you would happily sign up for anything. I gladly and consciously signed up for football and pool, and decided that I might as well try my hand at real tennis, whatever that was. I was then convinced by a pretty girl with a blonde ponytail that I was just what the mixed netball team was looking for, and told by a large boy with uneven sideburns that, whilst I was bent down with pen in my hand, I might as well put my name and email address down on the Quiz Society sign-up sheet.

Whilst happily sipping another cocktail and trying to understand Oisin, I was violently coaxed into taking part in a demonstration by the rowing club. I had been warned that Cambridge was mad keen on rowing, and that if you got involved you had to get up at some stupid time like six in the morning. With a determination to say no firmly planted in my mind, I found myself strapped onto an ergo, placed for all to see in the middle of the Hall, with instructions from a lanky lad with rosy red cheeks to row 500 metres as fast as I could. I obligingly pulled and slid to the best of my abilities, whilst he, and a few of the economists who had come to witness me making a prick of myself, shouted a mixture of support and abuse. After a couple of minutes I was completely knackered, feeling sick and fully signed up to the rowing club.

I managed to escape from the Hall with my fellow economist Mark Novak. On the way out we both signed up to a society that looked after babies at weekends or something, and then dashed off to the society-free fresh air. The next event on the freshers' agenda was karaoke in the college bar, which kicked off at 7 pm. It hadn't yet gone six, and Mr Novak and I were both starving and had both ruled out cooking something ourselves. We headed-off out of Catz in search of food. Neither of us really knew where we were going as we wandered along Kings Parade and took a right up a street that looked interesting. Stood under a pair of golden arches we weighed up our options. Neither of us were big fans of old Maccy-Ds, but then we were pretty hungry, and you did always know what you were getting (taste-wise, of course). Reluctantly, we pushed open the glass doors and ordered up a pair of bacon and cheeseburger meals (mine with no funny sauce, and a vanilla milkshake instead of the fizzy soft drink, Mark Novak's with whatever it came with). We chatted about the stupid things we'd signed up for today, and I told him about the preaching philosophising prophet from Bradford. We then discussed the fact that we had two pieces of work due in soon, and how work was the furthest thing from our minds. Again, I confirmed my first impression that I liked Mr Mark Novak.

Full of grease, and God only knows what else, we headed back to the bar just in time to catch the dying notes of one of the worst renditions of *I Will Always Love You* that I had ever heard. The bar was again packed to the rafters. Sitting was not an option, and neither was standing in space. With drinks in hand, we politely barged away over to the jukebox where my neighbours Mary Jane and Faye were standing. I introduced them to Mark. Mary Jane was clearly drunk, and had signed herself and Faye up to do the *Shoop Shoop Song*. Faye didn't seem half as drunk or half as keen as her hyper neighbour. As the three of us applauded the end of a *Let Me Entertain You*, sung by a lad who was loud enough not to need a mike, Faye kept saying, "Ooh no, ooh no", whilst frantically sipping at her Bacardi and coke. In the end, they did it. Mary Jane was really good, Faye was really awful, but it went down a storm, and both came off beaming with delight.

After the bar drew to a close, I took Mark Novak off to meet my Yorkshire nemesis that he had heard about at length over a burger and fries. Mark was a little reluctant as we lumbered up the millions of stairs to E-block, worried that he hadn't been invited. I told him that I had learnt that no-one was invited anywhere in this mad week; you just turned up and no-one seemed to mind at all. He wasn't convinced, but he was drunk and easy to persuade.

The Usual Suspects were all present and correct: the dark-haired owner of the room, who seemed to be getting less and less keen for me each night; the small girl who was crazy, but quite witty; my movie star girl, who sat crossed-legged clutching a glass of red wine; the All Mighty One, who tonight was explaining that he didn't drink, but had no problem with us all drinking, even though his stance was far superior to ours, of course; Caolan and Oisin, the former absolutely plastered, the latter stone cold sober and happily drilling away at anything remotely resembling a joke. After I introduced Mark Novak, I was introduced to a new member of our previously exclusive gang.

Even when sat down, with her legs folded neatly by her side, you could tell she was tall for a girl. She was sharing an ashtray with the room owner, and smoked every cigarette like it was the last one she would ever have. She came from Sheffield, and was studying English. She had big eyes and a pretty smile. She was called Francesca.

A Tale of Friendship, Love and Economics

Happily, the presence of a few new members seemed to propel the group to try something new instead of sitting around listening to the Great One. The small, crazy girl proposed a game of "Never Never", and I voiced my support, completely ignorant of what it entailed. A few had played the game, and a few hadn't, so luckily the rules were explained.

"Never Never" was a drinking game. You took turns in announcing to the group something that you've never done, and if anyone in the group has done the thing you said, they had to drink a load of their drink. The game's success relies on honesty and wise selection of things you haven't done (for example, "I have never walked on Mars" would not be a good one to get people drinking, although no doubt a certain person in the room would announce that he had taken a stroll on the Red Planet, spiritually, or something).

It didn't take long for the game to turn a wee bit raunchy. Mark Novak already had more than a few drinks on board, and was drinking for things he clearly had never done. Francesca, who had appeared quiet and reserved, was soon seen to be drinking for nearly everything that was put on offer. I found out things about the Sheffield Dark Horse that night that I didn't know about my best friend. She didn't boast about the things she'd done, she just did each alcohol punishment quietly, and giggled embarrassingly when pressed to reveal more. She was a much-needed breath of fresh air.

After an evening where I found out that I hadn't actually done much in my life, I trundled off to M-block in the company of Oisin and Mark. It turned out that Mark too was an M-block resident, and lived on the floor above me. I was not confident he was going to make it up all those stairs, but he assured me, in an unconvincing drunken way that would become all too familiar, that he would be just fine.

Mary Jane and Faye were still up, giggling away from inside of Mary Jane's room. I joined them for a quick cup of tea, listened to Mary Jane's plan of how she was going to seduce her Welsh Nanny, and then headed off to bed.

Chapter 11

The events of Freshers' Week were rudely interrupted on Thursday morning by the start of lectures. My first one started at nine o'clock, and again I was feeling and looking rough. Weetabix made me feel better, but the wind and the rain outside made me want to crawl back into bed.

At the meeting with Mr Stevens the other day, the economists had agreed to meet at the Plodge at 8.45 am so that we could walk to our first lecture together. I met Oisin on the stairs of M-block, and we soon caught up with Mark Novak on the lap of Sherlock Court, who was also looking a little worse for wear. All the Catz first year economists were lined up outside the Plodge overlooking Main Court. Some were armed with rucksacks or shoulder bags, others had decided to play it cool and opted for the minimalist pen-in-the-pocket and A4-pad-in-the-hand approach. A round of good mornings and a quick head count revealed we were one economist short. The missing tenth member of our mighty tribe was our one girl, Leila. At 8.55 am she appeared on the other side of Main Court, dressed sportily in tracksuit bottoms and a hoody, to a chorus of sarcastic grunts and groans. "Sorry guys" she shouted as she jogged the last couple of metres, simultaneously tying her long curly hair into a ponytail. With the group completed, we set off on our way.

Thankfully, the walk from college to lectures was only five minutes or so. This is because Catz is centrally located within the city, a feature pointed out by all well-practiced interviewees when asked why they chose St. Catharine's (along with friendly atmosphere, excellent facilities, strong academic reputation, blah, blah, blah). I immediately felt sorry for the poor buggers out at Girton College, who were faced with a twenty-minute cycle each morning to make lectures on time.

Economics lectures took place in the Sidgwick Site, a place also home to English, Law, History, Classics and some funny language subjects, as well as a lot of grass and a frequently visited little café called The Buttery. Our faculty building and library were also situated on the Sidgwick Site. Our faculty building didn't really have a name, and looked a bit like a block of flats. Our library, on the other hand, was bestowed with the grand title of the Marshall Library of Economics, and was named after the famous economist Alfred Marshall (1842-1924), who was, in fact, the founder of the

Cambridge Economics Tripos in 1902. Of course, I hadn't heard of him before I came.

A glance at the large notice boards revealed that our first lecture was in a building called Lady Mitchell Hall, and had the not-too-stressful sounding title of "An Introduction to Economics". Being the first day of lectures, everyone from all the colleges had turned up. Lady Mitchell Hall's wooden benches were taken up by the backsides of around 130 keen economics students. They looked a clever bunch, their faces kitted out with glasses and an air of intellect. Caolan and I pointed out that the girl boy ratio in the room was a reasonably healthy 40:60, which was a bit better than our 10:90, and a few of them were quite good-looking. Needless to say, Leila was not impressed when she overheard our conversation, even when we said that she wasn't bad-looking either. We sat together as a college and listened to a young-looking man explain convincingly into a microphone how economics was better than most subjects, and how it was neither an art nor a science.

Lectures were fifty minutes long, running from five past the hour until five to the hour, thus giving both students and lecturers sufficient time to get from lecture to lecture, and even squeeze in a cheeky coffee from The Buttery along the way. Naturally, some lecturers were good, and some were bad. Some were charismatic and interesting, some were boring as hell. Some tried as hard as possible to get you to understand what they were banging on about, even though the subject matter was difficult to say the least. Some seemed happy to stand in front of a room of confused faces, week after week, sporting a smug grin whilst banging on about a subject, not giving anyone else a chance in hell of understanding it.

Some lecturers, often the younger ones, mostly from abroad, gave you out a comprehensive hand-out, which meant that you didn't have to take that many notes, but also you had a tendency to switch off a bit, safe in the knowledge that all the key insights had been written down for you. Moreover, these lectures were put up on the internet afterwards, which often, especially if it was an early morning lecture, removed all incentives to go at all. If the lecturer was just going to read from a script, you might as well download the script back in college, and read it yourself sat in a comfy chair with a nice cup of tea. There was no register taken at lectures, and so as a result, the lectures with the "best" hand-outs, were more often than not binned in favour of more time in bed. Some of the older lecturers refused to produce such a hand-out at all, clearly missing the days of blackboards and chalk, days when computers weighed two tons and the earth was flat. This meant that if you didn't write something down in these lectures, you would forget it. You were forced to concentrate hard, but often ended up scribbling down points as fast as you could whilst trying desperately to listen, comprehend and remember the next five points that the lecturer had moved swiftly on to. You missed more than you got down. Anyway, to conclude this ramble, all I am trying to say is that the best lecturers gave hand-outs with the lecture outline and a few key points, but left you to fill in the detail. This way, you had every incentive to listen, but always knew where you were in the lecture. Any A-level student will tell you that economics is all about incentives, and yet even the great Cambridge minds seemed unable to apply this principle to their lectures.

We had an average of about three lectures a day, always in the mornings. Vets, medics and NatScis (Cambridge's term for those studying Natural Sciences) had far more. They often took place all morning, and until about 4 pm in the afternoon. My vet neighbour Mary Jane even had some lectures on a Saturday morning, the poor girl. Some subjects hardly had any lectures at all, and those that were scheduled were poorly attended. The beauty of having no lectures in the afternoon was that by the time you were sat in hall having lunch, you knew you had the afternoon free to yourself. Free to work, if you needed to, at your own pace, or play sport, or go back to bed.

The two lectures that we had that first Thursday morning put me in the mood for work; not exactly looking forward to it, but able to tolerate it. Good job, because I had a lot to do. With two pieces hanging ominously over our heads, I set off with Caolan, Mark and Oisin to the Marshall Library of Economics, and got out the recommended books for tackling our first macroeconomic essay on the key differences between Keynes and the neo-classical economists. The Marshall Library was full of books and foreign librarians, wooden desks and a musty smell. There weren't enough books for us all to have one copy of each, so we agreed to share, and took out a couple of different books each. Mark Novak pointed out, half joking, that we had implicitly put into practice an important economic lesson: cooperation is key in times of scarce resources. We told him to shut up and stop being a freak, but deep down nodded in appreciation of his observation.

I took my books home in my rucksack, and spent the rest of the afternoon reading and making notes in M14, with the sound of traffic and car radios seeping in from the street below. I had one brief tea break with Mary Jane, who was absolutely definitely going to pull her Nanny tonight, but apart from that I worked right through to tea time.

Chapter 12

Although I felt like I was working as though my finals were next week, I had to remind myself that it was Thursday, I had only been in Cambridge five days, and we were still in the middle of Freshers' Week. Tonight's scheduled event was the much-hyped Nanny-Nannettes Dinner. My Nanny Trevor had left me a scribbled invitation in my pigeon hole inviting me to his flat at 7.30 pm sharp. All I had to bring was a bottle of wine or some beer. I opted for beer.

The idea behind Nanny-Nannettes Dinner was simple. The Nannies cooked a meal for all their little Nannettes in their flat in St. Chads. It was another chance to bond with your Nanny, and to meet the Nannettes of his/her flat mates. One big, happy, extended family of Nannies and Nannettes.

Chads (for brevity the Saint part got the unholy drop) was the location of the second year accommodation for all the St. Catharine's students that had made it that far. It consisted of flats of four and five people. Interestingly, it had recently finished quite highly in one of those lists that newspapers are often keen on printing, about the UK's most architecturally pleasing buildings, or something. This was largely to do with the fact that every bedroom in each flat was octagonal in shape, which I guess was pretty rare as far as buildings go. Chads was about a ten minute walk from college, just across the road, in fact, from the place of our lectures, the Sidgwick Site. I had arranged to walk down to Chads with Mark, Caolan and Oisin, and we set off in good time, armed with beer and wine, and dressed in shirts and trousers.

Chads reminded me of a block apartments you might find abroad. There were three full floors of flats, each with about ten flats on them, and then a fourth and a fifth floor that were home to only a couple of flats. Each floor had its own path, which ran along the outside of each flat. The path was bordered on the other side by a wooden support on all but the ground floor, presumably to limit the number of people that fell off. The rows of flats were not in straight lines, but in fact bent around themselves to form what looked like three sides of a hexagon, and the space that was subsequently created in the interior of this incomplete polygon was filled with grass and benches. It as all very complicated, very Cambridge, but ultimately quite nice.

Trevor's flat was on the ground floor, which did not appear to be the best spot. It wasn't blessed with much light, and in terms of people-traffic levels, the ground floor was like a motorway. The way selection worked was once you had chosen the people you wanted to share a flat with, all groups of four or five were put into a random ballot to determine the order of picking flats. You then waited anxiously for all the people above you in the ballot to pick all the flats that you wanted, and you took the best of what was left. In this ballot, Trevor's crew had come out near the bottom, and were thus forced to live there. Each flat was almost identical inside, equipped with four pretty decently sized octagonal bedrooms, a couple of bathrooms, a kitchen and a wide corridor but, as in any housing market, it was all about location, location, location.

I bid farewell to my one London and two Irish friends, as they went off in search of their Nannies' flats, and pressed the small black buzzer by the side of Trevor Starkey's name. He promptly answered the door, shook my hand, made some joke about the wind that I didn't really understand, and led me through to one of the bedrooms. The room evidently belonged to a girl, unless Trevor or his mate used curlers and mascara, and was full of people. I said a group hello, and quickly counted up. There were six in the room, excluding me and Trevor, meaning the full compliment of Nannies and Nannettes were all present and correct. As I sat down and cracked open a beer, I was having trouble working out who in the room were Nannies, and who were Nannettes. My initial instincts, based solely on how much each person was talking and how comfortable they appeared, suggested there were six Nannies and two Nannettes in the room, which my Maths A-level told me couldn't be right.

After chatting and drinking, mostly with Trevor and mostly about football, we were summoned by a curly haired girl to move into the corridor as dinner was served. I liked the fact that the corridors in the flats were wide enough to just about fit in a table and eight chairs. I had visions of my flat

A Tale of Friendship, Love and Economics

next year having big "family" meals, like *The Waltons* or something, all sat together catching up with what had been going on in each others' lives. In the end it turned out to be more *The Osbornes*.

I was seated opposite a guy with short fair hair and a tendency to blink a lot, and sandwiched between Trevor and a plump lad with glasses, who was wearing a shirt and tie. I was told the first course was Mexican fajitas, which, needless to say, I had never had before, but as everyone else was eating them, I could hardly refuse. Luckily, as most of these strange meat foods that I had been avoiding most of my life tended to be, they were really nice.

I found the conversation tricky to get into. The blinking lad opposite me was dominating proceedings at my end of the table. Unbelievably, he too was from Yorkshire, and I was beginning to wonder whether there were actually any other places in England except for that awful county and London. He was also very loud and very arrogant, especially for a Fresher that blinked so much. He was explaining to Trevor, and the rest of us who were forced to listen, that he and his mates from Barnsley had written a load of comedy sketches for radio. He then proceeded to act one out for us. It was about as funny as sticking a fork in your eye, and I found the obligatory fake laughter hard to generate. I laughed for real when he announced, in all seriousness, that they would probably turn it into a TV show in the near future if he could find the time. The guy to my left was also annoying. He was a Fresher as well, and talked posh. His contribution to the evening was to insist on playing his Chopin CD at full volume, and encourage us all to close our eyes and absorb whilst he played air piano and swayed his head around manically. It was a good job the food was good. I hadn't really said much all evening, spending my time eating and smiling politely, and had already been labelled by the curly haired girl as "the quiet one". This time I didn't really mind.

Whilst taking a tactical toilet break, my fifth of the evening, my mobile started to ring. I answered before the sound had chance to make it to the table outside. It was the Movie Star Look-alike. Her name actually flashed up on my screen, so I must have somehow drunkenly coaxed her number out of her on one of the previous nights. Nice one, Josh. I answered the phone as coolly as one can when whispering in a toilet. She got straight to the point. She was having a terrible Nanny-Nannettes Dinner, she was making a break for it, and wondered if I wanted to be rescued. I didn't think twice. I gave her my location, and she told me to play along with whatever she said. Roger. Over and out.

I rejoined a table in the middle of some sort of drinking game. You had to tap your hands in a certain way and a certain number of times, depending what the person to your left had done, or something, and if you got it wrong, you had to drink. And sometimes you didn't have to do anything, and if you did, you had to drink. I didn't follow. I tapped and drank the next fifteen minutes away, until I heard the heavenly sound of the door buzzer.

"Hi, is Josh here?" she was shown in by the curly haired girl. "Hey Josh, we've got to go. It's Ellie's birthday party and we're already late." I looked at my watch.

"Bloody hell, you're right. Time flies, and all that. Ellie will not be happy." I stood up from the table. "Trevor, I'm really sorry but I've got to go. I completely forgot." I looked over towards the curly haired girl, "Thanks for a lovely meal", and then to the rest of the table, "It was nice to meet you all". Then I was off.

Safe in the darkness and solitude of the space under the stairs up to the first floor, we giggled like naughty children. I thanked her for saving me. She said she was glad of the company. We spent the next few minutes trying to better each other's stories in the quest to discover who had had the worst night. With nothing much else to say, we climbed the stairs and went looking for other escapees.

I did feel guilty for leaving Trevor's party early. He did look a bit disappointed. It wasn't his fault, it was the fault of those stupid freshers with their stupid stories and stupid conversations. It was also my fault, for being the way I was.

On the second floor we found music and an open door. There was a party going on inside, and all seemed to be invited. The Movie Star Lookalike found a man to talk to that I didn't know, so I wandered around looking for something to do. There were about ten or so people in each of the bedrooms, and a few more in the corridor. I strode around the flat purposefully to disguise my lack of purpose. Happily, I stumbled across Faye in one of the bedrooms, slouched on the floor, and propped up against the side of a bed.

"Well, hello there, Mr Josh. How are you on this lovely evening?" She was drunk and sounding more Scottish than ever.

"Not so bad. Yourself?"

"Aye, not too bad, not too bad. Me thinks I might have had a wee bit too much to drink" she ended the sentence with a hiccup.
"You've had a good night, though?"
"Aye, grand." She paused for thought. "Grand."
"Any sign of Mary Jane?" I gave up my painful crouching position in favour of joining Faye leaning against the bed.
"Not seen her. She sent me a text saying things were going to plan with her Nanny".
"Bloody hell. Poor bloke."
"I know."
We both laughed.

We were soon joined by Mark, who was in his floppy drunken state, and Caolan, who was in his loud drunken state. Oisin had gone home a while ago. The Group and my nemesis were also there, but we mutually limited contact with each other to a few nods and a few "alright"s.

The party was good as far as parties go, but the excesses of the week seemed to be catching up on everybody. Before the party was over, Caolan, Mark and myself were ready for home. Despite the walk from college to Chads taking just ten minutes earlier that evening, the walk back took closer to ninety. Caolan insisted that he knew exactly where to go, but then he also insisted that he could sing. The walk took in some parts of Cambridge that I had never seen before, nor seen since.

On our long and winding way back, and in between bursts of songs whose tune sounded familiar but whose words were certainly not, Caolan started telling me about some girl he'd met at his Nanny-Nannettes Dinner, but he didn't do anything with her because of his girlfriend back home. He repeated himself several times, and each time his point was made more passionately. Whilst we were bonding I decided to tell him about the Movie Star Look-alike. He silently considered what I'd said for a minute or two, and then told me, with fresh vigour and excitement, about a girl he'd met that night and how didn't do anything with her because of his girlfriend back home. Like I said, I didn't think we would ever be that close.

We eventually stumbled across a building that thankfully turned out to be our college and headed inside. Despite universal fatigue, there was still just about enough energy in the group to climb the stairs to Oisin's room and bang on the door. Not even a corpse could have failed to be awakened by the racket, but Oisin remained silent inside. Caolan sang him an Irish song, something about the town they loved so well, but even this failed to coax him out of his room. After a mouthful of drunken abuse, we got bored and tired and headed off to bed. There was a note on my door from Mary Jane saying that she needed to talk to me. I fell asleep wondering what it was about, and wondering how on earth I was going to get up for another nine o'clock lecture.

Chapter 13

Freshers' Week was as good as over, and normal college life began. Well, as normal as things ever got in Cambridge. Whilst I had had a really good time in Freshers' Week, I was also glad it was finished. I was looking forward to settling into some sort of routine. Even, maybe, looking forward to doing a bit of work.

I cut down the amount of time I spent with The Group. I was pleased that I found people to hang around with so early on, but I'd stopped having a good time in their company. I couldn't be myself, and to be honest I couldn't cope with all the late nights. The Group was also very exclusive. They seemed happy just to know each other. I felt like I should have applied for permission from the committee before I brought Mark Novak up to meet them. On top of this, all thoughts of a whirlwind romance with the Movie Star Look-alike were squashed by the philosophising preaching prophet from Bradford.

One day, whilst I was happily tucking into a Crunchie bar on the bench outside the college library, trying in vain to bite and suck the chocolate off and just leave the honey bit, the Great One came along and sat down next to me. After an initial hello and a routine observation about the weather, he began showing a remarkable interest in the posters in my room, posters that he'd apparently heard so much about. He explained that he had been told that I had achieved a remarkable effect with John Lennon and Martin Luther King staring intensely at each other and he really wanted to see them for himself. I wasn't stupid enough to believe him. The effect was good, but not that good. After unsuccessfully trying to get out of it, I reluctantly led his Royal Highness across Main Court and up to my room. After

A Tale of Friendship, Love and Economics

glancing at the posters for a microsecond, he got down to the real purpose of his trip up the stairs of M-block.

"Josh," he began, as patronising and condescending as ever, "how do you feel you've settled in?"

"Pretty good, apart from meeting you, you big dick." Only the first two words actually left my mouth.

"Have you met anyone special since you got here?"

"What do you mean?" I knew what he meant. How did he know?

"I mean, any girls, you know, that you like?"

"Well… I mean… erm…" he liked to see me squirm.

"You can tell me" He reminded me of an evil character in a fairytale.

"Well, I suppose I kind of like a certain girl… from Leeds."

"I thought so."

"Is it obvious?"

"Very."

"Oh."

"Listen, Josh, let me give you some advice. She's going through a tough time with her boyfriend from back home at the moment. The last thing she needs is you fancying her and making her upset. Try to forget about it. Yeah?"

"I wasn't planning on doing anything to upset her." Even I thought I sounded pathetic.

"Good. Just be careful, that's all I'm saying."

Neither of us spoke for what felt like a couple of minutes, then the Great One brought the proceedings to an end. "Their eyes aren't quite lined up properly, you know?"

Nob head.

Breaking away from The Group was hardly a big wrench. I got the feeling that the two Irish, Caolan especially, were also getting a bit sick of it, and Mark never really felt a part of it all anyway. We all wanted to meet new people, and that wasn't really an option in a club whose main strength seemed to be its exclusivity. Dark-horse Francesca had also been making fewer and fewer appearances as the weeks were going on.

Time saved by ditching The Group was more than offset by time taken up with Mary Jane. The thing she had wanted to talk to me about was her pending relationship with her Nanny, a Welsh lad called Gavin. She had indeed captured and kissed him after Nanny-Nannettes Dinner, and then again in the nightclub, Cindies, a couple of evenings later, whilst dancing to Take That. During the next few weeks the incestuous couple progressed from "just having fun" to "kind of seeing each other" to "yeah, definitely going out". Right from the start, I was told every detail, at every hour of the day.

As Freshers' Week petered out and my longed-for routine kicked in, I would often find myself shamefully but happily tucked up in bed pre-midnight, tired after a hard day's work, lying in the scratcher watching a bit of telly, or flicking through the pages of a book I wanted to finish. I have repeatedly found that my body, especially after a long summer, isn't designed for early starts. As I adapted to this new climate where people were regularly up at 8 am (and a strange species called "rowers" often rose around six), I found I needed at least a couple of these early nights a week to survive. So, I would be quite contentedly lost in a dream when I would hear a gentle knock at my door around 2 am. At first I would ignore it; half assuming it was part of my dream, and half because I couldn't be arsed getting out of bed to answer it. By 2.01 am, the gentle knock returned with a bit more force, and was often accompanied by a "Josh, are you awake?" Silence, apparently, was an unacceptable answer, and a shout of "no" seemed to lack credibility. A couple of knocks later, I would reluctantly roll out of bed and bundle my way to the door, only half opening my right eye, and keeping the left one firmly shut in the hope that I could still reap at least half the benefits of an uninterrupted night's sleep. The times often changed, ranging from 9 pm until about three in the morning, but the face behind the door was always the same.

In those early days Mary Jane was happy. She made the most out of Freshers' Week and thrived on the challenge of chasing her Nanny. During the day she would dazzle myself and Faye with her latest plans and schemes, and explain again and again to her sceptical neighbours how it was perfectly rational to read so much into the shirts Gavin wore and how he had started saying "see you later" to her instead of "bye". In our late night rendezvous in M14, with Faye snoring the night away a couple of doors down (no door or wall was thick enough to block out that sound), the strawberry-blonde vet would give me the latest update from that night, and tell me all the stuff that was on her mind. It was like I was addicted to a reality TV show, where following Mary Jane's life was becoming the main thing I did each day. And I enjoyed it. At first. When things were going well.

I liked the way Mary Jane felt she could talk to me about all this stuff. She said I was a good listener. She even sought my advice on relationships, which was like asking Stevie Wonder to choose you a new pattern of wallpaper. She encouraged me to tell her things as well. I told her I fancied the girl who reminded me of a movie star, but how I wasn't really too bothered because I knew it was just a phase and her friend was a cock. Mary Jane tried to make more of it, even mentioning the L-word that always made me cringe. She also wanted me to talk about my family, but I wasn't used to doing that. After a particularly heavy night to celebrate Mark Novak's nineteenth birthday, she even cleaned up my sick, patched up my arm (whilst minding my own business, I had been violently pounced upon by a ferocious holly bush) and put me to bed. She was fast becoming the best friend I had always wanted. Or thought I always wanted. Night after night, she would talk to me about everything, and expected me to do the same. This took a lot of getting used to. It felt strange to be so close to someone that I had only known for a couple of weeks, telling her things that I had never told anyone. My mates at home said I just wanted to get in her knickers. They didn't understand.

Chapter 14

I had to find time in my hectic schedule of going out, counselling Mary Jane, and doing to odd bit of economics, to play some football. I had decided against answering any of the countless emails concerning rowing, and after a while they happily went away. I had loved footy for as long as I could remember, but I was never really any good. My two main problems were that I lacked pace and I lacked ability. I wasn't that fit, either. In my favour were my height and the fact that I shouted a lot during matches. I could also kick the ball quite far (distance was bought at the price of accuracy, of course). I was never going to be a thirty-goal-a-season striker, or a cultured midfield genius, but as a centre-back, as they say to people who are crap, I "did a job".

Thankfully, my beloved St. Catharine's College had three football teams that I could try to do a job for. For its size, this was a lot, but then we were supposed to be a sporting college. As I signed up to the football list at the sports squash, I was told that as long as I could walk I would at least get into the thirds. Armed with the knowledge that I was quite good at walking, I set off to football trial a week or so after Freshers' Week finished feeling reasonably confident.

What I wasn't confident about was finding my way to the sports grounds. I couldn't make the Plodge rendezvous that was organised by the captain as it clashed with a lecture. I was supposed to be going with Oisin, but he pulled out at the last minute because he was behind on work. I tried to sign up Caolan as a replacement, but he politely explained that football was gay (not like his beloved polo, of course, a sport renowned for its masculinity and heterosexuality). Armed with my awful sense of direction and some vague instructions from Mary Jane, who'd thought she'd heard where Catz sports grounds were from a fat, ginger vet from Trinity College, I wandered with boots in hand across fields and ditches.

I arrived about an hour late. The grounds were about half an hour's walk from college if you went the right way, and twice that if you took my scenic route. I apologised to a chubby boy with a quiff who seemed to be the captain, and scurried off into the changing rooms.

The sports grounds were very impressive indeed. The centrepiece was a white-lined and lush-grassed football pitch. The groundsman was very proud of his little baby. There was no wear and tear around the centre circle or in any of the goal mouths, and there were even four yellow and red flags to mark the corners. The only clue to the pitch's summer metamorphosis was the sectioned-off cricket square that lay a small distance off one of the long sides of the football field. There was a rugby pitch, which doubled as a second football pitch, in the adjoining filed, as well as a mini football pitch which was used for training. There was a grass hockey pitch and three clay tennis courts, a sports hall, which was hiding a basketball court and a couple of squash courts, and a wooden pavilion that smelt of grass, mud and sweat. A few miles down the road, Catz was also the proud owner of an all-weather hockey pitch. We were the only college to possess such a thing, and it seemed to make our hockey players very happy, and our rivals very jealous. All in all, it is fair to say that the college remained significantly sports-orientated, despite the growing importance of various academic league tables, which favoured exam results over sports trophies. Indeed, a prominent fellow of St. Catharine's was once heard saying that he longed for a return to the days when the college had more Blues (people who had played a sport at university level) than scholars, and many people felt the same way.

I threw on my stuff, did a few token stretches and keenly jogged out onto the pitch. I tried my best to look devastated when the captain told me I'd missed all the (completely knackering) warming up and the (boring) drills, and only arrived in time to play a match. Luckily, one team was short of a centre-back, so I continued my jog all the way onto the pitch, to join my fellow orange-bibbed team-mates. About fifteen freshers had turned up for the trial, and so the remaining seven players were second and third years. I immediately recognised Simon, the Jewish economist, who had taken off his little round hat for the game. He looked like the type of person who would be rubbish at football and I was glad he was on the opposition. By the end of the game he had nutmegged me three times, made me fall over twice and scored four goals. He was ace.

Thankfully, much of the rest of the quality on display was of a lower standard. A much lower standard. The guy who was playing alongside me at right-back was the worst football player I had ever seen. He swung his leg with complete disregard to the location of the ball. On the few occasions when he did make contact, the ball either trickled out for a throw-in or went straight to one of our un-bibbed enemies. With him in the back four, we were always fighting a loosing battle in terms of stopping them scoring, but at least he made the rest of us look good.

My performance that day apparently warranted immediate selection to the mighty 3rd XI, an honour I received via email. Our first game was at home on a Saturday morning against Sidney Sussex 2nd XI, and I put myself on a self-imposed alcohol ban on the Friday night in order to be in optimal shape for my big debut.

I'd already factored in the very real possibility that I would ignore the beeping of my annoying mobile phone alarm, and so had made arrangements to borrow Faye's bike to get to the sports grounds in double-quick time. There were three noteworthy features about Faye's bike: it was tiny; it was called Isabelle (as in the apparently "classic" Scottish joke, "Isabelle necessary on a bicycle?" "Yes it is." Right...); and it did actually have a bell – a large red one with a picture of Minnie Mouse that stared up at me as I cycled, my knees brushing past my ears.

I arrived on time, and saw my new team-mates mingling outside the wooden pavilion. As I was soon to find out, the mighty Catz 3rds were a right mixed bunch. They were made up of eager freshers, not so eager second and third years who had usually been roped into turning up the morning of the game by a desperate captain who had only had four replies from people saying they could play, a couple of post-graduates who played because they lived next to the grounds and thus could roll out of bed onto the pitch, and a few of the kitchen staff who turned up so that they could kick some posh Cambridge boys without getting arrested. The captain was a third year who looked like he could be a third year at high school. He led us into the changing rooms and gave us our kit. There was a mass scramble for shirt numbers 7 and 9, but happily the 4 that I desired had been tossed aside by a Beckham-wannabe ready for me to scoop up. The kit was the claret and blue colours of West Ham and Burnley, and was dangerously skin tight.

The little captain, who had a surprisingly loud voice, gave us a team talk as we were getting kitted up. He explained that we were a new team, no-one knew each other, and no-one really knew what position to play in. He also explained that he was aware from the emails that at least seven of us were carrying potentially debilitating injuries and were thus unlikely to last more than ten minutes. Moreover, our opponents were a 2nd XI and were thus likely to have some first team ringers in their line-up. We nodded in agreement. Nevertheless, he explained less convincingly, we were going to win because we were playing "for the wheel", and that's all that mattered.

"Who the fuck are all these lot?" shouted a small member of the kitchen staff who wore glasses, had a hint of a beer belly, and was in possession of a strong cockney accent.

"Erm... good point Buzz," said the captain, looking like a parent trying to cover up for his child's inappropriate outburst. "Let's do a round of names."

"Right, I'll start," announced Buzz. "I'm Buzz, and I'm fuckin' brilliant. Pass to me, and we'll be alright."

"Buzz, you're shit," shouted the largest member of the kitchen staff, removing his fag from his mouth long enough to let the words come out, and then popping it back in. His name was Mick. Or to give him his full title, "Mick the Cook".

"Fuck off," replied Buzz, after some consideration.

We took turns to introduce ourselves. To everyone who had a southern accent, Buzz would politely enquire as to whom they supported, and if the answer was not Spurs, he would tell them to fuck off. To everyone who had a northern accent (that would be just me then) he would call them a northern monkey. Having been fully introduced and bonded, we marched out of the changing room and onto the pitch.

We didn't have a proper referee, so one of our substitutes was asked to do it. This provoked a negative reaction from our opponents, but was soon silenced when Buzz enquired what the fuck else we were meant to do. As the make-shift ref signalled that we were about to get underway, I took up my position in the back four alongside Mick the Cook, who was still sucking every last bit of life out of his cigarette, the worst footballer in history at right-back, and the lad whose surname began with S but had had to stand with the As for the Matric Photo as he was being sick at left-back. We looked a frightening force.

The game didn't get off to the best of starts for me when my first touch was a header that sent the ball hurtling onto my own crossbar. Seeing that I was more than a little nervous, Buzz offered some words of encouragement.

"What the fuck are you doing?"

After ten minutes I realised that if I kept running around like the proverbial headless chicken, I would die, so I transformed myself into a continental-style defender who just strolls around and uses his perfect reading of the game to ensure he is always in the right place at the right time. We were soon 3–0 behind.

The half-time team talk was a contest between our poor captain's interminable quest to draw positives from our appalling performance, and Buzz's insistence that we were all shit. Mick the Cook pointed out that if Buzz actually passed to the rest of the team instead of trying to take on the world and his wife every time he got the ball, we might have scored a few goals. After some consideration, Buzz told him to fuck off.

We were a little better in the second half and we ended up loosing 6–2. The captain said that he was pleased with how we all played and that we could learn a lot from the game. Only the naive believed him. Cramp in my right calf meant that Faye's Isabelle was too painful to ride, so I hobbled the long walk home with Duane, the central midfielder and fellow M-block resident, who went to a posh boarding school.

In the coming weeks we played and actually won quite a few third team games. We found ourselves sitting comfortably in fourth place in Division 5b, and through to the third round of the Shield competition. The spirit in the team was good. The right-back and left-back decided that football was not their cup of tea and tried their hand at rowing and sailing respectively. The captain found some decent replacements, and together with Mick the Cook we formed quite a tight unit at the back. Buzz started scoring goals, which thankfully resulted in the majority of his abuse be directed away from us and towards the opposition.

I soon discovered that Buzz, Mick and the rest of the kitchen staff were invaluable to the team. They would turn up to every single game at the drop of a hat, and play their arses off when they got there. They would also give you extra food in the canteen, which depending on what delicacies were on offer was either a good thing or a bad thing. Also, once you realised that Buzz took the piss out of everyone and didn't mind having the piss ripped out of him, you found he was a really nice guy. Honestly.

Anyway, I soon found myself electronically receiving a call-up to the Catz 2nd XI. It was the proudest moment of my undistinguished career to date, and so I printed out the email and Blu-Tacked it to the wall in my room.

It was whilst playing for the 2nd XI that I met two people who, for better or worse, remained friends throughout my time at Cambridge. Their reputation preceded them. After a "bad taste" party at St. Chads (everyone wanted to borrow Oisin's normal clothes for the night, and he couldn't figure out why) two first year geographers, Joe Porter and Nick MacLean, decided to go for a night-time walk around Cambridge. In the process of this walk they happened to come across a couple of traffic cones and a yellow diversion sign with a big black arrow painted on it. Nick and Joe transported the signs from their home in the town centre to a location just outside the front gates of our college and proceeded to set up an arrangement of their own. Their intention was to inform the public of a new diversion that directed vehicles and pedestrians off the street and through our Main Court. The result was a journey in the back of a police van. Nick and Joe's efforts to explain the benefits of the new route were in vain, and a caution and a gowned trip to see the college Dean was the unfortunate reward for an evening's hard work. The college Dean was the fearless and proud leader of the Land Economists, Dr Tinsley, and I just couldn't imagine anyone with as funny a Brummie accent as he had sounding the least bit scary. Nick and Joe assured me he did.

Looking back, it is hard to think of two people less likely to be involved in such an incident. Joe Porter would talk all day about doing it, but then

A Tale of Friendship, Love and Economics

not get round to it, whereas Nick MacLean would be far too sensible to try it. Drink was the only explanation.

Nick and Joe were nice guys, considering they were geographers. Joe liked to encourage people to suggest that he looked like Charlie Sheen ("You won't believe it, right, but do you know, some people say I look like Charlie Sheen? Crazy, isn't it?"), and Nick would often engage in conversation whilst fiddling about in his crotch area. Both had dark hair, and whilst Nick had successfully grown a pair of sideburns, Joe kept trying to. Joe was reported to have at least four showers a day, and Nick once claimed that, whatever the situation, two wipes with toilet paper was enough for him. Joe could play guitar and often talked about starting up a band. This never happened. Nick ran like a disabled duck, and made funny noises with his mouth just before he tackled someone. Nick was a right-footed left-back, and Joe played right-wing or upfront. Joe had ambitions to get in the 1st XI and would ruthlessly network with those in a position to make his dream come true, whereas Nick was happy where he was. Nick liked to remind people that as a child he had appeared on Going Live; Joe liked to remind people that he was from a state school. Both were a bit shy in their own kind of way.

I soon introduced the pair of geographers to my fellow economists Caolan, Oisin and Mark (Nick actually lived just two minutes away from Mark, which sparked off numerous conversations that interested no-one but those two), and they became regular members of the growing tribe that would watch *Neighbours* in my room every day at 5.35 pm.

Actual football for the seconds was not as fun as for the thirds. The standard was higher (after all, we were in the dizzy heights of Division 3), and the team spirit was lower, almost certainly due to the fact that we were routinely stuffed week after week. We lost heavily to John's 2nds, Queen's 2nds and Sydney Sussex 1sts, and only won 5–2 against Hughes Hall 1sts, a college renowned for being absolutely awful at all sports that weren't rugby. We were also tragically knocked out of the Shield competition whilst the Mighty Thirds marched on. The misfortune of the 2nds gave Buzz, Mick the Cook, and the rest of the culinary gang much material to pummel the second team players with each time they came into hall to eat. Playing for both teams, my loyalties were tied, but as the kitchen staff were bigger, and the sole providers of food, I sided with them.

So, for the majority of the first term, I was playing at least two games a week and going to training. All of which got me dirty, injured and sometimes a little behind on work.

Chapter 15

Whenever my friends from home asked me if I had a lot of work to do at Cambridge, my answer was always the same. Yes.

Five pieces of work every two weeks was a lot to fit in. Especially considering you had an average of three lectures a day, and had to go out at least three times a week, which, for me, normally made the following morning a write-off. The secret was not to waste time. If you were going to work for a couple of hours, then you had to make sure you worked properly for all of that time. For me, this meant not working in my room, as more often than not Mary Jane or Faye would knock on the door and demand a cup of tea, or else the radio or TV would magically turn itself on and distract me. One of the two college libraries, or the Marshall Library of Economics, were your best bet to get some proper work done, so that's where I often went.

Someone back home had told me that A-levels were far harder than a degree. The expression "yeah, bollocks" springs to mind. There was no doubt at all that this was the most difficult work I had ever done. You could read a paragraph in a book over and over again and still not have a clue what the author was banging on about. You could read book after book and not even begin to scratch the surface of a topic. You could search on Google for pre-written answers for your set questions and not find any.

Nevertheless, I was quiet pleased with my first essay about the differences between Keynes and the neo-classicists. Work usually had to be handed in twenty-four hours before the supervision, and so I proudly placed my first piece of work in a plastic wallet (Caolan and Oisin called them "Polly Pockets". Silly Irish) and dropped it off in the Plodge, marked for the attention of Mr Stevens. I then made myself a nice hot cup of tea to celebrate.

On the academic side, Cambridge's big selling point relative to other universities is its supervision system. The way things work is that you are given an essay title and a reading list, and then off you trot to write the essay on your own. You then hand it in, it is marked, and then you have a supervision on the essay topic. Supervisions normally take place with a maximum of five students and one supervisor, although scary one-on-ones were not uncommon in many subjects. They last an hour, and take place in the supervisors' rooms, which are often cosy and warm, filled with the aroma of coffee, complete with comfy sofas and chairs, and scattered with books. Some supervisors just teach like a lecture, but allow you to ask questions, some spend the whole time asking you questions, and some make you read out bits of your essay to the class and then proceed to rip it to shreds. Some supervisors made you coffee, some made you cry, some gave you a biscuit, some gave you a hard time. I generally found supervisions quite stressful, but very useful for making sure you understood a topic.

I had been playing football when we were deciding who would go in which group, and as a result I hadn't managed to get in either one of Mark's or Caolan and Oisin's. With an aching left knee and a 3–1 defeat hanging over me, I found myself stood outside Mr Stevens room at four o'clock on a windy Wednesday afternoon. Joining me in so-called Group Three were the hockey-playing economist, who was desperately trying to guess what questions Mr Stevens might ask and frantically asking our opinions on the matter, and the economist who was prone to wearing a bowler hat, who turned out to be from Cyprus. The latter was three years older than me, and had achieved the rank of sergeant whilst undertaking national service in his country's army. He could even drive a tank. As Group Two, containing four people, of which 50 per cent were Irish, and 25 per cent female, sauntered out looking weary, but reassuringly still alive, I led my group in.

The supervision was in C4; the same room where we had met Mr Stevens for the first time and where we had gathered for pre-Matric drinks. I made straight for the comfy-looking sofa and was joined by the hockey-playing economist, while the Cypriot ex-sergeant chose to go it alone on a hardback chair. I fiddled around in my bag for a pen, my pad of A4 paper and the notes I had made for the essay, and then had a quick look around the room. It was easier to notice things in the room now that there were fewer people. For a start, there was a full-size harpsichord in one corner. I never saw this being played in all my time at Cambridge and never got round to asking Mr Stevens why it was in his room. Never one to let anything go to waste, Mr Stevens used the instrument as a make shift table to hold anything from books to bottles of wine. There was also a portrait of an elderly college fellow laying on the floor and leaning against a wall. Again, the question of why Mr Stevens should have a picture of another fellow in his room was never addressed. There was also a sofa-bed, which I never saw in its bed form, and which nobody could ever sit on as it was always piled high with books and papers. There were books and journals scattered everywhere, although they tended to be the same ones open in the same places week after week, which led us to wonder just how much work our DOS was getting up to. There was a fireplace which was never lit, and a window which was never opened. All in all, Mr Stevens' room was quite a nice place to have supervisions; pretty homely and informal. However, on the whole, regardless of the comfy sofa, his supervisions were anything but relaxing.

Mr Stevens began our first supervision by handing our essays back. I quickly flicked through to the last page, where I found some scrawled handwriting that read, "Good essay. Policy implications? 63%". Sixty-three per cent sounded a bit on the low side. It might not have got me a B at A-level. I quickly glanced over at the hockey player who was sat next to me on the couch to see if I could see what he got, but I couldn't.

Experience soon taught us that Mr Stevens nearly always gave marks in the 62–68 bracket whether your essay was good or not. In the university marking system, anything 70 and above was given a first, 60–69 was a 2:1, 50–59 was a 2:2, 40–49 was a third, and below that you had things called "ordinaries", which was a pass but only just, and of course, the dreaded "failure". So, Mr Stevens tended to give everyone 2:1s. I guess his logic was something along the lines of, if you wrote a really good essay and he gave you a first, you might get complacent and start putting in less effort, so if instead he gave you a high 2:1 this would provide the incentive you needed to keep working harder and harder to try and achieve that elusive first. Similarly, if you wrote a bad essay, giving you the 2:2 you deserved might make you think there is no point in bothering and thus resign yourself to defeat, whereas giving you a low 2:1 gives you sufficient confidence in your abilities to keep trying to better yourself. Of course, the problem was once we figured out Mr Stevens system, we weren't psychologically influenced by his mark. We used to say that he had a random mark generator that he pressed once he'd finished reading through your essay that gave you a mark between sixty-two and sixty-eight. We also speculated that he had a stamp that said, "Good essay. Policy implications?" on it in his hand writing.

At first I found Mr Stevens' supervisions pretty intimidating, and I think Mr Stevens did too. This was largely because the Cypriot ex-sergeant had a habit of grilling our poor supervisor on every single issue. "No!" he would shout when Mr Stevens made a statement he didn't agree with. And he really knew his stuff. He had always read and fully understood every single reading on the reading list. I had rarely read and understood the reading list itself. Mr Stevens was scared of him, and I was too. As a result I kept pretty quiet in those early supervisions, scared that I would be on the receiving end of a Cypriot "No!" as soon as I opened my mouth.

However, it was not long before I had a brain-wave. Mark Novak's group went to supervisions first, and mine were last. This left one hour between Mark coming out and me going in. I arranged for Mark to come round for a relaxing cup of tea once he'd finished his supervision, and after a few sips I would subtly swing the conversation away from football and towards what questions Mr Stevens asked in his supervision. After a while, I couldn't be arsed being subtle, or making poor Mark a cup of tea. He would pop round, give me his notes, I would read them and then drop them off later. I would then rock up to supervisions armed with answers to questions that hadn't even bee asked yet. Sometimes I would pre-empt a question ("Mr Stevens, I was just wondering about..."), and then offer an answer ("Well, I don't really know, but maybe it's something to do with..."). Mr Stevens was impressed, the Cypriot ex-sergeant was suspicious, I was happy.

Mr Stevens was a good supervisor and a nice guy. He would always ask you how everything was going before the supervision kicked off. This was probably as much out of a desire to find out some good gossip as a concern for our welfare, but it was nice to see he took an interest in our lives. He was a left-wing socialist, and made no effort to hide it. His solution to every problem in the economy was government intervention. He hated Thatcher and hated free trade, and hated having to teach the economic benefits of each. His proudest moment was being called "a left-wing dinosaur" in the *Daily Telegraph*, a story he told us with a fresh smile and fresh enthusiasm over and over again.

Compared to other supervisions, I guess Mr Stevens' were fairly relaxed. Undoubtedly the most stressful were our Micro supervisions. Unless you knew absolutely everything about the topic, you were in big trouble. Our supervisor was pretty young, and he had the look of someone who had played rugby in his time. Five minutes into a supervision, just as you were getting settled, he would say things like, "Caolan, you've been pretty quiet so far, why don't you explain to us all about the significance of a concave indifference curve." Under normal circumstances I'd have tried to make

Caolan laugh as he tried to answer, but in these supervisions I didn't dare. Our supervisor also had a strange habit of saying words like "fastastimundo", "groovy" and even "Cowabunga". He only ever said these if you got something correct, which was a something of a rarity in our supervisions. Every fortnight we were subjected to one hour of pure grilling. At the end you were often tired and shaking, but safe in the knowledge that you now knew the topic inside-out.

Our Statistics supervisions were at the other end of the intensity spectrum. All ten of us were taken in one group into a tiny room by our bearded supervisor. After a few sessions, half of us were only recognisable to him by the backs our heads, as the lack of space meant we had to sit with our backs to him. Most of his supervisions lasted about six minutes. He would ask if we had any problems with the work. We would say no. He would say go. After a while, Caolan, Mark and I started doing the stats work together as, unlike an essay, it was the kind of work that could be made easier by a bit of collaboration. By the end of the term, collaboration had been redefined to mean Mark did the work, and Caolan and I copied it. I felt guilty, but Mark said he didn't mind as Caolan and I only slowed things down in the group work sessions.

Politics supervisions were like no other. They were taken by a guy from Anglia Polytechnic University, the only other uni in Cambridge. He was a really nice guy, and clearly very knowledgeable, but spent nearly all of our supervisions telling us about how he would like to throw his mother-in-law off the side of a boat, and how his lawn-mower was leaking petrol. What all that had to do with the rise in popularity of New Labour and the increasing importance of globalisation respectively was lost on most of us, but we enjoyed his supervisions all the same.

Finally, our History supervisions took place at the all girls' college that went by the name of New Hall. This was miles away from Catz (one and a half, at least), and involved walking up a massive hill. Our supervisor was a lady who was prone to wearing short skirts, and who the hockey playing economist apparently once said he fancied, although he has feverishly denied it ever since. Her room resembled a boudoir. It contained a bed, a comfy couch, nude paintings on the wall, all illuminated by subtle red lighting. Unbeknown to our supervisor, we sometimes played highly sophisticated games between ourselves in her supervisions. For example, we were all given a word before we went in that we had to say at some stage during the supervision, like Andrex or peanut butter or Nivea Moisturising Cream. Sometimes this sparked off big debates about the role of toilet paper or dry skin in the industrial revolution, and our supervisor seemed genuinely pleased with our original insights.

Supervisions and lectures meant that the economists were rarely out of each other's hair for long. It was a good job we all seemed to get on with each other okay. Definite sub-groups seemed to be forming within our band of ten, which I guess was always inevitable with such a large number; however, we were all proudly united under the banner of Catz First Year Economists, and I liked all my fellow subject buddies very much. Indeed, we seemed to get on better as a group than most other subjects, especially the vets who seemed to hate each other.

As the term went on, the attendance ratios in lectures were mixed across our group. At the bottom were the hockey player, the Malaysian, and a guy who allegedly had a burger and chips from Gardi's, the Greek take-away, every night. Within a couple of weeks, they had binned lectures all together in favour of sleep. Caolan, Oisin and myself were somewhere in the middle. We went to most lectures. The only ones we regularly binned were the crap ones or the ones that were at 9 am (and maybe 10 am) after a heavy night. People like Mark, Jewish footballer Simon and the Cypriot ex-sergeant went to nearly every lecture, even though we tried to apply significant peer pressure, especially to Mark, to try and make them come to their senses and stop making the rest of us look bad.

All in all, work played a significant role in my first term at Cambridge, as it would inevitably do in all terms, but thankfully it didn't dominate proceedings.

Chapter 16

Up until now I suppose I didn't really have a good reason for disliking the All Mighty Philosophising Preaching Prophet from Bradford as much as I did. "We just got off on the wrong foot," I suppose you could say. "Live and let live"; "It takes all sorts", "First impressions aren't everything". Well, as it happened, my good reason was waiting just around the corner.

I was watching *Match of the Day* in my room on a Saturday night with the two footballing geographers, Joe and Nick, as well as the ever-present economists Oisin and Mark (Caolan hated football, and was elsewhere) when the first text message beeped its way onto my mobile phone. It was from a mystery number not stored in my phone book, and read as follows:

Hey josh. I don't usually do things like this but its about time I started takin chances. I think ur fit & we cud have fun together. xS

Bloody hell, I thought, and I started grinning like an idiot.

Keeping things quiet was not exactly my strong point, so after contemplating for all of two seconds whether it was maybe time to start, I immediately told the rest of the football-watching contingent, before popping next door to tell Mary Jane and Faye. I had never had a secret admirer before, but I had always wanted one. As soon as a suitably poor match was on, we turned off the sound and started actively thinking who it could be. The problem was, I didn't think I knew any S's. In fact, the only one that sprung to mind was Mr Stevens, and I hadn't picked up any signs to suggest that he fancied me – he hadn't even been giving me good marks. As my crack team of detectives were going through the recently arrived Matriculation Photo and noting down likely S candidates, my mobile beeped again:

Hey josh. so r u single at the mo? I hope ur. xS

"Bloody hell, she seems keen," said Joe Porter, dribbling my mini football round the room as he spoke.

"Desperate, more like," chipped in Caolan, who had joined us once the news had reached him.

Although I was sceptical, the group consensus was that I should reply. Caolan suggested something along the lines of: "ru fit? If so, fancy a shag? xJ". I promptly exercised my veto. In the end, after a lively discussion concerning the psychological nature of text messages, I opted for the brilliantly crafted:

Hi S. thanks 4 your messages. can u tell me who ur? J

Moments later, back came the reply:

Not yet josh. but u'll find out soon. sweet dreams. xS

In the following days, more messages came. I managed to build a picture of S from the snippets of information contained in her sub-160 character electronic notes. S was a girl, from my college, and in my year. I gave her a bit of a quiz to prove that she was from Catz and that she knew who I was. She said that she was a bit hurt that I didn't believe her, but she nevertheless answered all the questions and passed with flying colours. It sounded

A Tale of Friendship, Love and Economics

promising. It soon got to the stage where I actually looked forward to her messages. I suppose, technically, she was a bit of a stalker, but again I'd never had one of those before, and as they say, try anything once (except for fish, mayonnaise and chopping your genitals off).

I continually asked her if we could meet and finally she replied, saying that she would be in the college bar tonight at 8.30 pm wearing something red. It felt like I was in a film. A really bad, low-budget one. I was there for 8 pm, positioned and ready, sat on a table in the far corner of the bar so I that could see everyone who came through either door. The rest of the gang were there. I surrounded myself with three economists and a feisty female vet for moral, physical and intellectual support. I brought the two geographers, Joe and Nick, along too.

There was a lot of red entering the bar that night; T-shirts, jumpers, scarves, gloves, hats. I even caught a brief and rather disturbing glimpse of a pair of red frilly knickers on a rather large girl as she bent over to pick up a few coins that she had dropped at the bar. None of the ladies in red came over to our table all night, and at 9.45 pm I had had enough and retired, defeated and deflated, back up to my room. Mary Jane made me a cup of tea to cheer me up.

The mysteriously elusive S texted me just as I was clambering into bed around midnight:

Hey josh. saw u in the bar tonight. 2 nervous 2 cum over with all your mates there. we'll meet when ur alone. sweet dreams. xS

The following evening I was rustling up a nice little delicacy in the kitchen when I was joined by a lad from down my corridor called Jude. He had black floppy hair that formed a pair of curtains that were never quite open. We had met several times in similar circumstances as he too was fond of a late-night bowl of cereal. We sometimes ate them in each other's rooms or just slumped in the corridor on the steps outside my room. He was a really nice guy, chilled, mellow, and far cooler than me. Apart from Mary Jane and Faye, Jude was the only person I didn't mind sharing my precious milk with. As I poured milk on my Weetabix, and he stood patiently in line with his Clusters ready for access to the fridge, I started telling him about my stalker. Jude's face was not one of surprise or excitement, more one of concern, one burdened by the weight of knowledge. He stopped me just as I was getting up to the red in the bar bit.

"Look Josh, there's something you should know."

"No, Jude! Tell me you haven't been eating your cereals with someone else behind me back?" He smiled, but not as much as he normally would have.

"No, Josh, it's about your stalker. I know who it is" And then he told me. And then we sat in the corridor and ate our late-night cereals until I calmed down.

The bastard. The smug, arrogant pretentious bastard. The All Mighty Stalking, Philosophising Preaching Prophet from Bradford had reeled me in hook, line and sinker and hung me out to dry. Jude studied history with him and had overheard him boasting about his brilliant little scheme in the history library the other day. Jude told me they were all in on it. The Group. Not Caolan or Oisin, he assured me. Or Francesca. She had left long ago. But the witty weird girl was involved, as was the girl who owned the room where we used to gather night after night in those dark days, as was the Movie Star Look-alike, so long the object of my affections. I could and should have blamed them all, but I only blamed him. If any one else had done it to me I would have found it funny. I would even have congratulated them, but not him. Not him.

Later that night, just as I was dozing, about to enter a Freudian dream involving Mary Jane, Mark Novak and my father, I was re-delivered to consciousness by an all too familiar beep beep.

Hey josh. i'm sorry but i don't think we should text each other any more. it's my fault. it's been good getting 2 know u. ur a great guy. take care. xS

I replied quickly:

It's ok. i understand. it's been nice getting 2 know u2. take care. J

I decided to let him have his fun for now. I figured that confrontation would bring me nothing. After all, to everyone else it was no more then a harmless prank. I couldn't be seen to take a joke badly. But I knew as much as he did that it wasn't just a joke. It gave him too much pleasure and made me too angry. But I would have my revenge. Not this year, but I would have it. And when it came, it tasted so sweet.

Chapter 17

Being single before uni is not entirely desirable, but it does have a few advantages. One is that you can drunkenly touch a girl's backside on a night out and only expect to get one slap. Another is that if you are single before uni you are, by definition, single when you get to uni (unless you start going out with a hitch-hiker you pick up on the way down). In my experience, this is definitely a bonus. Few home-grown relationships survive the duration of university. I guess it's partly because people change so much between the ages of eighteen and twenty-one, partly because of the inevitable months apart, and partly because of the innumerable temptations on offer. Also, evidence suggests that if something is going to go wrong with your partner back home, it is likely to go wrong pretty soon into your uni life.

I was pretty much single when I arrived at St. Catharine's College, as were Mark Novak, Oisin, Nick and Joe, and Faye and Mary Jane. I say "pretty much" because nobody is ever completely free from everybody, if you know what I mean. Anyway, the bottom line is that the only one of us with a steady partner was Caolan. She was a girl, she was from back home, and she was called Mary.

It didn't take us long to meet Mary. She came down from Liverpool, where she was at uni, on the final Saturday of Freshers' Week. Mark and I had spent the afternoon in the pub watching England loose 1–0 to the bloody Germans in our last ever game at Wembley Stadium. That had certainly not put me in the mood to read a book about Keynes, so I was more than happy to head out with Caolan and The Group as we showed Mary the delights of Cambridge. She was very pretty; tall with long dark hair. She had been seeing Caolan for a couple of years. You could tell immediately that she was Irish, as she had that look about her, and this was confirmed when she spoke.

The consensus within The Group was that we should go out for a meal to an Indian restaurant that was apparently very highly recommended. I was trying to drum up support for pizza, but my campaigning fell upon deaf ears. We were given a circular table and a set of rectangular menus. I had never had a curry before, and didn't fancy trying one tonight, so I opted for my favourite Indian dish of omelette and chips. The waiter smiled as I ordered and my great friend the Stalking, Philosophising Prophet from

Bradford made some snide, unfunny remark that again, incredibly, was well appreciated around the table.

Mary was lovely. As we were sitting next to each other, we decided to share a plain naan together, of which she kindly gave me the bigger half. She also sympathised with my burden of strange taste buds. Apart from the occasional crap that left the Great One's mouth, the evening was very pleasant. Caolan and Mary seemed to be able to take the piss out of each other and not get offended, which I always think is an important strength in a relationship. I decided there and then that this was a couple that was going to last the distance.

Within two weeks it was all over.

It was the birthday of the weird, witty, small girl, and again I had gone out with The Group for a meal. Another bloody Indian. Another bloody omelette and chips. Another bloody pile of shite pouring out of the Great One's great big mouth. It was a Sunday night, and Caolan had left Cambridge on the Friday to go up to Liverpool to see Mary. He was not back in time for the start of the meal, and only arrived as I was contemplating dipping my last chip into Oisin's chicken korma sauce to see what it was like. He arrived smiling, but his eyes looked sad and weary. He kissed the birthday girl, and sat down at the end of the long table. He turned down the waiter's offer of food, but ordered a pint which he drank like he really needed it.

When I knew him as well as I could, Caolan would still very rarely talk about stuff that was on his mind, and in these early days, it was virtually impossible to get the young Irish lad with boy band looks to open up. I made my attempt after the meal. Knowing that he was probably getting hungry, I told him that omelette and chips had made me thirsty and I was going to the Van to get a can of Fanta. He swallowed the bait and said he'd come with me and pick up a cheeseburger. In the end he even added a rasher of bacon.

There were two fast-food vans on Market Square. One was called the Van of Life, the other, predictably, the Van of Death. The Van of Life had its name proudly painted on its side, the Van of Death did not. The meat from the Van of Death was believed to be fatal, and hence the queues were normally longer outside its rival. However, after a night out, the prospect of dying the next day was second to being fed meat now, and, thus, around 2 am the queues were the same length. I wasn't fussy where I got my Fanta from, so I let Caolan lead the way, and he led us to Death.

On the way back to college I asked him what was up. After taking a bite of his death-in-a-bun, he reluctantly told me the bare details. He had broken up with Mary. I had to use the snippets of information he inadvertently leaked out, together with my A-level in psychology and my worldly experience, to form a picture of what might have happened. Freshers' Week, and Nanny-Nannettes Dinner in particular, I speculated, had made Caolan realise how difficult keeping a long-distance relationship going was. It was not that my good Catholic friend was desperate to bed everything in a dress. Indeed, he openly boasted about his long-standing "three-month rule", whereby he didn't sleep with a girl until three months after they had been going out. It was just that he realised no-one could predict what would happen or who you would meet at university, and it would be best if both him and Mary weren't constrained when faced with those possibilities. It was a tough decision to make, and it clearly had hurt him a lot, but I think he knew he'd made the right one. I think ideally he would have liked to sign a contract that stipulated that he and Mary were on a three-year break, and that whatever happened whilst they were at uni, they would get back together and probably marry once they returned to Ireland. Unfortunately, there was no lawyer in the room when he explained that it was over.

So, by the middle of the first term, we were all free to bed-hop, and do whatever we wanted. It was just a shame that no-one seemed to want to do it with us.

Chapter 18

My relationship with Mary Jane changed as she started going out properly with her Nanny, Gavin. Our actual time spent together remained pretty much the same, it was just that we saw each other less and less during the day, and more and more at night. We became closer in a dangerous kind of way. I don't know whether it was the darkness lowering our inhibitions, or the fact that we'd often had a couple of drinks, but the conversations were always more intense than they used to be. Talk of *Neighbours* and biscuits was replaced by questions of what was love and what was happiness.

It turned out that neither of us knew the answer to either, but I was sure Mary Jane wasn't happy. I just didn't know why. The confident, bubbly girl of Freshers' Week soon revealed herself to be a self-loathing wreck. She was convinced she was ugly, and convinced Gavin didn't like her. Every time I told her she was pretty and that it was obvious that Gavin really liked her, she told me I was just saying that to make her feel better.

Of course I was saying it to make her feel better, but it was also true. She was pretty. Without wishing to be too vulgar, she had a great body, and a nice face. She was also a lovely, lovely person. And of course Gavin liked her. He would come and visit her every day, and text her all the time. He would miss going out with his mates to see her, listen to her sing, help her with her work, make her tea and toast when she was ill in bed. Gavin was a really nice guy. He must have only weighed about six stone, and often looked like a lost little boy, but he was a good person, and treated Mary Jane well, which is what I wanted, and what I kept trying to tell her.

Pretty soon it would be every night that she came to my room crying. I was not used to my friends shedding tears in front of me, and I found it especially hard seeing a person cry for the first time. I didn't have any insight at the best of times, but when tears were falling I felt under even more pressure to come up with answers, and I could never think of anything at all useful to say. I would just hug her and stroke her head (I'd seen people employing this technique on the telly) and tell her everything was going to be alright. When she calmed down I would make her a magic cup of tea and then make sure she got into bed okay. Sometimes, through her tears, she said some terrible things. Things that I had never heard real people say before. Things that I had no reply to. Things that really scared me and flew around in my mind refusing to leave long after she had gone.

Mary Jane came around more and more, and stayed later and later. I grew very tired, and started missing lectures that I should have gone to. I was quite worried for myself and very worried about my neighbour. I'd never encountered anything like this before, and A-level psychology offered no answers.

Oisin noticed that I was looking knackered and told me to tell Mary Jane to sort her life out, or whatever, because she was clearly crazy. Oisin rarely said anything like this, always preferring to see the good in everybody, and I knew he was right. I was well out of my depth. I lay in bed knowing that the inevitable knock was moments away, and I tried to not answer it. But

A Tale of Friendship, Love and Economics

then I pictured her crying, and I worried that she might do something stupid, so I always answered it. I thought people like this only existed in films and Channel 4 documentaries, and I just didn't know what to do.

The only person I could really talk to about all this was Francesca. I wasn't a great fan of telling people my problems, and I could easily pass off my strange mood with a "No, I'm fine, I'm just a bit knackered, that's all" to Faye and the boys, but the English student from Sheffield could somehow tell there was something more to it. Mary Jane took up my time, and I took up Francesca's. I hadn't seen her much since we both left The Group, but fortunately she invited me in for a cup of tea one rainy Sunday whilst I was wandering the halls of Bull (just another block of rooms like M-block or E-block, but with a funny name) in desperate search of a toilet. We swapped phone numbers, and after that met regularly for cups of tea, and the odd biscuit.

I didn't want to burden Francesca with my problems. My experience with Mary Jane had taught me that excessive problem-sharing is bad for a friendship. But Francesca knew something was up, and wouldn't give me a biscuit until I told her. I said that I would swap some of my problems for some of hers, but she said that unless I had any insight into nineteenth-century English fiction, I couldn't really help. Apart from pointing out that the nineteenth century in fact encompassed the years 1800–1899, and not 1900–1999 – a point I was pretty sure the straight-A student from Sheffield was aware of, I didn't. Francesca was a very private person. All I knew about her was that she had a boyfriend back home, she fancied Jarvis Cocker, she took sugar with her tea, and that she said she was happy. I wished I knew more.

Francesca was a really good listener and lifted a great weight off my shoulders. She saw that I couldn't just bin Mary Jane, but also that I had to stop things going the way they were going. I ate my biscuit and assured Francesca that I would think of something.

Chapter 19

Sometime in the midst of all this, Sapphire came to stay. My two neighbours and I were having tea in my room with the Stereophonics wailing in the background when Mary Jane broke the news.

"Who the bloody hell is Sapphire?" enquired Faye, loudly. I would have probably said the same if I didn't already know the answer.

"My little sister," replied Mary Jane, before quickly returning to her tea as if she'd said something wrong.

"Oh," replied Faye, before the awkward silence set in. It went on for quite a while. Thankfully, Faye finally broke it. "That's a bit of a funny name, isn't it?" I had to laugh, and luckily Mary Jane did too.

I had spoken to Sapphire a couple of times, having answered Mary Jane's mobile whenever she was tied up doing something important like fixing up her make-up or sitting comfortably. I didn't know much about her. I knew she was two years younger than her big sister, and didn't sound half as posh. I was about to be told all I needed to know.

"Sapphire is beautiful," began Mary Jane, fixing her eyes on an unremarkable spot on the carpet. "She's done bits of modelling and stuff. Every boy that I'm friends with turns to jelly when they meet her, and when she's gone, she's all they talk about. No doubt you'll be the same." A quick sex count in the room suggested that Mary Jane was addressing that last point to me.

"Well, you know the only reason I'm friends with you is so that I can meet her." It was a bad time for a bad joke. It was met with silence and a disapproving but sympathetic look from Faye. It was time for one of those serious, corny moments that I hated and was really no good at.

"Look, Ms Mary Jane, your sister could be the most beautiful woman in the history of the world, and it wouldn't matter one bit. I'll never bin you. You'll always be one of my best friends." I needed a good swig of tea after that one.

Mary Jane seemed to think about it for a while, and then slowly lifted her eyes off the carpet.

"I know you won't, Josh, and I'm sorry. It's just that I've seen it happen so many times." She smiled a warm smile.

"Of course, if she's really fit..." Too far, Josh. Too far.

Sapphire was wearing nothing but a dressing gown when I first set eyes on her. She had come out of our M-block shower and I was waiting to go in. We were heading off to formal hall to celebrate her first night here and give her a big mouthful of the Cambridge experience. My God, she was gorgeous.

"Erm... (don't look at her breasts)... erm... (you're still looking)... I'm... (lift your bloody eyes up at least thirty degrees)... Josh. Yes, I'm Josh. Josh is my name."

"Sorry, didn't quite catch your name."

"J..."

"I'm only messing. I'm Sapphire, and I'm guessing that you're lovely Josh, my sister's neighbour?"

"No, I'm nasty Josh, her other neighbour. Lovely Josh lives on the other side."

Even the walls cringed. She giggled sympathetically. I told her I'd see her in a bit, and hurried off like an embarrassed school-boy into the shower.

Formal halls were one of those things that sounded like a ridiculously poncy, over-the-top Cambridge tradition, but were actually a really good idea once you got into them. They were like a mini Matriculation Dinner. On the minus side, you had to wear your suit and gown and listen to a bit of Latin. On the plus side, you got a three-course meal (plus crackers, cheese and coffee) for just £6, and you were even allowed to bring your own wine in. Once you got beyond the formal dress, the Latin grace, and the standing up when the college fellows entered, it just became a cheap and pleasurable way to have a really nice meal and get wrecked. Every college had formal halls, and they varied immensely in price (ours was one of the most expensive), quality (ours was up there with the best on the quality scale) and regularity (some colleges had them every day, ours were on a Sunday, Wednesday and Friday). They became a good way to celebrate someone's birthday, and an even better way to show a non-Cambridge guest some of the quirky extravagances of this funny little place.

Mark Novak had become sufficiently friendly with my neighbours to justify an invite, so as soon as I was out of the shower and dressed up in my suit, my fellow economist and I made the short trip to the Oddbins that was next to college to snap up a bottle of wine.

Before I came to Cambridge I had not been a wine drinker at all. Now, I can happily tolerate almost any wine, and I have three years of formal halls to thank for that. From the very start we upheld a long-standing tradition to buy the cheapest wine available. Oddbins always had a couple of bottles in the sub-three-pounds category that were promptly snapped up. Most of these were clearly bottled cat-piss, but that was half the fun. Anyway, it was not as if you could even enjoy a quality vintage wine in formal hall. Another Cambridge tradition was "pennying". There were some subtle rules concerning double-pennying and stuff, but the basic principle was that if someone dropped a penny into your glass of wine, you had to finish whatever was left in the glass. Usually the person dropping the penny in your glass was the very same soul who had, moments ago, kindly offered to fill your glass up right to the top with the aforementioned awful wine. On particularly good formal halls, the pennying got to the stage where by the time the main course arrived, nobody had any wine left. If you are going to drink wine that fast, no wine is going to taste good, and hence you might as well save yourself a few quid and snap up a cheap bottle. That was our logic anyway.

Wine and gowns in hand, our party queued up outside the Hall ready for the mad dash to secure seats so that everyone could sit together. Faye took no prisoners, and so our gang happily found itself as one on the centre table, with me sandwiched between Mary Jane and her sister, and Mark Novak sitting opposite.

At our college's formal halls the starter always seemed to be fish. I hated fish (not that I'd attempted to try it for more than fifteen years), and every time I sat down and saw the dreaded fish knife lurking ominously amongst my plethora of cutlery, I struck a deal with someone (usually Mark or Nick MacLean) to swap my fish for their bread roll. If, as sometimes happened, the main course was fish, I flicked it onto my side plate, and stuffed my face with loads of potatoes and veg. Luckily, there were never any fish-based deserts.

I am reliably informed by my mother that before I went to primary school I ate all meat and fish. It was only when the good old British education system informed me where these meat and fish things came from, namely that they were things that used to be alive, that I stubbornly refused to eat them. It was not that I had any particularly strong moral objection to animals being killed, in fact I never really liked animals that much anyway, it was just that I didn't like the idea of munching on something that had once been moving around. It was as if I could its face staring up at me before I ate, reminding me exactly what it was that I was about to put in my mouth. My worried Mum tried many methods to get her strange young son

A Tale of Friendship, Love and Economics

to eat meat and fish. She hid little bits of meat in the vegetables, but I would always find them. She reminded me that tomatoes and apples and grapes had all been alive one day as well, and I seemed to have no problem eating them. Her most successful technique was lying. For years I was convinced that "tomato" sausages were a vegetarian equivalent, and that the pâté that I happily slapped on my toast every morning was nothing more than a tasty vegetable-based spread. It was only when Mum sent me to the meat counter of our local supermarket to get some pâté that I found out her secret.

"May I have some pâté please?" I was always a polite child.

"Certainly, young man. Would that be fish pâté?"

"Erm... no, the other one."

"Well, fish pâté is all we do."

And then the tears came. It was years before I could trust my Mum in the food department again. I would sit on the kitchen table, keeping a close eye on everything she did, inspecting ingredients on packets, and making sure she kept both hands visible at all times. I was a very low-maintenance child.

This particular formal hall was a particularly drunken affair. It was a Friday night, and myself and Mark had just handed in a deceptively time-consuming and incredibly boring history essay on the role of entrepreneurs in the Victorian era, so we felt like we needed a drink. Once a few pennies start finding their way into glasses, a domino effect was set into motion, and soon the table was awash with circular copper pieces. Mark and I pointed out that the table was like an economy, and that at the start of the night it was in recession with no pennies flying around, but as soon as someone injected a few pennies into the system, loads of penny-activity was generated, and we had a boom. I tried to explain to Sapphire that the lesson we can all learn from this is that the government should inject expenditure into the economy in times of trouble, just like the great Keynes said. Sapphire told me to shut up and placed a penny into my over flowing glass of cheap Hungarian white wine.

Everyone seemed to be having a good time, and as soon as we had seen away a bottle of wine each (Mark and I also helped Sapphire to finish hers) and the odd bit of coffee and cheese, we headed off to the college bar, where we met up with Caolan and Oisin.

After an hour or so, Mark astutely pointed out that Mary Jane, Sapphire and Faye didn't actually come back to the bar. We got another drink to take out, and went off to look for them.

The Cambridge Diaries

We tracked them down to our floor on M-block, and more specifically, the toilet. Sapphire had been sick. Back in her room, Mary Jane was in tears, unable to believe that she'd been so irresponsible to make her poor little sister so ill. Faye was half consoling her, and half using the top of her head as a pillow. In the toilet, Sapphire was having her long blonde hair held back by none other than Adam bloody Sylvester. I had managed to avoid him since that awful first night in Cambridge, and now here he was, on my turf. I didn't believe that Mr Sylvester was of the type to regularly perform altruistic acts, and indeed his motives for helping Sapphire were soon exposed.

"You're probably best taking your top off as well," he suggested, "you don't want to get puke all over it."

I brought Mary Jane out to look after her sibling, and Adam Sylvester skulked off with an evil smirk, seemingly biding his time before he flew into my life again.

The rest of the evening was a drunken clean-up job. Faye and I took Sapphire's trousers and top down to the washers, whilst she lay in bed, with Mary Jane stroking her head and feeding her water. Mark did his best to clean up glasses and cans from Mary Jane's floor but was dismissed on the grounds that he kept knocking things off shelves.

Needless to say, I woke with an achy head and another vow not to drink again. In the morning Sapphire looked rough but still gorgeous. We went to breakfast in hall, where she managed to force down a banana and a glass of water, and I managed to squeeze in a full English, a pint of milk, and a thick 'n' creamy strawberry yoghurt.

The rest of the weekend went by at a more leisurely pace. We took Sapphire on the open bus tour of Cambridge, the same one that annoyingly passed under my window every weekend in winter and every day in summer. On the tour she learnt such fascinating pre-recorded facts as: Gonville and Caius College has two names because it was founded twice, first by the Norfolk parish priest Edmund Gonville in 1348 and then again by the royal physician and former student John Caius in 1557 after he was upset at the poor state of his beloved college; and in the Old Library of Jesus College there lies an autographed copy of the first edition of the Bible printed in America in 1663, autographed by its translator, Jesus fellow John Eliot, presumably because the original author, God, was unavailable (I added that last bit myself, and as Sapphire giggled, Mary Jane gave me a stern, disapproving look). I loved all these little facts and anecdotes; they were a constant reminder that you were in a place full of so much history and tradition, a point easy to forget when you were queuing up to get into Cindies on a Tuesday night. I wondered if the day would ever come when the tour guide would announce to a bus load of attentive pairs of ears that if they cared to look to their left they would see the first year room, M14, of the great Joshua Bailey. Probably not. We then took Sapphire on a walking tour of the big colleges, where she soon got tired and moany and learnt that Catz was quite small. Back in college and slumped on my comfy chair, we introduced Sapphire to her sister's boyfriend, Gavin. They didn't exactly hit it off, and by the end of the cup of tea, Gavin was half-jokingly calling Sapphire a witch, and she was one-quarter-jokingly calling him a puff. We all found it very funny. Sapphire, sufficiently recovered, even found time to fit in some girly shopping, which I managed to get myself out of. She left on the train home on the Sunday with hugs and kisses and happy tales to tell. Mary Jane said that she would miss her, but in a funny way she was kind of glad that she was gone.

Chapter 20

With the nights still bringing her sorrow, Mary Jane decided she needed to go home for the weekend, to get away from it all, and asked me if I'd like to come as well. To be honest, I had been feeling like I needed to escape from the Cambridge bubble for quite a while now, but my home was too far away. After weighing up the work and football situation, I decided that a trip to London was just what I needed, so I gladly accepted her kind offer.

We caught the train early Friday afternoon to King's Cross, and then a combination of buses and trains to the town of Croydon, the home of both Mary Jane and Adam Sylvester. I had only been to London a couple of times, so this was quite the big day out for the poor, wide-eyed northern boy. As we turned onto the street that contained her house, Mary Jane gave me a few pointers that would ensure I had a pleasant stay. Firstly, her Mum worked with victims of child abuse, so no jokes about that and, secondly, her little sister was still beautiful, so don't dare fall in love with her. No problem.

I was always nervous about meeting adults for the first time, and doubly nervous when they were parents of my close friends. Of course, I had briefly chatted to her Mum whilst washing my cereal bowl before the start of Freshers' Week, but that didn't count. I normally tried to make a joke whenever I met someone new, and more often than not, I died flat on my arse.

We were greeted on the street by her Mum and Dad, the latter was leaning over the opened bonnet of his car, whilst the former stood out of the way tutting. I shook the Dad's hand firmly, and opted for a lighter variety on the Mum (I was not one for kissing on the cheek). As Mary Jane hugged her mother, her Dad asked me if I knew anything about cars. I realised that in this particular instance, lying could end up costing the family thousands of pounds, and so I ashamedly admitted that I was not a practical man. He smiled and said that he wasn't either. Feeling reasonably content with the initial impression I had given off, I was led into the house.

Mary Jane's house had a tardis-like quality of appearing small for the outside but pretty big once you got in. It smelt of air freshener and cooking, a strange combination, but not at all unpleasant. The house had all the usual house things like stairs and rooms and carpets and pictures of the family standing proudly above the fireplace in the lounge.

A brief guided tour of the house was followed by lunch. Now, I think that part of the reason I was so scared about meeting parents was that more often than not food was involved. The mums and dads of my friends back home had grown immune to my inherent fussiness by that stage, and so they didn't try to give me anything fancy. Unless they were having burgers or bacon, they just gave me whatever the normal people were having minus the meat, and I was more than happy. New friends' parents just didn't understand. They often tried to get to the bottom of my strange eating habits. They thought that they could be the ones to change me, to cure me. They were always disappointed.

I wish I had a tape recording of the history of my food habits so I could just sit back and press play, instead of going through the usual routine: No, I didn't actually eat any meat at all until recently, and now I only really eat burgers and bacon. Yes, all the rest of my family eat meat. No, it wasn't for any moral reason, I don't really like animals in fact. Mum said it all started when I was too lazy to chew meat when I was little, so I used to choke and that kind of put me off it, then I went to school and the idea of eating something that had been alive just seemed a bit funny, a bit horrible. Yes, I know vegetables have been alive. Well, I got by alright because I used to drink about four pints of milk a day, and take vitamin tablets. Oh yeah, I'm well into dairy products. But not cheeses that aren't cheddar though, and not butter on sandwiches. No, that's not for any moral purposes either. Well, in the end, the smell of bacon was too much to resist, and burgers aren't really meat anyway, are they? Oh, and now I suppose I kind of eat chicken, but only if I have to as I'm not too sure if I like it or not. And I'm not really a fan of all those fancy vegetarian foods, especially those with onions in them. And I don't like cheese sauce or mayonnaise. Ketchup's alright, though. No, I will never eat fish. Mainly because of the smell and the eyes. Yeah, I'm a right pain in the arse. Poor Mum.

In the end, lunch was beans on toast, which was lovely.

That Friday night we stayed in chatting and watching telly. Sapphire came home from Salsa classes about 8 pm and joined us in the lounge. She politely asked me to promise not to tell her Mum and Dad about her alcohol-induced puking up when she was in Cambridge. I promised and tried not to look at her breasts.

On Saturday afternoon, Mary Jane's older brother took me to watch his beloved Crystal Palace play football. Every week he sold programmes before the game, and for his troubles he got 5p for each one he sold, and, more importantly, a match ticket. I grabbed a bundle of programmes and one of those orange luminous jackets, and sneaked into the ground behind him. We managed to shift six programmes between us, and then sat down with our hard-earned 30p to watch the game.

Her brother was a really nice guy. He clearly cared about Mary Jane a lot. He asked me if she was happy at uni, and if Gavin was treating her well. To save him from worry, and because I still didn't know exactly what was going on, I told him everything was fine. He made me promise to look after her, and although I was pretty sure he was not the kind of older brother to hunt me down and kick my ass, I promised anyway. Because I had every intention of doing so.

On Saturday night I sat in a cathedral with her parents whilst Mary Jane sang in a choir. It was a nice occasion, but not really my cup of tea. I find it hard to remain quiet for such a long period of time in any situation, something undoubtedly inherited from my Mum, and when the fat man in front of us farted I would have happily paid £5 to have Caolan or someone beside me to laugh with. Instead I had to hold my breath and smile politely.

On Sunday morning I had a bath, my first since arriving at Cambridge due to the unappealing organic "hair-carpet" that lined the floor of ours in M-block, and on Sunday afternoon we caught the bus and the train back to Cambridge.

It had been a really nice weekend, and just what we both needed. There was never any hint of tears in Mary Jane's eyes at any stage. For some reason we arrived back in Cambridge manically buzzing with excitement. It may have had something to do with the particularly strong coffee we snapped up on the train, or the kid with the funny accent who was sat two seats in front. It may have been due to the alignment of the planets, or the fact that I felt clean after my bath. Whatever the reason, Mary Jane and I were happy. Perhaps a bit too happy. We seemed to feed off each other's good mood, and the whole thing just spiralled out of control. Back in the safety of Catz we decided to call around to see Oisin, who was trying to do the Stats work that Caolan and I had copied off Mark Friday morning. Oisin was friendly and welcoming at most times, but even more so when he had work to do. Seeing that he was busy with work, I said I'd call round another time, but he explained that he was due a wee break anyway. Oisin was always due a wee break.

Mary Jane and I spent an hour or so publicly giggling and privately exchanging jokes in the Irishman's room. Oisin, quite reasonably, accused us of being drunk, to which Mary Jane took huge offence, succinctly explaining that it was bloody ridiculous to suggest she would even consider consuming a drop of alcohol on the afternoon of the Sabbath. I assumed she was taking the piss because she didn't believe in God, but Oisin was not to know that. After our little display, we went back to her room, had a cup of tea, and slowly came down from our strange, unexpected high. That evening I read about the nature of competition in oligopolistic industries. My come down was complete.

The following week the rumours began. I can only presume that Oisin phoned Caolan after we had left, and then Caolan told Mark, and more than a few other people, whenever the opportunity arose. By Wednesday, Mary Jane and I were going out.

This came as something of a surprise to me. Last time I'd checked, she was seeing Gavin, and I was very much single. When Adam Sylvester came up to me in the bar and asked me if I was going out with Mary Jane so that I could shag her sister, I knew I had to intervene. I called round to see Oisin. He was ready for a wee break.

"What? You're not going out?" The poor lad looked innocent and worried.

"Well, not that I know of."

"Oh, right... it's just that... well, everyone was sure that you were. Especially after London, or whatever."

"Everyone? London, or whatever?" I would have liked to have said this in his thick Irish accent, but it always sounded more German.

"Well, when you came round on Sunday, you were holding hands, or whatever, and I... well... I just assumed you were going out."

"Oisin, what happens when you assume?" I sounded patronising.

"I don't know?" Innocent and scared had turned to sorry and confused.

"You make an 'ass' out of 'u' and 'me'."

My boss at work had taught me this valuable lesson after I had wrongly assumed that a display of tinned baked beans that I had created on the shop-floor was structurally stable.

"But you two have pulled before, right?"

"No," I paused just to take in what he had said. "No. Of course we haven't pulled before. For a start, I am the world's worst person at keeping secrets, so I'd have probably told you, Caolan and Mark before the kiss was even over. And secondly, we are just friends. And thirdly, she's bloody going out with Gavin."

Oisin had been hanging his head in shame whilst I had been ranting on like a parent disciplining his unruly child. When I had finished he lifted up his shaggy main to reveal a pair of apologetic eyes.

"Hey Josh, I'm sorry, you know. It's just that, well, you know, I just thought you two were, you know, just because, well, just because, or whatever."

I think I knew what he meant. I suppose we did spend quite a lot of time together, and hold hands and stuff, and to the naive observer, I suppose we may sometimes have looked like a couple. I'd just never thought that other people would think it before. I mean, of course I had thought about what it would be like if we did start going out together, and the thought scared me a bit. Sure, she was attractive, and we got on really well, but I didn't really fancy her. Also, she was more than a little crazy, and she would probably have made the most high-maintenance girlfriend I had ever met. I was just happy being close to her. Being her best friend. And I think that she was too.

Mary Jane found it all very funny indeed. She particularly enjoyed that fact that I didn't find it funny.

"Am I not good enough for you, Mr Bailey?"

"Of course you are, it's just that... oh, shut-up, this isn't funny."

"No, it's hilarious. So, have you told your Mum yet?"

"Look, be serious. I mean, for a start, what will Gavin think?"

"Oh, he'll be alright. We'll invite him to the wedding. Anyway, lover-boy, forget Gavin, I'm going out with you now."

Against Mary Jane's wishes, I texted Gavin just to reassure him that I was not going out with his girlfriend. I put a smiley face at the end of the message. He said he'd heard the rumours and they surprised him a bit too, but he trusted me. His message ended with a smiley face as well.

In the coming weeks, I did my best to dispel the rumours. I started watching how I acted with Mary Jane in public, and whenever she knocked at my door at night, I made sure no-one saw her come in.

Chapter 21

My Mum had always said I'd make a good actor, but then it's a Mum's job to fill her children with self-confidence. Saying that, I'd always thought I was pretty good. My extensive repertoire included doing impressions of Roland Rat, a mean Marlon Brando from *The Godfather*, and Chris Tarrant's laugh from *Who Wants To Be A Millionaire?*. I could also do a fine Birmingham accent, a reasonable Mancunian, and I was currently working on my Scottish. When drunk, I could also do many more. So, when I saw the poster advertising auditions for the forthcoming Fresher Play, I immediately signed up. I didn't tell anyone I had put my name down in case I didn't get a part, and because Caolan would have ripped the piss out of me just for trying. The play was called *Hayfever*, by Noel Coward, and because I suffered from hayfever, I thought I stood an even better chance.

Auditions took place in the Octagon Theatre, out in the octagonal second year accommodation at St. Chad's. I had played football that morning (we had lost 4–2), and in the process of the match had picked up a ridiculous-looking limp.

A Tale of Friendship, Love and Economics

The St. Catharine's College Fresher Play happened every year, and was entirely run by freshers, with each year's budget determined by the cumulative profit made by previous years. Two Fresher directors were in charge of the auditions, both of whom were girls. One was a geographer who was quite friendly with Faye, the other an English student who was quite friendly with Francesca (it's not about what you know…), and both I had met briefly on nights out earlier in the term.

I hobbled in at my allotted time and found before my eyes a large room, with eight sides, two people, one table and three chairs. I made a bad joke about deciding to play my character with a limp, and I think the directors decided there and then that I was not suitable for the role. *Any* role. I went through the formalities of reading for various parts, but the play was set in a posh, rich, well-spoken, southern English household, a place where limping northerners were rarely found. They thanked me for turning up, and gave me the "don't email us, we'll email you" line.

As expected, I didn't get a part in the Fresher Play, but Mary Jane did. To my disgust, also cast in this joke of a production was none other than the Stalking, Philosophising Preaching Prophet from Bradford. He was obviously the right kind of northern (i.e. not northern) for a part.

But that was not the end of my role in the Freshers' Play of 2000. Oh no. You see, Caolan and I had heard rumours of a free after-show party for all cast and crew, and that was something we were not going to miss out on. We went along to the recruitment meeting for the backstage staff, and dragged Oisin along for good measure. Mark Novak was getting stuck into an essay and, not for the first time, refused to be torn away. After an hour of pondering and eating free custard creams, Caolan was signed up to do lighting, and me and Oisin were suddenly running food and beverages. Of course, not one of us had any previous experience in either role.

Oisin and I were given a budget of £100 to cover three nights' performances. Over a cup of tea in the floppy-haired Irishman from the 1970s' room, we discussed and debated exactly what we needed. Wine was chosen over beer, orange squash over coke and lemonade, biscuits over crisps, and plastic cups and plates over real ones. Sorted. I also declared myself boss, and Oisin my assistant. He said I could call myself what the hell I liked but I was still doing half the work and he was not taking any orders from me, or whatever. I smiled, happy in the knowledge that I was in charge.

We decided to buy the food and cutlery first, and then use whatever was left to buy the wine. So, on a Tuesday afternoon, after a morning of boring lectures and a Mary Jane-free night (she was rehearsing until late), Oisin and I hit Sainsbury's. I was outraged at the price of plastic cups, and the plates were not exactly a bargain either. As a result, my plans for McVities Milk-Chocolate Digestives were shelved in favour of the plain Sainsbury's Economy variety. After a hard-fought battle, I did get my way with respect to the custard creams and bourbons, though. We tossed a coin to see whose reward card we would use, and with my account seventy-six points better off, we set out in search of wine.

A flick through the Yellow Pages had revealed the location of an out-of-town wholesaler. Oisin reckoned we could easy walk it in half-an-hour, or whatever. The reality turned out to be the whatever, as we arrived, shattered, after nearly two hours of trekking. Bloody Irish.

The wines at the wholesaler where not actually the bargain of the century either. Sainsbury's – that's the one less than ten minutes away from college – had loads of wine around the £3 a bottle mark, and the expedition to the out-of-town/out-of-county wholesalers had landed our eyes open a range of wines mostly £4 or more. Having come all this way, I was determined we were going to buy something. We asked the man behind the counter, whose delusions that we might be a pair of young sophisticated wine connoisseurs were about to be shattered, to recommend us the cheapest wine that was actually drinkable, and he led us to a red wine and a white wine coming in at £3.75 a bottle. They were both described as fruity little numbers, ideal for parties and gatherings, and eminently drinkable. They were cheap, and we were tired, so we spent our remaining £62.46 on eight bottles of red and eight bottles of white. Thankfully, free delivery was an option for all orders above £50, and so the man took down Oisin's name (He had to spell it. Three times) and the address of St. Catharine's College, Cambridge, CB2 1RL. We just made it home before nightfall.

Oisin was summoned to see the Head Porter a few days later to explain why over £60 worth of wine had arrived at college in his name, when he was supposedly tee-total. Was he running a black-market wine racket? Was the workload getting too much? They were not impressed.

Unlike myself and Oisin, Caolan had to attend a couple of the rehearsals to make sure he had got the lights right. His co-worker was an eccentric engineer with curly ginger hair, who would often be seen talking to himself

A Tale of Friendship, Love and Economics

and swinging around lamp posts. My Irish assistant and I only had to go in to the Octagon on the afternoon of the first performance to set up our stall.

As a child, me and Mum would often do car boot sales to get rid of our old stuff. This, combined with three years in the retail industry, working in a local supermarket, meant that I was very capable at creating an environment where people (or "punters" as we call them in the trade) wanted to buy, buy, buy. Oisin didn't seem to realise how lucky he was to be working with and learning from such an expert ("retail is detail" I told him over and over again). We were given a large room underneath the performance area, and permitted to sell our goods before and after the performance, but primarily at the interval. We were given the kitchen area, complete with fully-functional sink and plenty of preparation space, and closed off to all non-food and beverages staff by a couple of wooden tables. I had hired freelance Faye for three nights' work on the condition that she was allowed a glass of wine and a couple of biscuits (custard creams if possible). With our biscuits covered with cling-film and laid out in the form of a wheel (as in the Catharine Wheel. A nice touch, if I do say so myself), our plastic cups laid out ready to be filled with sumptuous wine and orange juice, and my elite team drilled and motivated, we relaxed and waited for the public to arrive.

Stress levels amongst most of the cast and crew were running high as I stood behind my counter tucking into a digestive and a cheap, weak orange juice. One actress wasn't happy at all with her hair and was demanding the sole attention of the two make-up girls to fix something that didn't look too bad at all to everyone else. One of the directors was apparently in such a state that she required two (free) glasses of wine from our carefully allocated stock. Mary Jane was sure she looked awful and sure she would forget her lines, and I sure wished she'd shut-up. The All Mighty Stalking, Philosophising, Preaching Prophet from Bradford was busy calming everyone down with his mystical words of wisdom. The 2nd XI right-footed left-back, tonight in his new role as Props Manager, otherwise known as geographer Nick MacLean, was frantically trying to locate all his props that the cast and crew had been playing with. And one of Caolan's bulbs kept going out.

In the end it was alright on the night. Alright on all three nights, in fact. Loads of tickets were sold, and, by the final show, people were even being turned away. The audience laughed and clapped in all the right places, and there was even a hint of a standing ovation at the end of the final performance (in the end it turned out to be no more than a mad rush for the toilets).The university-wide newspaper, *Varsity*, had sent a journalist along to review our college's little production. In the write-up the following morning she praised the production in general, and the performances of all the actors, except for one boy, who she described as having "the worst Russian accent ever". Only thing was, the lad in question was actually Russian (yeah, I know, they could have a Russian but not a Lancastrian).

Apparently the only thing people weren't happy with was the food and beverages. Our own college newspaper, *Catzeyes*, went as far as describing our wonderful wine as "bloody awful". To be fair, it did taste like cat-piss, and nobody ever bought a second glass, but we had walked miles and miles to get it. As sales had started to dwindle, I was offering buy-one-get-one-free purchases, but no-one was keen. Anyway, in the end, mine and Oisin's Anglo-Irish catering venture, after a quick fiddling of the books, just about broke even, and the play as a whole made a significant profit.

Unfortunately, the left-over wine, and there was a lot of it, provided the sole refreshment for the after-show party. Thankfully, after a few glasses, you became immune to the taste. We ordered in loads of lovely pizza, and drank, ate, and danced the night away in our exclusive party in an eight-sided room.

Chapter 22

I love the build-up to Christmas. Whilst most people moan when a department store puts up its Christmas tree in October, I smile, knowing that the old 25th December is getting closer and closer every day. Yes, I just love Christmas, I do.

I soon discovered that Cambridge is a really nice place to be around that time of year. The old college buildings seem more suited to cold, dark nights, lit only by the faint glow of surrounding street lamps, than they do to the glaring midday sun. I enjoyed doing my twice-weekly shop to Sainsbury's after dinner, wrapped up snug and warm in my winter clothes, wearing my favourite thick, black gloves and a slightly stupid-looking hat, blowing out at the cold air pretending I was smoking, singing along to the same Christmas songs I have heard all my life escaping from the brightly lit

A Tale of Friendship, Love and Economics

shops, imagining what the city's festive lights will look like when they're turned on, keeping my fingers crossed that tomorrow will bring with it some snow. Most people seem to be in a better mood as Christmas approaches. I certainly am. I don't think I'll ever be too old for the magic of Christmas.

I also used to like counting down the days until school finished for the holidays, thinking how many double-physics lessons I had left before I could lie-in for weeks on end, play footy and pool as much as I wanted, and watch the good Christmas telly until late at night in the comfort and warmth of my bedroom. Now, as first year Economics students, we were all counting down the days until lectures finished and our last essay (a particularly festive politics one on the future of the Conservative Party) was handed in. Then we could relax and really get in to the Christmas spirit. Myself, Caolan, Mark and Oisin went to The Anchor with a few of the other economists to celebrate handing in that last essay, and over our pints (lager for us, coke for Oisin) and packets of crisps we smiled, thinking of the hard-earned nights coming up.

That's one good thing about Cambridge; any night out was usually a hard-earned one. If you had done a good day's work and then headed out in the evening, you tended to have a better time than if you had just binned work and pissed around all day instead. Although, when you were stuck in a stuffy library, buried in books and with a bunged-up girl sniffing away every five seconds, the latter option certainly was tempting. Knowing that this was our last week of work for they year 2000, and knowing that we had a fully booked week lined up afterwards, we had pushed ourselves hard, and with all the work now wrapped up, our pints of Fosters really did taste like the amber nectar the adverts continually insist on telling us it is.

First on the list came Christmas Formal Hall. Now, our Nanny sources in the second year had told us that these formal halls sell out faster than the proverbial hot-cakes, so we arrived weary-eyed in the Plodge first thing in the morning to snap up our tickets. There were three Christmas Formal Halls arranged so it took a fair bit of co-ordinating to get all of your friends at the right one. Caolan and I had both agreed that the best thing to do in these situations was to make sure our core group all got the right tickets and then hopefully all others would fall in line. This seemed preferable to the brain power needed to arrange anything more complicated. So, along with Oisin, Mark, Faye, Mary Jane, Nick and Joe, we handed over six English pounds each and were handed back our tickets for Wednesday evening's Christmas Formal Hall.

Christmas Formal Hall followed the same format as your bog-standard formal hall, but with a few festive twists. Firstly, the food was chosen with the occasion in mind. We had minestrone soup for starters (I didn't see the link, but it was very nice), followed by turkey and stuffing with loads of veg, followed by Christmas pudding, which I gave to Nick and just had a bowl of the white sauce instead. This was my first taste of turkey, and made a pleasant change to my usual Christmas meal of potatoes and veg (one year my poor Mum even made me a pizza). Finally, along with the coffee came a big plate of mince pies. I offered to swap mine for an extra coffee, but seeing as you could have as many as you wanted, no-one was keen. Also, we got a Christmas cracker each, and were even permitted to wear the paper hat inside.

It escaped the college authorities' attention that some of the little plastic toys that flew out of the crackers when they were banged open were a little unsuitable for such a formal gathering. Several little plastic fish, which could be loaded with water, wine, or gravy and then fired out of their little round mouths, were flying around the tables causing chaos. Now these were one type of fish I didn't mind getting on my plate. Any bits of plastic jewellery tonight doubled as a "Christmas-penny" and soon found their way into people's wine glasses. Soon, mince pies were being used as nuclear weapons for the fishless, and were being launched between tables. For once, the fellows and the kitchen staff didn't seem to mind. After all, it was Christmas. It was a great night.

Mr Stevens kindly threw us an economist's Christmas party of his own. It wasn't exactly the all-night piss-up that we perhaps wanted, but nevertheless it was a good night. There were mince pies and two metal vats of something called mulled wine, which I had never come across before, but it was hot, alcoholic, spicy, and not too bad at all; kind of like hot Vimpto with a dash of pepper. We sat around in a circle chatting and drinking until our Director of Studies subtly threw us out at just after 10.30 pm. Instead of talking about work, Mr Stevens again seemed quite keen to know all the college gossip. You got the feeling he wasn't like most of the other college fellows. He was a bit of a rebel. The fellows were the only ones permitted to walk on the grass of Main Court, but Mr Stevens would never do. He never ate in hall at lunch and dinner times with the rest of them. He didn't like the pompousness of many of the Cambridge traditions, or the internal politics that unduly influenced many of the University's decisions. He was almost one of us but not quite. Just the right balance to hold our respect as our superior.

Chapter 23

The most eventful night of the Christmas run-in was undoubtedly the Friday. It started in a waistcoat, involved a room full of pensioners, an unconfirmed number of kisses, and ended with confusion and a condom. Out with a bang, so to speak.

The first event of that colourful evening was the annual Football Christmas Dinner. Now football outings at Catz are not like most other nights out. There are certain rules and traditions. For a start, there is always a dress-code, chosen by the social secretary (an extremely prestigious position). The favourite dress-code is "bad-shirt-and-tie-combo", with "bad" meaning absolutely bloody awful. Anything remotely respectable would be frowned upon and result in the naive wearer being subject to harsh alcohol fines.

That leads us on nicely to the second important feature – fines. The social secretary also holds the position of Chief Enforcer on nights out. The club captain and maybe one other lucky sole are also Enforcers for the night. It is the job of an Enforcer to dish out fines to the other club members. Fines are alcohol-related and are delivered in the form of: "Two fingers for anyone who...", with two fingers referring to the amount of alcohol that is required to be drunk, shown by placing your middle and index finger on the outside of your pint glass to serve as a marker. It is the job of the other people in the room make sure you have drunk a sufficient amount to satisfy your allocated punishment. As a general rule, the more personal the fine the better. Nothing quite gets an evening going like "Two fingers for anyone whose girlfriend has pulled three people in this room who her boyfriend doesn't know about yet". Particularly serious crimes are subject to larger fines, such as four fingers, or even a large swig of the dreaded Kulov vodka (about four quid a bottle, and by the taste of it, seriously over-priced).

Such a fine might be for someone who missed a game of footy because of a lecture, or who doesn't know all the words to the college football song.

The only hope for the poor soul on the receiving end of a fine is to "Mob Rule". This is an incredibly risky strategy, but it can have a massive pay-off. A cry of "Mob Rule" signifies the receiver's objection to his fine. If more than half of the people in the room then signal their agreement that the fine was indeed unfair by shouting 'Mob Rule' as well, the Enforcer who dished out the fine must finish whatever is in his glass (this will often be kindly filled to the top for him, and normally contain more than a dash of Mr Kulov himself). If the Mob Rule fails, the receiver faces the same punishment.

There are also a few "Snitches" around the room who are selected by the Chief Enforcer, and whose job it is to extract information from people for potential fines, which are then whispered to an Enforcer in the process of the evening. On top of this, there is also the "Knife of Strife" and the "Spoon of Doom" doing the rounds. Basically, if the aforementioned items of cutlery should find their way into your pint glass, you have to finish what is in it.

Apart from all this going on, you can just sit back, relax, and enjoy your meal. I always felt sorry for the couples who had come to the restaurant for a romantic night out, and ended up coming face to face with the Spoon of Doom and a fine about the colour of someone's pubic hair.

Such football nights usually took place in our local Indian, The Curry Mahal. Above the entrance to the restaurant is a sign advertising the fact that The Curry Mahal caters for weddings. It would also need to cater for the imminent divorce of any couple who chose to have their reception there. The staff were very experienced in dealing with drunken louts like us, and even smiled and said thank you when clearing up our sick in the toilet. The Curry Mahal offered a £10 deal which entitled you to a poppadom, a curry of your choice, available with plain or pilau rice, a naan bread, and a pint of lager. Crucially, they didn't mind you bringing your own alcohol in, which generally saved a lot of money with all those fines flying around. It was the relaxed attitude of the staff and the bring-your-own feature that made the Mahal a popular venue for sport and drinking society outings. It was certainly not the food.

However, on two nights of the year, the St. Catharine's College Association Football Club moved out of the Curry Mahal, and into another

A Tale of Friendship, Love and Economics

restaurant. These nights were the Annual Football Dinner, held at the end of the second term after the season has finished, and the Christmas Dinner, held, as you might guess, around Christmas time. We often had trouble securing a non-Mahal restaurant for these special nights. Once a place had had us once, they didn't tend to want us again. With new places to try fast running out, the club had started booking in under other names, such as Trinity College Polo Club.

Tonight, we were trying out a local Turkish restaurant, which went by the name of The Erania. Suspicious of our given title of King's College Train Club, the management of The Erania had insisted we turn up in shirt and tie, as if this was supposed to guarantee high-quality clientele and a trouble-free night. Whenever twenty-five lads rocked through their doors at half-past-seven dressed in every colour of shirt and tie imaginable (Joe Porter was sporting a particularly grim fish tie, complemented nicely by an awful brown shirt), the mouths and spirits of the onlooking staff crashed to the floor.

Fortunately, The Erania had had the good sense to seat our party downstairs, which meant that we were only exposed to a couple of other diners, instead of the masses that lay safely unaware upstairs, enjoying their meals in peace. I took my seat opposite geographer Nick MacLean in the corner furthest away from the Chief Enforcer. Fellow geographer Joe Porter had the misfortune to find himself directly opposite His Lordship.

The menu of The Erania was like nothing I had seen before. They did everything from omelette to pizza, steak to curry, Turkish food to Chinese. The phrase "Jack of all trades, master of none" turned out to be particularly apt. Tonight, however, we were signed up for twenty-five traditional Christmas meals. Turkey, cranberry sauce, the works. We had already had a few quick drinks in the bar, and the freshers had already been the subject of a few slightly unfair fines ("Two fingers for anyone who didn't come to last year's Christmas Football Dinner on account of not being a member of the university yet"), and the sight of another bottle of wine sitting in front of me was not the most appealing. In addition, the water jug had now become the Kulov jug, with the plant at the side of the table getting an extra drink that evening.

The meal turned out as expected. Numerous unfair fines were dished out and reluctantly accepted, and our wine was finished before a bit of turkey crossed my lips. I felt more than a little off colour, but resisted going to the toilet to be sick in fear of what the fine might be if I was caught. Joe Porter seemed to be in a worse boat than me and Nick having had more than a few top ups from the "water" jug. The waiters couldn't understand what all the fuss and protests were about when Joe was politely asked to finish the half a glass of water that lay in front of him.

Having left most of our meals and been dismissed, Nick and I stumbled our way back towards college, because the evening had only just begun. Tonight was the last college bop of 2000, and everyone who was anyone was going.

Now, when I first heard the term "bop" I immediately thought of a really bad kids' disco, or a dance in a village hall that old people went to, i.e. something I didn't really want to be seen dead at. However, like many things at Cambridge, once you tried them out and didn't take them too seriously, you generally had a really good time.

A bop was basically a party. Each college had its own bops during the year; ours had about two or three a term, and lasted from 9 pm until the porters shut us down at about 12.30 am. For bops, Catz bar was transformed from a standard bar by day into a pumping night-club once the clock struck nine. Or at least that was always the plan. The pool table and table-football machines were carried out of the way and put in storage to create a dance-floor. Some of the tables and chairs were removed in a similar fashion to allow more standing space. A hatch was opened to the common room, and this formed the DJ booth. Speakers and lights were installed around the room and decorations were hung on the wall and the bar. Drinks were often cheaper at bops, and entry cost either £2.50, or £2 if you were game/drunk enough to dress up.

Each bop had a theme. The only other bop we had had that term was an S-bop, where you had to dress up as something beginning with S. This, however, was deemed too difficult, and thus after a barrage of complaints, the theme was extended to include famous people to encourage more people to get involved and dress up. Mark Novak put on his Spurs shirt (he had been wearing it during the day anyway) and went as David Ginola. He soon became Gary Lineker, however, when he lost his wig in the process of the night. Nick MacLean went as Tim Henman, an elaborate costume involving shorts and a tennis racket, and Adam Sylvester went as Ali G. I opted for my hero of former years, Mr Liam Gallagher, thus giving me a chance to swear and do my Mancunian accent that I was so proud of. Oisin didn't dress-up,

A Tale of Friendship, Love and Economics

but more than a few people complimented him on coming as Starsky out of the 1970s cop show *Starsky and Hutch*. During the night I also spotted a Mark Twain and a Laurence Llewellyn-Bowen flying around, as well as a girl who didn't really have the backside to accurately portray Kylie. Bops were really good fun. The music was very much of the cheesy nature – songs you never admit you like, and would never dream of dancing to under normal, sober circumstances, but always seemed to wrap you up in excitement and drag you onto the floor once the alcohol and the good times are flowing. Wham! and S Club 7 were always big Catz favourites. Most people danced, most people got drunk, and quite a lot of people got a little too friendly with each other. Very rarely was there ever a bad bop, or at least an uneventful one.

Tonight's theme was "Grannies and Grandads". My inability to walk straight suggested that the chances of me mounting the stairs to M14, finding something suitable to wear and then actually managing to get it on were minimal, so Nick and I begrudgingly forked out an extra 50p for the privilege of remaining in our lovely shirt-tie combos. The music was loud and of a 1980s nature, and the room was full of scary-looking pensioners, many in mini skirts, throwing shots down their mouths and bouncing around the dance floor. Upon entry, we were handed a condom (*each*, I hastened to add) and asked to make a donation to an AIDS charity. At first I thought I was being given Viagra, or something, and that it was meant to tie in with the bop's old-people theme. Nick pointed to the word "condom" on the square packet, and I nodded. I popped a few coins into the box, pocketed my newly acquired piece of male contraception, and thought nothing more of it.

Oisin, Caolan and Mark hadn't bothered dressing up for this particular bop, but the latter two had certainly had more than their fair share of drinks. Mary Jane and Faye had dug some old dresses out of somewhere and, combined with a pair of wigs and some horrible-looking yellow teeth, they looked quite the part. Peer pressure, despite our protests and against our better judgement, forced Nick and I to snap up another drink. Then we had another. And probably another. And then, who knows...

I vaguely remember demonstrating my groin-grabbing moves to a Michael Jackson number, and I think Caolan fell over at some stage, but that's about it. I woke up in my bed, naked, with a horrible headache, an empty condom packet and a bracelet keeping my lamp company on my bedside table, and absolutely no memory of how I got there or what had happened.

Sometime around midday, Nick MacLean popped round. He had no memory either. His mobile phone suggested he had made seventeen calls in the early hours of the morning to a girl he had never spoken to but somehow had her number. He didn't know what he'd said, but he knew she hadn't replied. Over a cup of tea, we tried to piece the events of last night together. He said he remembered something about me talking to a girl by the brick wall outside the bar, but, helpfully, he couldn't remember who she was. I told him about the condom packet and the bracelet, and he laughed for quite some time.

Nick was no help in remembering stuff, and neither were Mark or Caolan, although Mark said that Caolan definitely fell over whilst dancing, and the side burned Irishman had the bruise on his arm to prove it. In such situations, Oisin was very useful. Being a non-drinker, he often became like a video recorder at an office party, playing back the stupid things we'd done the night before in far too much detail as we all sat back and cringed. He remembered seeing me walking off hand-in-hand with Scottish Faye of all people, but he didn't see us kiss, or whatever. Faye! Bloody hell.

Fearing that the only option left was to ask Faye if I pulled her last night ("not that it wasn't memorable, or anything, but did we kiss..."), I made myself a bowl of Weetabix to pass the time and to help me think of a better option. Asking Mary Jane was no good as she'd just tell Faye anyway. As was often the case, Jude, the lad from down the corridor, was also making preparations for a gourmet dish of calcium and fibre of his own.

"Hey, Jude," even though by now I must have said it well over twenty times, the use of that little phrase still made me smile, "how's it going?"

"Not bad, not bad." He started to smile. "I heard about you last night. Casanova Bailey, I don't know."

I shook my head.

"Hey look, Jude, mate, I don't have a bloody clue what happened. What did I do?"

"Seriously, you don't remember?"

"Honestly. Cross my heart, and all that."

"Shit, mate, no memory, huh? OK, well, apparently, you pulled Faye and that girl who rows. Cassandra, is that her name? Good work."

"Bloody hell, I've only spoken to her twice." Then it sunk in, "Bloody

A Tale of Friendship, Love and Economics

hell, you mean I did pull Faye?". My mind immediately began racing. I pictured the condom and the bracelet. Maybe she had come with me back to my room. Maybe I found the condom in my pocket, she took her bracelet off, and one thing led to another. But you'd think I would remember sleeping with someone.

"I know, mate. We all thought you were just friends."

"We are just friends. Jude. We are just friends." I spilt milk on my right trouser leg and trainer whilst trying to make my point, but that was the least of my problems. "Did you see me pull them? I mean, where did it happen?"

"No, mate, I didn't actually see anything. I was busy dancing. Sly came around and told me this morning."

"Sly?"

"Yeah, you know, Adam. Adam Sylvester. We call him Sly now."

Bloody Adam Sylvester, the route of so many of my problems.

"Look, Jude, please don't tell anyone anything. I could well have pulled Cassandra, but I'm 100 per cent sure I didn't pull Faye. Well, nearly 100 per cent. And I'm even more sure that I didn't bang anyone. I just need to figure out what's going on, that's all."

"Okay, mate. If you say so." Jude spooned into his mouth a heaped helping of cereals. Some milk escaped and ran down his chin. "Look, Josh mate, don't stress about it. This is what happens at uni."

I was busy formulating a plan, almost certainly involving leaving the country, when there was an ominous knock at my door. This was followed by ominous shuffling, another ominous knock, and an ominous Scottish accent. It was Faye and Mary Jane. I had nowhere to hide. They knew I was in, and the jump out of the window would have killed me, unless I could somehow land in the open-top tour bus. Seeing as there wasn't one going past and I wasn't James Bond, I didn't fancy my chances. I greeted them with a nervous smile. Mary Jane brushed passed me.

"So, when you and Faye get married, I assume I can be maid of honour?" she began proudly. Faye punched her on the arm and whispered for her to shut up. My face turned a bit on the rouge side, and I lost the ability to speak.

"Hey, Josh" said Faye after a painful silence, "I know everybody is saying that we pulled last night, and I know you can't remember if you did or not, but I do, and I can assure you we didn't."

"Oh, thank God for that." I was supposed to just sigh, but the words I was thinking flew out into the open with the air.

"Well, that's a lovely thing to say, Bailey. Is my little Scottish friend not good enough for you, or something?" Mary Jane took a step forward as she spoke. She was very close to me now. I could feel her words as well as hear them.

"No, no, I didn't mean it like that. You know I didn't, Faye. I was just... you know... it would have... well... it would have messed up our friendship if we had pulled. I mean... pulling you wouldn't be a bad thing... I mean, not that I'm assuming I could, or anything, and not that I would want to... erm... I mean, not that I would necessarily not want to not pull you... if you know what I mean?" I offered up the kettle and a smile.

"Stop digging, Josh, and don't think a cup of tea will make this all better."

"Oh, leave the poor wee laddy alone MJ, you should know better." Faye turned to face me. "Don't worry about it, Josh, I do understand what you are saying. I think."

"Cheers, Faye. And I'm really sorry."

A cup of tea soon brought things back to the way they were, and I proceeded to tell my two neighbours about the bracelet and the empty condom packet. Faye started to laugh uncontrollably. Once she had calmed down, she began to explain.

"You see, Josh, you kindly offered to walk me home last night after I had helped you out of the Bop after you had tried to go asleep on one of the speakers." I looked shamefully into my cup of tea. "When we got back into your room, you suddenly got a new wee lease of life, and so you put on some Beatles and asked me to dance. Your dancing was a little on the wild side to say the least, so I took off my bracelet in case you ripped the thing off. My granny gave me that, you know. I must have forgotten to pick it up."

"And the condom? Or do I not want to know?"

"Oh, right, the condom... Well, you took it out of its packet and tried to blow it up. After seven attempts, you finally inflated it and then fired it out of your window. It flew around for a while and then flopped down. You then did pretty much the same, and I went to bed."

"I am a nob, aren't I?"

"A nice nob, though," replied Mary Jane.

Neither Mary Jane nor Faye had any insight on whether or not I pulled this Cassandra girl. Mary Jane told me not to believe a word Adam Sylvester said. She explained that he was a typical Croydon Boy, and this meant he was not to be trusted. I reluctantly chatted to Mr Sly himself in the college bar the following night, and he swore blindly that I did pull Cassandra, on the bench outside the library. He just happened to be walking past at the time. I had no way of knowing whether he was talking shite or not, and I didn't know Cassandra well enough at all to go and ask her myself. She was good friends with Faye through rowing, but I made my Scottish friend swear on Ally McCoist's life that she would not say anything to her. I thought it would be best to just let the matter fade away over the Christmas holidays. After all, it was not that big a deal and, as Jude said, this is what happens at uni.

Chapter 24

Pretty soon Saturday became Sunday, and it was time for me to go home. John had driven over to France at the weekend, so he called in to Cambridge on his way back up North to pick me up. I had left all my packing to the last minute, and all my washing was unfolded and dirty. Mum was not going to be happy. I went for a last walk with Faye and Mary Jane, and said goodbye to whoever was in their rooms when I did the rounds. I handed my keys into the Plodge and wished the on-duty Porter a Happy Christmas. I took one last look at Main Court, breathed in a final bit of Cambridge air, and helped John load my things into the car. I seemed to be bringing back more stuff than I came with, and Mary Jane and Faye had to feed boxer shorts and socks through the car window once I was firmly wedged into the passenger seat inside. I waved and blew a couple of kisses as we slowly pulled away and began the long journey home.

Chapter 25

At times it felt like I'd been away a life-time, at times no more than a day. Some things had changed, some things would forever remain the same.

The first thing Mum said as I gave her a big hug was, "God, look at your hair, you look like a tramp." And to be fair, she had a point. But I looked like a cool tramp. I hadn't actually had my hair cut all term. This was partly through laziness, partly through a lack of funds, and partly because, yes, I did think it looked quite cool.

I soon realised that I had missed my Mum. Whilst I had spoken to her a couple of times every week, it was still not the same as seeing her and talking to her face to face. There was no implicit pressure to keep the conversation going. Periods of silence in each other's company are perfectly acceptable in a way that they are not on the phone.

The house hadn't changed a bit. Mum told me she had done some decorating in the lounge, but I lied when I said I could tell the difference. My room was exactly the same as when I left it, only tidier. After a few goes on my piano, a few bounces of the basketball in our drive, and a few calls of, "Come on, Josh. Don't leave that plate there", it felt as though I'd never really left.

It was really nice to see my friends from back home. I was pleased that they all seemed the same as they always had been. I had talked to most of them regularly over the phone, and so we generally knew what each other had been up to, thus there wasn't much catching up needed. After a few lame jokes about my apparently new posh accent and questions about how many times I had been anally penetrated, things soon settled back down to normal. We went out, as we always did, on Monday nights around Preston, doing the local pubs first, then winding up at Squires, before calling in for a pizza (a mushroom one for me) and a taxi home. I even managed to successfully introduce the gang to the benefits of wine (i.e. its cheap and it gets you absolutely wrecked). Just to put the icing on the cake, fortunately, at least for me anyway, one of the lads from our Friday night footy team got injured, so I slotted right in at centre-back.

I soon got a job at the local supermarket where I been a faithful servant to the retailing cause for the last four years. The boss had called me up whilst I was at uni and offered me the highly prestigious post of Assistant Warehouse Manager. The hours were bad (six in the morning starts, and

A Tale of Friendship, Love and Economics

not many days off) and the pay was, as it always had been, pretty awful, but a lot of my old friends still worked there, and it was good to be back. The boss told me not to start trying to sell *The Big Issue* in the store. I think he was trying to make a hair-related joke at my expense.

I spoke to Mary Jane, Faye, Oisin and Mark over the holidays. I tried Caolan once, but he wasn't in and he never got back to me. I also received a bundle of Christmas cards from the uni crowd, including one from Francesca and her boyfriend, who I had never met. I spoke to Mary Jane the most. She was the first person I called when I reversed John's car into a parked car in an otherwise deserted Kentucky Fried Chicken car park. She was also the person I called as I walked home alone on New Year's Eve after having the same stupid drunken argument with my best friend that we'd been having for too many years. As much as I hated to admit it, I needed her as much as she seemed to need me. She was always there to talk to, and always ready to listen.

I enjoyed being home for Christmas. The holidays were just the right length for me not to get bored, but to do everything I wanted to do. I milked as much of Mum's generosity as I could, reminding her that this was only a fleeting visit, and soon her only son would be whisked away from her again, so it was probably best she made me that cup of tea and that bacon sandwich whilst she had the chance. There was the odd inevitable clash as I tried to explain that I had been used to a place where spilling a crumb was not a crime warranting death, and she explained that if I wanted my washing doing and my food cooking then I would abide by her rules. However, we both realised that time was too short for such silly little arguments, and they were soon sorted out and forgotten about. I lounged in front of the telly, catching up on all the soaps that I'd fallen behind on, and I went to the cinema a few times, bought a new batch of CDs and started to read *Harry Potter*. I thought about going to the gym, but decided to rule it out, reasoning that people were supposed to get fat over Christmas. I was having a great time, with so little on my mind. However, when the time came, I was good and ready to go back down to Cambridge, to see what trouble I could get myself into this time.

Second Term – January 2001

He saw her as he walked down the stairs. He was yawning and stretching in his usual exaggerated way, she was leaning over the sink, filling a rusted kettle with water. She said "Good morning, sleepy head," and turned herself around to look at him. She was still wearing her bed-clothes; baggy pyjama bottoms and an old red T-shirt displaying the faded name of a band that she didn't listen to any more. Her voice was high and pathetic, the way it always was first thing in the morning or last thing at night. Like a mother talking to a baby in a way she thinks it will understand. Her eyes had not fully opened, still adjusting to the light of this new day. As she squinted, her nose crumpled up and her eyebrows leant inwards as if trying to touch. Her hair was only brushed around the back of her right ear and she scratched the back of her head like it was an old shaggy dog. She asked him if he wanted a cup of tea or coffee, and he said no. Given more time he would have changed his mind. He constantly ruffled his hair, hoping that it would fall upon a decent style. She smiled. He smiled back. She looked beautiful in the mornings. She always looked beautiful.

Chapter 26

It was Dad's turn to drive me back down to Cambridge this time. He always insisted on setting off at a ridiculously early hour, explaining that this was the only way to avoid the traffic. He arrived at our house at 7am, with the back seats of his car flattened down, and armed with two atlases, an internet print-out of the best route to take, and a new little plastic clip thing that he had recently bought himself that attached to the dashboard and securely held in place another set of hand-written directions scrawled in pencil. He was always prepared.

I was tired and Mum was upset. I got the feeling that maybe it was a bit harder saying goodbye to me this time because she now knew what it was like for me to be away, living in the house on her own. She spent a lot of the time telling me what a pain I was to live with, but I knew she missed my dirty dishes and untidy room really, as much as I missed her nagging. I hugged her, kissed her and told her I'd call as soon as I got there. I bundled my suitcases, CDs, books and the rest out of the front door for Dad to load into the car.

Dad was wearing trousers, a shirt, and a green V-neck jumper. He had recently had his hair cut shorter than normal, but it looked better that way.

"Hiya mate."

"Hi, Dad."

"You alright?"

"Yep, you?"

"Yep." He looked at all my bags. "Bloody hell, Josh, you've got enough stuff here haven't you?"

"I need it all, Dad"

"What are all these books? All you student lot do is drink and go out isn't it?"

"We do some work as well, Dad."

"Have you forgotten anything?"

"No, Dad."

"Are you sure?"

"Yes, Dad."

"Really sure?"

"Well, now you come to mention it I have left behind this really important thing, but I can't be bothered going to get it."

"What?"

"Come on, Dad, let's go."

As we pulled away from the drive I waved goodbye to Mum, and goodbye to my home for another nine weeks or so.

I rubbed my weary eyes with the bones of my fingers, and tried to pick out quite a big piece of dried sleep that was nestling annoyingly in one of the bottom corners of my right eye. I talked to Dad about football and asked how my little sister was getting on. He told me that David Beckham was ridiculously overpaid and that my sister had just got her fifty-metre swimming badge. After a while I put on a tape.

Chapter 27

We arrived at college just before eleven o'clock. We had indeed avoided most of the traffic, but any time saved was off set by Dad's slow driving. Over the intercom, which was erected on a metal post beside the car-park barrier, the Porter told us that we had twenty minutes, and twenty minutes only, to unload the car and get out of the car park. Although he had never met them, Dad had decided he didn't like the attitude of the porters, speculating that they were just little men on a power trip.

I went to sign in and pick up my keys. We carried my stuff up to my room in three trips, and I told Dad that I would have made him a cup of tea but I had no milk. He helped me to unpack, constantly suggesting better places for all my stuff ("Look, Dad, that probably *would* be better but the thing is I need to know where everything is"), and asking me to turn the music down lower and lower as it was apparently giving him a headache.

Midway through unpacking Mark Novak knocked on my door. He was wearing his contact lenses today, and a T-shirt that I hadn't seen before, maybe a Christmas present. I greeted him with a handshake, even though I never seemed to do this to any of my friends back home. It was good to see him.

"Happy New Year, Mr Novak."

"Yeah, suppose it is, isn't it? Happy New Year. I see you haven't cut your hair then?"

"No, I suppose I haven't. I couldn't be bothered, you know."

"He looks a mess, doesn't he?"

"Mark, this is my Dad. He's out of touch with fashion."

Dad decided not to stay for lunch as he wanted to stop at an airport on the way back home and watch some planes. I thanked him for driving me down and helping me unpack, shook his hand, and asked him to call me or text me to let me know he'd got back safely. Mark had stayed in my room since he knocked and had now been roped into helping me slot the duvet into the duvet sheet. This was a task that was new to both of us, and by the time the Fab Four had gone through *A Day in the Life, All You Need is Love,* and *I Am the Walrus,* we still hadn't finished. We talked about work, my plans for my hair, and how his Mum had managed to get rid of the white paint that had been on the sleeve of his only black coat since Freshers' Week. She apparently used white spirit and a screw driver.

A Tale of Friendship, Love and Economics

I asked Mark if he needed to get anything from Sainsbury's. He said that he didn't, but that he would come along anyway. I snapped up the necessary milk and orange, and treated myself to a bag of satsumas and a tin of Ambrosia Custard, no doubt full of fat and sugar, but truly delicious and my absolute favourite. I also changed my preferred brand of coffee to a more expensive one because an unavoidable sign was offering me 500 reward points. Mark said that I was just the kind of shopper that these signs were aimed at and as an economist I should know better. "It's all to do with price discrimination," he explained, smiling. I'd missed these kind of conversations since I'd been back home. I knew he wouldn't be laughing when I had earned enough points for two-for-one on beauty products at Boots, or a family day out at a zoo. Mark almost bought a pack of Kellogg's nutri-grain bars, but in the end decided against it, even though they were on special offer and I knew he really liked them.

Mark Novak didn't need many things to get by in life. His room was definitely designed with a minimalist theme in mind. We used to joke that if he was ever in big trouble, maybe with the Mafia for offering some poor economic advice or something, he could clear his room of all traces of Novak and be out of there in two minutes. All he had was a few files for work, a couple of pens, a desk lamp, a little TV/radio/alarm clock that sat by his bed and could only seem to get BBC1 on Wednesdays, an *Abbey Road* poster, a jar of strong coffee, two coffee-stained mugs and a box of Nouvon washing tablets. That was it. No photos, no CDs, no books, no things from home to brighten up the place. He didn't even need milk or sugar or even a spoon for his coffee. And he was always happy. Never complaining, rarely ecstatic, but rarely in a bad mood, seemingly content and grateful for the hand that he'd been dealt.

Mark and I decided to treat ourselves seeing as it was our first night back. The rest of the gang were either coming back tomorrow or Monday, so we binned eating in hall in favour of a romantic meal for two at Pizza Hut. For a Saturday night it wasn't all that busy. I normally only frequented Pizza Hut establishments at lunch times to take advantage of the "eat as much pizza as you can" buffet that had happily been extended to include pasta, garlic bread and salad. However, I was pleasantly surprised at the normal prices and the improved quality of the non-buffet pizzas. I had, for a change, a mushroom pizza, Mark had a meat feast. After much debate, we both snapped up an ice cream factory, designed for greedy sweet-toothed kiddies, and felt duly sick afterwards.

The college bar was fairly quiet, and neither of us felt like drinking, so we headed back up to my room to watch *Match of the Day*, and have a cup of tea. Tottenham had lost in a home game that they should have won and, although Mark knew what the score was going to be, and when his favourite defender would give away the penalty, it still brought him great pain to watch it. At least Arsenal only drew.

Today's journey had made me tired the way that sitting down in the same place for hours on end shouldn't do but always does. I had started reading *Harry Potter* over the holidays, but didn't have the energy to do more than a couple of paragraphs. I said my prayers and sank into a deep sleep, with my head turned to face the wall, and my left foot hanging, uncovered, out at the side.

Chapter 28

There was no Freshers' Week at the beginning of this term, and although lectures didn't start until the Thursday, there was not much time for fun either. Despite Mr Stevens saying that he believed the holidays were for resting and recuperating, he had decided to set us some work anyway. I found it quite hard to work at home, with the TV and the comfy settee crying out that they were lonely every time I considered hitting the books, so, knowing that I was coming back early, I had left it to do now. Caolan had done the same. Oisin had forgotten we had the work to do. Mark had already done it.

So the next few days were spent in the library, reading and making notes on real business cycle theory, which is a very controversial topic in economics, as it happens. The lazy days of Christmas suddenly seemed no more than a distant memory.

The library provided a good place for the economists to catch up. News from the economists over the Christmas break included the fact that my hair had grown longer, Oisin had had his first alcoholic drink, and we had a new member of our group. On the latter point, a lad who started his Cambridge life a philosopher had finally seen the light and decided to transfer across to a proper subject. Mr Stevens had chatted to him at the end of last term and deemed his interest in the subject and his reasons for changing to be good enough to justify it. He was a dodgy-looking character to say the least. He had a skin-head and tattoos. He was from somewhere in London, and there were rumours circulating around that not only could he not tell his mates back home that he went to Cambridge, but that he also couldn't tell them he went to university at all. Apparently, he would say he worked away all week, and then come back home at the weekend. Presumably he didn't take his gown back home with him. He was a nice lad and very intelligent, but more than a little bit dodgy. Anyway, now we were eleven, and with a non-too-healthy girl-boy ratio of 1:10.

Oisin had always maintained that he would start drinking sooner or later and, for once in his life, it had been sooner. His Dad had bought him half a pint of lager in a pub a few days after Christmas, and apparently he was still drinking it come New Year. We constantly wound Oisin up saying that he drank so slow and so little that you still couldn't tell he'd started drinking. His reply would always be the same.

"Hey, I've only been drinking for a few weeks, or whatever."

The problem was he was still using this same excuse for his woeful drinking ability two years later.

My longer hair was getting mixed responses. As I had seen it every day, I hadn't really noticed how long it had got. It was only when I saw before and after photos that I could put some perspective on things. There was little doubt that it was long. It now covered over half of my ears. Whenever I tilted my head back and looked in the mirror, I could see it start to creep around at the sides, like a deadly animal ready to pounce and engulf my whole face. It had also started to go wavy and a bit curly, which was something of a surprise to me. It was nearly as long as both Oisin's and John Lennon's style from the *Imagine Sessions* depicted by the black and white poster on my wall. Mary Jane liked twiddling it, and Faye affectionately said I looked like a dog (this was considerably better than the response of my friends at home who said I looked like my Mum). Oisin said I suited it, but I got the feeling that he felt I had stolen his brand, like he had copyright over long hair, or something. Caolan said that he liked it, but had a sufficiently suspicious smile painted across his face for me not to believe him. Francesca said I looked like a cool indie-kid, which I would have taken as a compliment if I was fourteen and we lived in 1996. Mark said he liked it, but then he wouldn't have said so if he didn't.

And that was about the only news from the crazy economists, apart from a rumour that the Cypriot ex-sergeant had finished the whole first year course and started revising already. All four topics of conversation were more than sufficient to distract us from work every ten minutes or so in the library.

Everyone seemed to have a fair bit of work to do before the start of term, even the geographers. Mary Jane was up to her eyes in animal welfare issues, Francesca was trying to read and understand a book that was thicker than it was tall, and Joe, Nick and Faye were doing something pointless about volcanoes. There was still time for several cup of tea breaks, and the odd trip to the bar at night and, of course, everyone still stopped for *Neighbours*. However, the bottom line was that there was work to be done.

It was a shame, because I felt like taking a few days off with my friends now that we were all back together after the Christmas break. We were getting to that stage that I had wanted to fast-forward to in Freshers' Week. I now had my core group of friends who I knew lots about and could happily spend hour after hour in their company, talking about any old shite, and not pretending to be anything that I wasn't. They were a really nice bunch. Faye always made me smile, whether she was in a good mood or one of her "Jesus Christ, ooh no" bad moods. I loved Joe's endless plans for setting up bands and businesses, plans that never got off the ground, and Nick's camp sense of humour and infinite repertoire of awful jokes. Francesca would always be there for me with tea and time for me to tell her my problems, and had a special way of making everything seem alright. Oisin was one of those people who everyone thought the sun shone out of his arse, especially the girls, but to be fair you would need to apply a fair amount of sun cream if you stood behind him for too long. Mark was probably the most genuine and decent person I had ever met, an under-rated individual even then, and someone I considered myself very fortunate to know. Despite the time I had spent with him, I knew Caolan less well, and only really saw him as everyone else did – the good-looking Irish lad who got drunk a few too many times, had time to talk to everyone, and said he told everything to people's faces and despised those two-faced individuals that didn't. Above all else, I couldn't imagine being there and not having Mary Jane as my neighbour, and as my best friend.

No, at the start of that second term I was very happy with how things were working out. I had formed a stable base. I quite fancied getting to know a few more people in the coming weeks, oh, and if I had time, maybe falling in love. That couldn't hurt, could it?

Chapter 29

However, it was Faye, who had the first run-in with romance, and it was a run-in that she never really ran out of.

It was a romance that had planted its seed midway through the first term. She had become friendly with a boy called Duane, who lived next door to Jude along the same corridor in M-block that we all lived on. Jude did history with him, Mary Jane sang in the college choir with him, and I played football with him. We already knew Duane and soon, through all of us to varying degrees, Duane knew Faye. He would come around for tea with Mary Jane after choir and Faye would be there, or he would help me hobble into my room after a particularly painful football match and Faye would come out to see if I was okay. Pretty soon he would just call around to see Faye anyway, thinking of his own excuses, cutting out the middle men and women.

Duane was a nice lad and a shy lad. He had been to one of the country's most prestigious and poshest boarding schools, and you could tell. It just didn't sound right when he swore, like a foreigner struggling with English, especially when he used the f-word. He wore slippers at night and a dressing gown when he came out of the shower, ready to slip right into middle age at the drop of a hat. He would never speak on the football field and rarely when in a room of more than two people, slowly fading into the furniture. He had a lot of stubble, a permanent shadow on the lower half of his face, requiring two shaves most days of the week, compared to my two a month. He played guitar and wrote his own songs, but would never play them to anyone. And he was absolutely, 100 per cent, no question about it, head-over-heels, totally in love with our wee Faye McLaughlin.

We all knew about it, and whilst Faye did her best to play it down, Mary Jane and I especially did our best to build it up.

"So, what y' been up today, Faye?"

"Ooh, you know, this and that, nothing much."
"Any visitors?"
"Visitors? Hmmm, let me have a wee think... no, I don't think so... well, apart from Duane," she rushed the last four words out into a barely audible whisper.
"What was that? You say Duane called around. Again."
"Aye. He just popped round on his way back for a lecture. We had a wee cup of tea and that was that."
"Methinks little Ms McLaughlin has an admirer. What do you think, Josh?"
"Sounds like it to me, MJ."
"Oooh, pack it in you two. You know he's shy and he just seems to like talking to me, that's all. It's all very innocent, I can assure you."
"Whatever you say, Faye, whatever you say."
Mary Jane and I didn't know what to think. It was plain as day that Duane fancied the pants off the Scottish minx, but we weren't so sure that the feeling was reciprocated.
"She'd tell us, wouldn't she, I mean if she did fancy him?"
"Why would she tell *us*?"
"Why? Because we're her two best friends. Who else is she going to tell?"
"Look, MJ, not everyone likes telling their best friends everything. Faye's quite a private person. And besides, remember when she told us in confidence that she thought Nick MacLean was quite fit? It was round college before she'd even left the room. No, even if she did fancy him, I don't reckon she'd tell us."
"Well, there's only one thing for it then, isn't there?" she smiled as she spoke.
"What's that then?"
"We'll have to get her pissed. Then she'll soon spill the beans."
So, one Friday night a couple of weeks into second term, my two neighbours and I snapped up three bottles of suitably cheap wine, ordered in some pizzas and sat in Mary Jane's room with the door closed and our mobiles switched off. Neighbourly Bonding, Mary Jane called it.
Apart from finding out if Faye fancied Duane, the evening had a dual purpose. In the near future we would have to decide upon our flatmates for living in St. Chad's next year. About three weeks into the first term, Faye, Mary Jane and myself had decided to live together (we were drunk at a

A Tale of Friendship, Love and Economics

nightclub, and the suggestion led to a lot of hugging and kissing), the only problem was we needed either one more person for a flat of four, or two more for a flat of five. Seeing as the evening was young and we were not yet drunk enough to move onto the subject of lover-boy Duane, I decided to get the ball rolling on finding ourselves some more flatmates.

"Right, well, are we all agreed that Chip is a definite?" I began, holding a slice of mushroom pizza in my right hand as if it were some kind of conch.

"Who the bloody hell is Chip?" chirped Faye, making good progress through her first glass of wine.

"You know, the skinny lad with blonde spiky hair. He plays football with Josh. He's been up here a few times. He's allergic to peanuts," replied Mary Jane.

"Aye. It rings a wee bell. Is he alright?"

"Yes, he's a really nice lad, isn't he, MJ?"

"Oh, he's lovely. He'd be a really good flatmate, I reckon. As long as we keep him away from the nuts, or course."

"Aye. Sounds good to me. Sign the wee laddy up then."

"Okay. Problem is, he might still be moving into a flat with Francesca," I pointed out.

"Nah. He sent me a Christmas card signed: love, your future flat-mate, Chip," responded Mary Jane, and took a proud bite of her ham and pineapple pizza.

"I know. He sent me one too, without the love bit. And he sent a similar one to Francesca and the rest of her flatmates."

"Bollocks."

"I know," I took a big sip of my wine. Its awful taste was happily beginning to fade. "So, it would probably best if we could find another flatmate and go for a flat of five, and if old Chip does pull out, at least we can then drop down to a flat of four. What do you reckon?"

"Listen to Mr Organisation over here."

"Why thank you, dear Mary Jane, but do you agree that I have a point?"

"Yes, yes, you have a point. So who are we going to have?"

"What about Mark?" I suggested after a brief pause.

"Aye. I like Mark," chipped in Faye as she poured out a second glass and peeled away the strip of mozzarella cheese that had been stuck to her chin for the last minute or so.

"MJ?"

She thought about it for a moment, her eyes seemingly looking for the answer on the ceiling.

"No. I don't reckon it would be a good idea." She didn't smile, so I knew she wasn't taking the piss. My silence served the same purpose as asking why.

"Don't get me wrong, he is a really nice lad and everything, I just don't think it would be a good idea to have you and him in the flat together, that's all."

"Me and him? Why not?"

"Well, you'd be talking about work all the time. About the economy and unemployment and, it would be like, 'Oh no, the dollar's gone up, what are we going to do?' all the time, and all the other rubbish you are always banging on about. I want the flat to be a place where we can escape all talk of work. Somewhere we can relax, you know?"

"The dollar going up would have very serious consequences, you know... What do you think, Faye?" I asked, impressed and slightly intimidated by my strawberry blonde neighbour's response.

"Well, I don't know. I suppose Mary Jane has a point. I mean, what do you reckon, Josh, will you be talking about work all the time? I mean, do you really think living with Mark is a good idea, for you, I mean?"

I took a bite of pizza and a sip of wine before I spoke. As I opened my mouth, I didn't really know what I was going to say.

"Look, I know what you're saying, and believe me, I've thought about it too. Mark works far harder than me, and it makes me feel guilty and bad knowing that he's working even now when he's a floor above me, so I suppose it would be even worse in the flat. But look, he is one of my best friends, and apart from the fact that he is an economist, you've got to admit he would make a really good flatmate. I mean, you two get on with him well enough, don't you? And I promise that I will make a conscious effort to keep all talk of economics out of the flat, and if we do have to mention the dreaded E-word, we'll go in a room, close the door, and turn the music up, okay? And anyway, if we don't have Mark, who the hell else are we going to have?"

"Aye, he's right you know," said Faye, "as long as you are sure you can live happily with someone from the same subject, then Mark gets my vote?"

"And you, Mary Jane?"

"Well, I'm not entirely sure, but maybe you're right."

"I'm always right. You should know that by now"
"Yeah, bollocks. Okay, ask Mark tomorrow if he wants to live with us, and then we'll see what happens with the whole Chip thing."
"Nice one. Meeting adjourned."

And so it was. Mark Novak jumped at the chance to live with us. I explained to him the two-economists-in-a-flat problem, but told him not to worry about it. Being Mark, he did worry about it, and said that if he was going to cause problems, he would find someone else to live with. Again, I told him not to worry about it, and that everything would work out just fine. As it turned out, I don't think I could have survived living in that flat without Mark there, and talk of economics turned out to be the least of our problems.

We were not the only people having flat selection issues. Francesca, like us, was anxiously waiting upon a decision from Chip. I said that if she stole my flatmate I would never speak to her again, and she said the same to me, which meant that whatever happened we would not be speaking to each other very soon, which didn't seem the greatest of outcomes, so we had a cup of tea and said whatever happens, happens. Caolan and Oisin had signed up flatmates almost as early as we had. Way back in the first term there was already talk about the two Irish living with two Group members; the dark-haired girl who owned the room in E-block, and the small, witty, weird one. The only matter up for debate was where the Movie Star Look-alike was going to live. She had said openly that she couldn't live with Caolan, and Caolan said he couldn't live with her. This naturally left a problem. Implicitly the deal seemed to be that if Caolan goes, so to did Oisin, thus leaving further problems, and so in the end, and not exactly amicably, the Movie Star Look-alike went in search of another bunch of flatmates. Joe Porter and Nick MacLean had decided that they wanted to live together, but the problem was no-one seemed to want to live with them. At one stage they had signed up the curly-haired Yorkshire lad who blinked a lot and who had annoyed me for a few hours at Nanny-Nannettes Dinner, but he pulled out at the last minute to live with people he considered cooler, explaining that he was, in fact, not letting Joe and Nick down, but actually doing them a favour. They were not grateful. In the end, and influenced by mine and Caolan's recommendation, they decided to live with the Jewish economist Simon, and his equally Jewish friend, who also happened to be Caolan's next-door neighbour. We pointed out that seeing as Nick's Dad's family were also Jewish, the flat as a whole was five-eighths Jewish, and Joe Porter was the only one with his original penis fully intact. Joe smiled uncomfortably.

With nothing to gain by talking about flats any further, we had another glass of wine, polished off the remaining pizza, and moved onto the all-important topic of conversation. Using the flat theme, Mary Jane made the smoothest of links into it, not even turning around to face Faye as she put on a new CD, as if what she had said was the most natural thing in the world.

"Of course, we could always ask Duane if he wants to live with us."

Taken a little by surprise, I coughed, and a bit of wine found its way up the back of my nose.

"Nah. I don't think that would be a good idea" said Faye, swallowing the bait like a hungry, unsuspecting Scottish fish.

"Oh, why not?" I asked, trying to do as good as job as my neighbour, but having to avert eye-contact at the last minute.

"It's just that... Well..." she took a big swig of wine, cleared her throat, and, as if finally accepting defeat, began. "Right, before I start, this goes no further, you two, alright? Do you understand? Good, 'cos I mean it this time. Right, well, where to start... Well, I guess you guys were right, maybe Duane does like me, you know, more than as a friend."

We nodded simultaneously. Mary Jane nipped me to try and make me laugh.

"And I don't encourage it, you know. I don't lead him on, or anything. I'm just being friendly"

We nodded again.

"But recently, I don't know if you've noticed, but he's been coming around to my room loads and loads. And what's worse than that, anytime we're in a room together with a load of other people, he won't talk to anyone. He will just sit there and stare at me."

We tried to look surprised, but we had noticed. I remember one time when a few people had come back to my room after a night out. We had all taken a few drinks on board, and Faye had suddenly gone all sleepy. She was laid, curled up like a cat, on my bed, snuggling her head into my pillow. I asked her if it was maybe a good idea for her to go to her own bed, but she lucidly explained that she was certainly not about to fall asleep, she was merely closing her eyes for a couple of minutes and having a wee rest. Four seconds later she was snoring. Jude and I went out into the kitchen to get some cereals, and we took Mary Jane with us. Everyone else had decided to call it a night and had gone home. All except for Duane. He remained in my room, sat in my chair, with all the lights out, just looking at the small Scottish girl lying sleeping on the bed. We kept popping our heads around the door and trying not to laugh, but Duane didn't seem to notice. He just kept sitting there, watching the love of his life sleeping peacefully, no doubt dreaming of haggis and Ally McCoist.

Faye carried on.

"And it scares me a wee bit, you know. Not that he would hurt me, or anything like that. It's just that he's a bit, well you know, obsessed with me."

"Like a stalker?" suggested Mary Jane. I gave her a disapproving thump on her arm. Faye pretended not to hear.

"And you don't feel the same. I mean, you just see him as a friend?" I enquired.

"Well yeah. I mean, he's really nice, and everything, but I'm not looking for a boyfriend, you know."

And that was that. Faye realised Duane fancied her, but she just wanted to be friends. And Mary Jane and I had no reason to doubt her. I asked if she would like me to go and talk to him, but thankfully she said no. I wouldn't have had a bloody clue what to say. She told us not to worry, and that she would sort it all out. And again, we had no reason to doubt her.

But then something most unexpected happened. Just a week or so after our drunken meeting we again found ourselves a little worse for wear in Mary Jane's room, this time having been to a formal hall for no particular reason. There were a lot of people there; economists, Mark, Oisin and Caolan, chilled historian Jude, the footballing geographers, Joe and Nick, some of Faye's friends, some of Mary Jane's friends and good old Duane.

The conversations revolved around the usual topics. The geographers, led by a drunken protesting Joe Porter, were trying to argue that economics was worthless.

"It's all about money, money, money, with you guys, isn't it?" he would say, slapping the back of his right wrist into the palm of his left hand three times to coincide with his repetition of the word money. "You've no heart. No fucking heart."

"Aye, just leave the world in the hands of the geographers, that'd make everything better, wouldn't it?" replied Caolan, always one to defend our subject, and always one to disagree with Joe. "Jesus Christ, can you imagine?"

I tried to imagine. I tried to imagine Joe Porter as our Prime Minister, full of big plans that he never quite got around to doing, Nick MacLean as his loyal deputy, happily playing with his willy as he addressed Parliament, Faye as Foreign Secretary, trying to put Scotland at the centre of Europe, and a Cabinet full of geographers, drawing pretty pictures whilst the world crumbled around them.

Lost in my own thoughts, I had failed to notice the incident developing on the bed beside me. A well-timed, and not so subtle, nudge from Mark Novak soon got my eyes looking in the right direction and my mouth hanging wide open. I was sharing the bed with Mark, Faye and Duane, and, low and behold, the Scottish vixen and her shy adorer were holding hands right next to me. She was even running her thumb slowly up and down the side of his hand. I couldn't believe it. I tried to get Mary Jane's attention, but she was too busy trying in vain to bring the welfare of cows into the ongoing conversation.

I knew I couldn't sit there for long without laughing or saying something, so I released a large artificial yawn and announced that I was heading to bed. The rest of the room seemed suddenly reminded of their tiredness, and the party promptly trickled out of the door.

I made the five-metre journey from Mary Jane's door to mine last as long as possible, stopping to admire the paint work, bending over to tie the non-existent shoelace on my socks, and twirling around a few times, dancing with an invisible maiden whilst whistling a made-up tune, so that I could see what would happen next. Faye had turned left out of Mary Jane's room and was putting the key into her door. Duane had hovered for a while, like a lost motorist at a T-junction, and then opted for the safest route and was now wandering slowly behind me along the M-bock corridor, heading towards his room. Just as I was fiddling around looking for my key, I turned around for one final check. I couldn't believe what my eyes were seeing. I rubbed them a couple of times to make sure they were working okay. Faye was leaning half in and half out of her room, her left arm draped seductively along the door frame, and with her right hand in a fist all but for her hooked index finger, she was beckoning him towards her. Duane rubbed his eyes as well. When he saw that, rub over, the woman of his dreams was still standing there, still reeling him in with her coiled digit, he didn't need a second

A Tale of Friendship, Love and Economics

invitation. He turned around and walked nervously towards her. Faye, expressionless, like a woman who was there to get a job done, closed the door behind them. Bloody hell, I thought.

In the safety of my room I got out the old mobile phone. Within seconds Mark was down, toothbrush in hand. After a knock, Jude was there also. Coincidentally, the Movie Star Look-alike from Leeds was also walking the corridors of M-block when I opened the door, so I beckoned her in and got her up to speed on all the details. Mary Jane was unavailable, having scuttled off to Chads to see Gavin. The room was in shock and questioning my eyesight.

"Look, honestly. I promise. Cross my heart, and all that."

As soon as everybody accepted it, the domino effect kicked in and the room fell into mad hysteria. This was the most unbelievable thing anyone had heard. Faye was just about the last girl I could imagine draped against the frame of her door, coaxing young gentlemen inside. And what about Duane? That quiet, staring approach finally paid off. Maybe we should try it. After a while, Mark broke the laughter.

"Hey, she will be alright, won't she? I mean, she's not in full control, is she? I mean, I know Duane's a nice guy and everything, but what if... you know."

We knew what he meant.

"Shit. He wouldn't, would he?" asked Jude.

"Nah, I'm sure he wouldn't. But then if he thought Faye wanted to, I suppose he would have no reason to stop, would he?" I said.

"Fuck, we've got to get her out" said the Movie Star Look-alike, giggling slightly at how serious she sounded, like she was in a bad action film, or something.

"And how are we going to do that?" I asked.

"Easy," she replied, "I'll just go round and ask to borrow some Blu-Tack"

"Blu-Tack?"

"Yeah, Blu-Tack"

"That is the worst plan I have ever heard."

"You got a better idea Bailey?"

I hadn't.

"Exactly. Blu-Tack it is then. I'll be back in a sec."

And with that she was off, out of the door, in search of Blu-Tack at two in the morning. We watched her, huddled around the tiny peep hole of my door, taking three-second shifts each.

"What's she doing, what's she doing?"

She knocked at the door, and after a wait of about twenty seconds, we saw the head and arms of Faye. The Movie Star Look-alike mouthed something, Faye's face looked surprised, mouthed something back that could well have been, "Are you taking the piss?" And after receiving a shake of the head in response, disappeared into her room. Moments later the Scot was back, clutching a small blue ball. The Movie Star Look-alike then mouthed something longer than thank you, and after a moments thought, Faye mouthed something back that was longer than okay. Then, as the Movie Star Look-alike turned to come back to my room, she was followed first by Faye, and then by Duane. Bloody hell, I thought.

"Right, don't laugh, whatever you do. And don't make me laugh. Alright? Please."

"Fucking hell, Josh, I don't think I can take this."

"Shit, Jude mate, you have to. Just think of something bad, like death, or something."

Jude started laughing. I followed. Mark did too. It got worse and worse. Bloody domino effect.

The Movie Star Look-alike knocked on the door, and I took a big, deep breath, hoping the oxygen flooding into my lungs would push the laughter down with it.

"I thought Faye and Duane might want a cup of tea seeing as you were making one," she said as she passed me. She was good at this.

"Oh… right… erm… yep… tea, you say… tea, tea, tea… no problem… tea coming up for Faye and… erm… Duane."

I was not.

In the days and months to come, I was sure that that was going to be the most awkward cup of tea that I had ever had. Amazingly, I was to have a few worse ones in my time at Cambridge, but this would always stand out as being pretty damn awful. I just didn't know what to say.

"So, Duane, what have you been up to?" No.

"So, Faye, been getting into any mischief lately?" I don't think so.

The room was silent except for a few whistles and some "maybe-this-will-make-up-for-the-fact-that-I-am-not-talking" shuffling. Everyone turned to

A Tale of Friendship, Love and Economics

the window as a car sped past below, hoping that it would somehow take off and fly into the room to give us something to talk about.

"I tell you what, I'm really looking forward to Easter," was about the best I could come up with after ten minutes' thought.

After a few "yeah so am I"s followed by more painful silence, Duane decided it was time for him to go to bed. He bid everyone good night, and was greeted with a chorus of over-enthusiastic replies. There was momentary silence as he walked out of the room and slowly made his way along the corridor. When we eventually heard his door close, the interrogation began.

"Bloody hell, Faye, what are you doing?" I began.

"Ooh no, Josh, ooh no," she replied.

"Did you pull him?"

"Aye. I think so," she replied, curling herself up into a tight ball on one of my better chairs, hiding her eyes from the world.

"You think so?"

"Aye. I can't really remember, but I do remember his bloody stubble itching my face. Ooh no, Josh, ooh no."

"Don't worry about it, Faye. It'll be alright," I moved over to her and rubbed her shoulder.

"Did you use protection?" asked the Movie Star Look-alike.

"What, like anti-itching cream, or something?" Wrong time, Josh, wrong time.

"I didn't bloody sleep with him, alright?" shouted Faye, pulling her head up out of her body like a surprised tortoise, and staring straight into the eyes of the Movie Star Look-alike from Leeds. Once again, no-one knew what to say.

"Look, it's probably best if everyone goes now," I said. Realising that for once I might just be right, the members of Operation: Rescue Faye were discharged. I perched on the arm of the chair that Faye was still curled up in and put my arm around her.

"Don't worry Faye, don't worry."

"Ooh no, Josh" she mumbled, "ooh no."

Chapter 30

The whole Faye situation, whilst no doubt traumatic for her, was something of a blessing for me. It provided light relief from the ongoing saga of Mary Jane and Gavin. A saga that continued to require late-night visit after late-night visit to the M14 Counselling Service.

I honestly don't know why she bothered. As ever, I had no big insight into any of the questions posed to me. She would ask me how she knew if she really loved Gavin, and I would say that only you can know that. She would ask me how she knew that Gavin really loved her, and I would say that only Gavin can know that, why don't you ask him. She would ask me why she was so crazy, and I would say I don't have a bloody clue, maybe it's genetic, or maybe it's all that coffee you drink. She would say "No it's not, it's because of my bastard ex-boyfriend, he's messed me up for life." I would say, "Oh, he sounds like a right dick." She would nod and cry at the memory of him. Eventually she would stop crying thank me, and then go to bed. Then the next night it would start all over again.

Don't get me wrong, our friendship wasn't all about Mary Jane pouring all her problems over me night after night. When we saw each other during the day, everything was absolutely fine and how it always was. Whenever we were trying to sort out Faye's love-life, there was no better team in town. Also, if I ever had anything on my mind, she would be the first and only person I would tell. The problem was, because of the time she spent with Gavin, the bad times at night would increasingly take up a higher proportion of our time together.

But no, I still wouldn't have changed anything. I was still glad Mary Jane felt she could talk to me about all these things, and glad that she seemed to think that I was helping. I was pleased to be so close to someone, knowing that she would be there for me if I was ever that down. I still think I needed her almost as much as she seemed to need me. If you took away the emotional side of Mary Jane, you took away the essence of the person she was, and that was something I didn't want to do.

And our friendship managed to survive even the toughest of challenges. We were always falling out about the stupidest things, like when I hadn't washed up one of her cups, or when she had nicked my last bit of milk. However, we always sorted it out in the end with a couple of apologies and a hug. It was inevitable that two people who spent so much time together would fall out occasionally.

Sometimes, however, things were a little more serious. One particular Wednesday night Mary Jane and I, along with a load of others, were out clubbing in the party district of the city. Now, Cambridge is not not called the Ibiza of England for nothing. There are basically three nightclubs: Cindies, which was a bit of a hole, but was still the place to go on a Tuesday (that's if you wanted cheesy music and easy women); The Fez, which was by far the coolest club, especially on a Monday night when indie and rock classics, old and new, were pumping out; and then there was Life. Now, Life, called 5th Avenue in those dark days before we arrived and blessed Cambridge with our presence, was probably Cambridge's most famous club, and it was even more of a hole than Cindies. And yet, every Wednesday night, without fail, the foolish members of the university would arrive in droves and queue up in all conditions to gain access to this wonderful establishment, and every Wednesday night, without fail, we would do the same. The queues were absolutely ridiculous. The Life doors opened at 9 pm, and by as early as eight, come rain, sleet or snow, the queue would stretch all the way down the alleyway and onto the main street. If you were to join the back of it, you would not be surprised to be waiting close to two hours to get in. Of course, people tried to time their entry to minimise queuing time, coming just before the pubs shut, or even later, and once in the queue, everyone tried to subtly push to the front. But, no matter how you timed it or how well you avoided the beady eye of the bouncers when pushing in, you would still be lucky to get into Life in under half and hour.

Of course, by the time you got in you were stone-cold sober, and often wondered why you bothered. For Life was a drunken man's paradise, and a sober man's nightmare. The music was cheese all the way through, and the whole place was crowded, stuffy and had temperatures in excess of a 100 degrees.

And if you wanted to find someone from Catz on a Wednesday night, then Life was the place to start your search. Every week, without fail, the dance-floor would be dominated by a Catz-circle, strutting their stuff to bad song after bad song. We would jump to Jacko, boogie to The Bangles and whiz around to Wham, and every time another member of Catz was spotted walking past, whatever year they were in, they would be greeted by a cheer and dragged on over into the holy circle. Basically, if there was drink and bad music, you would never be far away from a fellow Catharian.

On this particular night, Mary Jane and I were taking a break from dancing. The first signs of sweat marks had begun to appear in the arm-pit region, and I was wearing a grey shirt. I knew it was time to take a drying-off break, and so headed to the one of the bars for a drink. My strawberry blonde neighbour followed me, and as I snapped up a VK-Ice (in no way a cheap copy of Smirnoff Ice, of course), she opted for a water.

"You stopping drinking?" I shouted, fighting for sound waves with Andrew Ridgeley and George Michael.

"No money left," she yelled back.

"I'll get you a drink if you want?"

"What you say?"

"I said, I'll get you a drink if you want."

"Nah, you're alright."

"Sure?"

"Yep."

And so, with bottle in hand, I left the bar and went over to talk to Oisin and Mark, who were also taking a break from the dance-floor. The Irishman was slowly working his way through his first drink of the night.

"That's evaporating quicker than you're drinking it," I shouted.

"What?" he shouted back, cupping his hand to his ear.

I repeated what I'd said, but it didn't seem as funny second time around. Thankfully the ever reliable pair of Mark and Oisin still laughed.

"Hey, I've only been drinking for a few weeks, or whatever."

"Shit, you've never mentioned that before."

And if this ever went to court, I would describe what happened next as follows:

Well, your honour, because I was fully engaged in conversation with Mr Novak and Mr Kerrigan at the time, I failed to notice Ms Catterall standing behind me. I only became aware of Ms Catterall's presence when she grabbed my bottle of VK Ice... sorry, your honour, VK Ice is the vodka-based drink that I was consuming at the time. It comes in a glass bottle, about 300ml, or something around that. I believe mine was raspberry flavour, but I could be mistaken... and started drinking it herself. Well, your honour, I'm afraid to admit that this made me more than a little angry. You see, I had only just offered to buy Ms Catterall a VK Ice drink of her very own, and she had assured me that she didn't want one. I was very thirsty, your honour, and it was very hot in the club, and I really wanted all my VK Ice to myself. I just snapped. I tried to grab the bottle of VK Ice from Ms Catterall's mouth, so that I could have it back before she drank too much of it. Unfortunately, as the court has been made aware, in the process of removing the bottle from Ms Catterall's mouth, I succeeded in knocking out approximately 50 per cent of the lower segment of her left front tooth. Ms Catterall seemed to be in shock for a few minutes, and I'm afraid to admit that I started laughing, thinking she was playing a joke on me, you know, pretending she was hurt. She'd done that sort of thing before. However, I was soon to learn otherwise when she burst into tears, held the bit of tooth in front of me, and said, and I quote, "You bastard. You bastard. My teeth are the only bit of my face I like. You bastard." Although the music was still pretty loud, I am quite sure that these were her words. She then proceeded to run off into the ladies toilets, and the bouncer prevented me from following her in. She later emerged, still tearful, and told me that she was going home, and that I better not dare and try to follow her. I hung around with Mr Novak and Mr Kerrigan for a while, and then I left the club to go for a walk on my own. I am deeply regretful about this whole unfortunate incident.

And I was truly, truly sorry. I suppose laughing as soon as her tooth fell out was not the optimum response, but I didn't realise how serious it was, and it did look pretty funny. But it was just an awful accident, and one that I felt terrible about for the next few days. The thing Mary Jane said about her teeth being the only part of her face that she liked didn't exactly help me to feel much better. The next day I bought her a bunch of flowers and a card saying sorry. I also offered to pay for any treatment. I even declined the countless opportunities presented to make tooth-related jokes. After a few days, and a successful visit to the dentist, my beautifully toothed, strawberry blonde, neighbour had officially forgiven me. Weeks later I still cringed and felt awful whenever she mentioned it, and never laughed whenever my friends brought it up.

So, our friendship survived countless arguments and freakish accidents. But as Mary Jane started spending more time with Gavin, I started spending more time with other people.

I had started to make friends with a lot more of my year during the past weeks, widening my circle in the way I wanted to. There were Faye's rowing friends, both those I knew I hadn't pulled and those that I wasn't so sure about; the football lot, enforcers and all; Mary Jane's band of vets, medics and NatScis that she knew the names of only when drunk; Francesca's English crowd, who couldn't believe how few books I had read; the M-block gang, united by bricks and mortar; the other economists, who although they mixed in different circles (they liked R'n'B and Hip-Hop – or Shit-Hop as Caolan liked to call it – whereas we liked cheese) would always happily meet up in the bar with us for a few drinks and a chat about supply and demand; and anyone who was a fan of *Neighbours* who had joined the growing party that watched it in my room every day at 5.35 pm.

Indeed, it was the pulling power of the Aussie soap, combined with the fact that I had a TV, that more than anything else brought me into contact with so many different people. Friends of friends would turn up, and maybe bring their friends along too. I used to make tea for everyone, but once numbers got above three, I soon put a stop to that. It was crowded to say the least. For the episode where Madge Bishop died, we had a record attendance of thirty-one. We even took a photo to celebrate. People started coming earlier and earlier to make sure they got a seat, or even just a sitting space on the floor. If you wanted a chair, or a place on the bed, you had to turn up at least twenty minutes early. Pretty soon, a crowd of about half the size were turning up for 5.15 pm to watch *The Weakest Link*, and soon you had to turn up before 5 pm to make sure you got a seat for that.

The *Neighbours* crowd were a right mixed bunch. Representatives were there from every subject and every social circle. Historians mingled with mathmos, medics with geographers. It was beautiful. Some just sat there quietly, answering any questions you should ask them whilst keeping their eyes glued to the screen, others were loud and spoke more than the characters we were watching. One small girl, a friend of a friend of Mary Jane, had an inability to sit in one place for more than a minute, or to keep quiet for more than thirty seconds. I soon christened her the Loud One. One time when the Loud One didn't turn up and we enjoyed a peaceful episode, there was a movement started to permanently evict her from our little club, but the rebels were defeated and she got away with a warning.

I liked having all those people around. If I ever had too much work on I would just leave the door on its latch so people could let themselves in. I had to play host. I had to be at the centre of things. It was a role I was suited for. A role I was happy to undertake. Most of the time.

A Tale of Friendship, Love and Economics

But my new group of friends did not come at the price of my old ones. Oh, no. If anything, they complemented each other. Established friendship groups were looking to expand, and over an episode of *Neighbours* seemed like the ideal place to do it.

I suppose it was my nineteenth birthday that symbolically represented the official unity of this new, extended group, although no-one in their right mind would have been sad enough to make such an observation. I decided that it would be quite nice to have a formal hall to mark the occasion as this was cheaper and easier to organise than a restaurant, and it seemed somehow appropriate to celebrate my first birthday in Cambridge in such a unique, traditional setting. My actual birthday was on the Saturday, so a good old Friday night formal hall fitted in almost perfectly. I electronically invited everyone I knew and liked. I sent a big group email around telling people to get a formal ticket for Friday, and thankfully most people managed to get off their arses and do it.

We met in the bar at 6.30 pm to get in a few early drinks. Even at this stage, Oisin's "Hey, I've only been drinking for a few weeks, or whatever" excuse was wearing a little thin, and peer pressure ensured that he had two drinks in the bar just like the rest of us. The proven strategy for success in such a situation was a pint of larger to line the stomach, and then a double spirit and mixer to get you going. Caolan always had double vodka and diet coke ("Remember, it has to be diet. Make sure it's diet, alright?"), Mark had a double anything with anything, Oisin's doubles always looked suspiciously like singles ("Jesus Christ, it's a frickin' double, alright?"), and I went for a double vodka lime and lemo (lemo, being, of course, the cool short-hand terminology for lemonade). Now, as soon as my uni friends started taking the piss out of me for drinking such an apparently "girlie" drink, I told them that this was what all the hard northern lads drank back home. Whenever my friends back home took the piss out of me for drinking it, I told them that this was all the trendy uni lot drank. The truth was I was probably the only male on the planet that drank double vodka lime and lemo, but it tasted really nice, and I was sticking to it.

So, with a couple of drinks on board, and with the majority of the party all present and correct, we moved from the bar to the hall to make sure we all got seats together. Once again, largely thanks to the take-no-prisoners, these-are-our-bloody-seats, attitude of Faye, and the cringe-inducing, sweet-talking technique of Caolan, we all found ourselves sat together. I plonked myself down between Caolan and Mary Jane, with Mark, Oisin and Faye in pennying distance across the table. And boy, where there some pennies flying around. Whenever it is someone's birthday, wherever you are in the world, it always seems to be the rule that they have to get absolutely smashed. The birthday boy or girl, assuming they are not still at primary school, are obliged to drink and be grateful for anything that is put in front of them. Tonight was no exception. By the time my starter had arrived (fish again, which I traded for a bread roll, and even got given another one seeing as it was my birthday), my incredibly cheap and rank bottle of wine was one glass away from completion, and I knew that although it was gone it would not be forgotten.

The rest of my wine was gone a few mouthfuls into the main course of pork something with lovely mashed potatoes and veg. Just as I thought my drinking was done for the rest of the meal, geographers Joe and Nick kindly gave me some of their wine as a gift; a sweet little white Chilean wine costing £2.89 a bottle, and a dry Bulgarian rouge coming in at a bargain £2.69, were lovingly mixed to form a rosé liquid with a taste that should have been illegal. Fortunately, I was at that stage of an evening when I was seemingly becoming immune to the taste and the effects of the wine continually being placed in front of me. I was not immune, however, to what came next. Caolan politely asked me to pass him the gravy, and as I took hold of the silver gravy boat, full to the brim of a cold, lumpy brown liquid, upon which a considerable skin had formed across the top, my good Irish friend proceeded to drop a shiny copper penny into it. He smiled. I didn't. I looked into his eyes pleadingly, but it was too late. Word had spread around the table, and now all eyes were focused upon me and the gravy. Bloody hell, I thought. I shut my eyes, said a little prayer, held the poisoned chalice to my lips, and started drinking. Words cannot describe just how awful it tasted. I tried not to think about what the solid bits of matter that were constantly brushing past my tongue during the downage actually were. I could feel gravy dribbling down my chin, but I could also feel the end getting closer, and so I kept going. I also knew that was not the last time I would be seeing that gravy this evening.

As the deserts were cleared away and the fellows departed, I put all my concentration into staying upright and keeping my food down where it belonged. Then Caolan clinked his wine glass with a fork, and started calling for a speech. Bloody hell, I thought. If he had called for a "stand", I

A Tale of Friendship, Love and Economics

would have struggled to oblige. Once again I looked at him pleadingly but, as I was fast beginning to learn, such a look had no effect on the cold hearted Irishman. Peer pressure kicked in once more and up I got, slowly, and uncertainly, using the chair and the shoulders of my neighbours as support. The room fell silent and people turned their chairs around to see what was going on. I took a deep breath and swallowed down a mouthful of sick that was coming up to say hello. I didn't have a clue what to say.

"Erm... hello everybody... (good start)... as you probably know, I'm Josh and it's my birthday... (there were about 120 people in the room, and only thirty or so probably knew these facts. The rest just knew me as the strange boy who had just downed a jug of gravy)... erm... and I'm an economist... (I did not have a clue where this one was going)... now us economists work our arses off... (this got a cheer from the economists in the room, so I carried on)... unlike some other subjects I could mention... (this got an ooooooh!)... the Mickey Mouse subjects... (this got an even bigger ooooooh!)... you know what I'm talking about... (I looked around the room to remind myself just what I was talking about)... I'm talking about Geography... (this got a few boos, notably from Nick and Joe, and I got assaulted by a few high velocity green beans launched by Faye, but mostly it got cheers)... I mean, put away your colouring pencils and do a proper degree... (this went down well. Now I was on a roll)... and what about History?... (oooooh!)... I mean, oh no, don't give me more than one essay every week or I might die... (not great material, but it got a cheer)... and SPS, oh no, don't give me more than one essay a term, and please give me an extension on that... (luckily there weren't any SPSers in the room to defend themselves)... and don't even get me started on bloody Land Economy. Jesus Christ, what the hell is that subject all about? (even the good old Landies themselves were cheering this one. I was in luck. I looked around, and I couldn't see any more subjects to take the piss out of)... and so, to close this ramble I'd just like to thank everyone for coming to my birthday. I've had a lovely night. And can I please ask all of the economists to raise up their glasses... (ten glasses and my own were suitably raised)... this one's for Keynes and the best subject in the world... (the rest of the hall looked bemused, but cheered anyway. I could have gone on, but no doubt my luck would have run out very shortly. I decided to quit whilst I was ahead, and slumped back down into my chair. That could have gone a lot worse, I thought, and swallowed a bit more sick down)."

I staggered out of hall, aided by a sober Oisin Kerrigan and a floppy Mark Novak, and found myself in the bar. Bloody hell, I thought, I've got to kiss the cat. I looked up to his lair on top of the bar, and his battered papier-mâché face stared right back down at me.

"Not a chance in hell of you getting up here tonight, mate," he seemed to say.

"I know," I replied, and slumped down in the corner of the bar amongst the discarded coats and gowns.

The rest of the gang sat drinking in the bar, whilst I happily dosed in the corner. Oisin, who would still have passed a breathalyser test, decided that it was time for me to go to bed. Caolan and himself provided an Irish walking frame, and I shut my eyes and moved my feet whenever they told me to. Back in my room I ruled out all talk of brushing my teeth and getting undressed, and instead collapsed onto my bed.

Just before I drifted off to sleep I was sure there was something I had to say. I opened my mouth to see if any words were forthcoming, and then out it came. Sick, all over my bed and up my wall. Sick on my pillow and duvet cover. Sick stuck to the side of my face. I half-heartedly appealed to Caolan for help, but he was laughing and making phone calls with my mobile. I immediately fell to sleep.

I awoke with the sensation that one side of my face was peeling off, but a blurry inspection in my mirror revealed that it was merely dried puke on my cheek and the right-hand side of my chin. Then it all came flooding back to me and I was sick again. And again. Happy birthday, Josh.

I spent the rest of the morning half-heartedly cleaning sick off my wall, stopping every five minutes or so for a moan and a sleep. Footballing geographer Nick MacLean came round after lunch to see how I was, and I used the "I think I might be dying" trick to rope him into giving me a hand.

It was the first birthday that I had been ill for, and was glad my Mum couldn't see me now. How disappointed she would be in her only son. Mum phoned me in the afternoon to pass on her best wishes, and I did my best to receive them in as lively a way as I could. I thanked her for the presents she had sent me, presents that I had taken down to uni with me at the start of term and had successfully resisted the temptation to open for all these weeks. She had got me a few CDs and a new video player to replace my old one that I had had for years and had not successfully played a tape since 1997. She asked me if I had had a good night last night, and did I feel rough this morning. I answered yes to both questions. I opened Dad's package that had arrived in the post on Wednesday. He had collected together cards from all his side of the family and stuck them all in a big brown Jiffy-Bag envelope. The majority contained money, which was just what I needed. I texted him to say thanks and he called me later that evening. I guess it seemed strange not seeing either of them on my birthday, but then I suppose it was no stranger than not seeing them on a Sunday afternoon or a Wednesday evening.

During the day, Mary Jane called me around to her room for a cup of tea. She hadn't popped in to see me that morning as she was feeling rough too. We had spent four text-messages each trying to better each other in who was feeling worse. She complained of a killer-headache. I asked her if she had woken with sick on her wall, pillow and face, and she conceded that I had probably just about won this one. When I got to her room, all my friends were sitting round, and everyone was looking up at me. It was one of those times where I knew what was going to happen, but pretended that I didn't to keep the game going and keep everybody happy. I sat down on the bed and asked what was going on. Mary Jane pulled a large white carrier bag out from behind her comfiest chair. She presented me with a big card, inside of which everybody had put a few words. Comments were either the safe "Have a great day", something funny about Lancashire ("Have a happy Yorkshire birthday"), or something economical from the economists ("We have *supplied* you with the birthday which you *demanded* and I hope you reach a happy *equilibrium*"). Caolan, Mark, Oisin and I were at that stage in our friendship where we put quite nice things in each other's cards. In a year's time, my birthday card would make quite different reading. As well as the card, they had all chipped in to buy me a bundle of goodies. I got *Magical Mystery Tour*, one of the only Beatles albums I didn't already have, a huge poster of Jim Royle from *The Royle Family* saying "My Arse" on it, a load of "special" coat-hangers that you could not only hang your clothes on but you could also spin round your finger really fast and even painfully fit your head inside them (I had discovered this during numerous cups of tea with Mary Jane because she had some of the very same hangers), and a bundle of boxer shorts because recently I had been running really low, and having to go commando in jeans, which was both extremely painful and had the potential to inflict long-term irreparable damage. I could tell that Mary Jane had organised it all, and I was very grateful.

It's strange, but I far prefer giving presents than receiving them. I can never seem to find the right words to say when I get a gift. If I don't like it I am usually alright, because I am quite a good liar. However, if I actually do like the gift, which is usually the case, I can never seem to convey my delight to the giver. I either sound corny, and people presume I'm being sarcastic, or I try and make a joke, and the person takes great offence. On the other hand, I suppose I am not much of a fan of giving presents either. I like buying them and wrapping them, and it's not that I'm a tight arse who doesn't like parting with his money, it's just that I absolutely hate the moment when the person sets eyes on your carefully thought-out gift for the first time. Even when they say they like it, and then promise they like it, and then cross there heart and hope to die they like it, I still find it hard to believe them. I'm a bit strange like that.

Anyway, the bottom line was I was really touched by the presents people had got me, but whenever I said those very words, Caolan started laughing thinking I was telling a joke. He always laughed in the wrong places. But I was extremely grateful for the effort everyone had gone to. Especially Mary Jane.

So, in summary, I was extremely happy to have met a load of new people in the first few weeks of that second term, whilst still staying close to my group of friends from first term. I was settling in good and proper, and everything was rosy. And although I was seeing less and less of Mary Jane, no major crisis was imminent. Or so I thought.

Chapter 31

I knew that it was only a matter of time before I started to fancy someone. Since the Movie Star Look-alike, and that one didn't really count as hindsight suggested it was more of a way to get the ball rolling, there hadn't really been anyone. I mean, of course when we were on nights out I would look at girls and think, "Yep, she's pretty fit," and things like that, but nothing to keep me awake at night.

Me fancying someone tended to be quite cyclical; I would usually like them for a period of about three weeks, and if nothing came of it, I would take a couple of days break and then move onto someone else. Variety is the

A Tale of Friendship, Love and Economics

spice of life so they say. It was only when I started getting, or at least perceiving, some positive feedback from my fancee that problems emerged. I would normally handle this by becoming good friends with them, in an effort to get closer to them, and pretty soon that's all they would see me – as my friend Josh, good old Josh. Whoever says that all the best relationships start with friendship is talking a load of bollocks. Anyway, this wasn't going to happen at uni. Oh, no. If I fancied someone and it didn't seem like anything was going to come of it I would forget about it and move on, end of story. If it seemed like something was going to happen, I would cut to the chase, maybe ask them out straight away, and step right past that "good-friends" rubbish. That was the plan, anyway.

So, as January took an eleven-month holiday and gave way to February, the various chemicals in my body went into overdrive, and put me on the hunt for someone to fancy. It was like some wizard had cast a spell on me that said I would fall for the next person I set eyes on. Fortunately, I didn't call round to see Mark, Oisin or Caolan the moment spell was cast, and instead I found myself sat having a cup of tea with Cassandra.

I had become quite friendly with Cassandra recently. Partly this was because I was hoping that I might be able to discover from our conversations whether or not we had actually pulled on the night of the Granny Bop at the end of last term, but also because I thought she was a really nice girl. Whenever she popped round to see my favourite wee Scot, Faye, I would stay in the room and happily chat away, and if Faye was going to visit her she would often invite me along, and so long as I thought the world of economics could survive without my input for an hour or so I would gladly go. Pretty soon I would call around to her room on my own, without my little Scottish chaperone, and Cassandra was soon a fully fledged member of the ever expanding Team Neighbours.

She was indeed a really nice girl, and we soon found out that we had a lot in common. First there were the small things, like we both liked pasta and U2. Then there were the bigger things. Cassandra's Mum and Dad were divorced too. My parent's divorce was not something I particularly enjoyed or felt the need to talk about. It had happened such a long time ago, that I had just accepted it as a part of my life. It was only when you talked to someone who had gone through the same kind of thing that you realised talking helped. Amazingly, despite the countless statistics that would have suggested otherwise, none of my close friends' parents' marriages had suffered the same fate. Hence, whilst they could appreciate certain aspects ("but you get *two* sets of birthday and Christmas presents every year!"), the more everyday things were incomprehensible. Just the small things like having a different surname than your Mum, being careful not to say that you had too good a time at the other parent's house, only having one of them at parents' evening or watching you play football, constantly defending the actions of one to the other, not knowing how to introduce the person your parents were now with ("partner" made it sound like they were gay, and "boyfriend/girlfriend" like they were seventeen). These were the things that reminded you day after day that you did not live the so-called normal family life. But what is normal these days, Mum would say, and of course she was right. Also, upon reflection, I would not have changed anything. Getting divorced was the best thing my Mum and Dad ever did, and both were infinitely happier, with their "special friends" (by far the worst) in the long term as a result. And it's not as if I am from a broken home or unstable family background, or anything like that. It's just that you didn't have some of the simple things your friends took for granted, and for the first time in my life, I found that talking about it helped, and I think Cassandra felt the same too.

It was hardly the most light-hearted foundation for a friendship, but it brought us closer together nonetheless. And then one day, low and behold, I started to see her as more than a friend. I don't know why it happened. There was certainly no significant event that kick-started things. I was drinking tea and eating a custard cream at the time. I just remember there suddenly being a few awkward pauses in our conversations as if space were being made for something more important to be said, and after that I started feeling nervous every time I knocked at her door or saw her in the bar. Bloody hell, I thought, you fancy her.

But then I wasn't sure I did. You see, I was fully aware of the cyclical nature of my affections, and the fact that I hadn't fancied anyone for a while. I couldn't decide whether I really liked her, or if she was just the next girl along the conveyor belt, a necessary being to restore inner karma to my body. I didn't talk to anyone about it. It was the kind of thing that was too hard to explain to even the most willing, understanding set of ears, and I knew that if I tried to explain it to Caolan he would have said something like: "Look, Josh, it's perfectly simple. You either want to shag her or you don't." He already said I was too emotional for a normal male. I decided to leave it a week and see what happened.

Seven days later I still liked her. I decided to talk to Faye about it. Mary Jane was busy with Gavin at the time, and confiding in my Scottish neighbour also had a hidden advantage. As a good friend of Cassandra, the wee detective could find out if she liked me, without me having to make a dick out of myself, and with the Duane situation still weighing heavy on her mind, she was more than happy to fully embrace another distraction (after all, her geography degree was hardly proving time-consuming).

Taking her inspiration from the late, great Scottish detective, Jim Taggart, and throwing in a bit of female intuition for good measure, Faye began amassing clues to determine whether Cassandra liked me. Apparently just asking her was too easy. Faye carefully observed her behaviour in situations when we were all together, and analysed her reaction when she slipped my name into the conversation when I was absent. After a week's work, for which I had to pay her two cups of tea and four custard creams a day, she handed in her report. Faye was 93% sure Cassandra liked me, and she advised that I should go ahead and ask her out. She was also pretty sure that I had pulled her at the Granny Bop, but this remained unconfirmed. I thanked her for her tireless work and gave my wee Scottish neighbour her final payment whilst we listen to a bit of Coldplay.

Whilst this whole affair had been in progress, and in what I took to be a sign from above, the calendar had plodded along to 12th February. Being the old romantic that I am, I decided to launch my attack on Valentine's Day.

I had never sent a Valentine's card asking someone out before. In fact, I had only sent two Valentines cards in my life, and both were to my girlfriend at the time. Likewise, I had only received one back (we had fallen out pretty badly one year so my card was more of an apology, and her lack of card was a gesture that she was still not happy). This was quite a while back, when I was young and foolish, and since then 14th February had been but a day of big plans that I was too scared to carry through, and big disappointments when the postman failed to deliver.

In fact, when I came to think about it, I was quite looking forward to sending a Valentine's card again. I'd been out of the old Valentines Game for too long, and it was about time I jumped back into it. Clinton Cards seemed the place to start, full to the brim with all sorts of cards, as well as heart-shaped balloons, paper flowers, teddies, and special chocolates. I am one of these people who do not like pissing around when choosing a card, no matter what the occasion. As soon as I come across one that looks vaguely suitable, I snap it up and get out. I think the economic term for such behaviour is "Satisfying", when you chose the action that might not necessarily make you the happiest out of all the choices of actions available to you, but brings you an amount of joy that you are happy enough to stick with. I think that's right, although I could well be mistaken. Anyway, whatever it is called, this is my attitude to most forms of shopping, which is in stark contrast to any female I have ever met. However, on this particular day, I thought it best to exercise a certain amount of care over the choice of card, seeing as it was important and there were so many to choose from. Some were about a metre high and cost about as much as my student loan. They were quickly ruled out. Others were funny but filthy, and, despite a little voice saying go on it'd be funny, they were eventually deemed inappropriate and ruled out also. In the end I opted for a non-offensive little beauty, which even came with a free red envelope. The front of the card was made up of a red heart beating away against a subtly patterned white background, with the words: "To My Valentine" sprawled in a suitably elegant and posh font across the top. The inside was left annoyingly blank, thus requiring imagination on my part.

    I took the card back home to the safety of my room, and with the door well and truly locked and secured, I thought about what I was going to write. I took out a piece of rough paper first to lay down a few preliminary ideas. Bloody hell, it was not easy thinking what to say. I was really bad of thinking what to write in birthday cards, but this was on a whole new level. And then, like a cartoon light bulb popping on above my head, I had it. Yes, yes, that's it. I'll write a poem. Brilliant idea.

    And so, hitting my pad of A4 paper with all the naïvety and enthusiasm of someone who had never written a poem before, I started. And after half an hour, or so, I had it. Before I had time to change my mind I transferred the beautiful piece onto the card in my finest handwriting, signed it "Love, Josh" at the bottom, and sealed it. I then put the kettle on and read the showbiz gossip pages on Teletext.

    The poem reads as follows:

>   Sometimes I don't know what to do,

A Tale of Friendship, Love and Economics

Should be working, but thinking of you,
Close my eyes and see your face,
When open you're gone without a trace,

I love your smile and your curly hair,
The way I'm happy when you're there,
The way you hiccup when you get a joke
The way you swore when your soup bowl broke,

The way your eyes can't hide what you think,
How easily you can tell when I've had a drink,
I'm trying so hard just to say,
You brighten up my every day.

    Bloody hell. Where the little voice in my head had gone that was supposed to stop me doing stupid things like this, I had no idea. It sounded like a Ronan Keating song, and a really bad one at that. Of course, with the benefit of hindsight, it was a shit poem and an even shittier idea, and it makes me cringe like hell now to even think of it. However, at the time I was really proud of my efforts, utterly convinced I had done a really good move. I decided there and then that I was wasted as an economist, depriving the literary world of my wonderful whimsical verses.
    On the night of 13th of February, I slipped out of my room, dressed in a black T-shirt and an equally black pair of jeans, and went on an undercover mission to put the card in her pigeon hole. Thankfully, the coast was clear, so I didn't have to kill anyone on the way. Equally thankfully, there were no other Valentine-looking cards lying in Cassandra's pigeon hole, just a small flyer advertising Reiki classes at Queen's College. I took the red enveloped out from its hiding place down the front of my jeans, and slotted it right to back of her pigeon hole. I then picked up the info on Reiki that was lying waiting patiently for me in mine and retired to my room, where I had tea with Faye. I told her about the poem, and she asked me if I was taking the piss. I ashamedly said no and made her promise not to tell a soul. Not even Mary Jane.
    And then I waited. Waited until night gave way to morning, lying there in my bed playing over the various scenarios that could happen, practicing my lines and my facial expressions, starting, or course, with the worst case.

With four Weetabix in my belly and a lecture on the use of the Gini Coefficient under my belt, I wandered into the pigeon holes on this day of love with Caolan, Mark and Oisin.

"Do you reckon any of us will get any?" I asked, casually.

"I might, but you losers have no chance," replied Caolan.

"Cards from your Mum don't count, Caolan," I explained, and turned to the other two, "how many did you guys send?"

"None" said Mark.

"None, or whatever," said Oisin.

"Nah, me neither," I lied. "Right, let's get this over with and see if the females of this world have come to their senses and sent us fine economists a bundle of cards. Get the shovels and the wheelbarrows ready."

"You digging yourself a hole to bury yourself in when you get no cards?"

"You are piss funny, you know, Caolan, you really are."

We went straight over to our pigeon holes. I must admit, I was kind of expecting a card. If not from Cassandra, then from someone else who had been hiding a burning desire for me. I mean, come on, there must be someone. I was to be disappointed. My pigeon hole lay unromantically bare. Luckily, so did the p-holes of the other three.

"It's a load of bollocks this Valentine's Day, isn't it?" I said, after confirming that each of the others withdrew from their holes equally empty-handed.

"Well, if you don't send 'em, you can hardly expect to receive 'em, can you?" explained Caolan in the annoying all-knowing way he often did when he was making a big point. I nodded.

Seeing as ours were empty, we decided to have a look if anyone we knew had been visited by the love gods. Purely by chance I found myself looking in Cassandra's pigeon hole. It was empty. She had got the card, or it had been stolen. Mary Jane had a card, presumably from Gavin, although Caolan asked if I was sure I hadn't sent it. Faye was cardless, and I could only assume she hadn't sent one to Duane. Geographers Nick and Joe's were suitably empty. A lot of the girls in our year had a single red rose popping out of their pigeon hole, which turned out to have come from Jim the barman, the small, balding old man who enjoyed flirting with the girls as they ordered their drinks. Feeling adequately informed about the love lives of our year, and indeed the non-existent nature of our own, we retreated to hall for lunch, where I enjoyed a very well-cooked jacket potato topped with beans and cheese.

I felt nervous and generally unpleasant for the rest of the day. I had an essay to write about the reasons for the differences in unemployment trends between Europe and the USA, but trade unions and unemployment benefits were far from my mind. I was already beginning to regret sending the card. By 2 pm I would have happily paid £10 for someone to have removed my actions from the history books, and the figure was increasing at about £15 an hour. I couldn't believe I had sent a girl a poem, and such a woeful one at that. If ever me and my friends were watching a film and a one of the male characters did something similar, it would be met with the universal cry of "what a dick". God, I was a dick. I knew that I couldn't change what I'd done, but it didn't make me fell any better.

I didn't know what I was supposed to do now. Was I supposed to wait for her to make contact, or should I take the decisive step and pop around to see her? The former option seemed much less daunting, but I didn't fancy just sitting around in my room. It was like waiting on Death Row, or something. With little else to do I called round for Jude to see if he fancied going to the gym.

Jude and I had been getting into the gym recently. Neither of us were fat, but both of us were far-sighted enough to see that the combination of excessive drinking combined with not much else was bound to lead to a few spare tyres appearing around our midriffs sooner or later. We always went to our college gym, and tried our best to go every other day. To be fair, Catz gym was rubbish, but it was free and literally a stone's throw away, unlike the fifteen-minute bike-ride and the signing-on fee at the uni gym out by Parker's Piece. To gain access to our college gym you first had to go and see one of the lovely college porters. You handed over your room key and signed your name in one of their books, and if they couldn't think of a reason not to, they would give you a gym-pin in return, which also doubled as a key to get you into the locked gym. As a sign of our growing maturity having come to university, and quite a prestigious one at that, Jude and I always signed our names in the gym book as Jude Slug and Josh Bug respectively, for no particular reason.

The gym was in a small, stuffy room underneath Hall. A pathetic-looking fan hung in the far corner, that blew even more stuffy air into your face if you stood right up against it, but apart from that had no effect. The equipment was pretty basic. There were a couple of ergos to satisfy the college rowers, a few free weights, a bench-press, a leg thing that didn't really work properly, and a few pulley-down things that tended to erode the skin off your hands pretty quickly. Thankfully, and perhaps unsurprisingly, it was often empty, so Jude and I could put on his *Rocky* soundtrack tape and work out like the great fictional boxer who single-handedly ended the Cold War to our hearts' content. We were once caught in the act of shadow boxing in front of the mirror, with our sleeves rolled up trying to find some biceps in our arms, and squealing along to *Eye of the Tiger*, but that was about it.

Midway through the Great Work-Out of 14th February, Mr Slug and I again found ourselves with company. We heard the rattle of a key in the door, and girls' voices outside.

"Right, don't let them see how little we can lift," instructed Jude with panic in his voice.

"What exactly... do you want... us to do... grow some... new muscles... in five... seconds?" I replied, struggling to get through my final set of bench-presses.

"No, we'll just add a good few kilograms onto each of the machines and look like we've just finished. Easy."

And with that Jude set about making the necessary adjustments to the room, kilo after kilo. He was more tired after doing this than after a normal work out, but he finished just as the band of females started streaming in through the door. I couldn't believe it, it was Catz first year rowers, a frightening-looking troop that contained, of course, Cassandra. I smiled as they walked in, nodded at a few of them, made an exaggerated sigh of exhaustion, and flew out of the room as quickly as I could. I managed to avoid all eye contact with her. Jude grabbed my gym-pin and followed me. He caught me up and asked me what the big rush was. I told him I didn't want to be late for Hall.

"Well, laddy, you sure handled that one well," said Faye sarcastically in the post-gym-incident analysis.

"I know, but I didn't know what to say. And even if I did, I wasn't going to say if in Catz gym with an audience of female rowers and *Rocky* music in the background".

"When exactly are you going to confront her, Josh?"

"Soon, soon. Maybe in the bar tonight."

"You better bloody had do."

"Yes, boss."

Faye wouldn't let me pull out of going to the bar that night, unemployment essay or no unemployment essay. She said I had to go to make sure she didn't let slip to anyone she should meet in the bar about a certain poet in our midst, masquerading as a northern economist. So reluctantly along I went, taking Faye and an unsuspecting Mark with me for moral support. The three of us sat on a table in the corner of the bar with two pints of lager, a vodka and coke, and a pack of dry roasted peanuts for company.

Every time I saw somebody coming through the door of the bar my eyes focused in, analysing whether or not that somebody was Cassandra, and if it wasn't, whether it was a person who was likely to be walking into the bar five metres in front of Cassandra. Mark said I looked on edge. I told him that I mulling over in my mind whether shocks or institutions played a bigger role in the rise in post-war European unemployment. He seemed happy enough with my answer, and admitted that he was concerned too. Then, just as I was beginning to relax, beginning to let my guard down, sitting back and enjoying a handful of peanuts, in she came. Faye nudged me under the table, just to make sure that I had seen.

She walked into the bar, stopping briefly to hang her coat up, for it was chilly outside, and then began taking the most efficient route to the bar, between the table football and pool tables. I put my head down. Not for the first time I looked into my drink for the answer. I knew she must have spotted me by now because the bar was fairly quiet, and also because Faye was waving like a mental woman trying to attract her attention. I didn't know what to do. I chose to do the first thing that came to mind; the manly option, the thing that I often did in these situations. I pulled my mobile out of my pocket and faked a phone call.

"Yes mate... how's it going?... what, it's really important, you say?... right, well give me a sec, I'll just go outside... yeah, I'm in the college bar... no, mate, it's no trouble."

And I was out of there, out into the open on this bitterly cold Valentine's night, shivering away with my drink in my hand, my coat and my friends inside, talking away to myself on my mobile.

I walked back to my room, shut the door, and sat down with my head in my hands. You are such a dick, Josh, I thought and said out loud, talking either to the walls, John Lennon and Martin Luther King, or the fictional friend in need who was presumably still listening as much as he ever had done at the other end of the phone-line. I knew either way that it was best I knew how she felt as soon as possible, but at the same time it was the last thing I wanted to know. I would now happily have paid £100 for this whole thing never to have happened. Then there was a knock on the door.

"Erm... hi... Cassandra." It was Cassandra. "Come in."

And she walked into my room. I closed the door behind her.

"How are you?" I asked.

"Good," she replied, smiling sweetly. "You?"

"Yep, pretty good, you know."

"I've brought your coat. You left it in the bar."

"Oh, right. Thanks."

And then there was silence. Painful silence. I exhaled air through closed lips as if I was trying to blow up a balloon, and swung my arms and tapped my hands together, first behind my back and then out in front. Cassandra searched for the eye-contact that I was reluctant to give.

"Hey," I began, still breathing, still swinging my arms, and now staring at a spot to the right of her feet, "did you see United's goal the other night?"

I saw the shadow of her head shaking. She had absolutely no interest in football. Without looking up, I continued.

"Well, it was amazing, right, Giggs had it on the left, right, and it looked like nothing was on, right, and so he looks like he's just going to lay it inside to Keane, right, but instead he rolls the ball back, right, and..."

"Look, Josh, about the card..."

I stopped dead in my tracks. It was the phrase I knew was coming all along, but it still paralysed me with surprise. I contemplated denial ("What card?"), and lying ("Yeah, it was just a joke, you know, pretty funny, eh?"), but in the end opted for, "Oh." Then more silence. There was no way I was speaking next.

"Josh, it was lovely, and the things you said inside were... well, they were lovely. *Really* lovely."

It was a sentence crying out for a "but".

"But, I'm afraid... I don't feel the same."

I still couldn't look at her. I started swinging my right foot around the back of my left one like I was rehearsing a dance routine. I was still not prepared to talk.

"You see, I'm kind of seeing someone at the moment... well, not really *seeing*, but, you know."

"Oh."
I didn't really mean to speak.
"Yeah, it's been going on for a while now, but no-one knows about it because we weren't so sure ourselves, you know."
"Oh."
I didn't know what else to say, but then she didn't seem to either.
"Is it anyone I know?"
"Does it really matter?"
This was turning into a really bad soap opera script.
"Not really, but seeing as I've made a complete prick out of myself, you might as well tell me. I won't tell anyone, you know. Cross my heart, and all that."
"You haven't made a prick out of yourself, Josh. Okay? You've been very sweet, and it's nothing at all to be embarrassed about. And if you really want to know who it is, then I'll tell you. It's Charles."
"Charles?"
A little laugh escaped from my insides. I looked up at Cassandra for the first time in the conversation. She didn't look impressed.
Bloody hell, Charles. Now don't get me wrong, Charles was a really nice lad, an engineer in our year as it happened, but for a boyfriend? No way. He was like a giant special needs child. He was about six-foot-two and always had a smile on his face surrounded on both sides by a pair of rosy red cheeks. He could often be seen running around college with a water pistol, or a pea shooter, or a bow and arrow, or a potato gun, or a Viking set, complete with horned-helmet, sword and shield. He also had a habit of tickling you instead of shaking your hand, and calling you names like Joshy-Woshy. I mean the lad was totally harmless, but come on?
I wasn't too upset about the whole thing. You kind of had to see the funny side. I had lost the girl to a real life clown, a kiddies' entertainer doing an engineering degree at Cambridge, a two-year-old who had some how gotten hold of a twenty-year-old's body. I told Faye about it, and after trying to keep a straight face in case I was upset, she then proceeded to piss her sides for an hour.
"Oh Jesus Christ, not Charles, ooh no, not Charles," she repeated whenever she had saved up enough breath in her body. And I laughed too. I couldn't get mad or upset about it. It was too ridiculous.
In the end their relationship lasted about four weeks, with most of our

year completely oblivious to the whole thing. Thankfully, and amazingly in a place where gossip travelled faster than light, most were equally ignorant of my failed poetic seduction. If the football lot had found out, I would have been finished. By the time the happy couple split up, they had already signed up to live in a flat together next year in Chads. This was yet another household destined for frictions, but hardly in the league of our one. In the long run I didn't regret asking her out at all. After a couple of weeks of the inevitable awkwardness, Cassandra and I stayed pretty good friends and, looking back, I don't think the relationship would have worked anyway. I think I liked her for all the wrong reasons; more out of a desire for any kind of romance than for a romance with her in particular. I think it was something I needed to get out of my system, get the "asking-people-out" ball rolling at Cambridge. And boy, did it roll.

Chapter 32

In the days immediately following my Valentine's tale of woe, I needed something to take my mind of Cassandra, and preferably something that didn't begin with "E" and end in "conomics". The answer came in the form of the annual RAG Blind Date.

RAG is a very prominent student-led charity that exists in a number of British universities. Cambridge RAG raises a significant amount of money each year by organising a whole host of events, such as Pyjama Pub Crawls across the city, paint-balling, parachuting, bungee jumping, parades, variety shows and various themed nights out. The worthy charities to benefit from all this fund-raising are spread far and wide and include the Breast Cancer Campaign, Make-A-Wish Foundation and even Hearing Dogs for Deaf People. In Cambridge, each college has its own set of hard-working RAG reps, and, as with most things, there was a lot of inter-college rivalry to see which reps could raise the most money (an economic example of incentives working in the right direction, I thought to myself. And kept to myself). But by far the most popular and well-known RAG event each year was the university-wide love-fest that was RAG Blind Date.

Whenever I had been approached in the bar by our bubbly RAG rep and asked to buy an entry form, I immediately said no. At first I thought she

A Tale of Friendship, Love and Economics

might have heard about my poetic misadventures, and thought a manufactured meeting with an unseen member of the opposite sex would be just what a ruined Romeo like myself needed. Even when she promised that this was an event that everyone who was anyone signed up to, regardless of their position on the spectrum of singleness, I still ruled it out. As did most of my friends. I mean, the whole thing sounded absolutely ridiculous.

Entry cost £3, with each boy given a blue form to fill out, and, in keeping with the traditional stereotypes, each girl a pink one. Not too bad so far. On these forms were a series of questions, ranging from the straightforward (name, age, college, email address), to the quite difficult (choose five words to describe yourself), to the bloody difficult (draw your ideal woman), to the come-on-now-you-must-be-taking-the-piss (write a short poem). You then handed in the completed form back to your college RAG Rep who then – wait for it – rated you out of ten, and then pretty much auctioned you off like a piece of meat. This was obviously the ethically dubious side of charity. Each pair of college RAG Reps took along their rated bundle of forms to a big hall one afternoon and when the whistle sounded, frantically exchanged a St. Catharine's seven for a Girton seven, a Homerton nine for a King's nine, a New Hall zero for anyone unlucky enough to still have forms to swap at the end of the afternoon, and so on. With all the swapping complete you would then find, lying waiting patiently in your pigeon hole on the morning of your date, the pink form of the girl you were due to meet. Hours were then spent drawing upon all resources, trying to find out if your prospective date was a minger, or not. If she was, you started planning your excuses, if she wasn't, you then got yourself ready to meet at the time and place she had chosen that evening. For safety reasons, I guess, the girls always got to pick the time and the place for the date. This often resulted in gangs of girls from the same college gathering together in one place to form a fierce tribe ready to interrogate and intimidate an unprepared band of male strangers. It sounded like absolute hell to me, and there was no way, absolutely no way, I was going to do it. None of us were.

And then, one by one, we were picked off by eager, persuasive RAG Reps and coerced into exchanging three golden coins for one blue form. To be honest, the Cassandra thing had instilled in me a "couldn't give six shits" attitude to the whole thing, so in the end I didn't actually need that much persuading to sign up. If it stopped them nagging me in the bar, I would do it. Soon, Caolan, Oisin, Jude and Nick had all signed up. Joe Porter refused, and could not be swayed no matter what the reps, and us, tried. Mark was the final one to fall. He really didn't want to do it at all, but he was not as strong as Joe. We asked him what the hell else he was going to do that night whilst we were all out meeting and greeting the future loves of our lives. He explained that he had a bit of game theory to finish off, so he would probably stay in and do that. Even as the final words left his mouth he knew he wasn't going to be allowed to get away with that one, and promptly, and extremely reluctantly, purchased a form.

We left it until the last possible moment to complete our forms. They had to be in the RAG Reps' pigeon holes by midnight, and we had been to the bar and had more than a couple of drinks each. I signed up Faye and Francesca to analyse our potential answers from a female perspective, subsequently advise otherwise, and hence enable us to produce the perfect forms, and thus get the perfect ladies. Neither of them were doing the blind date themselves. Francesca chose not to because of her boyfriend, and Faye because "Ooh no, it's not my cup of tea". So, the expert panel gathered in M14 and, armed with a bundle of forms, a few biros, and a cup of tea each, we set about putting pen to paper, and setting the wheels of love in motion.

We rattled through the first questions without the need for consultation. Name, email, college, no problem. If they had of been representative of the rest of the form we would have been finished in ten minutes. Of course, they weren't. The first stumbling block came when we were asked to choose our current "status" from the following list: Married, What she doesn't know, Recently divorced, Single, Desperate.

The Married option was to make sure even people who were going out with someone would sign up. The plan was that they would then get paired up with other married blind daters, and they could enjoy a platonically pleasurable evening. Naturally, none of our lot could claim to be married. Oh, except for Caolan, of course.

Yes, the Irish boy-band wannabe had recently started seeing a lovely girl from our college who was in the year above. Caolan had thus been the first to break the implicit bond of singleness that united our group, a bond that I had tried to break but failed miserably. The girl in question was a good friend of his Nanny, and he had met her, and probably fallen for her, at Nanny-Nannettes Dinner. She was apparently from Scotland, but had an accent that Faye was disgusted with ("Scotland, my arse" she often commented). They had only been seeing each other for a couple of weeks, and he had never brought her around to meet us all properly. When pressed, all Caolan would say about the relationship was: stop calling it a relationship, that it was nothing serious, but things were going well. Caolan would not talk about things like that – proper things – to any of us. It was apparently not serious enough to warrant the sending of a Valentine's card, but nevertheless serious enough for the Irishman to circle Married on his form, resulting in jeers and jibes from the rest of the room. Not that we were jealous, of course. We all circled Desperate.

Making rapid progress down the form, and after taking a well-deserved slurp of our tea, we moved onto the trickier stuff. Choose five words to describe yourself. Right. Some thought was definitely needed here. The thing was you couldn't exactly rattle-off stuff like "considerate", "sensitive", "charming", "generous" etc. one, because they weren't true and, two, because it made you sound like a right tosser. No, you had to somehow pick words that made it seem like you didn't take yourself too seriously, but at the same time that you weren't a total freak. Basically, and this was the case for all these kinds of questions on the form, you couldn't make yourself sound good, but you could easily make yourself sound like the biggest nob on the planet. As the minutes ticked on we soon gave up all hope of charming the pants off our ladies with our forms. Damage limitation was declared the order of the day.

Just as we reached the forty-minute mark of time spent trying to answer this stupid question, Francesca suggested the following:

"Why not go for something like: charming, romantic, intelligent, athletic, liar."

There was a moment's silence around the room whilst we considered the Sheffield English student's suggestion. Then, like a stand-off at the end of a Western, we all reached for our pens in an effort to be the first to write it down on our forms. In the end we all had some variation of Francesca's brain-wave as our answer.

Right, next one: draw your ideal woman. Bloody hell. Again, a perfect answer did not spring immediately to mind, and Faye promptly filled up the kettle. Drawing a huge pair of breasts and a tiny brain was certainly an option, but one that could easily back-fire if the form fell into the hands of the wrong woman (i.e. one who did not share our immature sense of humour). Still, this was a chance that Nick and I were willing to take. It required little thought and little artistic prowess. Oisin refused the sink to our level, and instead drew a pretty-looking girl with a flower in her hand. Even Francesca and Faye had to admit they liked our big-tit, small-brain portrait better. Soon, married Caolan had jumped upon our bandwagon, and shortly after, a resigned Mark put one leg on board by drawing a less extreme version of ours – a smiling girl with a smaller cup size and a larger IQ.

Now we were on to the trickiest of all, and we only had fifteen minutes before the forms had to be handed in. Write a poem to your date. Faye gave me a wink which I ignored. A poem, eh? Any pretentious ode would make you look a fool, but then a rude limerick could cause offence. Again, it was all about striking the right balance to minimise the damage. Francesca, the English student, was as good as useless, and Faye was struggling for air in response to one of young Nick's earlier efforts that ended with the word "muff". It seemed we were all on our own for this one. I toyed around with a few ideas in my head, but they were not exactly awe-inspiring to say the least. Then, one by one, the other members of the group suddenly seemed to be hit by a gust of poetic genius. All the good lines were being taken up. Caolan, inspired by Seamus Heaney he explained, was using vegetables to portray sexual innuendo in a tasteful, and yet quite humourous, way. Nick was using his unappreciated talent for telling the worst jokes on the planet to create a poem that built up to a climatic, and necessarily awful, punchline, which unbelievably worked a treat. Even Mark, the least imaginative of souls, had created a little four-line wonder that I would have happily paid £5 for. I had to think fast before Oisin, the last in our group in most things, stole any remaining good lines.

And then I had it. Yes, Josh, brilliant. I quickly wrote it down on my form without saying a word to anyone, keeping my right arm coiled protectively over the form as I wrote to guard my verse from prying eyes. There was no way I was going to let the shaggy-haired Irishman nick this one. And when it was safely there in front of me, neatly printed in black biro, a satisfied smile fell upon my face. I read the words back to myself, and then out loud to the group:

Roses are red,
Violets are blue,
If you aren't a minger,
I might just nob you.

A Tale of Friendship, Love and Economics

"Tell me you're joking, Josh," said Francesca, "please just tell me you're joking."

"Ooh no, Josh, ooh no," said Faye, shaking her head and tutting like a disapproving parent.

"You dickhead," said Caolan.

I wasn't exactly expecting a standing ovation or the Nobel Prize for literature, but I was hoping for a slightly more positive response. What was their problem? And then I thought about it. I suppose there was the slightest possibility that the girl on the receiving end of my sweet little verse might not see the funny side. Indeed, she might even be a little scared. But there were only five minutes to go, and I had no Tippex, no spare forms, and absolutely no desire to write another poem. I resigned myself, against my better judgement, to sticking with it.

Then, just as it looked like things couldn't get any worse, a tiny little voice in my head started talking.

"Go on, Josh," it said, I think for some reason in a Manchester accent, "do it, do it."

And I did it. I ran the idea by the group, and there were no objections. Caolan and Nick seemed very in favour of my idea. Even Francesca and Faye were silent, probably partly because they assumed I was joking, and partly because they realised the form was beyond salvation already. And what did I do to my lovely blue form that was all finished and ready to be handed in? I wrote the word "nob" nineteen times on it. I wrote it vertically around the side of the form, I wrote it in a speech bubble coming out of the mouth of my ideal woman drawing, I even squeezed it in as my middle name. It was everywhere. Why, I do not know. I'm a bit strange like that.

Almost as soon as I had written the b of the nineteenth nob I started to realise what I had done. On the morning of the blind date, a blue form would be waiting in the pigeon hole of an excited, innocent, unsuspecting Cambridge student, and as she tried to psychoanalyse the personality of her date by his answers on the form, his image in her mind would probably be dominated by a certain three letter word repeated twenty times (for it was in the poem too). I wasn't sure if she could legally have me put in jail, but I was certain that she wouldn't turn up. The boys in the room started laughing, the girls shook their heads. It was too late. The forms had to be handed into our RAG Reps' pigeon hole in three minutes, and there were no other forms available. It was all over. I was finished. I put the form in with all the others and prayed for a miracle.

The morning of the blind date came around, and with it a nine o'clock lecture on national income accounting. Caolan, Mark, Oisin and myself called in to the pigeon holes on the way to lectures to scoop up the pink forms that lay waiting for us. And whist the young American lecturer was projecting an equation onto a white screen that only the freaks in the front row understood, we, along with the majority of the students in the Lady Mitchell Hall Lecture Theatre, scrutinised and analysed the forms that lay on the bench in front of us. The lecture theatre was a sea of pink and blue. Each form had its top right hand corner torn off, as this was the place the unethical mark out of ten had been written.

It was hard to gage what kind of person you were destined to meet from the answers they had given. After all, we had given some pretty dodgy answers that Freud would have had a field day with, and we were all fairly normal. Well, relative to most people in this place anyway. So, as our eyes wandered down the form, our minds remained open. And yet, it still was pretty clear that I had gotten a bum deal.

The evidence was plentiful. Her name was normal enough, Margaret Allsop, although perhaps a little old-fashioned, sounding like it could have been a character on *Last of the Summer Wine*. Her email address was also pretty inoffensive, she was my age, and I had no negative preconceptions about her college, Selwyn. No, I was happy enough with the start of the form. It was when you carried on reading down it that the problems started. Firstly, the time she wanted to meet was 10.30 pm. I thought that this was a little on the late side, and a quick glance across at other people's forms confirmed that the majority seemed to have a rendezvous of about 8.30 pm or earlier. Most people seemed to be meeting in a restaurant as well, where they would enjoy pleasant conversation over fine food. Margaret Allsop wanted to meet in the stuffiest, most crowded pub in Cambridge, The Granta. This only left me half an hour of talk-time in the pub before last orders were called, and considering people often took more than a little time to warm to me (a period of about three weeks was sometimes required), things were not looking good. One of the words she had used to describe herself was "voluptuous". Now, a childhood of reading football magazines instead of the classic novels had left my vocabulary ashamedly limited, and I had to ask our only female economist, Leila, exactly what this voluptuous word meant. She

A Tale of Friendship, Love and Economics

explained that it was used by fat women when describing themselves to avoid saying they were fat. Nice one. With her form also saying that I would recognise her because of the long black coat she would be wearing, it sounded like I was off on a date with a voluptuous vampire. Next came her poem. Now a quick glance at the other lads' forms revealed that their girls did not seem particularly averse to the odd smutty limerick. The same could not be said for Margaret Allsop. Whereas other girls rhymed "I like the odd cig" with "you better be big" and "if you start to snore" with "I'll do you some more", Ms Allsop had opted for the raunchy:

I like a man to treat me right,
Buy me flowers, walk me home at night,
Get me a drink from the old man's stand,
Feed the ducks in the park, hand in hand.

I suppose you could say that the voluptuous Margaret Allsop's poem was in a slightly different genre to my little verse. I wondered if perhaps her grandma had given her help with it.

On top of all that, there was not a nob in sight. Not a single thing that could be misconstrued as slightly sexual. My only hope was that she thought I had a strange obsession with door-opening devices.

So, whilst everyone else set off on their dates, I sat alone in my room regretting my actions, and regretting my rotten luck. We all agreed to meet up in Cindies afterwards for the post-mortem, and to keep our mobiles on at all times for emergencies. Faye and a good friend of Jude's, Elizabeth, kindly said that they would follow me and rescue me whenever I gave them the sign (tapping the back of my head three times with my right index finger, or bursting into tears, whatever came sooner). Elizabeth was very pretty, and very small, so much so that she reminded me of my little sister's favourite doll. Elizabeth lived on the bottom floor of M-block, made a good cup of tea, had stood next to me in the Matriculation Photo and was a fully signed-up member of Team Neighbours. She was a medic, and had one of the squeakiest and poshest voices I had ever heard, sounding like the Queen after Her Majesty had inhaled a large quantity of helium. And so, with my two undercover agents well drilled, I reluctantly set off at 10.10pm along the quiet streets of Cambridge, armed with my wallet, my mobile, and

Margaret Allsop's pink form, and dressed in black trousers and a dark purple shirt, my mind running through possible scenarios, none of them good.

The Granta was surprisingly quiet. Pub regulars must have been put off by the deluge of blind-daters standing at the bar, nervously looking for a girl with a flower in her hair or a boy with a rip in his jeans. But this deluge had since subsided. Happy couples had gone off arm in arm to the night club, and those who didn't fare too well had long since gone their separate ways. I walked up to the bar and had a quick look around. Margaret Allsop's form had said that she would be wearing a long, black coat, but none were to be seen. I spotted Faye and Elizabeth sat on a table in the corner, with a couple of vodka and cokes and a packet of prawn cocktail crisps, trying to look inconspicuous. Faye gave me her usual mad-woman wave, to which I responded with a look that was supposed to say: not now, I don't know if she's here yet, and if she is I don't want her to think I've brought along two female bodyguards for protection, so stop bloody waving. I also spotted Nick MacLean sat on a table of six, with the *Friends* ingredients of three girls and three boys. He smiled and beckoned me over. I had another quick look around to make sure the black-coated, voluptuous Allsop had not swoon into the bar, and then ventured over to his table.

"How's it going? Any sign of her yet?" you could tell Nick had had a few drinks. He wasn't drunk, but his voice was a bit higher and a bit camper than usual, and his hand movements a bit looser.

"Don't think so, mate. Wouldn't be surprised if she didn't show. Please may I have a peanut?"

"Oh, are you the boy who wrote nob nineteen times in his form?" The blonde-haired girl who was sitting opposite Nick entered into the conversation.

"Yep, that's me. And it was twenty times."

"Yeah, it was probably that last one that put her off."

"Yeah, good one Nick," I took a handful of peanuts just to spite him.

"Josh, this is my blind date, Carol. Carol, this is Josh."

Again, I opted for the shaking-hands approach, partly because it always seemed more appropriate for first-time meetings, and partly because I had salty lips and a mouthful of peanuts.

"Nice to meet you, Carol. And how are you enjoying your date with young Mr MacLean?"

A Tale of Friendship, Love and Economics

"I am enjoying it a great deal. Nick is a gentleman. Or at least he is being tonight."

It was clear that Carol was older than us. She looked older and sounded older. Whenever I went to the bar to get a drink, Nick told me that she was in fact twenty-six.

"Twenty-six? Bloody hell. Nick the toy boy, eh?" I said, ensuring we were out of earshot, and having another quick look to see if my one had decided to turn up yet.

"I know" he said quietly, with a nervous giggle

"So, do you reckon you'll pull her?" I said, as I took my first sip out of an over-priced pint of Fosters.

"Don't think so. She's really nice, and everything, but she's more like an older sister, if you know what I mean?"

"I see, you're talking a bit of incest?" I knew this was the last thing Nick was talking.

"No, I don't think so. But we're having a nice evening, you know."

At least one of us was. If she wasn't going to show up I wished she would have let me know, so I could go over and join Faye and Elizabeth and relax. Instead, I had to stay on my toes, stay looking cool, on the off-chance that Margaret Allsop should walk through the wooden doors.

And then, at 10.50 pm, she did. I knew it was her straight away. She had a long black coat on like the FBI wear in American movies, and she was holding a crumpled blue form. My form. My bloody form smothered in male genitalia graffiti. She was also accompanied by a small Chinese girl and a slightly bigger Asian lad. Nick wished me good luck and went back to join his older woman. I took a deep breath, which I disguised by bringing my fist to my mouth, and wandered over.

"Erm… Hi, are you Margaret Allsop?" I had to tap her on the shoulder as she was locked in conversation with her two friends. I took out her pink form from my trouser pocket, and showed it to her like a policeman might present a search warrant. She glanced at it, glanced at me, and nodded.

"And you must be…" she took out my form again from her hand bag and straightened it out, "Josh Bailey?"

"Yep, that's me." I laughed a little, for no apparent reason at all, and then took a prolonged gulp of my pint. This was going to be awkward, I could tell. If I had been the one who had been late, I could open up with something like: "Sorry I'm late". But, seeing as she was the one who was late,

I could hardly say: "So, you're late, why?" I didn't know what else to say. The silence had lasted so long that I felt confident that saying anything at all would be better than nothing.

"I wasn't sure you were going to turn up." I said, and smiled like a guilty little child.

"Oh, and why's that?" she replied, very formally, seemingly successfully fighting off any inclination to smile back.

"Well... because of my form."

I had planned to bring this up a little later in the night, but as time was ticking on and as I didn't really have anything else to say, I thought I might as well go for it. Shit or bust, you might say.

"Yes, I did wonder about that." She replied, sounding like a teacher and still not smiling.

"Yes, it was all a bit of a joke, you see. My friends got hold of my form, and filled it in without me knowing. It's not even in my hand writing, you know?"

"Yes, I figured it must be some kind of a joke."

I got the impression that Margaret Allsop didn't like jokes, especially ones about nobs. I also got the impression that Margaret Allsop didn't like me. I mean, it was early days in our relationship, but things were not going well. As the conversation progressed she would not look me in the eye whilst I was talking, she gave short, sharp replies, she didn't start any conversations of her own, and she did not laugh, or even smile, at some of my best jokes.

From the tiny bits of information she did reluctantly divulge, I managed to find out that her Chinese friend had, in fact, been stood-up by her date, and by the resigned expression on her face, it was not the first time. The next piece of information was more of the visual kind. It seemed that Ms Allsop and her male Asian companion were quite good friends. Whilst I was trying to woo her with tales of football and economics, he would fiddle about with her hair, blow into her ear, and on occasion, slap her backside. She carried on not listening to me regardless.

She then informed me that she was not, in fact, going to Cindies tonight because she had a headache (surely it was a little early in our relationship, and the wrong setting, for that particular excuse?), so if I wanted to go, I was probably best to go now, on my own. This wasn't the most subtle way of saying piss-off that I had ever heard, and in response I tapped my head with

A Tale of Friendship, Love and Economics

my right index finger three times as a signal for the back-up troops to arrive. They arrived at speed, and a little unsteady on their feet.

"Oh, hello you two. What a surprise seeing you here! Margaret..." I had to tap her again as she was giggling away at something her male companion had said, "...Margaret, these are two of my friends, Faye and Elizabeth."

Margaret Allsop gave them a polite nod and then returned to her previous conversation. Faye rather loudly informed me that she didn't like her, and Elizabeth, in her squeaky posh voice whispered in my ear that she was a bit of a minger. I told Margaret, when I again had fought hard for her brief attention, that I was off to Cindies, and proceeded to shake her hand. By this stage, her male companion had moved behind her and was now groping her breasts with his hands. Faye's eyes nearly popped out of her head, and Elizabeth had to promptly place her hand over the Scottish one's mouth before the inevitable "Jesus Christ!" fully escaped into the bar. I just smiled, and shook her outstretched hand.

"It was nice to meet you," she said.

"You too," I replied with an equal lack of conviction.

And then I walked home arm in arm with my two friends, leaving the voluptuous (and yes, in this case "voluptuous" could quite easily have been substituted for "podgy") Margaret Allsop behind in The Granta, where she could continue to be fondled to her heart's content.

Faye and Elizabeth tried to convince me to come to Cindies, but I was no longer in the mood. I wasn't expecting romance tonight, just someone pleasant to spend a nice evening with. I did not want to talk to a voluptuous brick wall for ten minutes and then be witness to a live sex-show. No, the night had been a complete failure, and I just wanted to go to bed. And that's what I did.

In the end it turned out that none of our lot found true love that night. Caolan's married lady turned out to be an old hag, and not a very pleasant one at that. Mark said that his one was quite nice, but he didn't think she liked him very much. Oisin told us that he had a really good night and that he was definitely going to stay in contact with her, send her an email, meet up for a drink, or whatever. Alas, he never got around to it. When all the love dust had settled, one thing was clear; there was no way we were doing this next year. No way.

Chapter 33

It all started one day when I was in a bad mood. This was not the kind of bad mood that I was often subjected to; the kind where I awake in a bad mood for no apparent reason, the kind that makes me go quiet and I know that nothing can bring me out of it, only time. No, whilst this particular bad mood also had no apparent cause, I was pretty sure it could be banished with some affirmative action. And so I wrapped up warm, for it was a biting February afternoon, and took myself off into town to do some shopping.

Clothes were an obvious option, but seeing as my Mum said I had too many already, and because I always take a girl with me whenever I am contemplating a purchase (I was born with bad taste), I decided against it. CDs were the next on the obvious list, but seeing as I begrudge paying high-street prices when you can get the same CD on the internet for four quid less, and seeing as there were no big sales on to tempt me otherwise, this too was ruled out. And so, purely by chance, and with no real purpose I wandered into Woolworths. Immediately my eyes fell upon videos and Easter eggs. I didn't know what I was looking for, but I knew it was neither of these, and so I bombed quickly along through the centre of the shop, avoiding irresponsible trolley drivers and wildly swinging baskets, and headed upstairs. It was there I found the answer I was looking for, the golden shrine at the end of my quest. A board game was what I needed. Yes, a board game.

I hadn't bought or been bought a board game for years. The last one I remembered getting was Dungeons and Dragons. It looked really good on the adverts leading up to Christmas, with excited kids metamorphosing before my eyes into brave warriors armed with swords and shields, having deadly duels with each other, with their lounge transformed into a Gothic cave with green lights, smoke and scary music. However, it turned out to be a right pile of shite once I cracked it open on Christmas Day, and I was bored within five minutes. Since then, I assumed I had grown out of board games. I used to absolutely love them, especially Monopoly, where my natural flare for economics came in handy (it's all about asset values, cash flows and returns on investment, you know), and Scrabble, where my ability to make up words, lie convincingly and successfully hide the dictionary proved equally useful. But teenagers just didn't play board games. Young kids played them, and parents who had dinner parties played them, but no self-respecting teenager would ever sit down with a couple of dice and a plastic figure. Whenever my mates and I complained of boredom in the school holidays and my long-suffering mother suggested a board game, we would either grunt back our disapproval, or utter the incredibly witty reply of: "Why do you think they're called *board* games, Mum? Because they make you bored." It seemed that there was a thirty-year void from putting down your last board game as a child to picking up your next as an adult, a void filled with getting a Playstation, getting a girlfriend, going out and getting drunk, getting a more serious girlfriend, getting married and getting old.

But as I stood now on the first floor of the Cambridge branch of Woolworths, a nineteen-year-old in a bad mood, I was convinced that the only thing that would alleviate my sorrows was the purchase of a board game. But which one to choose? There were so many. There were ones from TV shows I had never even seen, ones with flashing lights and moving parts, even ones that came with a DVD. Then there were the old classics: Operation, Trivial Pursuit, Go For Broke, Monopoly, Snakes and Ladders, Ludo, Guess Who?, Scrabble, Jenga, Uno and then, right in front of my eyes, the answer to my problems, the game I had always wanted as a child but had always moved on to something else, the latest fad, whenever it was time to draw up the Christmas list. But I was not going to be denied the chance to get it now. Oh, no. I picked it off the shelf, handed over the money, and marched off back to college with a large white plastic bag in my hand and a smile on my face. I had just bought Kerplunk, and inadvertently given birth to a phenomenon.

Like all good games, the brilliance of Kerplunk is its simplicity. The plastic main frame, or "mainbody" as it came to be known, is shaped kind of like a bee hive and is full of little circular holes. Flexible plastic sticks are then placed at random in these holes so that they go right through the inside of the mainbody and pop out of a hole at the other side. They can be placed in at any angle at all, and the sticks' flexible nature even allows them to be bent slightly. The plastic mainbody, with its protruding sticks, is then placed upon a plastic base with four compartments, one for each player, for Kerplunk is a game for up to four players. Once all is secured, then comes the important part. The packet of thirty-two marbles is tipped carefully into the top of the mainbody, where they are held securely in the air by the criss-crossing mesh of plastic sticks. Then the game begins. Each player takes it in turn to remove a stick. Once he or she has touched a stick, then this is the stick they must play with. The player must carefully remove the stick from the mainbody by means of pushing or pulling until the stick is completely out, from whence it is returned neatly to the box. Any marbles that drop during the go fall into that player's compartment. Once the stick has been removed and any marbles have fallen, the player must then rotate the main body clockwise, so that marbles will now fall into the compartment of the player to his or her right. Once this process is complete, the player's go is over and he or she can count their marbles and relax for a while. Like golf, the player with the lowest score once all sticks have been removed is declared the winner.

I envisaged Kerplunk at best giving my friends and I a couple of hours of enjoyment. I certainly did not foresee that it would be the dominant feature of my second term at Cambridge. From the first game played in M14 that very afternoon with Faye McLaughlin, Mark Novak and Nick MacLean, a game which Faye won with only two marbles, and Nick lost with a disappointing eighteen, there was a feeling around the room that we had discovered something special. We played twelve more games that day. Kerplunk was a game of skill and luck, a game of tactics and chance, a game that kept you on your toes from the moment the first stick was removed right up to when the last marbles inevitably fell to the ground, it was a game that girls and boys could play together on an equal par, it was a players' sport and a spectators' sport, it could be played in your spare hour between lectures, or in a drunken state after a night out, it was a way of bonding and a socially acceptable way to release the day's pent up aggression, it was a revolution, and it came along just at the right time.

The word of Kerplunk spread from the four walls of M14, and soon competitors were coming from the far reaches of college, from E-block and Bull, K-block and Gostlin, to play the game. Every night the numbers grew. Soon we were having morning, afternoon, and evening Kerplunking sessions. We knew we had to enforce some order before they whole thing got out of hand, and so the Kerplunk Society officially came into being, along with the Kerplunk Committee, the Kerplunk World Championships, the *Kerplunk Bible*, and an official set of rules, complete with space for amendments, to iron out the numerous grey areas in the game. We noted down official Kerplunk terminology, such as: "Cross Pollination" – when you attempt to remove a stick that cuts diagonally across a sizeable grouping of marbles; "Damage Limitation" – when you know you are going to drop some marbles with your next go and it is a case of picking the stick that releases the fewest; and "Perfect Game" – the rare event when you drop not a single marble in the course of a game.

Positions on the committee were decided in a democratic fashion, but seeing as I bought the game and each match was held in my room, I declared myself President. Only the so-called "Founding Members" were permitted to stand for the more prestigious positions and, after an election as legitimate as those that occur in the Middle East, the Official Kerplunk Committee was decided. I was President, geographer Nick MacLean was Vice-President, my posh, squeaky blind-date saviour Elizabeth was Treasurer, cool dude Jude was in charge of Publicity, Scottish Faye was social secretary and Mark Novak was simply Secretary (there were no gender stereotypes in the ultra-modern world of Kerplunk). Within a few weeks, the Movie Star Look-alike was installed as Artistic Design Officer for the the *Kerplunk Bible*, a sailing medic of unconfirmed sexuality was appointed Statistics Co-ordinator and Oisin Kerrigan was Irish Ambassador. At this stage, Caolan was still maintaining that he was too cool for Kerplunk, and would not be seen dead on our gay little committee, or playing our gay little game.

Jude, being the cool guy that he was, held the position of Arts Editor for the fortnightly college magazine, *Catz Eyes*. One week he was struggling to find a serious article to write about. In previous editions he had reviewed various college societies like the Shirley Society, a very prestigious English society, and the Steers Society, the geography equivalent. But Jude was all out of societies. It was then that Elizabeth had the brain wave that Jude should write about the Kerplunk Society. Technically, we were not a proper society, we had no history to speak of, and knew nothing about the evolution of the game. Still, we had good imaginations, and a few drinks on board when Jude wrote it. Before Jude's article we knew we had something big on our hands, but it was only after its publication that we realised just how big Kerplunk was and could be. This is what he wrote:

The Kerplunk Society
President: Josh Bailey
Email: Catz_Kerplunk@hotmail.com
Motto: *"vini, vidi, kerplunki"*

Kerplunk is a game of strategy and skill that has a phenomenal worldwide following. It is a simple game for four people that is played by removing sticks from the mainbody, with the aim of having the least marbles in one's tray at the end.

It is believed that the game originated in the southern mountains of Nepal around AD 7. The original game was played with the bones and testicles of mountain goats by wandering minstrels and shepherds. The Nepalese realised that the game had a cathartic effect on the mind and even today it is often used as a relaxation technique. Indeed, Henry Winter was prompted to say that, "if the English players had been playing Kerplunk in the evenings of Euro 2000, they would have progressed much further in the tournament". Originally the game was called Kepileshvilli. However, it was changed in 1837 with the untimely death of the seventeen-times world champion and the undisputed "Greatest Player of All Time", the German Kerr Plunk. It was Herr Plunk who was the ultimate victor in the longest ever game of Kerplunk, which lasted a staggering forty-seven weeks, two days, three hours, thirteen minutes and seventeen seconds (indeed, two players had to resign due to cramp and fatigue).

The St. Catharine's College Kerplunk Society was only founded this term, but has met with overwhelming success. Meeting most nights in M14, to be a member requires a dedication and commitment that only a few can muster. St. Catharine's is the only Kerplunk Society in Cambridge, and thus, hopefully, soon the St. Catharine's team will acquire full Blue status. The society runs a league and a cuppers tournament each term, and applications to join the league for next term will be considered from now on, via the above email address.

The Society is dedicated to preserving and expanding Kerplunk's international reputation. With this in mind the founding members will embark upon a college tour, hoping to proselytise other colleges to the Kerplunk way of thinking, so that inter-collegiate leagues may soon be established. However, not satisfied with merely domestic Kerplunk, the members are planning a trip to Africa in an attempt to set up the African Academy of Kerplunk. With innovative plans like these for the future, Catz Kerplunk is looking to build upon the success of this term, and help perpetuate the international Kerplunk phenomenon.

The emails came flying in. Many wanted to know the source of Jude's extensive research, some wanted to sponsor our proposed Africa trip, and everybody wanted to join the Society. We had to restrict the first ever Kerplunk World Championships to just eighteen players, otherwise we'd have had to stay down at Easter to finish things off.

For the World Championships, it was decided that only matches consist-

A Tale of Friendship, Love and Economics

ing of four fully affiliated players would be permitted, with the winner receiving four points, second place three points, and so on down to one point for the player that lost all his marbles. These points would then be translated into a league table, which Nick MacLean drew up every week without fail and sent round on an email as an Excel file (how he could find time to do this *and* his incredibly demanding geography degree was beyond me). The person sitting at the top of the league table come the end of term would be crowned Kerplunk World Champion 2001. Each game was meticulously recorded by a Founder Member, who had to be present for the duration of the game, in the *Kerplunk Bible*. The following are extracts from that most sacred of books, chronicling the inaugural Kerplunk World Championships, taken over a five-week period of extreme, intensive Kerplunking:

World Championship Match 1

Date: 18/02/01   Time: 21:05
Weather: Very Damp   Attendance: 1

Players:	Nick	Josh	Simon	Mark
Marbles:	15	1	2	14
Points:	(1)	(4)	(3)	(2)

Comments/Quotes:
- First official Kerplunk World Championship game.
- 23 sticks removed before any marbles fall. World Record!
- "You'll never see Kerplunk like that again" – Josh Bailey.

World Championship Match 5

Date: 23/02/01   Time: 23:52
Weather: Variable/Cold   Attendance: 3

Players:	Faye	Nick	Mark	Josh
Marbles:	8	7	9	8
Points:	(2.5)	(4)	(1)	(2.5)

Comments/Quotes:
- The danger of the "Flipper Effect" first noted by Mark Novak.
- The first game of Kerplunk to start on one day and finish on the next.
- "Piss off Nick" – Faye McLaughlin.

The Cambridge Diaries

World Championship Match 6
("The Battle of the Sexes")

Date: 25/02/01   **Time:** 14:33
Weather: Windy, Overcast   **Attendance:** 2

Players:	Elizabeth	Faye	Josh	Jude
Marbles:	7	1	19	5
Points:	(1)	(4)	(3)	(2)

Girls: 8   **Boys:** 24

Comments/Quotes:
- Josh Bailey breaks Nick MacLean's record for worst ever score.
- "I hate this fucking game. I should have bought Hungry Hippos" – Josh Bailey.

Item 85: Ideas for Modifying the Original Kerplunk Game
The Committee met to suggest ideas for modifying the original Kerplunk rules, possibly for use in a cup competition:

i. The Magic Marble
A single marble (possibly pink, possibly big) is placed into the mainbody with the other thirty-two, which when felled counts as ten marbles.

ii. The Sock
The top of the mainbody is covered, possibly by means of a sock.

iii. Erotic Couples Kerplunk
Sticks must be removed by both partners (possibly naked) by means of teeth for pulling, and tongues for pushing.

iv. Food Kerplunk
Ideas for sticks: dried spaghetti
Ideas for marbles: Maltesers, frozen peas, those funny bollock-shaped potatoes we get in Hall, grapes, cherries, gooseberries, Ribenaberries.

v. Original Kerplunk
Taking the game of Kerplunk right back to its roots by using the bones and testicles of mountain goats, or an available equivalent.

It was decided unanimously that the well-established rules for the Kerplunk World Championships would remain unaltered for the duration of the 2001 tournament.

A Tale of Friendship, Love and Economics

World Championship Match 8

Date: 25/02/01
Weather: Still Windy & Overcast
Time: 15:02
Attendance: 0

Players:	Elizabeth	Josh	Nick	Oisin
Marbles:	16	8	3	5
Points:	(1)	(2)	(4)	(3)

Comments /Quotes:
- Not one marble enters Nick MacLean's compartment directly.
- Seven marbles held up by the last stick.
- "There's a funny-looking hair amongst the marbles" – Elizabeth Braithwaite
- "Oh yeah. I think it's pubic" – Nick MacLean.

World Championship Match 10

Date: 26/02/01
Weather: Dark
Time: 23:47
Attendance: 3

Players:	Mark	Francesca	Jude	Julie
Marbles:	9	12	4	7
Points:	(2)	(1)	(4)	(3)

Comments/Quotes:
- First ever use of the "Francesca Crisp Packet Manoeuvre". It is not successful.
- First World Championship match not involving President Bailey (he explains that he couldn't give six shits about the result).
- "I'm going to get a Perfect Game" – Mark "Perfect Game" Novak just before Kerplunking an embarrassing five marbles. What a tosser.

World Championship Match 14

Date: 28/02/01
Weather: Brrrrr!
Time: 00:27
Attendance: 1

Players:	Anthony	Faye	Elizabeth	Joe
Marbles:	5	20	0	7
Points:	(3)	(1)	(4)	(2)

Comments /Quotes:
- First ever Perfect Game, by Elizabeth Braithwaite.
- There are fears that one of the thirty-two sacred marbles has been lost, but thankfully it is found in Elizabeth's shoe. The Committee is confident that she wasn't trying to steal it, and the matter is not taken any further.

The Cambridge Diaries

- "Oh shit, oh shit! I'd bloody won until I fucking manoeuvred! Bollocks! Bollocks!" – Faye McLaughlin eloquently describing the art of Manoeuvring.
- "Jesus Christ, I've bloody lost again. I can't even fit my bloody marbles into my bloody container" – Faye McLaughlin, again.

World Championship Match 17

Date: 29/02/01   Time: 23:58
Weather: A bit Pearl Harbor   Attendance: 3

Players:	Faye	Mark	Simon	Dale
Marbles:	7	17	3	5
Points:	(2)	(1)	(4)	(3)

Comments/Quotes:
- Mark "Perfect Game" Novak has now gone ten consecutive games without victory. Because of this abysmal fact, Mr Novak's case is to be brought before a tribunal consisting of the other five Founder Members. The investigation continues pending further enquiry.
- "There's no point having a quote for quote's sake" – Simon Joseph.
- In other news, Dale Harrison has removed his official complaint lodged against President Josh Bailey for excessive verbal abuse (it is believed that President Bailey described Mr Harrison as a "nob" after Mr Harrison defeated him on his debut in World Championship Match 15). Present Bailey apologised publicly for his remark but chose to make no further comments.

Item 117: Action to be Taken Against Mr Mark Novak for being Rubbish at Kerplunk
Each Founding Member is to be given three votes to be distributed however he or she sees fit amongst the following options:
     i. Start Mr Novak again with a score of zero.
     ii. Ban Mr Novak from all Kerplunk matches until the end of term.
     iii. Test out "The Pineapple Theory."[1]
     iv. Kill Mr Novak by maiming.
     v. Ban Mr Novak form the next five games that he is present for.

Official Result: Kill by Maiming – 2 votes
                          Pineapple Solution – 6 votes
                          Five-Game Ban – 7 votes

Hence, as by the judgement of the Founder Members, Mr Mark Novak is officially banned for the next five games of Kerplunk which he attends. In an official statement, Mr Novak accepted the Founder Members' decision, adding "I'll try better next time".

A Tale of Friendship, Love and Economics

World Championship Match 24

Date: 02/03/01
Weather: A Wee Bit Chilly

Time: 20:28
Attendance: 6

Players:	Anthony	Jude	Josh	Mark
Marbles:	11	3	6	12
Points:	(2)	(4)	(3)	(1)

Comments/Quotes:

- The unsuccessful return of Mark Novak.
- The first time the Kerplunk mainbody has been applied with deodorant, after a Committee vote deemed unanimously that it was getting a bit smelly.
- The first ever application of "Solomon's Baby Principle". There was an element of doubt concerning the exact instance when Anthony Oldfield's go ended and Jude Richards' go began. During the changeover period, two marbles fell. After a brief meeting, present Committee members agreed a compromise whereby each player accepted one of the marbles. Mr Oldfield accepted the offer, whilst Mr Richards refused, thus revealing the guilt of the former. As a result, Mr Oldfield was ordered to take not just one, but both marbles.
- "Jude, you are an arse, and what the fuck has that got to do with Solomon and his baby?" – Anthony Oldfield.

[1] "The Pineapple Theory" refers to the ongoing debate within Kerplunking circles that if you were forced to insert a whole pineapple up your backside, which end would you insert first, the thin spiky end, or the fat flat end? Answers were spread pretty evenly across the group. I was very much in favour of flat end first, as it avoids the spikes and the worst bit is over quickly. Similar debates include, "Would you rather be invisible or have the ability to fly?", and "If you could have an extra eyeball on any part of your body where would you have it."

The Cambridge Diaries

World Championship Match 27

Date: 08/03/01
Weather: Sore Throat

Time: 23:15
Attendance: 2

Players:	Jude	Josh	Nick	Elizabeth
Marbles:	0	2	12	18
Points:	(4)	(3)	(2)	(1)

Comments/Quotes:
- Second ever Perfect Game, this time for Jude Richards
- At the end of the game, a disheartened Elizabeth Braithwaite made a direct attempt on the life of Vice-President Nick MacLean. In front of the present Committee members, she pleads not guilty, but is found guilty on the grounds that everyone in the room saw Ms Braithwaite throw twelve plastic sticks at Mr MacLean's face in what can only be described as an aggressive manner, and because she laughed as she said "Not Guilty." Ms Braithwaite accepted her three-match ban, and Mr MacLean was advised, on medical grounds, to sit out the rest of the night's Kerplunking.
- "It's a sad day for Kerplunk" – Josh Bailey.

Item 223: Proposed Change of Venue
Having apparently had a "bloody awful day", President Bailey announced to The Committee that it might be about time we moved Kerplunk to somewhere other than his room. The Committee has come up with the following possible locations:

  i. A Punt
  ii. The Top of St. John's Chapel
  ii. Wembley Stadium
  iv. Shakespeare's Globe
  v. Millennium Dome

By the end of the meeting, and after a cup of tea and two biscuits, President Bailey announced to the Committee that there was no immediate need to find another venue, it was just something to think about for the future.

A Tale of Friendship, Love and Economics

World Championship Match 31

Date: 18/03/01 **Time:** 00:05
Weather: Moony **Attendance:** 2.5

Players:	Nick	Faye	Josh	Jude
Marbles:	10	14	1	7
Points:	(2)	(4)	(4)	(3)

Comments/Quotes:
- Jude Richards faces a possible ban for saying what is widely regarded as the "worst of all swear words" (otherwise known as the "c" word) fourteen times during the game, especially when ladies were present.
- Oisin Kerrigan provides refreshments midway through the game, and when asked who he thinks will win this particular match announces that he is not a betting man.
- The general feeling around the room is that the smell emanating from the mainbody of Kerplunk is becoming unbearable. Deodorant no longer seems to be enough. Fabreeze may have to come into play. On top of this, another suspicious-looking hair is found nestling amongst the marbles.
- "A week is a long time in Kerplunk" – Nick MacLean.

In the end, I happened to win the Kerplunk World Championships, and hence be bestowed with the prestigious title of Kerplunk World Champion 2001, but this did not really matter. Kerplunk was about so much more than winning and losing. It was about bonding and friendship. It was about bringing people of different backgrounds and friendship groups together, building bridges with flexible plastic sticks and thirty-two marbles, and uniting all in the good name of Kerplunk. It built upon and furthered the work that Team Neighbours had done and was continuing to do every weekday at 5.35 pm. People felt more comfortable discussing their problems over a good old game of Kerplunk, and no problem was too big that a perfect game couldn't solve. Also, every time I boasted about being World Champion, and the Greatest Player of the Modern Era, I was reminded that I only finished top of the league because of the fundamentally flawed nature of the Kerplunk Scoring System. I had played far more games than anybody else, and thus I was guaranteed at least a point every time I crouched down to play the great game. I failed to see the relevance of my fellow players' points. Anyway, like I said, Kerplunk was about more than winning and losing, although I was more than happy to win.

Chapter 34

By the end of that second term, almost half of the year of St. Catharine's College, Cambridge had played Kerplunk at one time or another, either at a professional or an amateur level, in the birthplace of the game, M14. Also, by the end of term, I had fallen out beyond repair with one of my closest friends, Mary Jane, and the two events were not entirely unconnected.

I hadn't seen Mary Jane much of late, although it was only when people asked me how she was that I really noticed. She had been busy with Gavin, and I had been busy Kerplunking. Mary Jane tried the game once, but couldn't see what all the fuss was about. Faye told me that my strawberry blonde neighbour had recently split up with Gavin, but she had split up with Gavin about twenty times in the past two terms, so I had no reason to suppose that this one would be any less temporary. Basically, I didn't really see that there was a major problem brewing. So what? Mary Jane and I were seeing each other a little less than we used to. It wasn't as if we were going out, or anything.

It was then that I got the letter. I had just come back from a riveting lecture on the decline of the British manufacturing industry, and was about to have a little lie down on my bed before I went off to the library for another fun-packed afternoon when I saw it pinned to my door in a sealed white enveloped. Closer inspection revealed the word "Josh" on the front, and "Read on your own – important" on the back. I loved getting letters. Whenever they flew through the letterbox at home, or lay patiently waiting in my pigeon hole at uni, I used to cross my fingers hoping that there would be something interesting inside, maybe a large cheque or a love-letter from a beautiful woman, even though they clearly had the address and logo of the mobile phone billing company marked on the back. But I think anyone would have gotten excited about this letter. Who was it from? What could it be about? Why did I have to read it in private? I took the letter inside, made sure no-one was hiding under the bed or in the cupboard, and sat myself down in the comfiest chair in the room. I was no good at recognising hand writing, so I opened it completely clueless. This is what it said:

A Short Story

Once upon a time, in a town called Preston, there lived a guy called Jez. After

A Tale of Friendship, Love and Economics

much hard work, combined with a high IQ, Jez gained a place to study Economics at Cambridge.

In late September 2000, Jez arrived at Cambridge, whereupon he instantly made two very good friends – Scottish Frances and Martha. Martha was going through an emotional time that term and turned to Jez a lot for support – crying in front of him numerous times. Although she thought she might be taking advantage of his kindness somewhat, she thanked her lucky stars every day to have found such a good friend, so trustworthy and dependable, so quickly. A friend who she could rely on, have fun with, and all the things good friends do. As the term drew to a close, Frances, Martha and Jez sat in his room waiting for his parents to pick him up, and one thing in the future seemed certain: nothing could come between the close bond between them.

And indeed, during the Christmas holidays, Martha and Jez texted and phoned and emailed each other and kept in touch. Jez even called Martha at 3 am on New Year's Day because he had fallen out with his friends at home. Not that Martha minded, because friends are there for each other – aren't they?

However, a funny thing happened second term, Jez changed. He stopped knocking on Martha's door to see how she was. In fact, he stopped taking any notice of her altogether. It seemed that Jez had found new friends and the old ones didn't matter any more – even though he had referred to her as a "best friend".

Martha felt them growing apart, and tried on several occasions to sort things out. Jez would only reply that he didn't know what she was talking about, that the only reason he didn't knock any more was because every time he did, she was either working or with her boyfriend, Garth. Which Martha knew was complete bollocks because:

a). She didn't work that hard.
b). Garth only ever came over late in the evenings because he was either working or out with his friends.
c). Martha saw Frances all this time without work or Garth getting in the way.

Now things are unbearable. Martha feels invisible around him. In fact, it is safe to say that in the last few weeks Jez hasn't come round once for a cup of tea, just her and him, nor shows any signs of doing so, although it used to be a regular occurrence. Even when Jez knew that Martha had split up with her six-month boyfriend, Garth, whom she was in love with, Jez never asked her how she was doing, although everyone knows that the one thing you need after a relationship break-up is your friends.

Martha feels lonely and neglected by the one person in college she was sure she could trust, dropped like a hot potato for newer, cooler, better friends. Perhaps Josh, sorry I mean Jez, was not in fact the lovely, kind, thoughtful, selfless person he seemed in the first place, and was in fact a self-centred bastard. Perhaps he has just changed. But whatever it is, Martha really wishes that things could go back to the way they were, partly because they will be living together next year, but above all, because she misses him. Lots

Bloody hell, I thought. I guessed there was some kind of hidden message buried somewhere deep inside Martha's – sorry I mean Mary Jane's – fanciful tale. To be honest, after the initial shock had subsided, I was still a little surprised, and more than a little bit hurt. Needless to say, I had never received a letter quite like that before. I didn't know what to do. I didn't know whether I should call round for her now, give her a huge hug and a kiss, and tell her I was sorry for everything, or call for the men in white coats.

But the thing was, I wasn't actually sorry for everything. I mean, of course I was sorry that she was upset, but I was not sorry for how I had acted this term. I didn't think I had done anything wrong. I had done my best to mix Mary Jane in with my new friends, and I thought it was working fine. She came round to watch *Neighbours* with us all, and seemed happy enough to substitute Kerplunk for Gavin, and after all Faye was one of my so-called old friends, and I still saw her as much as ever. Moreover, I took the fact that she hadn't been coming around to my room night after night to cry as a good thing, as a sign that maybe things were getting better for her.

But then again, maybe she was right. Maybe I was using the time she spent with Gavin as an excuse to justify seeing her less. Maybe I didn't like how intense our relationship was, how we would talk about emotions and feelings all the time. Maybe I didn't always want to tell her what was on my mind. Maybe she was getting too close. Maybe I didn't like how she would make me face up to the fact I went quiet sometimes, telling me I had a problem that needed sorting out. Maybe I did prefer spending time with my so-called new, cooler friends, talking about shit, keeping the other things hidden safely inside, just having a good time. Maybe I liked the way that theirs was a friendship requiring not a word of analysis or effort of maintenance, a friendship that would have caused embarrassment if we were asked to define it because no words were needed and none were appropriate, we were just friends, simple as that. Maybe I had finally decided that she was using me, coming round to see me only in the bad times, and getting on with her life when all was rosy. Maybe I thought it was time I had a life that she didn't dominate. Maybe I didn't think she had all the problems she claimed she had. Maybe I was sick of her attention-seeking behaviour when there were lots of people with far worse problems. Maybe I was in love with her, like everybody seemed to think I was, and not seeing her at all was far easier than trying to be friends with her. Maybe, maybe, maybe. I just didn't know. All I knew was that at the moment, when I thought long and hard about it, and as ridiculous as it sounded, I preferred my life the way it was now, without my best friend in it.

And that was that. The seemingly unbreakable had fallen apart. I didn't reply to Mary Jane's letter. I didn't know myself why we had drifted apart, so I figured it was pointless trying to explain things to her. She got back together with Gavin, and I carried on with my life. We would say hello to each other when our paths crossed in the kitchen or the queue for the shower, but there were to be no more cups of tea and no more tears. For whatever reason, our relationship was dying a long time ago, and Mary Jane's letter just put it out of its misery. Above all, I think the whole thing was hardest for Faye. She was like the child caught up in a messy divorce, having to divide her time between the both of us, always watching what she said. I regretted how things had turned out, and regretted not having seen this coming, but I knew that they were for the best. After the intense relationship Mary Jane and I had had, it was always going to be all or nothing, and the latter just seemed the more favourable option at that time. One thing I did regret, however, was signing up to live in a flat with her next year.

Chapter 35

Often, the careers of the world's great politicians have the humblest of beginnings, and the same could be said for the career of young Caolan O'Donnell. Whilst the rest of us had been wasting our time playing with marbles and plastic sticks, or writing short stories about our neighbours, the Irish boy-band wannabe had been meticulously plotting his rise to the top.

Not only is JCR the acronym for the undergraduate's common room, it is also the name of the elected undergraduate committee, a group voted in every year. The JCR Committee, following a similar power structure to the obviously superior Kerplunk Committee, consists of a President and a Vice-President, and then a host of more specific positions including Food and Beverages Representative, Treasurer, Welfare Officers, Entertainments Representatives, Green Officer, Communications Officer and so on. There were not a great deal of benefits for those elected onto the JCR Committee, with "it looks good on your CV", and "you get a free meal and free wine once a year in a nice restaurant" probably being the two biggest attractions, along with the honour of representing the needs of your college, of course. The President and, more controversially, the Vice-President, were also elevated into the Scholar's Ballet which guaranteed them a better room in college in their third year. As well as fulfilling the duties attached to their specific role, which like Cambridge degrees varied immensely in terms of work load, with Food and Beverages Rep and Communications Officer being the Geography and Land Economy of the Committee, each Committee member also had to attend a general meeting every fortnight.

Each Cambridge College had its own JCR Committee, and the Presidents of each would meet on a fairly regular basis. Some colleges were well into student politics, and hence the JCR Committee was an important vehicle for expressing the views and opinions of the college members. King's College JCR Committee, for example, would always be protesting about something or other, usually more rights for lesbians and more rights for Communists. The JCR of our lovely St. Catharine's college, on the other hand, tended to be more apathetic. We rarely registered our votes on whether Cambridge as an institution was pro-abortion or pro-US military action in the Middle East, and our President rarely attended all those general meetings. The student body of St. Catharine's were easily satisfied so long as they got at least three college Bops a term, and as long as college food didn't kill them. Indeed, even failure with respect to the latter issue would be forgivable as long as the Bop count was high enough.

Now, running for a position on the JCR Committee was not as simple as just putting your name down on a piece of paper. Oh, no. First you had to find two upstanding, well-respected members of college who were happy enough, or drunk enough, to propose and second your nomination for whatever position you were going for. Once you were officially signed up, you then had to give a speech at Hustings and answer questions from the floor. Hustings was held in the college bar and was always a popular night, both for those people interested in democracy, freedom of speech and the structure of the collegiate political system, and also those wanting the hurl abuse at the nervous candidates, and try to make them cry. Presidential Hustings had taken place late into last term, and had resulted in the election of a skinny lad, who once took a rather harsh three-finger fine at a football dinner for looking like he was HIV positive, to the position of JCR President. Now, midway through the second term, with a new President at the helm, it was time to oust the old committee and bring in some fresh blood.

Caolan O'Donnell wasn't interested in improving communication within college, or protecting the environment, he didn't want to be a mere understudy to the President, or sit and listen to people's problems (I could not imagine a less-suited human being for that particular role), he wanted the so-called glamour position; Caolan wanted to be First Year Rep.

First Year Rep was always the most hotly contested position at the non-Presidential Hustings, and always the event that brought the night to a close. There was often only one candidate standing for positions like Green Officer, and the crowd soon lost interest. But for First Year Rep there was always a good number standing and, more importantly, they were always the so-called Big Names of the year. There were two First Year Reps elected each year, one boy and one girl. They were the ones who wrote to the new Freshers over the summer, and their first point of contact if they needed anything. To be a good First Year Rep you needed to be lively, bubbly and friendly. You had to know everyone and get on with everyone. You had to meet and greet the cohort of new first years and look after them in Freshers' Week, organising countless activities to keep them entertained, making sure everyone was having fun and getting involved, especially the quieter ones. You had to be out and about every day and night of that hectic week, often with a drink in your hand and more than a few in your stomach. It was certainly not a job for the shy, reserved type.

Caolan was certainly suited to the job. He knew almost everyone in our year, was always going out, and was generally liked by most people. Although he often got more than a bit abusive to his friends when he was drunk, he could put on a good act in front of everyone else. He couldn't dance but he tried, he couldn't sing but he tried, and he was great at meeting people for the first time. Caolan could chat away to anyone about anything, and would always try to bring everyone in the group into the conversation. No, he was certainly the man for the job.

The problem was, so too was his rival. Caolan signed up the day the sheet was pinned up outside the pigeon holes, and within hours his traditional Irish name had been joined by a Mr Jake Vincenzi. Everyone knew Caolan, and everyone knew Jake. Or at least everyone had heard Jake. You see, Jake Vincenzi was probably the loudest person on the planet. His laugh would have to be heard to be believed, and if you were stood within a fifty-mile radius of Cambridge, you would have heard it. If you imagine the biggest grizzly bear you have ever seen finding a joke really really funny, and then turn up the volume a couple of notches, then you are close to how Jake laughed at anything. And it wasn't just his laugh that was loud. You could hear Jake coming a mile away whether he was chatting, singing, whistling, or just walking along thinking. Even his whisper required earplugs, resulting in a movement to ban him from every library in Cambridge, which unfortunately failed. Buildings shuddered and children ran for cover when Jake Vincenzi was around. But he was a nice guy. He too would talk to anyone and everyone, and was always there in the thick of things on a night out, tending to stay on his feet longer than the Irishman.

The main difference between them was that Jake Vincenzi was a little too much in your face, a little overbearing, tending to dominate every conversation, often taking over four at once with one comment. Caolan knew his limits, he knew when to take a step back, when to be quiet, and, of course, he had a bit of the old Irish charm. Personally, I couldn't see it, but the girls seemed to think he was lovely, with his funny name, quiffed hair and well-cared-for sideburns.

Caolan was never one to ask favours, but in the days following his signing up he dropped enough hints for us to know he wanted a bit of help with his campaign.

"Aye, it's going to be a well lot of work, this campaign you know?" he would say and then take a sip of his pint.

"Really?" I would reply, not taking the bait.

"Aye, there's a lot to do. More than you think."

"Really?"

"Aye, there is."

Then silence.

"Look, Caolan, do you want a bit of help with things?"

"Nah, I'll be fine... but if you insist I suppose you could..."

And so Caolan hired Oisin, Mark, Joe, Nick and myself to help him beat the human fog horn.

If Caolan was going to do something, he would always do it properly. Underneath his apparent carefree attitude lay a dedicated, motivated, ruthlessly driven individual. This was a quality that not many people gave him credit for, for he kept it well hidden, presumably due to a fear of failure having been seen trying so hard, and it was a quality that I had witnessed in very few people. There were some things that Caolan was just not bothered about, like whether he won at sport or whether he got the top mark in a test, but when it came to something that he really wanted, he would work hard to make sure he got it. And from the outset, it was very clear that Caolan O'Donnell wanted to be First Year Rep, although he would never admit it to any of us ("Aye, I suppose it would be grand if I got it, but there are more important things").

Caolan's Nanny had been the female half of our set of First Year Reps, and so the Irish one went to her for some advice and, in a shrewd political manoeuvre, got her to propose him for the position.

Caolan didn't plan to make his campaign a lavish one, explaining, and already sounding like a boring old politician, that it was best if people just heard what he had to say at Hustings and then made their own minds up from that. Then, Jake struck. One evening college was a Jake free zone (apart from the sound of his voice, which seemed to echo 24-7), and then the next morning the St. Catharine's students and Fellows awoke to the sight of Jake Vincenzi's face staring back at them from every wall and every door in college. He was in the library, the Plodge, even smiling at you from above the urinals whist you relieved yourself. And even the posters were loud. They contained the simple tag-lines: Vote Jake, or Vote Vincenzi in bold type, and a large head-shot of the Irishman's rival sporting the cheesiest of grins with his arm around some other notable names in college. Caolan tried to play it down, but you could tell he was not happy. It was time to strike back. After a discussion over a cup of tea, Team O'Donnell launched its own batch of posters, nothing fancy, nothing too obtrusive, just a friendly, smiling Irishman dotted in various places around college. Then Caolan went for a bold move. The boy-band look-alike's room faced onto Main Court and was situated quite high up on the third-floor of a block called Gostlin. His window, if you knew which one it was, could thus be seen by all who walked across Main Court heading towards the bar or the library.

It was the kind of advertising space that money couldn't buy. With the permission of his friendly Jewish neighbour, who was to be Nick and Joe's future flatmate, the Irishman plastered the phrase: "Vote Caolan" across both windows in bold, brightly coloured green and red lettering for all to see. To be fair it only stayed up a couple of hours before the Porters, ever neutral and ever protecting the image of the college, told him to take it down, but its effect was far more permanent.

In the days leading up to the election, Team O'Donnell remained strong and united. We sat together at meal times, and fired dirty looks towards Vincenzi and his cronies, even going so far as subtly booing them as they walked past putting their empty trays away. Caolan, fast becoming the experienced politician, always kept up a friendly front when in the presence of his rival, and always told us off for being so childish, sounding just like a parent disciplining his child for doing something he wished he was in a position to do himself. We were loving it all, especially Joe and Nick. Although the two geographers were normally quite reserved (apart from their infamous run-in with the police and the traffic cones) and would never openly say that they disliked anyone, they had absolutely no qualms about admitting they hated Jake Vincenzi.

"He's just so bloody loud," Joe would say, screwing up his face at the mere thought of the man. Then, one night, without the consent or even the knowledge of Caolan and the other Team O'Donnell members, Joe and Nick went all around college, under the cover of darkness, and ripped down or graffitied many of the Loud One's posters. By the morning, Jake Vincenzi's cheesy grin was now complemented by a penis protruding from his forehead. Caolan, quite rightly, denied all knowledge, and was a bit pissed off when he found out who'd done it. However, even he couldn't hide the smile on his face when his eyes fell upon the poster pinned outside the library displaying a grinning Jake Vincenzi and the tag-line: "Vote Vincenzi, he's the biggest tit on the planet".

On the day of Hustings, Team O'Donnell put together the final pieces of our preparation. Lectures were binned in favour of a trip to the joke shop to snap up a powerful hooter and a load of those annoying whistle things you get at kiddies' parties (the ones that you blow into and the paper end uncoils). I put myself in charge of the hooter, and distributed one of the little whistle things to Oisin and Joe. I had to confiscate Nick MacLean's as he kept licking the end and blowing it in my ear all the way home,

A Tale of Friendship, Love and Economics

explaining that he was only giving me a "wet willy". Despite a torrent of abuse, traitor Novak did not come to the joke shop, again managing to maintain his 100 per cent record attendance at lectures. Only when he gave us the lecture hand-outs that he had kindly picked up for us did I issue him with his whistle.

Hustings were due to start at 7.30 pm, so Team O'Donnell rocked into the bar just after seven and secured ourselves a seat near the front, a few pints, and a few packets of peanuts. Caolan claimed he wasn't nervous at all, but he was talking really fast, drinking even faster, and twiddling about with his hair more than normal.

At about 7.33 pm, the pool table was moved out of the way to create more floor space for the speakers, and the JCR President, who was looking particularly frail tonight, got proceedings underway. He explained that each speaker would be given about two minutes to state their case, and then the candidates for each position would convene together to face questions and answers from the audience gathered in the bar. He asked people not to shout out too much during the speeches, and to try and keep the questions serious. He knew he was wasting his breath, but I suppose he had to say it anyway.

There were other notables striving for a prestigious position on the JCR Committee. First up was a lad running for Green Officer. He was the only other male first year geographer apart from Joe and Nick, and they informed the table that he was a bit strange but we had to support him because of subject loyalty. He was uncontested for the position, and as he spoke passionately about his Five-Month Plan to introduce a red bin for recycling old clothes and the promising enquiries he'd already made about fitting energy-saving light bulbs around college, the audience chatted amongst themselves. There were no questions for him to answer, and he walked back to his seat with a mere smattering of applause. Whenever a position was uncontested, the only way the sole candidate could fail to get onto the JCR Committee was if more people voted for RON (standing for Re-Open Nominations) than for him. This was the ultimate vote of no confidence and, whilst there were always a few RONs flying around from the disgruntled members of college, very rarely would Mr RON have enough support to be elected.

The next position was also uncontested. It was for JCR Treasurer, and who should be running but my good friend the Stalking, Philosophising

Preaching Prophet from Bradford. I was tempted to get the hooter out, but feared I might be prematurely evicted. He opened up his speech with one of the worst jokes I have ever heard, something about Asians fiddling the books, and once again, to my absolute disgust, it got a good laugh. I looked around our table for someone to give a knowing look to, but unfortunately no-one else hated him. I was now convinced that his sole purpose on this earth was to torment me. As our resident Prophet prattled on about investments and the absolute importance of transparency, I transported myself off to a dream land where good old RON ran a sterling campaign for Treasurer, won a landslide victory, and permanently wiped the smug grin off his face.

Another member of The Group from first term was running for Entertainments Officer. She was the small witty one, who I thought was a bit weird, but since I had left The Group, I had decided that she wasn't so bad after all. Her partner in crime was her absolute double, only a bit taller, a bit weirder, and a lot louder. She was the Loud One who was always shouting and moving around during *Neighbours* and the general feeling was that she didn't approach the Kerplunk World Championships with the respect they clearly deserved. Nevertheless, this combination of Ents Officers was far more preferable to the alternative; a duo out of the Vincenzi camp, who were cooler than cool, and also pictured on posters displaying perfect teeth and perfect smiles, with their arms flung around characters such as Vincenzi. In order to counter their opponents superior popularity, the small weird duo had launched a campaign focusing solely on their lack of popularity and their weirdness. They had posters with them grinning and their arms flung around cones and bushes. They explained on their posters that: "We are not cool, or popular, and we don't really have that many good ideas, but if you want to vote for us, then you can do". It captured the imagination of the college and made the other two look a bit stupid, and in the speeches, it was the small weird duo who got the laughs and even seemed to have the better ideas.

The Movie Star Look-alike was running for Welfare Officer along with fellow Group member, The Girl Whose Room We Used To Hang Out In Who Didn't Really Like Me. Call me sceptical, but I didn't think they were as interested in caring for the welfare of other college members as they were about the free piss-up that came with the package if they were elected. Moreover, they only wanted to do the job if they could run as a pair.

A Tale of Friendship, Love and Economics

Unfortunately, unlike for the position of Ents Reps, the College Constitution did not allow such pairings in the Welfare Officer category, and thus the Movie Star Look-alike, drawn to speak first, recited the words that the two of them had worked long and hard on, leaving her would-be partner, quite literally, speechless.

With all the other positions accounted for, attention turned towards the night's Main Event; the battle for First Year Rep. Now, as well as the much-hyped Vincenzi – Donnell encounter, the night also played host to the contest for female First Year Rep, and in the running for this position was a girl named Emma.

Emma was a bubbly blonde-haired girl who bore a tiny resemblance to Buffy the Vampire Slayer, and who was always completely wasted after two drinks. She came from Southport in Lancashire, and had even once been for a night out in Preston, but these big plus points were massively offset by the unfortunate and unforgivable fact that she spoke as posh as any Londoner. Another point of interest as far as our story goes was that Emma was the sole and long-standing object of desire of our very own footballing geographer, and serial moaner, Joe Porter. Right from Freshers' Week Joe had liked Emma and had successfully managed to pull her one drunken, sweaty night in Life, and walk back with her to college afterwards. In the inevitable grilling that followed the next day, Joe, when asked how far things went, uttered the phrase: "Yeah, I spent the night with her", and then winked. In later days it transpired that Mr Porter had indeed spent the night with the lovely Emma, but not in the way he might have hoped or implied. Joe had drunkenly fallen asleep in her chair whilst she slept soundly, and alone, in her bed. He, quite rightly, took a few fines at subsequent football dinners for this little piece of attempted deception. Anyway, the bottom line was Joe still liked Emma, and would do for quite sometime until events would take an unexpected turn, but unfortunately she didn't see him the same way. Perhaps he should have written her a poem.

Emma's opponent was, in fact, one of her closest friends, a brown-haired girl who divided her time between going out, studying law and getting up early to row. The girl in question was also best friends with Vincenzi, and thus, whilst she was nice enough, she was our sworn enemy on that night and, using the same logic, Emma was adopted as one of us. Of course, the ever neutral Caolan would not be drawn into saying who he would prefer to have as his female counterpart, but it was obvious it was Emma.

The boys went first, and having stupidly picked heads, the Irishman was put into bat. He rose up from our table to an expectant round of applause and several pats on the back, and as he shuffled past the many chairs that lay in his path he turned to me, his faithful companion, and said: "Bailey, if you blow that bloody hooter before I've finished, you're dead." I put his rather harsh comments down to nerves, smiled back and wished him good luck.

He didn't look at all comfortable stood up facing his audience. This wasn't the same man who repeatedly fell over with a smile on his face on the very spot he now stood every time a Bop was on. He had nothing to lean on, and started swinging his arms around nervously. I thought he was going to choke, and so I crossed my fingers and turned away. Then, finally, he spoke. He read his meticulously prepared speech from shaking hands with a slightly quivering Irish accent. He was not a natural, but he was good. He spoke clearly and looked into the eyes of those listening. He forced himself through the jokes we'd convinced him to keep in, and got a reasonable response back from the crowd. He wouldn't make a good comedian, but he would make a good First Year Rep. His apparent nervousness made him come across more genuine, more trustworthy. He said all the right things, but then everyone always said the right things in these speeches. He talked about how he loved to meet people, how he was going to make sure that every Fresher had as good a time as possible, and that he was not afraid to leave the outgoing ones to their own devices whilst he focused his attention on the shy, quiet ones. The older members in the bar had heard the same speeches every year and shook their heads and mumbled cynically, but Caolan had a humble nature that made you believe him. He ended with a bad joke, one of Nick MacLean's, that went down well and, as soon as I was sure he was finished, I unleashed the hooter that had been by my side for the last five minutes, ready and waiting like a cowboy's cocked pistol. The rest of them were more than a little reluctant to blow into their party blowers, but that didn't matter as the sound of the hooter pretty much blocked all other noise out, and caused a girl on the next table to spill her vodka and orange all down her white top. I threw in a few wolf whistles for good measure, and the rest of the bar thankfully joined in the applause. The Irishman returned to his table with a rouge tint to his face, wearing a nervous smile, and asking over and over again: "Do you think it went alright, do you think it went alright?" The boy done good.

A Tale of Friendship, Love and Economics

Next up was Vincenzi. He was clearly a man who had spoken in public before (but I suppose with *that* voice, every conversation he had ended up being in public). He strode up to his position purposefully, and marched up and down the bar, keeping the audience wondering when he was going to speak. Then, just as I sensed he was about to begin I "accidentally" fired off one last hoot of the hooter. Caolan gave me a dirty look and a dead leg, and I smiled apologetically at Jake Vincenzi. It was a dirty trick, and very uncharacteristic of me, but after all politics is a dirty game. Anyway, Mr Vincenzi wasn't going to let a little hooter stop him. He began: "Well, thank you for that. Ladies and Gentlemen, boys and girls. for those of you who don't know me, I'm Jake. Jake Vincenzi."

The JCR President looked over to see if Mr Vincenzi was miked up, or something. He was loud; too loud for an unassisted human. He sounded like a narrator of a Shakespearean play or a ring announcer at the boxing. Everything was loud and everything was exaggerated. With his hands making passionate, forceful movements, he yelled about how he was going to meet and greet all the Freshers, he screamed about how important it was to include absolutely everyone, and it felt like Concorde had flown into the bar as he explained some of the events he had in mind for Freshers' Week. He was certainly a good speaker, and his jokes were better than Caolan's, but he was too in your face. Caolan looked worried, whispering, "He's good, Josh, isn't he? He's good", and then quickly sipping his vodka and (diet) coke, but I knew the Irishman had it won. However, Vincenzi had one last surprise for us. Out of nowhere – well literally out of his pocket – Jake Vincenzi produced an orange. He held it out in front of him in his right hand for all to see. In the next few minutes the Loud One proceeded to explain to a captivated but bemused audience how this orange represented his group of Freshers. I tried to follow, but I lost it once he started beginning to peel of the layers and throw them at people. His punch-line, much to the surprise of those watching, was to eat the remaining orange whole, somehow linking this act into what he would bring to the role of First Year Rep. I think most of the applause that followed were for the fact that his gob was temporarily plugged. We clapped along sportingly, and I threw a knowing look in the direction of Nick and Joe. They smiled back. Vincenzi had just dug himself a citrus grave.

The two girls followed the boys, with Emma's rival being drawn first. She too looked nervous, but spoke well. She had all the right lines, and a nice smile, and her performance was received well by those still able to hear after the human megaphone had finished. Our table applauded graciously and threw a round of smiles of support in Emma's direction as she prepared to step up.

Emma too was very nervous. It was always trickiest going second or third for one of these positions for you inevitably ended up repeating most of what your predecessor had said, thus boring an already bored audience, and making you look like a little copy-cat. But once Emma had run through the standard points, she unleashed a refreshing bit of originality. She summed up what she would bring to the role of First Year Rep not with an orange, but with a poem; a poem written in the style of the annoying song that was big at the time, *Mambo No.5*. It was an inspired choice for such a cheese-loving college, and her words and the actions that went with them – oh yes, there were actions too – were as corny and as cheesy as could be. It was wonderful and woeful at the same time. A little bit of this, a little bit of that. It made the audience cringe in pain, but also want to vote for her. It was either a brilliant piece of tactical warfare or a fantastic bit of luck, but whatever it was, it certainly worked. As Emma's *Mambo No.5* remix drew to a close, the bar erupted. They had to endure no more, the pain was over, and looking back over the last couple of minutes through rose-tinted glasses, they were very appreciative of the young girl's efforts. They simultaneously breathed sighs of relief and clapped and whistled loudly. Emma smiled her pretty smile, and Nick nudged poor Joe in the ribs.

With the speeches wrapped up, all four candidates then returned to the floor to face a grilling from the audience. Most questions and answers were pretty standard and often repeated what had been covered during their speeches. The only question of interest was the one that came up every year: "Who would you prefer to be your fellow First Year Rep?" And was met with the same answer that was given every year of: "I would be equally happy whoever was elected", and a subsequent groan from the audience. Candidates also refused to be drawn upon commenting on their rival's flaws, prompting yet another cynical boo from the floor. All in all, in that question and answer session Jake Vincenzi continued to talk a bit too much, and young Caolan O'Donnell did himself no harm at all.

We stayed in the bar for another drink, Caolan graciously accepting the good wishes of a few who came over to see him and shaking the hand of Jake Vincenzi, and then we all went to bed, for unlike most in the political jungle, we had a nine o'clock lecture on statistical hypothesis testing to get up for.

Voting took place at breakfast, lunch and dinner on the following day. The procedure involved you picking up a ballot paper in Hall, being issued with a pen, and having your name ticked off the register by a JCR Committee official once you had posted the slip of paper into the makeshift wooden box. The voting system was one I had never come across before. It certainly was not the good old "first past the post system" that was traditionally employed in elections. Instead of just voting for the person you wanted to win and leaving it at that, you had to rank the candidates, including the ever-present RON, in order by means of a number, with a mark of 1 for your favourite, 2 for your second choice, and so on. In the first round of counting, the candidate with the least number of 1s was then knocked out, and all his 2s then added on to the other candidate's totals, and then the person with the lowest amount of 1s and 2s was knocked out of the second round and thus his 3s were then brought into play, and so on. This bizarre system opened the opportunity for some tactical voting, because whilst you might have thought that a candidate was indeed the second best for the job, if he was a close rival of your preferred candidate, then it was best to put a 4 by his name, or even no number at all, instead of the 2 that he probably deserved. All this was very complicated and a bit too much for many of the Cambridge intellectuals, many of who just put a tick and left it at that.

I registered my 1 vote for Caolan and, much as I would have done most things I could to ensure my Irish friend won, I did give Vincenzi the 2 nod ahead of Mr RON. I also opted for Emma as Caolan's female equivalent, the Movie Star Look-alike and her friend who didn't like me for Welfare Reps, the small weird duo for Ents Officers, and Mr RON for Treasurer. I quickly whizzed down the rest of the list, placing numbers here, there and everywhere.

The rest of the day was spent working, Kerplunking, and having cups of tea. Then, at 9.30 pm, the news came through. Team O'Donnell was gathered in M14 when Caolan received the phone call, with Faye having just Kerplunked eight marbles and Mark Novak busily perusing an economics textbook with a worrying grin across his face. Caolan smiled almost shyly as he returned his mobile to his pocket. He had won a landslide victory, getting over twice as many votes as Jake Vincenzi. Jake graciously phoned to congratulate the new Irish First Year Rep, and we had to restrain Joe and Nick from shouting anything out whilst he took the call. You could tell Caolan was delighted, although he tried his best to hide it, and genuinely surprised, although most in the room took it as false modesty. He phoned his Mum to tell her the good news, and we abandoned Kerplunk in favour of the bar.

Most of the other results had gone as expected. RON failed to prevail in any of the categories, thus meaning the Stalking, Philosophising Preaching Prophet from Bradford was indeed now a man with too much influence over college finances. The Movie Star Look-alike got the nod as Welfare Rep, but her mate didn't, meaning the problems of the students of St. Catharine's college would soon be in the safe hands of a girl who didn't really want the job, and a very strange guy whose advertising campaign had revolved around penguins and turtles. Happily, the small, weird duo successfully defied the popular vote and were elected as Ents Officers, and Emma was voted in as Caolan's better half. All in all it was a great night for us, and not the best of nights for Vincenzi's crew.

Team O'Donnell had been a success, and I had really enjoyed all the campaigning, and not just because it was a welcome change from the toils of an economics degree and a faltering football career. I even felt quite proud of Caolan, although I would never be stupid enough to admit it. No, I had had a good time, and our single, all too brief taste of election fever was never going to be enough. We would be back, bigger and better than before.

Chapter 36

I was happy being single. Cassandra and her overgrown baby of a boyfriend were old news, and any regret had long since been replaced by relief over how well things had actually worked out. I looked at Mary Jane and Gavin and all their troubles, and compared that to my happy-go-lucky, free-as-a-bird, crazy Kerplunking, football playing, looking-at-anything-in-a-skirt lifestyle, and I knew which one I preferred. But then something changed. I don't know whether it was because Caolan had his lady friend, or because of all the trouble with Mary Jane, or just the old cycle coming around again,

A Tale of Friendship, Love and Economics

but as the term was reaching its midway stage my internal Powers That Be suddenly decided it was about time I fancied someone again.

Once again the object of my affections was a young lady from our year. Her name was Julie, and she was best friends with her English compatriot, and the final resting place of all my Mary Jane-related whinges, Francesca. She was from Wales but her accent had been eroded over the years by a constant storm of private education.

Julie wasn't like any girl I had fancied in the past, or even like anyone I had been friends with. She was an occasional member of Team Neighbours, but gave the impression that she was above it all, chuckling away at things no-one else did whilst shaking her head and muttering something about irony. She also, and quite amazingly, never really got into the whole Kerplunk thing, despite Francesca's and the Committee's best efforts. She preferred to spend her time reading the classics, watching plays, and talking about things that I didn't understand. To be honest, Julie and I never really got on that well. We were certainly pleasant enough to each other, making each other numerous cups of tea over the two terms, but we were just too different, and in fact didn't appear to have a single thing in common. She didn't like football, and I didn't read books. She didn't like nob jokes, and they were the only ones I knew. It was quite strange how Francesca could be so close to both of us, whilst we were worlds apart.

So it was somewhat of a surprise to me to discover that I fancied her. I was having a cup of tea with her and Francesca at the time, and I suddenly realised that I had been staring at Julie's chest for the last five minutes whilst Francesca had been trying to make some typically left-wing point criticising New Labour. Worried, I quickly finished my tea, made my excuses, and left to room to figure out what was going on. In the safety of M14 with the door shut and another cup of tea in hand, I ran through all the usual tests, and they all confirmed that yes, bloody hell, I did indeed fancy Julie.

I now had to decide just what I was going to do about it. Firstly, I decided against telling anybody; Mary Jane was off limits, Francesca was too close to the source, Faye had no useful connections and often very little insight, and the boys would have just taken the piss. No, I was on my own on this one. Secondly, I needed a strategy. Any kind of poem was immediately ruled out. For a start, I didn't think my little verses, especially the nob ones, would impress a self-confessed lover of Keats and Milton, and secondly, the chances of me getting away with it for a second time without anyone finding out were minimal. No, this time I had to try a different approach to impress her. I quickly made a mental list of all the things I was good at and weighed up whether or not they were likely to win favour with Julie: I could do six, maybe seven, kick-ups? – Julie hated football and I was shit anyway, our survey says, uh-uh. I could recite the order the contestants were voted off *Big Brother* – unless I made some kind of clever Orwellian link, which I couldn't, this almost certainly would die on its arse. I could do a really bad Welsh accent that often turned Pakistani – Julie was from Wales and seemed like the kind of person who would take offence, so probably not the best of ideas. I knew the lyrics to every Oasis song ever written, including B-sides and bootlegs – Julie, of course, didn't like Oasis. And that was about it.

This little exercise lead me to one conclusion: I was going to have to change who I was to impress Julie.

Now looking back, I should have seen this was an accident waiting to happen. As all good agony aunts will tell you, if you had to change for a person to like you, you were obviously not a match made in heaven in the first place. But at the time all I could think about was how much I liked Julie and, as often happened, the feeling grew and grew with each passing day and with each brief encounter, until I was certain she was all I wanted. And if changing was what I had to do to get her, then change was what I would do.

I took myself off shopping, looking for items to fit my sophisticated new image. I snapped up a jumper that said to me "sophistication", and more importantly "50% off". I dragged Nick MacLean along with me to see a play, our first one ever, called *On the Breast of a Woman*. Neither of us understood what the hell the play was about, but we were surprised and very pleased that it did actually contain a rather nice pair of breasts. Whilst fellow thespians and theatre connoisseurs remained stone-faced, Nick sat there giggling like a six-year-old who has just discovered the word "sex" in the dictionary. I bought myself a brilliant little book that amazingly appeared to be aimed at frauds just like myself. It very briefly summarised the plot and the main points for discussion from fifty classic novels that I would not have dreamt of touching in fifty years. Some of them actually sounded pretty good and I made a mental note to have a perusal of them properly when I had more time. I made myself read and memorise five book summaries a night, and then tested what I had learnt out on the gang during the day.

A Tale of Friendship, Love and Economics

"Hey Caolan, isn't it strange how Harper Lee had *two* actual mockingbirds in her classic Pulitzer Prize-winning work?"

"What the fuck are you on about?"

"You know, not only Tom Robinson, but Boo Radley as well."

"You don't half talk some shite, Bailey."

Yes, but it was learned shite that I now spoke. Mission accomplished.

Within a week of my self-imposed makeover came the chance to test it all out. It was Faye's birthday, and she had opted for a Wednesday night formal hall that both myself and Julie were invited to.

Formal halls on Wednesday night took place in the smaller room that lay alongside the main hall. It was a very cosy room, wood panelled, with yet more portraits of important people hanging from its walls. Space constraints meant that the college could only seat about forty students in this particular room, so tickets had to be snapped up early. There were only two tables, and luckily our party managed to secure a table all to itself. I sat myself down next to my good friend Mark Novak, with Julie sat on the opposite side of the table, easily within earshot, at a bearing of about 32 degrees.

I decided not to begin my performance until the wine had started flowing, thus raising my confidence and hopefully lowering Julie's standards. By the time the main course arrived and the majority of my wine was gone, I was ready to begin. I struck up a conversation with an unsuspecting Francesca about her favourite books. She knew very well that I didn't read, often voicing her disapproval at this fact, and thus was more than a little surprised by my line of questioning. Any book that she suggested that had not been extensively covered by my fifty page pocket guide was quickly brushed aside. I was flying out with insights about everything from *Pride and Prejudice* to *Dubliners*, via *The Grapes of Wrath* and *The Catcher in the Rye*. Francesca looked sceptical and asked what was going on, and Joe Porter started making rude signs behind my back, but I just kept smiling and talking. Eventually, my hard work paid off, and Julie began listening intently. I seized the opportunity.

"I know it's a near impossible question, Julie, so please forgive me for asking, but whom do you consider to be your favourite author?" I even had a new voice. Mark started laughing so I punched his leg under the table.

"Well, Josh, it would have to be Mr Shakespeare, of course," Julie replied, smiling pleasantly.

"William Shakespeare?"

"Yes."

"Well, of course..."

I didn't know what else to say so I took a long sip of my wine.

"Are you a fan, Josh?"

"Of Shakespeare? Of the finest playwright of his era? Of any era? But of course."

"And what would you say is your favourite play?"

Shit. I had only read one, and that was for GCSE, and I thought it was a pile of shite.

"Well, as I'm no doubt sure you can appreciate, it's a most difficult question that you pose, but if pushed, I would have to say *Twelfth Night*."

"A fine choice. That was the second Shakespearean comedy I went to see."

"Oh really, I believe it was my ninth. A most wonderful production." Mark Novak began to choke and had to quickly cover his mouth to stop his drink flying out onto the table. I punched him again.

Well, that had gone fairly well. With Julie's attention firmly secured, I moved on to the main act. Having read it for GCSE, William Golding's *The Lord of the Flies* was my literary speciality, my *pièce de résistance*. I suppose it was the only proper book that I had read, and I remembered vividly how our class had spent hour after hour and essay after essay going into the finer points of the text, reading between the lines to figure out what Golding was getting at with his little tale of young boys stranded on an island. I was definitely onto a winner here. I subtly whispered into Mark Novak's ear.

"What do you want me to ask you?" he replied, loudly.

"Keep it down, you dick," and I repeated my initial whisper at a slightly increased volume. Mark looked at me strangely but I gave him a reassuring nod. He quickly finished what was left in his wine glass and began to speak.

"So... Joshua Bailey... I was wondering if you had any insight... into the role of God, or something... in that Fly book... what's it called?" Mark Novak was pissed. Our game of Chinese Whispers had broken down after one go. Most of the table were now looking at him and looking at me. I smiled embarrassedly.

"What I think my good friend Mr Novak was asking was whether or not there was an underlying religious message emanating from William Golding's classic, *The Lord of the Flies*?"

A Tale of Friendship, Love and Economics

"*Lord of the Flies,*" repeated Mark excitedly, nodding away and swaying from side to side. The rest of the table, including Julie, remained silent.

"Well, Mark, I am no expert on the matter, but I believe Golding actually used the character of Simon to portray Christ. In the book he is the messenger who comes down from above, in this case from a mountain, to tell the groups of children, who have since become divided tribes of savages, the news of the pig's head on a stick. The children fail to comprehend the message and inadvertently kill Simon, in much the same way that humanity failed to understand Christ's message to us and ended up crucifying him on the cross. It's something like that, anyway."

"What the fuck are you on about?" whispered Joe Porter.

"Shut up and keep smiling," I replied.

Conversations around the table were a little stifled after my brief lecture. I tried to gauge the reaction from people, especially Julie, and what I got back seemed to be more confusion than awe. Still, I was happy with how things had gone, and tucked into my desert with a smile forming my mouth as I chewed. I also made a mental note never to hire Mark Novak for such a task in the future, especially when alcohol was involved.

I didn't see Julie for the next couple of days. Apparently she was too busy with work to watch *Neighbours*, and offers of a late-night Kerplunking session didn't seem to appeal to her. I was again at the stage where I wanted to know whether or not I had a chance with her, and I needed to know soon.

In the end I conceded that the best policy was to get Francesca to find out if her well-read Welsh friend was interested in anyone in college, without even mentioning my name. As long as you could trust the middle man, and in this case I definitely trusted Francesca, this was a no lose policy, and a technique that I had employed several times in the past. I could find out if Julie liked me, without Julie ever needing to know that I liked her. After my performance at formal hall, Francesca had somehow guessed that I might just fancy Julie, and said that it would be no trouble at all for her to find out if the feeling was reciprocated. I asked her if she thought we made a good couple, and whilst her words said yes, everything else said no.

It was never going to work. Julie didn't want a boyfriend, and she certainly didn't want me. Francesca broke the news to me over a cup of tea in her room. I ended up feeling worse for her than I did for myself. Francesca looked so worried when she told me, with concern and comfort glowing in her pretty eyes. I assured her that I wasn't upset, and that in the days to come I would realise that all had happened for the best. I said this to make her fell better, and not because I believed it myself.

But I should have believed it. All the signs were there to suggest that I would get over this one pretty quickly. I didn't even know Julie that well, I was having to change who I was to impress her, she didn't laugh at my jokes, and she didn't enjoy doing the things that I liked to do. Moreover, I had been in this situation before and got over it easily enough. I should have known better by now than to get all upset about girls I fancied. I should have just accepted what had happened, knowing that in all likelihood things would be better in a few days. But I just couldn't see beyond my immediate pain. Economists call it "static expectations", when an individual learns nothing from the past, is unable to infer things about the future, and consequently makes exactly the same mistake over and over again. In real life it is called being human.

There was nothing concrete or substantial to my feelings for Julie, but I couldn't have known this at the time. At the time I knew beyond all doubt that she was the only one I wanted, the only one I had ever wanted. But it always felt like this with any girl I fancied. It only became apparent that there was not a great deal to these feelings when it was all over and it didn't take a long period of time to get over them. I then knew it was a nothing more than a cyclical impulsive thing, just like with Cassandra and the Movie Star Look-alike before her. Perhaps it was just a desire to have something else on my mind apart from the wonderful worlds of economics and Kerplunk, more than thinking about going out on a Wednesday night and trying to get up for lectures on a Thursday. Perhaps it was the desire to see what a relationship at university was like, or just something to fill the void left by Mary Jane. Anyway, it ended before it got going, and it was certainly for the best. No, I was yet to fall for someone properly in Cambridge, yet to fall in way that felt exactly the same as the others in the build up, but then hurt like hell when it was all over. For it was only when you realised what you couldn't have that you found out just what it was and how much you really wanted it. Maybe that's what love really is. Oh God, I've gone from sounding like Ronan Keating to sounding like a script from *Dawson's Creek*. Anyway, love or not, I had all that to look forward to.

Chapter 37

Faye didn't like talking much about her private life, and she certainly didn't like talking about Duane. This was, of course, in complete contrast to my other neighbour; the strawberry blonde open book. I tried asking Faye what was going on, but she would either quickly change the subject or, if I persisted, tell me to mind my own bloody business. I respected the fact that she was a private person, but it just frustrated me to see my wee Scottish pal with things on her mind and not being able to help.

I could only infer and speculate as to what was going on. Since the infamous night when the Scottish vixen lured the shy, obedient historian into her lair, and was subsequently rescued by means of Blu-Tack, the college's very own star-crossed lovers had not seen much of each other at all. Duane no longer popped around for tea, and now made less than subtle excuses to leave the room if Faye ever wandered in. They would still be friendly to each other in passing, but that was about it. I assumed that this was what Faye wanted. After all, she had admitted under the influence of a bottle of rancid wine that she didn't like the way Duane was obsessed with her, and was clearly regretful about her itchy kiss, so the fact that they rarely saw each other any more should have been a good thing, right?

The problem was, not only did Duane *see* Faye less, he also appeared to be obsessed with her less, even to the point of moving onto other people. And quite a few other people at that. You see, after the night that the Scottish one beckoned him in only to leave him out to dry, Duane underwent a bit of an image change. He got a new shorter haircut, and a few new clothes. It was no Clark Kent into Superman, but it did make him look a lot cooler, or at least a lot less public school. But it wasn't just the clothes. Within a week, rumours were circulating around the corridors of M-block that Duane had a woman on the go; a Polish girl who lived on the floor below us. Then, the following week, the block buzzed with talk of yet another female who had fallen for the historian's silent charms, this time a small girl with rosy red cheeks and a strange walk. Then, to top it all off, Jude and I were witness to a most unexpected scene. We were sat in our usual position on the steps outside my room tucking into our midnight bowls of cereals, discussing what songs we should put on our *Gym Tape – 2001*. Then, from the door that separated Duane and Jude's part of the corridor from mine and my two female neighbours', emerged a leggy blonde dressed in Duane's dressing gown. We knew Duane owned the stripy garment because he always wore it in the queue for the shower, whilst Jude and I opted for the more manly, but more chilly, towel-around-the-waist approach. She smiled at us as she headed into the bathroom, and we nodded in shocked unison. I had to spit a bit of chewed-up Weetabix back into my bowl to save myself from choking.

"Who the fuck is that?" I asked, having got my breath back, and wiping my cereal and milk covered chin on the sleeve of my T-shirt.

"Never seen her before in my life," replied Jude. "You know that's Duane's dressing gown?"

"I know."

"Dirty bastard."

The girl emerged from the bathroom and headed back along the corridor. Jude less than subtly stood up so that he could see which room she went into and, sure enough, straight into Duane's she did go. She was tall and quite pretty, and looked much older than most of the girls in college. Jude was claiming she was in her thirties, but I opted for a more conservative guess of twenty-five-ish.

Minutes later, as Jude and I had abandoned our cereals and talk of tapes in favour of discussing what the hell was going on in M-block and why no girls ever emerged from our rooms dressed in our clothes, out came Duane. He did not look happy. He was wearing a typical Dad's pair of pyjama bottoms, and a pale blue T-shirt. Jude nudged me and I nudged him back. I said hi, and Duane nodded ashamedly in our direction, keeping his eyes fixed firmly on the floor. He too went into the bathroom and came out a minute later. Without acknowledging us, he returned to his room with his head down. Bloody hell, I thought.

"He must have a huge cock," said Jude.

By lunch time the next day everyone in college knew about the late-night comings and goings along the M-block corridors. Jude had told Adam Sylvester and, adding a few bits of his own, he had told the world. In lectures, Caolan was telling me about it before I had a chance to tell him. Nothing stayed secret for long in Catz.

Pretty soon, Faye found out. I went round to her room to see if she wanted to watch lunchtime *Neighbours* as I had a supervision at 5 pm. You could tell she was not happy. She was sitting at her desk with a screwed up face and Radio One on in the background.

"I don't have time for bloody *Neighbours* today." She didn't look up from her desk, her eyes focused on the muddled heap of papers in front of her.

"Faye, you always have time for *Neighbours*."

"Not today, alright?"

"What's up?"

"Nothing."

"You can tell me, you know."

"Nothing, *alright?*"

"Come on, Faye." God, I was annoying. I knew this was just the kind of persistence that annoyed me in other people.

"Look, I've loads of work to do, Josh, now can you please just leave me alone?"

"Faye, have you suddenly changed degree, you never have loads of work to do. Is this about Duane?"

"Is *what* about Duane?"

"This grumpy mood you're in."

"I wasn't in a 'grumpy mood' until my lovely neighbour Josh came in to brighten up my day."

"I'm only trying to help."

"I know, but the only way you can help right now is by going away, okay?"

"Okay."

And so away I went, with my tail between my legs.

Faye came round later that night, just as I was lying in bed flicking through the stupid book I had bought to impress Julie. Apparently *Animal Farm* was about more than just animals. I hadn't had any late night-knocks in the last few weeks, and it made me jump a little. I looked through the peep-hole before opening the door, just in case it was Mary Jane wielding a large axe, or something. I smiled a little smile when I saw it was my wee Scottish neighbour, dressed in her usual red fluffy dressing gown.

"It's not too late for me to come round, is it?"

Whenever Faye tried to look into your eyes she often drifted up to your forehead. In the early days I used to go straight to the mirror after our conversations, armed and ready to wipe off whatever foreign body was residing between my eyes and my hair. She said she couldn't help it, and by now I was used to it. But as she spoke tonight, she looked only down.

"Nah, I was just reading."

"Anything good?"

"Nah, it's a pile of shite."
Then silence.
"Look, Josh, I'm sorry for snapping at you before."
"No probs, Faye. I'm so sorry for being a nob."
If it had been Mary Jane, we would have hugged, but for some reason Faye and I didn't hug each other. It wasn't that any of us were against hugging each other in principle, it was just we had never done it, and now the idea seemed somehow strange. We smiled at each other instead.

"I promise this will be the last ever time I ask, and feel free to punch me or something, but do you want to talk about it?"

"Yes, Josh, I do."

And when we were both sitting comfortably with a nice cup of tea in our hands, Faye talked and I listened.

Faye explained that she was upset about how Duane was behaving. She didn't know why but she knew that she had been sad in recent weeks, weeks when he had not been around. She didn't think that she was jealous of these girls, just annoyed. Annoyed that Duane seemed to be able to move on so easily, and annoyed at herself for being annoyed. She knew she had no real right to feel this way or expect any kind of behaviour from Duane. He had made his feelings for her as well known as his shy nature allowed him, and had then had them seemingly rejected through Faye's willingness to let the present situation of not seeing each other continue. She had led him on, kissed him, and then said no, and now he was only doing what she had wanted him to do from the start; getting on with his life, a life not dominated by her. But if this was the case, why was she so angry and upset?

"Why am I so angry and upset, Josh?" she asked.

Bloody hell, I thought. I was alright at the listening part, quite good in fact, but as soon as a question came along, I was no longer the man for the job. I thought about it for a while and had a sip of my tea. Faye perched forward on her chair, staring at my forehead, eagerly and naively awaiting my big insight.

"Well, Faye, just taking a wild stab in the dark, but don't you think there is a chance that you might just like him?"

"Do you think?"

"I'm no expert... well, apart from my A-level in Psychology, of course... but it seems to me like a classic case of not knowing what you've got until it's gone. You didn't realise how much you missed Duane, or how much he meant to you, until he was no longer around. You know, the grass is always greener and all that."

"You could be the next bloody Jerry Springer."

"Do you think I might be right?"

"Aye, I suppose you might be. It's about bloody time you were. Maybe I do like the stupid boy. But I've bloody blown it now, haven't I?"

"Have you bollocks. Again, not wishing to get too technical, but this seems to like a classic case of the man in question, in this case Duane, trying to make the lady in question, in this case you, jealous. Duane doesn't want to be getting off with a load of girls. You know as well as I do that he's not like that. They probably took advantage of him, especially that old blonde thing. Apparently, according to Jude's friend at least, she's absolutely rampant, and she's twenty-six. She's had nearly everyone in the choir. And Duane looked so sad when we saw him that night, you know. He could probably file for sexual assault. Everyone knows he only wants you. He'd probably marry you right now if he could, and then you, him, and his slippers and dressing gown could live happily ever after."

"I'm not marrying a man who has bloody slippers like those."

"I'm sure he'd get rid of them if you asked him."

"Oh, what am I going to do, Josh?"

"Just talk to him, tell him how you feel."

"Now you sound like a bloody girl."

"Now you sound like my Dad"

"I'm no good at talking about that kind of thing, and he's even worse."

"Well, then my expert advice would have to be to wait until you are both pissed. Drink sorts everything out. What do they say, *in vino veritas*, or something?"

"Aye, or *in vino pukeias* in my case."

"You'll be fine. I'm sure it'll all work out."

"I hope so, Josh, I hope so"

In my experience, few things work out as they are supposed to do, especially things that I am sure will work out. Happily, the case of Duane and Faye proved to be an exception. A week or so later, and just in the nick of time, along came another Catz Bop. We all went to formal hall beforehand which served the dual purpose of giving us a valid excuse for not being dressed up to match the ridiculous theme and enabling us to arrive with a bottle of wine on board. Faye realised that if she was going to act at all, then tonight was going to have to be the night. We sank a couple of Aftershocks to steady the nerves, doing the swilling and gargling until our eyes watered, and then Faye swaggered back to her room quickly to brush her teeth. I didn't bother, partly because I liked the taste of Aftershock and also because I figured the chance of any females getting close enough to pick up on the aroma of my breath that night was minimal.

The Bop proceeded in its usual fashion. As soon as we were drunk enough and the music was cheesy enough, we all took to the dance floor. Nick MacLean and I were always the first up, partly because we loved all the shit songs and partly because drink affected us more than the others. Joe Porter liked a dance, and was actually quite good, but was a bit more selective about the music and the people dancing around him. Caolan would happily dance and fall over to anything, and most of the time did. Mark and Oisin were always the most reluctant, preferring to chat at the bar about how the rest of us looked like dicks. However, the former would do absolutely anything if he had enough drink, and the latter, though often sober, was not averse to the odd mad, unexplained burst of wild Irish boogying.

Anyway, Michael Jackson's *Billy Jean* was on, which meant all my attention was focused on grabbing a willing girl, and getting my feet movements and nob thrusts absolutely right. Consequently, I didn't notice the main event that was developing just a few metres to my left on the crowded, sweaty dance floor. The ever reliable Oisin, in the midst of taking a wee break, or whatever, brought it to my attention. Faye and Duane were dancing together, and more importantly, they were holding hands. I shuffled over to have a closer look. They were clearly both very drunk, but I figured that on this particular occasion this was by no means a bad thing. I prayed for a slow song to come on to give the would-be couple the best chance in the world. If this was a movie, Jacko would have been faded out to be replaced by *Angels* or *I Will Always Love You*, and the magic would have unfolded before our eyes. But this was no movie, it was a Catz bop. The DJ slapped on *Reach* by S Club 7, the dance-floor erupted in approval, and the two pairs of hands separated to do the actions for the high-energy chorus. I got engulfed by a large human circle that was gaining new members every second, and resigned myself to screaming along with the rest of them.

It was only when the porters came to bring the Bop to an end that it finally happened. As I was carried along in the wave of people through the

A Tale of Friendship, Love and Economics

door I looked back onto the dance-floor. Faye and Duane were stood together, holding hands once more. Then, after a moment's hesitation, a stooping and a stretching, and a closing of the eyes, they were kissing. I tried to tell Mark, but he was putting all his concentration into staying on his feet, and not doing a very good job. I don't know how it happened; if Duane came up with a killer line, or if their eyes simply told them that the moment was right, but whatever it was, that kiss signalled the start of something.

Faye and Duane were soon officially going out. They would have tea together most nights and go for bike-rides together most afternoons. It certainly wasn't the wild, passionate affair of the novels and the movies, but it seemed to work for them. It did Duane the world of good. It brought him out of his shell a little, made him more talkative, more confident. And it seemed to make Faye happier too, although she rarely talked about it. It was a relationship that didn't have the most normal of starts, triumphing over allegations of stalking and late-night requests for Blu-Tack, but looked like it might just last. Only time would tell if the wee Scottish vixen had found her man, and if this part of the story truly would have a happy ending.

Chapter 38

I was more nervous than I should have been when Andrew came to stay. I'd built it up in my mind to be some kind of monumentous event, the bringing together of two vastly different species; my friends from home and my friends from uni. My only comfort was that Andrew was the first one. To the best of my knowledge he got on with everyone he met, and although I knew he would be worried, thinking he would spend the weekend having to listen to conversations about quantum physics and the wonders of seventeenth-century French fiction, I was pretty sure he would like my friends.

Andrew arrived at a strange time. I was hosting a quiz show in the bar, and a boy was doing breast-stroke on the pool table.

The recent JCR Committee elections had elevated the role of the two small weird girls from obscurity to college Ents Reps, and they were desperate to make their mark. They had promised creativity and originality, and were yet to deliver. Then one night, over a quiet game of Kerplunk, which I was losing due to an annoyingly shaky hand, they hit me with a proposition.

"Josh?" the smaller one of the two began in a drawn-out, whiney way that could only be the prefix to asking a favour.

"One moment... oh bollocks! Bollocks, bollocks, bollocks!" I had just Kerplunked six marbles from what appeared to be a reasonably safe position, and was now dangerously close to being beaten by Mark "Perfect Game" Novak. "What do you want?" I snapped. Obviously it was their fault.

"How would you fancy being Chris Tarrant?"

"Oh yeah, well keen." I figured this was leading to some joke at my expense so I returned my attention to planning my next crucial Kerplunk move.

"No, we're serious," the taller weirdo now joined in. "We are going to do *Who Wants to be a Millionaero?* in the bar, and we want you to be the host."

I averted my attention away from Kerplunk on the off-chance that they were being serious.

"Who wants to be a what?" I asked.

"A *Millionaero*" they replied in unison as if it was blindingly obvious. "Instead of giving out money, the prizes will be increasing quantities of Aeros, some mini and some full size, and probably some Haribo for the easier questions."

"Are you being serious?" I already knew they were. They were mad enough to come up with an idea like this.

"Yep, so are you up for it?"

"Aye, why not."

"Good. It'll be in about a week. We'll discuss the finer points at a later date."

"No probs."

"You are going to look like a right retard," pointed out the ever supportive Caolan.

I was always signing up to do stupid stuff like this at school, so I didn't see why I shouldn't give it a try at uni. I had once done a bit of compèring for a variety show, and even dressed up as Lulu for a painful rendition of Take That's *Relight My Fire*, and I loved every minute of it. My friends said it was the inherent attention-seeking nature of my personality, probably stemming from the fact that I was an only child. They were just jealous.

And so in the coming days posters popped up around college advertising the event and asking for contestants. To be fair to the girls, they had done a good job. They had got the *Who Wants to be a Millionaire?* circular logo from the internet, and changed the last word to reflect their original chocolaty twist (I'm sure they had sought the permission of the company that made the show). Unfortunately, despite their best efforts, the emails from people wishing to be contestants were not exactly pouring in. The strange lad who had run his ultimately successful campaign for Welfare Officer based around penguins and turtles signed up straight away, but he was not exactly the crowd puller we were after. I signed up a reluctant Nick MacLean, promising, with fingers crossed behind my back, that in return for his participation I would review the controversial Kerplunk scoring system that was keeping me on top. A bit of pressurising and a bit of drink eventually gave us our four contestants, with a hockey-playing girl from the first year and a well-renowned quiz show expert from the second year completing the illustrious quartet.

Everything was left to the last minute and, come the afternoon on the day of the event, I didn't have a clue what was going on. I was told to dress up in a suit with a shirt and tie of the same colour, like the great Mr Tarrant often wore, and come to the taller weirdo's room for six o'clock. The show started at 7.30 pm. I chose a lovely red shirt, red tie combo, got Faye to tie it properly, slapped a bit of polish on my shoes, cleaned my teeth, slapped a bit of gel on my hair, and headed up the stairs of Bull block to receive my instructions.

It was the first time I had been in the room of the taller weirdo – who was probably more loud than weird, but still definitely very much on the weird side – and it was as weird as expected. She had a bed and a sink and normal stuff like that, but she also had photos of nearly everyone in our year stuck randomly around her four walls. More worryingly, they were the kind of photos that gave you the impression that the subjects were not aware they were being taken. She had even managed to take one of Caolan not posing. Then, on the back of her door, she had constructed a mini shrine in honour of an actress girl in our year. There were photos of her and newspaper reviews of her shows, arranged in a cross shape and illuminated by a desk lamp. Now, to be fair, the girl in question was very attractive, but a shrine to her was perhaps going a little bit too far. No, the room was definitely strange, and as I stood their dressed in red and black, I felt more than a little uncomfortable.

The room owner offered me some vodka and coke to steady my nerves. I explained that I was not nervous. She explained that I probably should be as I was a virtually unknown first year about to host a ridiculous quiz show in a crowded bar. I took the drink and asked for another. We then got down to business. The two girls had copied down a load of questions from *The Official Who Wants to be a Millionaire Quiz Book – Volume 3* and written them on various pieces of paper. Some were illegible but I got the general gist of the questions. For the first couple of easy ones we made up our own questions, with a 'humourous' Cambridge theme. Let's just say they sounded funny at the time. The girls then tipped out the prizes onto the desk from two full Sainsbury's carrier bags. We quickly devised a scoring system by which a successful answer to Question 1 got you one single Haribo all the way through to two full packets of Mini Aeros, plus five packets of Haribos if you went the distance to Question 15. Whoever got the furthest on the night was to be given a bottle of the cheapest champagne available in addition to their sugary winnings, and any Aeros and Haribos left at the end would be divided equally between the two girls and me. Finally, we rigged the draw for the order of contestants to try and sustain the audience interest level for as long as possible. With another quick vodka drink inside me, I was ready to head to the bar.

It was both good and bad to see so many familiar faces in the college bar. Whilst I had little doubt that people like Francesca, Faye and Elizabeth had come along to offer their support, I was sure that Caolan and Joe's reason was more along the lines of: no way am I missing him making a complete prick of himself. The motives of Oisin, Mark and Jude lay somewhere in the middle. Contestant Number 2, Nick MacLean, was also present, looking very much like a man who was regretting signing up to do this. As I took a final look at myself in the bathroom mirror, adjusting a wayward bit of hair first to the left then to the right, I felt exactly the same.

The bar was reasonably busy, but few gave the impression that they were there for the game show. Some were playing pool, some were putting extremely bad songs on the jukebox, and others were chatting amongst themselves. The louder of the two girls gave me an intro, and to a mere smattering of applause and a few sarcastic wolf whistles from Oisin and Joe, I walked onto the stage, narrowly avoiding Caolan's outstretched leg. I say stage, but with no expense spared in this lavish production, the centrepiece of this event was, in fact, a small part of the left-hand side of the bar, and consisted of a table and two extremely uncomfortable stools. In order to try and emulate the intensity of the hit TV show, the lights in the bar were turned off, but then had to be turned back on again when no-one could see what was going on. Having seemingly blown the budget and their imaginations on Aeros and Haribos, the Ents Officers had not prepared any of the synchronised dramatic music and dimming lights that were characteristic of the hit TV show. Instead, just before the start of each question, one of the girls made the "de-de-de-le" sound with her mouth, whilst the other one swung a lighted torch down from her above her head. Let's just say it didn't have quite the same effect. There was no way Tarrant would have put up with this.

First contestant up was the hockey-playing girl from the first year. She had been chosen in Position One as kind of a warm up act. We reckoned that the bar would only start really filling up at eightish, so the plan was that I could hone my untested technique on this poor girl, and if it bombed, there wouldn't be too many witnesses. She was a lovely girl, with a sarcastic sense of humour and quite large breasts for her petite size. She supported Derby County football club and often wore woolly hats. She studied Natural Sciences and had pulled Adam "Sly" Sylvester in Freshers' Week. She had regretted it ever since. She was a fan of both Kerplunk and *Neighbours*, and having not met each other until the start of this second term, we now got on very well. Her name was Rachael.

"Ladies and gentlemen, please give a warm round of applause for our first contestant." Her reception was good, and a fair few degrees hotter than mine. "Welcome to *Who Wants to be a Millionaero?*. If you'd just like to take a seat on this wonderfully comfy stool. That's it. Now, why don't you tell the audience a little bit about yourself."

"Well, my name is Rachael, I'm eighteen years old, and I'm a student, studying Natural Sciences at Cambridge University."

She got a round of applause and a few woos.

"Cambridge, hey? Isn't that place full of puffs?"

My first lame joke got more jeers than laughs, but at least it showed people were listening.

"Only those from Lancashire," she replied and got a far better response. It was a shame I wasn't witty, otherwise I might have been able to come up with a reply. Instead I just grinned like an idiot, and moved swiftly on.

"Right, Rachael, let me explain the rules of *Who Wants to be a Millionaero?* As things stand you are fifteen questions away from winning two packs of Mini Aeros and five packets of Haribo." The crowd wooed sarcastically, and Rachael smiled sweetly and fluttered her eyelids. "To help your cause tonight, you have three life-lines: Fifty-Fifty; Josh's Special Clue; and Ask Jim the Bar Man. Use them wisely. There is no time limit for each question, so take your time, and can I please ask the audience not to call out any answers, and if they do, please pretend you didn't hear them. Okay, that's about it, so if you are ready, Rachael, let's play *Who Wants to be a Millionaero?*".

The two girls did the dramatic noise and lowering of the torch thing. The audience laughed, more out of sympathy than anything else.

"OK, Question 1, for one Haribo: Which of the following is a Cambridge College?

(a) New Hall
(b) New Balls
(c) Nude and Tall
(d) New place to store lesbians and easy women"

"Well, Josh, it's a tough one. All sound very plausible, but I'd have to go for (a) New Hall."

"Is that your final answer?"

"Yes, Josh, (a) is my final answer."

I paused to allow the tension to build.

"You said (a) New Hall."

I paused again. I was even annoying myself.

"You've just won one Haribo!"

The crowd applauded and Rachael gave me a kiss on the cheek. Bloody hell, I thought, I wonder what she'd do if I gave her a pack of mini Aeros.

There were a few more questions along similar lines, mostly slagging off other colleges who were not present to defend themselves, and then once we moved onto the big money prizes (I'm talking a full-size Aero here), the questions got a bit trickier.

A Tale of Friendship, Love and Economics

"OK, Question 7, for all the Haribos on the table, plus an Aero, and remember, if you get it wrong, you loose thirty two Haribos. Take your time. Rachael, when was the first *Human Genome Project* completed?
(a) 1998
(b) 1999
(c) 2000
(d) 2001"

It was obvious that Rachael didn't know. She had used her Fifty-Fifty on Question 5 about Chinese emperors. I reminded her that we were playing for a lot of confectionery items here.

"I'm not 100 per cent sure, Josh, so I'll have to use another life-line and Ask Jim the Bar Man."

"Okay, Rachael. Let me explain how this works. I am going to repeat the question to Jim, together with the four possible answers. He will then, hopefully anyway, suggest an answer. You are under no obligation to take his answer. Are you ready to Ask Jim the Bar Man?"

"I am."

I called over to Jim.

"Hang on a bloody minute, Josh, I'm serving here. What do you want anyway?" Like I said, I bet Chris Tarrant wouldn't have put up with this. Eventually, when Jim had poured two pints and a rum and coke, I reminded him that he had agreed to be a part of this game, and repeated the question to him. He thought about it for a moment.

"I'd go for (b) if I were you darling."

"How sure are you?" asked Rachael

"I haven't got a bloody clue, love," replied Jim.

Rachael thought for a while and then smiled.

"Well, Josh, I came here with nothing, and now look at all this I've won. It's certainly going to be life-changing, and I don't want to risk it. I think I'll take the Haribos."

"Are you absolutely sure? Can I remind you that you still have Josh's Special Clue left."

"Yes, but I dread to think what I have to do to get it." She said, and winked. "No, Josh, I think I'll take the Haribos."

"Okay, I can tell you that the answer was in fact (c) 2000, and specifically on a windy 4th April, I do believe [I made that bit up]. Anyway, give her a big round of applause, as Rachael goes back to Cambridge with sixty-four Haribos."

The audience clapped, Rachael gave me another kiss on the cheek, and I took a sip of my pint of larger. That didn't go too bad.

Next up was Nick MacLean, who looked more than a little bit nervous. He shuffled his way past chairs, tables and legs, and joined me on the stage. I shook his hand.

"Welcome to the show."

"Thank you."

"Tell the audience something about yourself."

Nick had gone a bit red and spoke softly. I tried my best to look reassuring.

"My name is Nick, I'm from East Sheen, and I am a first year studying geography." He got a few sympathetic applause.

"Well, Nick, I'm afraid there's no colouring-in round in this quiz."

Nick screwed up his face in disapproval.

"And what would you do if you went all the way and actually won two whole packs of mini Aeros?"

"Well, Josh, I haven't really thought about it, but I'd probably eat them."

"Sounds like a good plan, Mr MacLean, so let's try and get you there, as we play *Who Wants to be a Millionaero?*"

"Question 1, for one Haribo, and it's a fizzy cola bottle." The crowd wooed. The bar was filling up now and they were getting into it. "Which of the following statements is not true:

(a) $2 + 2 = 4$

(b) $2 + 3 = 5$

(c) $4 + 2 = 6$

(d) Geographers work hard"

Nick had been listening intently to each option, evidently thinking it was one of those trick questions, like 'What do cows drink?" "Milk?" "No, water," and he gave a weary sigh when the final option was read out. The crowd laughed, and fellow geographer Faye's cry of "Piss off, Bailey" was happily muted.

"You need some new material, Josh," moaned Nick.

"Is that your final answer?"

"No."

"Do you want me to repeat the question?"

"No. I think the answer is (d)."

"So, young Nicholas MacLean, you are saying that the statement geographers work hard is *not true*?"

"Yes, because they correct answer is that we work very hard."

It got a general moan from the crowd. Nick grinned like he'd made the best joke in the world ever. I gave him his Haribo and moved on.

Nick was actually quite sharp. He was always better than me at *The Weakest Link*, although I could normally make up an excuse why I got the questions wrong. He had breezed his way through the first seven questions, used his Fifty-Fifty on Question 8 about signs of the zodiac, and used his Ask Jim the Bar Man successfully on the tenth question by choosing a different answer to the one suggested. He was looking a good bet to go all the way. Indeed, Faye had already bought him a drink, a very rare action indeed from the stereotypically tight Scot, on the presumption that Nick would be able to keep her in Aeros for the rest of the year. Then came Question 11.

"Okay, Nick, you're going along very well. Here's Question 11, for three packets of Haribos, four full-size Aeros, and twelve mini Aeros: A plant, for example a strawberry plant, with the ice minus strain of *P. Syringae* can withstand temperatures as low as:

(a) 0 degrees Celsius
(b) Minus 5 degrees Celsius
(c) Minus 10 degrees Celsius
(d) Minus 15 degrees Celsius"

"How the shit am I meant to know that?"

I sensed that Nick might not know the answer. I repeated the question and reminded him that he was only five correct answers away from the jackpot. He thought about it for a moment, and then a resigned look was washed upon his face.

"Right, I'm guessing I'm going to regret this, but can I have Josh's Special Clue, please?" No matter what the circumstance, Nick was always polite.

"Of course." I smiled, knowing he would indeed regret it. "Now, Nicholas, as I am sure you are aware, nothing in life is free, so in order to receive Josh's Special Clue, you must do a teeny-weeny little task, okay?"

"What?"

"Don't look so worried, you'll enjoy it" I winked at him. "Now, Mr MacLean, as well as being a geographer and the Dennis Irwin of the 2nd XI football team, it is perhaps less well known that you do a mean Michael Jackson impression."

"What?" Confusion, concern and anger were now evident across his face.

"Oh come now, don't be so modest," I smiled at him, and he did not smile back. "So, I thought it would be a good idea, for our pleasure and for yours, if you were to share your talents with us here tonight."

"No way."

"Oh come on, Nick. What do you all think?" I turned to the audience and they obediently shouted their approval. Peer pressure was a wonderful thing sometimes.

"All I'm asking you to do is sing one verse and one chorus of the Jackson classic *Bad*, complete with dance moves, and wearing this hat." I produced the hat that I had borrowed from the Cypriot ex-Sergeant economist. Once again the crowd wooed in approval.

"I fucking hate you," said Nick as I handed him the hat. I kept smiling.

Nick often came across as a shy, sensible, pleasant lad. He would always reply if talked to, would always be polite, but wouldn't be intrusive firing up the conversations left, right and centre with strangers. He was the kind of friend that your mother wanted you to hang around with, a good influence. As he got to know you better, he became more talkative, and generally more camp. Nobody actually thought Nick was gay, but if somebody said one of our group was definitely homosexual, then all money would fall upon Mr MacLean. He would probably even bet on himself. Familiarity, for better or worse, also encouraged Nick's sense of humour. His self-proclaimed best ever joke was when he "brilliantly" changed the name of the dish Chicken à la Don to Chicken à la Don King. Like all of his jokes, it was so bad you had to smile. Nick was also always the sensible one, making us think through the likely consequences of throwing a water bomb into the passing tour bus, or planting a mobile phone on Oisin when he was in the library and then ringing it. As such, he hated being reminded of his encounter with a traffic cone, the police and the Dean. If Nick MacLean was drunk, his inhibitions fell, and he was a stupid as the rest of us. Indeed, if drunk and in the crowded anonymity of a Bop, he would have had no problem at all fulfilling my present request. However, he was stone cold sober, there was no music, and all eyes were on him. Even Jim had temporarily closed the bar to bare witness to this.

A Tale of Friendship, Love and Economics

Nick stood in front of the audience looking like a lost little child. He stared at the bowler hat he was holding in his left hand as if it was something that was going to kill him. He turned to look at me hoping there may be a way out, and I gestured that it was best just to get on with it and get it over with. Then, he started to sing. When I thought about it, I couldn't actually believe he was doing it. He was stood in front of the whole bar, singing "your butt is mine" in a high-pitched voice, and shuffling his hands and feet like he had Parkinson's disease. The audience found it hard to watch, it seemed to go on for ever and ever, and all were thankful when it was all over. Nick returned to his stool red-faced and handed me back the hat. I got the audience to give him a second round of applause, and promptly told him the answer to the question. (It was apparently (b) Minus 5 degrees Celsius. Obviously). I failed to see how any amount of Aeros could have been worth that.

I was a lot like Nick in some ways. I was shy sometimes with new people, and even shy with friends I'd known for years; an unannounced cloud of silence suddenly falling over me, and with it an inescapable desire to be on my own. Then at other times I was completely different. I wanted nothing more than to be talking and for the whole world to be listening. I wanted to be the centre of everything, acting the fool, playing any part that would get me noticed, happy to dance along to any tune that might be playing. Later, Caolan would call me an attention-seeker, both when I fell into unexplained silences and when I preformed for all who would listen. But he was wrong, partly anyway. When I was quiet I did not want to be noticed, I wanted to disappear. Concern and sympathy brought only guilt, and guilt made me feel worse. I didn't like this part of me or understand it. I knew it wasn't depression or anything proper like that. I'd read a book on depression and in it there was one guy who was so depressed that he couldn't even get out of bed, and when he finally managed to progress to one leg hanging over the side, he then couldn't get it back up and under the covers again, and so he would lay there in bed all day long, depressed and with a cold leg. No, it wasn't anything like that. Then again, I knew it wasn't just a case of having normal bad moods, because these feelings I had didn't seem to have a cause and didn't seem to follow any recognisable pattern. I don't know, maybe it was the price of intelligence, or the price of having a good life, a life with nothing substantial to worry about. I wondered what price my friends had to pay, especially Caolan, who was never anything less than happy.

Eventually Nick bowed out graciously of *Millionaero* by passing on Question 12, which was a tricky one about the setting for James Bond films. He returned to his table to a generous reception of applause and a sea of heads shaking in disbelief and sympathy. The two weird Ents Reps smiled at me. The all-singing, all-dancing geographer, Nicholas MacLean, had been just what the show had needed.

The departure of Nick brought about the turn of our Star Attraction. His name was Sid, he was a second year economist, and his quiz show CV was second to none. He had done all the big shows: *Blockbusters, Countdown, The Weakest Link,* and he had recently won a whopping £10,000 on a new show called *The Enemy Within*. But tonight, the stakes were a lot higher, as Sid was playing not for cash but for Aeros. I was a little less comfortable talking to Sid than Rachael or Nick, not wishing to sound like a cocky Fresher getting too big for his boots, but he was pleasant enough and seemed game for a laugh. Which was a good job.

Sid rattled through the first questions with ease and at pace. He was clearly very good. Whilst Sid was mulling over in his head the possible answers to Question 7, a mobile phone started to ring.

"Can someone please turn that off?" I said, making sure I sounded serious enough to not be taken seriously.

"It's yours, Josh," shouted Faye, "It's your Mum."

"Bloody hell," I said, "just press cancel."

"Why don't you answer it?" shouted a rugby playing third year in the audience.

"Yeah, answer it, answer it," seconded someone else, and soon the whole bar was united by the belief that the best thing I could possibly do at this moment was to answer my mobile phone. And so, as the bar fell silent, that's what I did.

"Hello."

"Hi, Josh."

"Hiya, Mum, you alright?"

"Yeah, you?"

"Aye, not too bad."

"What are you doing?"

"I'm hosting a quiz show in the bar."

"Oh."

"Don't ask. Can I call you back later?"

A Tale of Friendship, Love and Economics

"Well, I'm off to your Auntie Mary's in about an hour, but you can get me on my mobile."

"Okay, will do... hey, you don't know anything about former communist states do you?"

"Do I heck. I can do *Coronation Street* if that's any help?"

"No, I'm only messing. Speak to you soon"

"Okay. Good luck with the quiz. Love you."

"Lo... yeah, bye Mum."

I handed the phone back to Faye, and wished I could hand her my red face as well.

"Right, can we make sure all mobiles are turned off, there are some serious prizes up at stake after all."

The audience clapped. At least it went down well.

Sid had made his way to Question 12, using up two life-lines in the process, thus leaving him with just Josh's Special Clue. After witnessing the trauma Nick MacLean had just gone through Sid was understandably reluctant to use this lovely little life-line. However, he did not know the answer, and needed only this question to overtake Nick's score, and move into pole position in the race for the ridiculously cheap champagne.

"Right, let's get this over with. I'll take that bloody clue thing."

"Well, seeing as you asked so nicely... right Sid, now there have been some question marks raised over your current state of physical health (Sid spent his days smoking and sitting on benches). So, with that in mind, I thought I would offer up a physical challenge. I would like you to lie on the pool table and complete each of the four strokes that comprise swimming's individual medley event. That's: butterfly, front crawl, backstroke and breast-stroke. Please spend a good fifteen seconds on each one."

"You're taking the piss." It was more a statement than a question.

I smiled.

With even more reluctance than Nick before him, Sid brushed a few loose balls aside and mounted the pool table. He did not smile once throughout the whole process. I released a feeble wolf whistle to signal the start of the challenge, and Sid waved his arms around and wiggled his legs unenthusiastically. The crowd cheered him on through each stoke.

"Do a tumble turn," one of Sid's mates shouted.

As Sid was swimming away Andrew walked into the bar. God only knows what he must have thought and also why he didn't just turn and run back up to Lancashire. Luckily I caught his eye and gestured for him to go over and join the gang. Although few could understand him, Oisin was very good at meeting people for the first time, seeming able to chat away and drill with laughter all night. As soon as Andrew was settled and Sid had swam enough of the final leg, I brought the challenge to an end, led a large round of applause for the embarrassed swimmer with a chalk mark on his black jeans, and returned to my stool. Sid passed on the next question, but had seemingly done enough to win this very strange quiz.

Once Sid's go was over, I could sense that the audience was loosing interest. We had been going for about an hour and a half now, and people were getting restless. Moreover, the formal hall lot were seeping into the bar, and with a bottle of wine each on board, they were not exactly keen for silently observing the quiz in progress. One of them walked right passed the table and lifted a pack of Haribos. Needless to say, I had not been provided with the security necessary to get the prize back. I knew I needed to wrap up proceedings pronto, and that meant getting rid of the final contestant as soon as humanly possible. It was the strange penguin-loving Welfare Rep.

I shot through the first questions at breakneck speed, not stopping for any small talk or jokes about how strange he was. He did request Josh's Special Clue on Question 5, and I gave him the correct answer in return for kissing the louder of the two Ents Reps, who had made it very clear over the last two terms that she detested him, for thirty long, sloppy seconds. He seemed very happy, she was not, and shone the desk lamp in my eye for the next ten minutes in a vicious act of revenge.

Anyway, despite this humourous interlude, the whole thing was still dying a slow and painful death. I needed to act fast. I decided to cheat.

"Question 10: Which of the following Cabinet positions did John Major hold immediately before becoming Prime Minister in 1990:
(a) Home Secretary
(b) Chancellor of the Exchequer
(c) Foreign Secretary
(d) Deputy Prime Minister"

Best case scenario was that the penguin-obsessed lad got the answer wrong, but even if he didn't, he was still going back to his seat after this question. He thought about it for a moment.

"I think I know this one," he said.

That won't help you, I thought

"I reckon the answer is (b) Chancellor of the Exchequer, because he took over straight after Nigel Lawson resigned."
He was right.
"Is that your final answer?" blah blah blah.
"Yes, Josh, (b) is my final answer."
"Well, I'm afraid the answer is... erm... (a)... yes (a) is the answer. Unlucky. Thanks for playing. Here are your prizes. Thanks everyone for coming. Well done, Sid, you win the champagne. Goodnight."

There were a few keen ones on the front row who were raising protests about that last answer, but I was already off back to my room, Aeros and Haribos in hand. I felt no guilt; it was for the greater good. I dumped the goodies, quickly got changed, and headed back to the bar to try and offer some kind of explanation to a no doubt bemused Andrew. On the way I looked at myself in the mirror and gave myself a cheeky wink and a smile. I had survived, and not completely died on my arse. I was feeling quite proud of myself.

To be honest, I hadn't really missed my friends from home too much in all the time I had been there. I was annoyed at myself for thinking it. It made me sound like a stereotypical Cambridge snob, who ditches the old friends he has grown up with for his culturally and intellectually superior new ones. But it wasn't like that at all. It was probably because I was too busy. Each week seemed to bring with it a new drama and a new set of essays, and there just wasn't any time to waste missing people. However, I found it was always so good to see them whenever I did. I wasn't one for drawing up fanciful analogies, but there was this one that I quite liked. University friends were like a meal cooked on full power in the microwave, whereas friends from home were the same meal but prepared in the oven, on the stove, and in various pots and pans (bear with me a minute). At the end of the day, you got the same meal, but the university one came quicker, and the home one often tasted nicer. You see, we were all flung together at uni, forced to share every waking minute in each other's company. Friendships were fired up a bit too quickly, the whole process was a bit too intense, there was no time for anything to mature, for anything to settle into place, for anything that went wrong to sort itself out. It wasn't the deepest thing in the world, and there were probably a thousand and one better ways of expressing the same simple point, but in my experience it certainly rung true. Maybe Mary Jane and I were a three-minute TV dinner gone wrong, maybe the right ingredients were never there in the first place, or maybe one can take a crappy analogy a bit too far.

As I'd hoped and expected, Andrew was happily chatting away to my friends in the bar when I re-entered, removed from my guise as the sexy game show host who got kissed on the cheek, and transformed back into plain old Josh. I winked at him and shook his hand.

"How's it going, matey?" I asked.

"Not too bad, not too bad. Shit, your hair's long."

"I know. Good journey down?"

"Long journey down."

"The bloody South is a long way away."

"Tell me about it. Hey, what they hell was all that about?" It didn't take eight years of friendship to know what he was referring to.

"All for a good cause, mate."

"It would have had to have been."

"Yeah, yeah, whatever."

"It's good to see you mate."

"Yeah, it's good to see you too."

I gave Andrew all the introductions, and he shook the hands and smiled at faces with names he would inevitably forget, as I had done not so long ago. I started him off on a conversation about football with Nick MacLean, whilst I went to the bar to get us some drinks.

I felt guilty that I had nothing planned for Andrew. I only found out he was coming a few days before he arrived, and indeed he was only down here at all because his parents were visiting someone in Cambridge and had offered him a lift. But Andrew was a low-maintenance kind of friend and I knew he would be happy doing anything. At home we tended to just watch TV with a few drinks instead of roaming the streets of Preston in desperate search of entertainment. I had warned him not to expect much, but I had not warned him about Kerplunk.

We left the bar as the porters flashed the lights and headed back to my room. Andrew was a little surprised to see the tribe of people following us, and more than a little surprised, when, in the confines of my room, they got out from the cupboard what looked like a kiddies board game.

"You ever played?" asked Nick.

Andrew smiled and did not know how to answer, probably assuming this was a big joke that he was at the centre of.

"They're serious, Andrew," explained Caolan, "the dicks waste their time playing this stupid game night after night. No wonder none of them have got a woman."

"You'll like it Andrew, trust me," I explained with a grin. "Have I ever let you down?"

"Don't get me started," my good friend of many years replied.

And so Andrew was both witness and participant to an evening of Kerplunking that lasted until one in the morning. It could have gone on for much longer, but I could see that Andrew was knackered after his long journey, and so I called proceedings to a halt. I was losing anyway. Andrew couldn't believe how seriously some people took it, especially Nick MacLean. I nodded in agreement, knowing full well I too was one of the main culprits.

I offered Andrew my bed, safe in the knowledge that that he would undoubtedly refuse. I took the cushions from mine and Mark's chairs, grabbed a spare duvet from Jude, and constructed for my friend a very comfy-looking bed upon my floor. We didn't chat for long, although Andrew did spent a good five minutes ranting and raving about how untidy my room was and how he would never have let it get into this state. Soon, like a large blanket falling from the sky, sleep was upon us.

Chapter 39

It was not easy being a northerner down in Cambridge. For one you had few northern allies, and any that you did have tended to be from the wrong side of the Pennines, and hence a tribe you did not really want to be associated with. Secondly, it was often hard to make yourself understood. I had lived all my life in Preston, only venturing out the odd time to go to school an hour away in Blackburn. We didn't mix with any southerners; we just watched them moan on *EastEnders*. We knew this one lad from Nottingham who talked a bit funny, and rightly got the piss ripped out of him for it, but that was about it. The rest of us all talked the same, and whilst the Burnley lot tended to say "fssst" instead of "first", and the Blackburnians had a tendency of calling "hair" "hurr", at least we knew what each other was talking about We were all reading from the same page.

That all changed when I went to uni. Suddenly I had a funny accent. Suddenly people would want me to say the most mundane things over and over again and be laughing their heads off as I spoke, and often, once their giggles had subsided saying things like: "You're putting that on, right?" Moreover, things I had taken for granted all my life were suddenly thrown into disarray. People had dinner at tea time and lunch at dinner time, and as for what afternoon tea was I had no clue. Girls wore pants instead of knickers and wore trousers instead of pants (the morning following a night when Mary Jane had got mud on her "trousers" having stumbled into a flower bed, I enquired over breakfast how her pants were doing and received a room full of strange looks). People didn't roll their Easter eggs down hills, or eat mushy peas from the chippy, or even parched peas on Bonfire Night. People had "barrths" instead of "baths", ate "parstar" instead of "pasta", and said "fire" and "poor" with only one syllable. At first my friends back home didn't believe me, and then they couldn't believe I had stuck it out for so long. "You poor bastard" they repeated sympathetically, and with emphasis on the "poo-wer" for my benefit.

At least Caolan and Oisin were different as well, but then they were foreigners. Instead of saying "What is his name?" the Irish pair would say "What do you call him?", which would often be met by a barrage of personal nicknames. Caolan also had a habit of saying "Yes" instead of "Hello". One time I was walking down Kings Parade with him and he yelled across the street to a girl from our college: "Yes Vicky". Vicky smiled and gave a confused wave back, and then went on her way no doubt wondering what question of hers the Irishman had just answered positively. Oisin had a whole repertoire of strange phrases. He said "Jeepers!" when he was surprised, "I don't have a baldy notion" when he didn't have a clue, "Take your oil" when somebody moaned about something, "You're an egit" whenever someone was being a dick, "fricking" whenever the other f-word was deemed inappropriate, and "or whatever" when a full-stop would have sufficed for most people.

There were also various "Cambridgeisms" that developed in our time there. People were "keen" for everything, and "massively keen" for some things, unless of course something was "rank", in which case people were not keen for it at all. The word "random" was used in the most unlikely ways. People had random days, were in random moods, had random supervisions, met random people, ate in random restaurants where they were, of course, served random food.

It was like the Tower of Babel, only the languages were biased southwards. My friends from home always said I sounded posher each time I came back up north for the holidays, but I was pretty sure that they were joking. I would have hated to lose my accent, and I consciously made an effort to keep it. I picked and chose the bits of people's dialects that I wanted to incorporate into my own, and pretty soon I was keen for the odd frickin random yes. However, I still had my tea when everyone else was having their dinner.

Chapter 40

If my home-grown buddy Andrew had thought that the previous night was a late one, he was in for a big surprise, for it was time to queue for tickets for Trinity College May Ball.

Cambridge is a place of extremes. The ultra-modern Law Faculty building stands in contrast to the fourteenth-century buildings of some colleges, the university is ahead of its time in its development of societies for all sorts of minorities and movements and yet only the privileged may walk on the grass, students spend nights out on the street to raise money for the homeless and then the following week enjoy a five-course lavish formal hall, and the intense build-up to exam periods leaves little time for anything else but work whereas in the week after exams there is no time for anything else but non-stop partying. For Cambridge was the home of May Week, and May Week was in June.

May Week was the thing that kept you going through the latter part of the third term, and it often helped you keep going during other terms. As first years we only had the tales of our seniors to go off, but they were enough. May Week was often talked about whenever the work load was heavy, regardless of the time of the year. It was portrayed as a kind of utopia, the Promised Land we may one day reach, and it certainly seemed a world way from the depressing reality of textbooks and libraries. We were told about lavish society gatherings, with each society trying desperately to better the others, about garden parties with delicious food and plenty of drink, starting before lunch time on gorgeous summer mornings and, above all, we were told about May Balls, and about one in particular.

May Balls were yet another of those Cambridge things that sounded ridiculous the first time you heard about them. You paid up to and above £80 for just one night's entertainment, and you often had to queue for hours on end just to have the privilege of handing over your money. But, once again, they turned out to be an amazing and unforgettable experience. Most colleges had their own May Balls. Some, like ours and Queen's, had theirs every two years, and others, such as Trinity and St. John's, had theirs every year. Other colleges, like New Hall and Trinity Hall, just had May Week Ents, which were like giant Bops. This latter group also contained the ever different King's College, whose principles would have been severely violated by playing host to anything as extravagant and traditional as a May Ball. Come on, they didn't even wear gowns.

It was common knowledge that the two best May Balls were those of Trinity and St. John's, and these were also the two most expensive. We asked around, and the general consensus seemed to be that if we were going to go for one of the Big Two, we might as well try for Trinity. There were various rumours about Trinity May Ball, neither confirmed nor denied by those who had attended in previous years. According to the *Guinness Book of Records* it was officially the second best party in the world lying just behind the Rio Carnival. Although the tickets cost around £90 each, each person was in fact subsidised to the tune of £1000, with the total budget for the one night being a hefty £2 million, thus making it something of a bargain. To put this figure in context, the budget for our little May Ball, which was having its year off that year, was around £60,000, the amount, in fact, that Trinity spent on security alone. With rumours like these, and the guarantee of big name acts, a spectacular firework display and free-flowing French champagne and caviar all night, the lure of Trinity May Ball was hard to resist.

The Ball itself was about three months away, and getting tickets was no easy task. They first went on sale to the students of Trinity College, with each person allowed to buy two each. Then, however many were left, and there were always a decent amount, were allocated on a first come first serve basis to the masses. These tickets went on sale at 9 am in one of the halls of Trinity, which meant starting queuing at about 8 pm the previous night.

A Tale of Friendship, Love and Economics

"Eight o'clock? No bloody way am I sitting in the freezing bloody cold for thirteen bloody hours."

"Well, I think we know how Faye feels. What about everyone else?"

We were sat in my room after lunch on the day of the queue. It was something of an emergency meeting as no-one had realised that tickets went on sale so soon. It was only because Caolan's girlfriend had told him about it that we had any clue at all.

"I know it would be shitty, but the Ball would be frickin' amazing. So if we are going to queue at all, we might as well start early and make sure we get the tickets, or whatever," said Oisin, after first clearing his throat.

"For once the shaggy-haired Irishman is right, and you never know, queuing might be fun," I offered. Mark Novak did not look convinced.

"We could get pissed. We could bring a bottle of vodka and some mixers," said our resident alcoholic, Francesca.

"We could buy a barbecue and cook loads of sausages and things," said Elizabeth, her posh voice becoming even higher and squeakier with excitement.

"Oooh, and some marshmallows, like we did in Brownies," Faye was quickly warming to the idea of queuing.

"We could bring Kerplunk," said Jude.

"Yeah, yeah, yeah," I said, sounding like a little kid whose just been told he can go to the zoo, "we should do this queuing thing more often, it sounds ace."

"Just remember, it will be very cold, and we will be out there for a long time."

"Piss off, Mark. We'll have vodka, a barbecue and Kerplunk. We'll be fine."

"I was just saying, that's all."

"Right, if everyone is in agreement, we will start queuing at 8 pm, so come to my room for 7.30 pm sharp. We'll sort out now who needs to get what."

I felt like an army commander preparing my troops for battle. I allocated jobs and delegated responsibility in such a way as to leave myself with nothing to do and so that I would be completely free from blame if all went wrong. Whenever anyone questioned my effort in this complex operation I explained confidently that I was supervising.

Andrew had sat quietly through the meeting, presumably not wanting to get in the way.

"Right mate, whilst they're all busy getting things ready, I'll take you on a quick tour of this strange city. Keen?"

"Sounds good to me. Hey, do you want me to come and queue all night as well?"

"Nah, mate. Just come down for the start, have a bit to drink and eat, and then you can go back to my room whenever you want. You can even have my bed. How does that sound?"

"It sounds like a plan."

"Hey, I'm sorry I've nothing big planned whilst you're here, it's just that I didn't realise tickets were going on sale and stuff, you know?"

"Don't worry about it mate, I'm having a good time."

And so, whilst Mark went to get a barbecue, Francesca to get vodka, Elizabeth to get sausages, Jude to get mixers, Faye to get marshmallows and Oisin to get all the things I had forgotten, like buns, plastic cups and matches, I took Andrew around all the colleges, filling in any gaps in my knowledge with made-up stories of ruthless kings, beautiful maidens and mad professors.

Mark, Caolan, Oisin and I took Andrew to our favourite eating establishment for the Last Supper before our all night pilgrimage along Trinity Lane. For the majority of term we had been going to Wetherspoons about three times a week. Because it was apparently the biggest pub in England, there were always plenty of seats, and because it was a Wetherspoons everything was always cheap. We always went there armed with the good intention of buying something healthy and nutritious off the menu, but in the end always opted for a round of Beer-Burger meals. Back in those golden days you could get a huge burger (the menu printed some favourable comparison to the size of a McDonald's burger under the heading of "Sorry Ronnie!"), complete with lettuce and tomato and thankfully no funny sauce, together with chips and onion rings and a pint of Fosters for just £2.99. For a limited time you could also upgrade to such delights as cheese and bacon for a mere 30p extra. It was too good a deal to resist, and we rarely did. Andrew bumped the order up to a round of five, and seemed suitably impressed. We bemoaned the fact that we didn't have one of these in Preston. With our bellies full, but with sufficient room for a few sausages and marshmallows of course, we felt well and truly ready for a night of queuing.

Faye, as usual, was running late, and I, as usual, was getting stressed. I undoubtedly inherited my obsession with time from my father – well, certainly not from Mum anyway. She hated getting anywhere early, and would even go as far as to lie to her darling, precious only son (i.e. me) about the time movies started, adding on a good fifteen minutes, so that I wouldn't be all worried and moany that we would be late. As I matured, I relaxed slightly, but apparently not by enough.

"Faye, any bloody chance?" I banged on her door.

"Keep you're bloody hair on, Josh. I'm coming, I'm coming," she squeaked from inside the safety of her room.

If Nick was here, he would have been doing the same. He got annoyed when people were late or if they were messing around. But Nick was back at home for his brother's birthday, and thus the position of Mr Unpopular was all mine.

"Look, Faye, if we miss out on a ticket by one place in the queue, you are dead."

"Alright, alright! I'm here, I'm bloody here! Jesus Christ."

"Good. Right, are we ready to go?"

"Please sir, can I go to the toilet?"

"You're a funny man, Jude, you really are."

And so, armed with sleeping bags, blankets, pillows, food, drink, a barbecue and a board game, we marched out of college, our body-heat sealed in at all angles by coats, trousers, gloves and hats. Not all of our gang were present. Caolan had ditched us in favour of queuing with his girlfriend and her mates, and Joe Porter had gone to a cocktail party that the new First Year Rep and love of his life Emma was also going to, explaining that he'd be along later. Mary Jane was queuing with her boyfriend and thus Faye could guiltlessly queue with us. Mary Jane and Gavin only wanted one double ticket and thus were doing shifts of which Gavin was signed up to do the first.

There were still a few doubters within the group, including myself I must admit, who thought that we were starting queuing far too early. All doubts were soon subsided when we set eyes on the queue. It was over twelve hours until tickets went on sale and it was a bitter cold night, and yet the queue of people was already about one hundred bodies long. They looked like a line of refugees, all huddled together shivering, some eating sandwiches, some drinking from steaming flasks of coffee. It was only the odd glimpse of a mini-disc player or the latest mobile phone that reminded me we were actually in affluent Cambridge. We swore as a group and scurried off to the back of the queue to secure our spot. The thought soon crossed my mind, as I'm sure it did everybody else's, that there was quite a good chance we would be queuing all night and in the end not get a ticket. I decided to keep this thought to myself to sustain morale.

We laid our blankets on the ground and our pillows against the stone wall of one of Trinity's buildings. We decided to make friends with the people in front of us as well as the people who soon joined the queue behind us, our logic being that we could strike a mutually beneficial deal that allowed toilet relief and subsequent re-entry to the queue for all concerned. There was a strong sense of comradeship between groups of queuers; after all we were all in the same freezing, all-night boat. We introduced ourselves and promptly signed the Toilet Agreement. The group in front was from Queen's College, and the group behind from Homerton. Having seen the steam and smelt the aroma being emitted from the Homerton lot we cursed the fact that we hadn't remembered to bring a flask of coffee, and I made it clear that, not wishing to place the blame upon anyone, it was definitely Oisin's fault. They were impressed by our supply of vodka, astounded by our barbecue and confused by Kerplunk. They seemed a nice bunch, and we swapped some of our crisps for some of their biscuits.

The first hour or so of the queue was really good fun. Oisin and I were kicking a football around with some of the Queen's lads, Francesca was tucking in to the vodka, and Mark had found someone to talk economics with. Then, in what seemed like the best thing in the world at the time, it started to snow. Everyone whooooed and cheered as the first flakes became visible in the golden glow of the street-lamp in much the same way as a football crowd cheers when the floodlights go out during an evening match. Underlying this reflex response was a slow realisation that no good could possibly come of this situation. Snow was cold and snow was wet, and we had to be outside in it all night. I pointed this out to Elizabeth.

"But it's so pretty," she replied.

I had brought along my camera and I decided to get a picture taken now whilst everything was all smiles in the snow. It came out like a Christmas card, and yes I suppose it did look pretty. I put the camera away and we arranged ourselves in the positions we were planning to sleep in. I strategically wedged myself in between Elizabeth and Francesca, my thinking being that it would be good to say in years to come that I went to bed with two pretty girls outside the great Trinity College, and if we needed to huddle together for warmth I would rather squeeze up close to them than to Mark and Oisin.

The snow became heavier and we became colder. Andrew asked if it was alright if he went back to my room. I asked him hopefully if he needed me to show him the way, but he said he would be fine, and set off on his journey back to the warmth, wishing us luck. Francesca's hand shivered as she poured herself another cup of vodka and she decided that it was now too cold to add any coke to it. Oisin, our resident barbecue expert, explained that we should wait for the blizzard to pass before firing her up, and unable to hold out any longer, Faye ripped open the packet of marshmallows and began munching them cold. I didn't even bother suggesting that we play Kerplunk. I looked at my watch. It was not even ten o'clock, meaning we still had eleven hours to go. After a while you could tell nobody really wanted to say anything to each other. It was too cold to be optimistic. I exchanged frozen smiles with Francesca and closed my eyes, hoping and praying that sleep would fall upon me.

I opened my eyes and looked at my watch knowing full well I had only had them shut for three minutes at most. I was so cold, and if someone had suggested there and then that we call it a night and go home, I would have been right behind them. Protecting the immediate future of my balls had to take priority over going to one. Again, I'm sure that others felt the same, but pride prevented any of us from being the first to speak. Then, after another twenty freezing minutes, we were joined in the queue by some familiar, and clearly drunken, faces.

"Hello, hello, what have we here then? Is that you Josh?"

It was probably a combination of his drunken, bleary eyes and my snowman appearance that caused Joe Porter to have doubts over my identity. He was dressed in a tuxedo, with the bow tie long gone, and the bottom half of his shirt fully escaped from the confines of his trousers. Joe was not alone. Among the group of about eight that was currently leaning dangerously over us was his beloved Emma and the not-so-beloved Adam "Sly" Sylvester. The latter was a pain in the arse at any time, but double trouble when he was drunk and I was freezing.

"Any chance we could squeeze ourselves in here?" asked Joe with a politeness that belied, but was also explained by, his present state. Francesca gave me a nudge in the ribs that was easily interpreted as: don't you bloody dare, we've been in the queue for two hours freezing our arses off whilst you lot have been getting smashed in the warmth, it is not fair on the people behind and it is certainly not fair on us. I gave her a resigned shrug of the shoulders. I knew she was absolutely right, but these people were my friends. More importantly, they were so off their faces that all reason and compassion had deserted them. They only had one thought, and to refuse them would have probably led to more trouble than it was worth, especially with the unpredictable Sly around.

"Look, Joe", I decided to direct all correspondence through him, "I don't think it's really fair, but I won't stop you. If you get chucked out, then don't blame me, and don't you dare get us chucked out as well."

"You're a gent, Josh Bailey, a real gent." Yes, he was definitely pissed.

And so, with all the elegance of a herd of elephants, Joe, Emma, Sly and the rest of the drunken amigos fell into the queue. I turned away so as to avoid the glares from the group behind, our former allies, who not so long ago had signed the Toilet Agreement and had welcomed the free trade of biscuits and crisps.

We were soon also joined in the queue by another couple of familiar faces; The Girl Whose Room We Used To Hang Out In Who Didn't Really Like Me, and would you believe it, the Stalking Philosophising Preaching Prophet from Bradford. Yes, the Great One seemed more than happy to sidestep any ethical or moral considerations concerning pushing-in in a queue, and sat himself down happily in hypocritical bliss. Even one of his biggest admirers, Mr Oisin Kerrigan, looked on with disgust. The Great One just grinned smugly and made some smart-arsed comment that was thankfully smothered by the unrelenting snow.

The minutes seemed to pass even slower now that our group had multiplied. I just couldn't relax. Adam Sylvester was on the phone to his rugby mates inviting them along to join the queue, Emma had fallen asleep with her leg dangling in the road only to have a car miss it by a matter of centimetres, Joe had turned from polite drunk to aggressive drunk and was now referring to me solely by the title of Northern Monkey, the group behind were making their objections known to a frightened Mark Novak, and Elizabeth was demanding more than her fair share of our blanket. I was cold, hungry, tired and in a bad mood. I prayed for a miracle, and for once it came.

There was a ruffling and shuffling in the queue ahead of us. A few people began getting to their feet, and a wave of Chinese Whispers made its way slowly backwards. Oisin went to the head of our group to try and get a grasp of what was going on – perhaps not the best man for that particular task, but the only one of us who was prepared to move. The smile on his face seemed to lift the temperature a couple of degrees. It turned out that the local police had informed the powers that be in the Trinity May Ball Committee that the present conditions were not safe (i.e. too bloody cold) to have people staying out on the streets. Hence, the Committee decided to come around and issue us with raffle tickets in the order of our positions, and told us come back at 9 am in the morning. There was a bit of pushing and shoving as the ticket allocator approached, a small lad with a gap between his two front teeth, but we managed to hold our ground and secured a batch of tickets in the mid-nineties. Joe and his gang had the good grace to allow those of us that had queued the longest to get the first tickets. And as quick as that, before the hour of eleven was upon us, we were off on our way home, smiles slowly replacing shivers, and still laden with an unlit barbecue, a bag full of cold meat, and an unused board game.

Faye asked the obvious question of why the bloody idiots couldn't have just issued us with the bloody raffle tickets as soon as we bloody well got there and cut out all that bloody pointless queuing (she wasn't in the best of moods). This was a job for the economists. In a convoluted way that we put down to tiredness, Mark and I tried to explain. Indeed, we began, queuing did appear to be an inefficient way of allocating the Trinity May Ball tickets. Having secured our position in the queue we were certainly then all wasting our time waiting for the clock to tick around to nine in the morning, in much the same way that passengers waste their time standing in line to board an aeroplane long before the gates will be open. However, it was the best way and the only way for two reasons. Firstly, it led to an efficient allocation of resources, because those who wanted the tickets the most were given the opportunity to ensure they got them by queuing earlier than anyone else. People were able to show how highly they valued a ticket by the amount of hours they were prepared to put in queuing, thus meaning that a person who valued a ticket at two hours queuing time was less likely to get a ticket than someone who valued it at fourteen hours, and this is the way things should be. Such a system was generally regarded as a much fairer way than allowing the price of a ticket to fluctuate so that those who valued the ticket the most would be forced to pay however many hundreds of pounds to secure it. Secondly, if it were to be known that raffle tickets were to be issued as soon as the queue reached a certain number, then a kind of time inflation would occur. People would readjust the time that tickets effectively went on sale from 9 amto 11 pm, or whatever, and simply start queuing twelve hours before this new time. The Committee could play this trick one year, claiming tickets were going on sale in the morning, and then issuing raffle tickets as soon as the queue reached the number of tickets available, thus ensuring that the people who valued the tickets most got them, and at the same time cutting out the bloody pointless queuing referred to by Faye. However, in subsequent years their stated time that tickets went on sale would no longer be credible, and people would simply queue earlier and earlier. No, we were all convinced, well at least Mark and I were, that as stupid as it seemed, queuing overnight was indeed the best way to allocate tickets for Trinity May Ball. Our explanation took us all the way back to college, by which time Faye and everyone else had long since stopped listening. Nobody ever listens to economists.

I had given Andrew my key as I was not intending to be back that night, and to my horror my fellow Prestonian had locked my door. I didn't really want to wake up the poor lad, even though it was technically his fault, and so I asked if I could kip on someone's floor. Elizabeth, clearly having enjoyed the experience of snuggling up to me under a blanket in the snow, was the first to offer. She even said that I could have her bed as she often enjoyed sleeping on the floor. I didn't know if she was just being nice or if she was actually a bit mental, but I was soon too warm and comfy to care. I said a quick prayer of thanks that I was not still out there in the cold, then an extended prayer of thanks that I was not a homeless person, and then I fell into one of the best sleeps of my life.

Being a rower, Elizabeth was good at getting up in the mornings. Being a lazy male teenager, I wasn't. Her annoying mobile phone alarm penetrated my dream about swimming with a dolphin that could talk and had yellow ears at about ten to eight, and before I had even contemplated opening my weary eyes, Elizabeth was bouncing up and down, opening curtains and turning lights on, and generally flying round the room like a demented dog.

"Bloody hell," I groaned.

"Bloody hell, what?" she replied, as squeaky posh as ever.

"Bloody hell, nothing. I always swear first thing in the morning. It's my way of welcoming in the day."

Elizabeth looked confused and decided to ignore my comment.

"Come on, come on, get up, get up, we've got to get these tickets."

"Yeah, yeah, five more minutes, just give me five more min…" I fell asleep before finishing the sentence, only to be rudely awakened by a fierce blow to my nose from a pink pillow.

"Get up now, alright?"

Due to the pitch of her voice, it was hard to take Elizabeth seriously when she was angry. Her voice just got higher and higher, until it turned into an inaudible squeal. I started to laugh, mulling over in my mind potential jokes about shattering the window or calling all the local cats, but then she threw me a look that made me think it was best to keep these ones to myself.

"Yes, sir, Elizabeth, sir." I saluted and rolled out of bed like a subdued fish being rolled back into the sea.

Remarkably, by eight o'clock, the gang, including Faye, was all present and correct, armed, on this occasion, with only a cheque book and a precious green raffle ticket. It was a chilly morning, and the ground was damp and littered with puddles where a pure white carpet had lay not so long ago. When we reached the street that had become all too familiar the previous night we were told by a bespectacled official sporting an orange band over his slung shoulder and resting diagonally across his body to join the queue in the order of our tickets. We guiltily greeted the group behind us, who had lost a good few places because of our extended group. The culprits soon turned up, looking deservedly pale-faced and ill. The Great One was there also, dressed in a coat that someone had obviously told him looked cool.

At nine o'clock, as promised, the doors opened and the queue began to steadily trickle through. By about half-past we had reached the front, where we were handed a biro and told to fill out the form and to paperclip a cheque to it. On the form we filled in our name and college, and then placed a tick by the type of ticket we wanted, either dining or non-dining.

The dining option meant you got a fancy seven-course meal before hand, but were still let into the main part of the Ball at the same time as the non-diners, thus ensuring you didn't miss anything. The dining was £30 extra per person, thus bringing the price of a double ticket up to a scary £246. Seeing as it was free food and drink when we got in, well not technically free I suppose, but you know what I mean, and seeing as I would probably end up eating seven courses of bread rolls, we unanimously opted to bin the dining option, and wrote out a batch of cheques for £186. We were told that if the money was taken out of our bank accounts within the next two weeks, then we had got the tickets. We asked if there was any details of who the Big Name acts were, but we were told by a stone-faced lad that that was a secret to be revealed a couple of weeks before the Ball. We took a photo outside on some of the college's steps to mark the occasion, smiling and waving our receipts around proudly. We went back to college and cooked up a big fried breakfast using all the left-over food from the aborted barbecue, and stealing a tin of baked beans from an unseen guy who marked his possessions as "Kip".

Over a tasty and much-needed breakfast, for which Andrew joined us, we discussed exactly what we were going to do with our tickets. Everyone who was queuing in our group had bought a double ticket. We were told by everyone we asked that this was not a risky policy at all, because you could easily flog the other half of your ticket in the weeks leading up to the Ball for at least double the price, such was the demand for this extravagant event. Ideally, however, we wanted as many of our friends to be there as possible. People started deciding who to give their other half to. Mine was easy; I had promised it to Nick as he couldn't be there to queue, having gone home for his brother's birthday. In return, Nick had promised to queue for me next year. Faye was giving hers to Duane, and Elizabeth had a friend from home coming up for the Ball. Nobody else was really sure. It was kind of tricky, because as much as you wanted your friends to come, you couldn't help thinking that they had as much opportunity to queue as you did, so why should you now give them half of your ticket when you could easily sell it for twice as much as it was worth to a desperate stranger, thus ultimately end up going to the Ball for free. Whilst considering this tricky conundrum, Oisin also raised the valid point that if only half of us got tickets, then it was only fair that they gave their half to the others that queued, or whatever. Everybody agreed that this was fair enough, and I gladly ate the half sausage that Elizabeth couldn't.

Andrew went home later that day, after insisting that I tidy up my room a bit before I showed it to his parents who were coming to pick him up. He said he had had a really good time, and though I failed to see how he could have had, and felt more than a little guilty for it, I believed him.

There was one final twist left in the Trinity May Ball Saga. Two weeks after we had queued, the money still had not been taken out of any of our bank accounts. It was a strange feeling going to the cash point each day and praying that your balance had suddenly dropped overnight by just under two hundred pounds. To make matters worse, Caolan, who was about forty places ahead of us in the queue, had had money taken from his. After another week of selecting the "balance enquiry" button, and coming away with a frown, we started to resign ourselves to the fact that we weren't going to Trinity May Ball after all. Then, in what was almost a second miracle, everyone got a phone call. I got mine at half-time in a 2nd XI football game that we were already losing 6–2, Jude got his in a history supervision having forgotten to turn off his phone, and Oisin got his whilst he was taking a wee break from work. A well-spoken lady on the other end of the line explained to us that we had missed out on non-dining tickets, but we could have dining ones if we wanted. Whether it was great minds thinking alike or fools seldom differing, we all reasoned that an extra £30 was not too much to pay to go to an evening that was universally regarded as unmissable. Having had our assumption that having queued we would simply be assured of tickets refuted in the last week, it had made us all realise just how much we really wanted to go to the Ball, and thus, after only a moment's thought, we all said yes. All apart from Faye, that is. I don't know whether it was just an inherent Scottish reflex action, passed down and strengthened from generation to generation, or just Faye being Faye, but when my neighbour was asked for even more money on top of the fortune she was already expected to dish out, no bloody way did she reply. Of course, when she found out we were all going, she regretted her decision terribly, and more than a few tears were shed. Luckily, Oisin and Mark had not promised their tickets to anyone, and thus Faye and Duane were able to go after all.

So, we all had tickets to the second best party in the world, a bargain at £123 each. Oisin didn't spend a penny for a week afterwards, drinking only water and eating only stale bread, and Faye had to be resuscitated several times when the harsh reality of her bank statement came through. But everyone was excited, and it remained a hot topic of conversation for weeks to come. Now all we had to do was earn the right to go by working hard next term and surviving the exams.

Chapter 41

Whenever my Mum, or my friends, or anyone else asked me what I had been up to at uni in any particular week, I would try to keep my tales as interesting as possible, focusing on nights out, or birthdays, or the many soap opera-style dramas that were forever unfolding. The problem was that this gave the impression that we did no work, and it was all one big party. This was by no means the case. It was just that a story about going to three boring lectures, then spending five painful hours in the library reading and making notes about trade unions, and then maybe going absolutely crazy and having a cup of tea *and* a biscuit, was not something that made the greatest of stories and was, in fact, something that I would rather forget. Cambridge was an amazing place, and I had the best of times there, but there was no escaping the fact that it was, as it should have been, very hard work.

But it was not all doom and gloom. Lectures during the second term had become particularly boring, mainly given by young American lecturers who recited from textbooks we had already read and then gave us out hand-outs that reproduced the same information yet again. Whenever we did bother going to these lectures – and I'm talking about myself, Caolan and Oisin, here as Mark *always* went to lectures – we did our best to entertain ourselves.

I rarely got into trouble at school, but whenever I did it was always for talking and laughing at the wrong times. I had a habit of not being able to stay quiet for too long, undoubtedly inherited from my mother. Whenever I knew I wasn't allowed to speak, talking was all I wanted to do, and whenever I knew I couldn't laugh, I exploded into fits of giggles. Whether it was in class, or assembly, or the library, or church, if I was sat next to one of my friends, after trying to concentrate for a few minutes we would soon be talking and giggling away to ourselves, and the quieter we tried to keep it, the louder and more noticeable it got. Whilst boys were sitting in Thursday night detention for throwing stones at teachers, I was there for laughing at a really bad joke about a killer potato.

In Caolan I had found a kindred spirit, and at that time I thought it was just about all we had in common. We would sit together every lecture and laugh at the most stupid things, the kind where you had to be there and even then you probably wouldn't have found it funny. We went bright red and hid behind the desk giggling uncontrollably whenever the our Nobel Prize-winning lecturer said a word that sounded remotely like the male sexual organ, and nearly died when we discovered to our horror that the quiet girl who always sat in front of us seemed to be keen on wearing a purple thong on Wednesdays. Oisin and Mark wouldn't join in. Mark was there to listen and learn, but never got mad at us for acting like fools. Oisin, on the other hand, pretended he was trying to follow the lecture, but it was very clear that he wanted to join in with us. The shaggy-haired Irishman would tell us to behave ourselves and stop acting like a pair of frickin' egits whenever he caught us laughing at something he didn't get. This, of course, made us laugh more. The economists from other colleges must have thought we were very strange, but we didn't care as we rarely talked to them anyway.

It was strange how we didn't mingle with the other economists. It was probably because the Catz economists were such a large bunch relative to other colleges – there were eleven of us in total – and thus we tended to just sit together, self-sufficient in each other's company, probably intimidating any would-be acquaintances. Seeing as we didn't talk to them, and we needed things to talk about in the lectures, Caolan and I started trying to guess what they were like, inventing stories about their past and speculating what they had gotten up to the previous night. We identified people who looked like nobs, and talked about them like we'd known them all our lives. Soon, seeing as we didn't even know their names, we christened them with names of our own creation (I was pleased I was finally growing up). There were two stunningly attractive girls, one brunette and one blonde, and observing them took up most of our time in lectures when we were not laughing, talking, thinking up with nicknames, or copying down from Mark the key point that we had just missed. We cleverly christened the brunette "The Egg" as her surname was "Easter" and the blonde "The Russian" as she was Russian. "Terminator" was the name bestowed upon a mean-looking Eastern European girl who asked too many clever questions and was never satisfied with the answers, "Street Fighter" was a girl who looked like a character from the popular computer game of the same name; "Stare" was a lad who had a tendency to stare at us; "Westbrook" was a girl who looked a tiny bit like Daniela Westbrook if you squinted and the room was poorly lit; "Deep Throat" was a girl with a deep voice; and "Cock Head" was someone we didn't like. In years to come there would be more, until eventually we had put names to the faces of nearly all our fellow economists. Whenever some of our lot eventually started to mingle with them, we found their real-life names just didn't seem to fit, and were only used in times of absolute necessity.

It was less easy to have fun in supervisions than in lectures as you were now one of four in a room instead of one in over a hundred, and giving nicknames to people you knew well wasn't half as much fun. We still had mostly the same supervisors from the previous term, and not a lot had changed. Our Director of Studies, Mr Stevens, was still our Macro supervisor, and Mark still gave me the answers to the questions he hadn't asked yet. Mr Stevens also continued the habit of telling us the same stories over and over again, each time with fresh enthusiasm. This term's best-seller was undoubtedly his one about the Japanese manufacturing industry; a tale that he managed to link into everything from business cycles to unemployment, and from trade to growth. It went something like this.

"Let me tell you a little story about the Japanese manufacturing industry that is quite relevant to what we are doing at the moment." At this point, having heard the story 300 times, knowing looks were exchanged around the room. "An American company decided to import ball-bearings from a Japanese manufacturing company, and told them they would accept an absolute maximum of five bad ball-bearings in each batch of a thousand. That's just *five* bad ones in a thousand, right? And do you know what the Japanese company replied? The Japanese company replied: "Would you like the bad ones packaged separately, sir?" he paused for laughter, and then continued "And it's stories like that that show just how efficient the Japanese manufacturing sector is, and that's exactly why I advised the college to invest in it a few years back." Mr Stevens thought a solid manufacturing sector was the key to every economy, and thought that the ability to produce things such as perfect batches of ball-bearings would drag Japan out of its slump. Thankfully the college did not take Mr Stevens' advice, and

Japan's economy, manufacturing sector and all, plummeted into deeper recession.

Our Micro supervisor was still loud, intense and prone to saying Cowabunga, and his supervisions continued to be both the most rewarding and the most terrifying. Our Statistics supervisions were still short and overcrowded, and Caolan and I, as well as Oisin who tried to do it without us knowing, were still copying Mark religiously. One difference was we now also had extra Statistics supervisions given by the Dean and Leader of the Land Economists, the Brummie Dr Tinsley. These supervisions were designed to prepare us for the Stats project we were due to receive at the start of next term. However, after a couple of supervisions, it became apparent that the main advice Dr Tinsley had to give was to choose the right font. In his comical accent he would enthusiastically drum into us: "Yeah, yeah, it's all about the package, get yourselves a nice font, yeah, a really, really nice font, and you'll be fine, yeah." Bloody Land Economists. Our Politics supervisions were still more about our supervisor's mother-in-law and his household appliances than the course. Our History supervisions still took place in a boudoir, and our supervisor, who lived on top of the hill, continued to wear short skirts. In one of these History supervisions, Caolan was handed back his marked essay, and after perusing it for a while, asked the supervisor what the comment on the top said.

"It says, 'excellent essay', Caolan," she replied in front of everyone. We never let the smug Irishman live that one down.

Chapter 42

There was still enough time left in that second term for a few final romantic twists and turns within our group. Indeed, I think everyone apart from Joe and Mark were involved. Joe was still pining over his beloved Emma, and Mark had no time for girls unless they came with a free subscription to the Economic Journal. Maybe they should have got together.

First up was young Nicholas MacLean. Nick had rarely shown any interest in women, thus partly explaining the question marks often raised over his sexuality. Whilst Caolan, Jude, Joe and I would act like good old Neanderthal men at the sight of a leggy blonde in a short skirt, Nick would remain silent, often sporting a little embarrassed grin. However, it turned out that he did indeed like someone of the opposite sex, and it was a someone that I knew all too well. I confronted him one drunken night in the bar. It was a freezing cold Wednesday night, and we were desperately trying to get ourselves drunk enough to take on Life, knowing full well that the queue would be massive, and its survival would require a beer jacket at least seven pints thick. I had no grounds for thinking Nick might fancy someone, I was just making drunken conversation.

"So, Macca, who's the special lady in your life then?" I put my arm around him, as if trying to emulate all the features of a stereotypical male drunk in deep conversation.

"I don't have one."

"Course you do."

"I bloody don't, alright?"

"Me thinks the Macca doth protest too much?"

"Is that line from the tenth or eleventh Shakespearean play you went to see?" I let him have that one.

"Come on mate, you can tell me."

Nick hesitated long enough for me to conclude that my perseverance would eventually be duly rewarded.

"Come on."

"No."

"Come on."

"No."

"Come on."

"You are a dick, you know?"

"I'm only trying to help. Talking about this kind of stuff helps, you know."

"You just want something to gossip about."

I tried to look hurt, and Nick must have been really drunk as it worked.

"Alright, alright, I'll tell you. But if you tell anyone else then I'll tell the football lot about a certain poet in the ranks."

I tried to look indifferent, but did a poor job. How the hell did he know about that?

"Cross my heart, and all that."

"Okay," Nick took a long sip of his pint and had a quick look around to make sure nobody else could hear anything, "I do kind of like a girl."

A Tale of Friendship, Love and Economics

"Who, who?"

"Calm down, will you?" He leant in closer, and for a minute I thought he was going to try and slap the lips on me. He whispered her name into my ear.

Bloody hell, I thought.

"Bloody hell."

"What do you think?"

"Erm... well, it's a good choice, I suppose. You know, I used to fancy her myself."

"I know."

"You do?"

"Josh, you're not exactly the best in the world at covering up that you like someone."

"Oh."

I thought I was.

Anyway, it turned out that Nick MacLean had gone and fallen for the Movie Star Look-alike, although he didn't think she looked at all like Kirsten Dunst. Now I thought about it, I had noticed him flirting a bit with her during the Kerplunk World Championships, but I had been too busy with marbles and plastic sticks to think any more about it. The only other person who knew about it was fellow geographer Joe Porter, and he had advised the same thing as me.

"It's the best way."

"What about a poem? I hear that's a sure fire success," I decided to let him off for a second time, but then that was it. "I know, you're right, and I will ask her out, just not tonight."

"Why not? You're pissed and she is. Perfect."

"Maybe, maybe."

In the end, and somewhat against the nature of the shy Nick MacLean, he did indeed ask out the Movie Star Look-alike that very night. He went and sat down next to her in the bar, as Joe and I looked on knowingly and Caolan thought we were staring at her breasts.

"Aye, not bad, but I prefer them a bit firmer, you know?"

After ten minutes or so, Nick came back not looking too happy, and in the privacy of the men's toilets he told me and Joe what she had said.

"Yeah, she just wants to be friends for now, but then maybe more next term. She's still trying to get over her boyfriend. You know what girls are like?"
"But you're okay, yeah?"
"Oh, yeah. Like she said, next term."
Predictably, next term came along and the Movie Star Look-alike got herself a new boyfriend who was not Nick. Indeed it was none other than the Enforcer from the football club. Each football social from then on I prayed that Nick wouldn't get fined for asking out the Enforcer's girlfriend, but thankfully it seemed that some areas were off limits.

Jude had better luck, at least for a while. I often doubted that men and women could be close friends and nothing more. In my experience, at least one of the parties usually had far stronger feelings, often unrequited and hidden down below, resulting in a somewhat unstable friendship that was just waiting to explode. In the case of Jude and Elizabeth, I was pretty sure that the feelings were mutual. Not wishing to sound like a corny old romantic, but it was the way they acted around each other, the way his eyes followed her as she left the room and she maintained eye-contact long before his point was over. Jude seemed like a man who wouldn't mind talking about this kind of stuff, so over a late night bowl of cereals sat on the steps outside my room, using the elusive Kip's milk, I brought the matter to attention.

"Jude?"
"Josh?" He replied, mimicking the whiney way I had said it.
"Look, I'm just going to come out and say it."
"You're gay?"
"Of course I am, but time for some new news. Look mate, do you fancy Elizabeth?"
"You know what, Josh my old matey, I think I do."
That was easier than I expected.
"And does she know?"
"Don't think so."
"And do you think she feels the same way?"
"I don't know." He paused for reflection and had a spoonful of cereals. "Sometimes I think she must, and then others I just think she is being a close friend. Who knows with women?"
"Tell me about it. For what it's worth, I reckon she fancies you."

A Tale of Friendship, Love and Economics

"Yeah?"

"Aye, course she does." I was falling behind on cereal consumption so paused to consume three spoonfuls of soggy, sugarless Weetabix. "Look, mate, feel free to say no, but I could try and find out if you want me to?"

"And how would you do that?"

"I'd be as subtle as ever and just slip it into the conversation. Whatever she says I'll promise her that I won't say anything to you, but I'll cross my fingers behind my back, and text you as soon as I know. She need never know you've said anything to me. What do you reckon?"

"You wouldn't mind?"

"Jude, are you kidding? I love all this teen drama stuff. It's like living in bloody *Dawson's Creek*."

"Only the girls here are not as fit."

"I know. Anyway, so should I do it?"

"Why not? Cheers, mate."

And so, officially hired as the M-block cupid, I waited patiently for the opportunity to strike. After a late-night game of Kerplunk in which I again amassed more points than anybody else on the night by insisting on playing every game, I asked Elizabeth if she would stay behind for a moment. She looked worried but agreed. When everyone else had retired to their humble abodes, armed not with a bow and arrow but with a cup of tea and a custard cream, I began trying that "subtle" thing that I had never been too good at.

"So, Elizabeth…"

"So, Josh?"

Good start.

"Erm… erm… how's it going, yes, how's it going?"

"Very good, thank you."

"Good, good, that is good."

I took a sip of my tea and thought about my next brilliant line.

"Good, good, that is good."

"Josh, what's up?"

"Bloody hell, Elizabeth, I'm shit at this. Look, do you fancy anyone at the moment?"

"Look, Josh, you're a lovely guy, you really are, but…"

"Not me you nob, although I didn't like where that 'but' was heading to. I'm talking about Jude. Do you fancy Jude?"

Elizabeth didn't speak for a moment and looked into her cup of tea. You could see the thin wisp of steam get drawn up her nostrils every time she breathed in.

"We're just friends. Just friends."

"I know you are now, but wouldn't you like it to be more?" She didn't answer, so I added, "He's not a bad catch, you know?"

"I know. He's a great guy, and he's good-looking, and I do fancy him" a pause signalled yet another "but" lurking just around the corner, "but he's also my best friend. Going out might mess everything up, you know, and I couldn't imagine losing him as a friend."

I knew she was right, even though those two not going out seemed so wrong.

"Look, Lizzy," that was the first time I had tried to shorten her name and I wasn't sure if I liked it, "the bottom line is you have not ruled out going out with Jude, have you?"

"Well... no, I don't suppose I've ruled it out as such."

"So" I paused for effect, "if he were, hypothetically speaking of course, to ask you out, you wouldn't necessarily say no." Again, this was more of a statement than a question. Elizabeth thought about it for a while.

"No, I suppose I wouldn't, hypothetically speaking."

"Good."

I spent the next ten minutes trying to explain why people from Lancashire hated the Yorkshires so much, and why them lot from over the hills did not technically win the War of the Roses, and then we went to bed.

As promised, I told Jude what Elizabeth had said, and he seemed quite pleased. Jude wasn't like most lads our age. He was thoughtful, sensitive and there was far more too him than met the eye. He understood Elizabeth's point about not losing their friendship, because he was worried about it too. In the end he plucked up courage to call around to her room and talk to her about it one night whilst the rest of us were dancing to Duran Duran in Cindies. The next day they were officially going out together, and everyone agreed that it was a perfect match. Within two weeks it was all over, with Elizabeth ending it.

Jude was devastated. He thought everything was going along fine, but evidently she didn't agree. Elizabeth explained that something just didn't feel right, and that they were better off just staying friends. After she had told him it was over, Elizabeth assumed that they could simply go back to

A Tale of Friendship, Love and Economics

how they were before, reasoning that a few kisses weren't going to change anything. The naïvety and stupidity of intelligent people has always amazed me. Jude dug out an old *I've Just Been Dumped* compilation tape that we were now obliged to take to the gym as the soundtrack to our work-out in place of the previous *Rocky* number. *All By Myself* didn't exactly give you the push you needed to get that final weight up and down on the bench-press, in fact it was more likely to make you wish the bar would fall on your windpipe and put you out of your misery. After a few days of being really upset and not wanting to talk about it, he decided the best course of therapy was to slag off Elizabeth at every possible opportunity, whenever she was not present, of course. I had grown so used to Jude's rants and raves that I had to be careful not to call her "the Bitch" whenever she came around for tea. Thankfully their friendship proved strong enough to recover, but never reached the point along the road that it once had been. By the end of second term Elizabeth had a new boyfriend, which was a surprise to everyone, and temporarily sent Jude into relapse. Her new man was a really nice lad from Churchill College, but for the first week or so of their relationship he was simply known as "The Cock". To make matters worse, and in what was now getting way beyond the joke, Jude and Elizabeth were yet another mismatched pairing who had signed up to live in a flat together in Chads next year.

Perhaps the biggest surprise of all was the next entrant into the Love Game, a certain shaggy-haired Irishman from the 1970s, with a laugh like a drill and a name from another planet, Mr Oisin Kerrigan. Now a lot of girls liked Oisin, but often more in the way that they liked cute little puppies than the way they liked Brad Pitt, wishing to sleep with the latter and ruffle the hair and tickle under the chin of the former. Oisin was widely regarded, and quite rightly, as the Nicest Guy Ever. He was always smiling, always ready to listen if you needed to talk, and would never say anything bad about anyone, even when the rest of us were. The problem was that nice girls don't fall for nice guys, and whilst few could resist the charm of the Irishman with the funny name, the fact that he had long hair with cute wings at the side, dressed like he was from another decade, and spoke in a language that nobody understood, made him seem like some kind of full-size novelty doll; something to sit on a chair and play with when you got bored. Oisin didn't seem to mind all this, however. He liked being liked, but was at Cambridge to work, and with his tendencies for taking wee breaks all the time, he had enough trouble fitting that in without the added time-sapping complication of a high-maintenance woman to contend with.

All that seemed to change, however, with the persistence of the louder of the two Weird Ents Reps. She was a lovely girl, but not Oisin's type at all. She was loud, crude and often completely smashed. Whilst Oisin was staying up into the early hours trying to finish off an essay after taking a few too many wee breaks during the day, she was busy getting drunk, going out and adding to the list of men she had pulled in college – and there were quite a few. More than this, however, was the fact that she had a tendency to get obsessed with people. In the two terms so far she had already been obsessed with Jude, the female actress who she had a shrine for and even little old me (completely understandable, of course). The thing about these obsessions was that they lasted for about a week, and then her attention was abruptly shifted onto someone else. At this particular time, as second term was rapidly drawing to a close, the strange, loud girl decided she was obsessed with the shaggy-haired Irishman. Now, Oisin was all too aware of her obsession-soaked history, the quantities of alien saliva that had entered her mouth, and his own good Catholic background, but he got on really well with her, and seemed to be enjoying the attention, simply waiting for the moment to pass. The moment didn't pass, however, and next thing we all knew, they had agreed to start going out in May Week. From what I could gather, she wanted to start the relationship there and then, but the ever sensible Derry Man had somehow managed to defer the arrangement until the end of next term, explaining as clearly as his accent allowed him, "I'm here to work, or whatever, and not to mess about with girls," whenever anyone asked.

We were all a bit confused with the whole situation.

"So, let me get this straight. You fancy her, yeah?"

"Aye."

"And she fancies you, yeah?"

"I hope so."

"But you don't want to go out with her yet. Properly, I mean."

"No."

A Tale of Friendship, Love and Economics

"So why don't you just pull her every now and again?"

"Or give her the odd ride." That was Caolan's contribution.

"I don't have the time. I'm here to work, or whatever."

"Change the bloody record. Anyway, how long do you usually spend pulling someone? Surely you can fit it in."

"It's not that, it's just... well, it might get out of hand, you know? You know what girls are like, especially her. I just think it's best to stay friends, and then if we still feel the same way in a couple of months, then we'll start going out."

"Or whatever?"

"Aye, or whatever."

Doubts were raised as to the stability of the moral high ground that the Irishman had placed himself on, however, when Caolan, bursting into his room without knocking in desperate need of a calculator, inadvertently caught Oisin and the loud lady messing about in the shaggy-haired one's cupboard.

"Erm... jeepers... erm... I was just... erm... she wanted to borrow a tie, and I was just getting one for her, or whatever."

Knowing Oisin, he probably was.

Caolan was having romantic problems of his own. His relationship with the pretty second year geographer had ended. Caolan did not talk about it to anyone, such was his nature and such was the way he expected everyone else to be. All we knew was that it had ended on good terms, and the two were still very good friends. Caolan didn't seem too upset about the whole thing, but then again he never really seemed to be too upset about anything. It did not take long, however, for the Ronan Keating-loving boy-band look-alike to get himself mixed up with another *femme fatale*.

Before Caolan met her, we all knew New Hall as the all girls' college on top of the hill where we had our History supervisions once a fortnight with the lady who liked to wear short skirts and put "excellent work, well done" on Caolan's essays. After he met her, the phrase "New Hall" would strike fear into the bones of all of us, for this was the start of the Catz-New Hall Bond, a bond that we were all involved in some way or another over the three years, and a bond that brought drama, misery, but above all, hours of laughter.

There are two all-girl's colleges in Cambridge; Newnham is one, and New Hall is the other (there is also Lucy Cavendish College, but this is a bit of a funny case as it only admits "mature" undergraduates over the age of twenty-five). In 1948 – a dark year in the eyes of many of Cambridge's old guard-women were permitted to be full members of the university. Women had been allowed to sit university examinations since 1881, and indeed a woman even gained the top in mathematics in 1890 leading to frantic re-checking and re-marking, but they were not awarded proper degrees like their male counterparts until 1948. With Newnham already up and running, and Girton College originally designed for women, the imaginatively named Association to Promote a Third Foundation for Women in Cambridge was formed in 1952 to investigate the possibility of founding a new college for women. By 1954 the Association had raised enough funds (£25,000) to get cracking, and after a ballot they came up with the name New Hall – it seemed that naming things was not this group's speciality. The college officially opened its doors in October of that year, with just sixteen undergraduates and two Fellows. Since then, the college has expanded in both numbers and grounds, and it is now hard to imagine the university, for better or worse, without New Hall as a part of it. I wonder if the Association had any idea just what they were about to unleash onto the world.

It all started one Tuesday evening in the nightclub Cindies. It was a night like any other; we were all drunk apart from Oisin, I was trying to avoid Mary Jane, Joe was complaining about the music and looking for 1st XI footballers to talk to, Mark had fallen into his floppy pissed state, and a huge Catz Circle had formed in the middle of the dance floor into the centre of which people were being pushed one after another to display thirty seconds or so of their best drunken dancing to their rotating audience. As the circle was spinning around, I caught a quick glimpse of what looked like Caolan talking to a girl I had never seen before. I had to wait another 360 degrees to have another look, and it seemed I was right. On the walk home, via a couple of burgers from the Van of Life, I asked the sideburned Irishman who she was.

"That, my friend, was the lovely Lauren from London."

"And who's she?"

As was often the case at this stage of the night, Caolan was walking anything but steady and his burger was going anywhere but in his mouth.

"She is an economist in our year from New Hall, and I think you'll agree, she's pretty fine."

"I didn't get a good look. She looked pretty big."

A Tale of Friendship, Love and Economics

"Big in the right places, Josh, big in the right places."
"Okay."

On the Wednesday, Thursday and Friday of that week, Caolan waved to the lovely Lauren in every lecture. I woooed like a primary school-boy, called him a nob, and quickly looked around for someone that I could wave at. By Monday they were sat next to each other, by Wednesday they were texting each other, and by Sunday a group of us found ourselves dressed in suits and gowns, clutching pairs of paper tickets, and welcoming Lauren and her New Hall friends into Catz bar for a formal hall.

I don't know whether I would describe Lauren as "lovely". Don't get me wrong, she was certainly no minger, I guess she was just not my type. She was very tall, not slim, but not certainly not fat, had long brown hair that she sometimes wore in a ponytail and sometimes just let hang free, and she was indeed "big" in the place I guessed Caolan was referring to. She also had the rather unfortunate surname of "Broad", but as we were soon to discover, this was the first and by no means the worst in a long line of dodgy surnames that were housed in the all-girls college on top of the hill. From the few times that I had chatted to Lauren I had decided that she was very pleasant but not overly friendly. She talked quietly and avoided eye-contact, making me a little suspicious of her for no good reason.

Whenever you played host at a formal hall, as we were doing tonight, etiquette deemed that you bought the tickets for your guests, and they bought your wine. Given that formal hall tickets cost six pounds at the time, and none of us had ever dreamt of buying a wine costing more than four pounds, the hosts always got the bum deal. It also meant that you had to find a girl to give your spare ticket to before you went into formal hall, and she gave you wine in return. This was a good way of breaking the ice, but there was always a scramble to give your ticket to one of the better looking-ladies.

Lauren had brought eight girls along, including herself, meaning Caolan was obliged to match this with an identical number of boys. He signed up me, Mark, Oisin, Nick, Joe, and a couple of the economists. Oisin explained that he wasn't going to drink as he had to finish an essay that night. Mark, Caolan and I had just finished an essay so we explained that we planned to get absolutely battered. It was one of those good feelings where you had worked all day and felt that you had earned a cheap bottle of disgusting wine in the evening.

However, to say that this particular formal hall was not a classic does not quite hit the mark. That particular group of girls were some of the most pompous and obnoxious individuals that I had ever had the misfortune to meet. It wasn't that they were bad-looking, or anything, it's just that you couldn't have a decent conversation with them. They took themselves too seriously, and didn't seem to find my hilarious jokes funny at all (a terrible character trait if ever I saw one). Joe Porter and I were stuck down at the end of the table with these two girls who spent all night explaining how much work they did and how they very rarely drank and how when they did it was a single glass of some funny French wine, which neither me nor Joe had ever heard of although we nodded knowingly, on a Saturday night. Somehow, Pennying their glasses of water was not much fun. Then, over a main course of fish, "my" girl proceeded to text her boyfriend, reading out the text message as she wrote it, and then waited anxiously for honey-buns to reply and say how much he was missing his little chicken too. By the time desert arrived, Joe and I had given up and started chatting about football amongst ourselves. At least Caolan seemed to be having a good time. He was sat next to Lovely Lauren Broad, and talked to no-one else all night. At the end of the evening he gave her a hug and a kiss on the cheek, whilst the rest of us waved at our lot unenthusiastically and gave them the finger under the table.

"Well, they were a lovely bunch of girls, don't you think?" Caolan said after his eyes had followed them out of the bar.

"Are you taking the piss?" Joe asked.

"No, I thought they were dead sound."

"Aye, that's because you only talked to bloody Lovely Lauren all night whilst the rest of us were bored off our tits," I said in a slightly more heated tone than I had intended, and then took a sip of my pint to cool things down in there.

"At least we don't need to see them again," added Joe, and the rest of us nodded in relief.

"Well..." began Caolan.

"You dick" I said, "what have you done?"

What Caolan O'Donnell had done was to arrange another get-together with Lauren Broad and her New Hall cronies, this time at a local restaurant called Old Orleans. I tried to get myself out of it, but Caolan was very persuasive when he wanted to be, using every trick he had at his disposal, like "Are we friends or not?" and "I'd do the same for you" and "Did I hear something about a poem?" In the end, presumably after the Irishman had employed similar tactics on the rest of them, the same eight boys ventured out on a Friday night to the restaurant, all of us expecting to have a terrible night, all of us thinking evil thoughts about our Irish friend, and all of us absolutely determined beyond all doubt that this would be the last time we ever agreed to meet anyone from New Hall again.

It was still just about Happy Hour in Old Orleans when we arrived, and we quickly snapped up two cocktails each in a race against the clock. As it was a Friday night, the restaurant was busy, mostly with couples seated intimately on candlelit tables for two. Then there was us; planning to sit as far apart as possible on a not-so-intimate table for sixteen. The girls arrived a few minutes after the concerned manager had asked us if they were definitely turning up. We were already sat down in alternate seats, so it was something of a lottery which girl sat where, although, given the feedback from our previous encounter, it was a lottery that none of us were destined to win. The girls walked into the restaurant, clutching handbags and coats, and all of us averted our eyes in the hope that maybe they were a few short tonight and the seats next to us would remain free.

A girl sat down in the seat to the right of me. I was still pretending to read the menu, so I didn't get a chance to have a proper look at her, however I did catch a glimpse of blonde hair. That's funny, I thought, I don't remember any of them having blonde hair. I had a sneaky peek down the other end of the table, and low and behold I saw more faces that I didn't recognise. Ever the pessimist, I assumed that maybe these were the wrong group of girls and were about to be whisked off to a table full of King's boys or something, and the New Hall bores would swoon in to take their place. But then I saw Lauren Broad hanging her coat on the back of the free chair next to Caolan, and then I saw another of the girls from the formal hall. No, these were definitely New Hall, but they appeared to have binned some members and shipped in a few replacements. I was convinced that they couldn't possibly be as bad as the last lot, and immediately my spirits rose. I stopped pretending to read the menu and decided to introduce myself to the mysterious blonde who was sat next to me.

"Hi, I'm Josh."

"Hello, Josh, I'm Imogene. Pleased to meet you."

Again, I didn't know whether to go for the kiss on the cheek or the handshake, but as usual I played it safe and offered my hand, which she accepted with a smile. I giggled a little for no apparent reason. She was gorgeous.

I wondered how I would describe her to my friends back home when I told them about her. What words would I use, what features would I focus on? I wished I was an author or a poet, one who could write page after page, verse after verse, describing someone's beauty, using metaphors to convey the seemingly unimaginable, descriptions that would make her face emerge from the page. I knew that I would just end up saying that she was well fit, and my friends would be happy enough with that.

I looked at her as she made some small talk about how bad the weather had been lately, trying to work out in my head what made her attractive. She had wavy blonde hair that stopped about halfway down her neck, and which she continually tucked behind her two ears whenever it crept forward without permission. She had pretty eyes, kind of a bluey-green colour that looked right at you and sparkled whenever they caught the light. She seemed to blink more quickly when she spoke than when she listened as if her jaw and her eyelids were connected. She had a lovely smile that she used generously and always revealed her well-kept white teeth. I couldn't really tell what the rest of her looked like as she was sitting down and I had purposefully avoided looking out of an ultimately misguided fear when she walked in. However, I was pretty sure she was slim and, for no particular reason at all, I reckoned she had good legs. I had decided that she was attractive in about three seconds, and fallen for her completely before the minute was out.

Lost in my thoughts, and whilst Imogene introduced herself to Mark Novak, I overheard Caolan and Lovely Lauren from London having a conversation about the new faces. Clearly, the Irishman hadn't noticed that some of the tonight's girls were different from the formal hall, but as ever he covered up well.

"Ah yes, Lauren, I was just about to ask you about that."

It turned out that Lauren Broad was the head of the New Hall first year drinking society, and had hoped to bring her finest women to the formal hall the other night. However, due to various complications such as essay crises, sore throats, and a Johnny Depp film on at the cinema, a lot of them couldn't make it, and she had had to rope in anyone she could at the last minute, thus explaining the below-standard selection. I even heard her apologise for it, to which Caolan assured her that they were perfectly lovely. I made a mental note to remind my Irish friend that he had used the phrase "perfectly lovely". First impressions suggested this lot seemed a whole lot better, especially Imogene.

I unashamedly talked only to her all meal. The girl to the left of me was engrossed in a drill-infused conversation with Oisin, and Mark was happily chatting away to a brunette with an unusually large smile. Imogene was incredibly easy to talk to. She laughed when I made the poor waitress promise three times not to put any mayonnaise on my burger, and even seemed quite interested in my football stories, even though I knew they were boring as hell and she admitted that she hated the game. God, I even started going on about the beauty of Kerplunk and she didn't make her excuses and leave. Imogene was a historian, who absolutely detested maths, and came from a town down south whose name I'm afraid went in one ear and out the other, having been instinctively dismissed as "somewhere near London". Her voice lay somewhere on the border between well spoken and posh and made her sound a bit like a news reader, especially when she read the menu out loud. Even though I had never met an "Imogene" before, she kind of fitted the bill of what one would be like.

I didn't usually go for blondes as a rule. I found them to be stunning and eye-catching at the first glace, but quite plain after that. Dark-haired girls were a far better long-term choice in my experience. As is happened, blondes didn't seem to go for me either. Unfortunately, a similar policy appeared to have been adopted by girls of all hair colours. Anyway, in Imogene's case I was quite happy to make an exception. She didn't seem to be one of those flashy blondes. I was the world's worst at telling, but I was pretty sure that her hair was naturally that colour (she confirmed at a later date that it was, but I suppose she could have been fibbing) and that she didn't wear much make-up (although I'm often told that the girls who don't look like they're wearing make-up are the ones who have spent hours putting make-up on to make stupid naive men think exactly that). She just seemed to be a pleasant, intelligent, funny, down-to-earth girl, who happened also to be very pretty.

That particular Friday night had been chosen for our get-together by Caolan and Lauren as it coincided nicely with a Catz Bop. This time the theme was the 1980s, and the New Hall girls, all with a few cocktails and a lot of wine on board at this stage, seemed very keen. We walked with them back to college, and whilst Caolan led the band of women into the Bop, I sneaked back to my room to have a think about just how I was going to play this one. I needed to make my move, and tonight's Bop was the perfect place. There are few things I regret in my life, but what happened next was definitely one of them. No sooner was I leant over my sink, looking at myself in the mirror and starting to form a rough plan in my mind, than there came a knocking upon my door. I opened it up and in walked in Mark Novak, Nicholas MacLean and Joe Porter.

"What are you guys doing here? How come you're not at the Bop?"

"Don't know if we can be arsed. Thought we might have a drink here first," said Joe, and held up his right hand to reveal a clear glass bottle with the word "Vodka" written in bold black font on a white label, without a design or any hint of colour. Something told me that this was not the finest variety of the spirit ever produced.

"Erm... we can't, we've no mixers."

Nick produced a two-litre bottle of coke that for some unknown reason he had been hiding behind his back, looking like a magician who had just done the worst trick ever.

"Nah, come on, let's go to the Bop."

"How comes you're so keen?" asked Joe

"Erm... no reason." I couldn't tell them. They were drunk enough to either tell the poor girl I was madly in love with her, or make me look a total prick in front of her, which experience had shown I was more than capable of doing myself.

"Well then, there's nothing to stop us drinking here then?"

"I suppose not," I said reluctantly.

And drink there we did, watching a particularly dramatic episode of *The Bill* until the bottle was empty. We then staggered down to the Bop, getting lost twice on the way.

The lad on the door, a third year who needed a good haircut, explained that we were not dressed to match the 1980s theme and tried to claim an extra fifty pence off us. We were dressed in shirts with T-shirts underneath, for it was bloody freezing, and a mixture of trousers and jeans on our bottom halves. I quickly convinced myself and the others that 1980 bands like Bros always wore unbuttoned shirts with T-shirts underneath in their videos. In a matter of seconds and with minimal effort we transported

A Tale of Friendship, Love and Economics

ourselves back two decades and, after a bit of persuasion, saved ourselves 50p.

The Bop was as jammed as it always was. We had arrived late in the day with only an hour to go and most people were throwing themselves about on the dance floor. The downside of this was you got a few elbows in the ribs and girls' hair whipped in your face as you walked past, but the bonus was the bar was empty. We ordered a round of Aftershocks and, much to the displeasure and jibes of my good friends, a round of double vodka lime and lemos. We were at that dangerous stage of the evening where additional drink appears to be having little effect and slips down like ice-cold water on a stinking hot day. With our drinks downed we hit the dance floor, quite literally in the case of Mark who stumbled over an invisible foot. We kept dancing until the very end, and joined in the "Boo!" when the nasty porters arrived to bring our fun to an end.

It was only when the Bop was over and we were ushered outside into the cold of the night by the Porters that I remembered about Imogene. It was like a light bulb flickering on and off in my head whilst I tried desperately to remember the thing I knew I needed to remember. It finally remained lit when I saw her stood around chatting with her friends, as well as with Caolan and Oisin just outside the library. I hurried over.

"There he is. Where the fuck have you been?" asked Caolan

"Erm... dancing and stuff, you know."

"Oiseen... Ois... Oisin (she couldn't quite say it right yet, but it wasn't a bad effort) tells me you're quite the dancer. It's a shame I missed it," said Imogene, smiling the smile that I couldn't believe I had forgotten about.

"Erm... I do my best, you know," I tried to smile back as best I could but I was too annoyed at myself and too drunk to hide it properly.

"Right ladies, it's time we were off home," said Lauren more authoritatively than I thought she was capable of.

"Are you sure you don't want me to walk back with you? The streets are very dangerous these days," said Caolan, and I made another mental note to remind him of this woeful line in the morning.

"No, we'll be fine. We're big girls, you know."

I don't know why I said what I did next, but I was glad I did, and it made me feel a bit better in the morning.

"Hey, Imogene, you look cold. Do you want to borrow a hat for the walk back? I've a nice pink one you could have."

"That would be lovely, Josh. Thank you."

I walked back calmly towards my room, and as soon as I was out of sight I ran as fast as I could to make sure she hadn't given up and gone before I got back. I flew into my room, cracking my right knee on the corner of my desk, swore three times, and then dug the hat out from the bottom of my "random bits of clothing" draw. I had bought the hat for use at bad taste parties and football outings. It was a luminous pink woolly hat and had cost me £2 from a sports store that had been closing down for the last seven years. I ran down the stairs of M-block and across Main Court, remembering to stop just before I passed through the gate that led to where the girls were stood. Imogene was still there. I composed myself, walked over coolly and tried to grab a hold of my breath.

"There you go."

"Thank you, it's very sweet of you, and she kissed me on the cheek. Only the dark of the night kept my red face hidden, but my joy was more apparent. The girls left college through the Plodge and made their way through town and up the big hill that led them back to New Hall. I said goodnight to everyone and made my way back to M-block with fellow block-mates Oisin and Mark. I went to bed feeling happier and more excited than I could remember, so much so that I forgot to have a glass of water and awoke the next morning with a deservedly stinking headache.

It transpired that Caolan had indeed pulled Lauren Broad that night at the Bop. He said he quite liked her and he didn't know what was going to happen. I said he was in love. He told me to piss off.

It was the last week of term, and I didn't see Imogene again until after the Easter break. I didn't think there was much point trying to get her phone number or anything like that as it was too near the holidays and, knowing my luck, she would be on a different mobile network and it would end up costing me a fortune. And I certainly wasn't going to write her a poem or woo her with my vast knowledge of Shakespeare. No, I was going to wait, and this time I was going to make sure I didn't do anything stupid. Imogene returned my pink hat via Lauren in lectures and with it a little note saying thank you and praising my choice of colour. I put Imogene's note in the box where I kept all my important things. It would not be her last entry.

Chapter 43

Since Mary Jane had left the now infamous note pinned to my door earlier in the term, it had become quite the popular thing amongst my friends to pin up similar notes upon the door of M14. They all had the words "Important – read in private" on the outside, and usually contained incredibly hilarious and witty messages such as "You're gay" and "You've got a small nob" on the inside. So, when I came back from lectures only to find another note pinned to my door, I took it inside and opened it indifferently.

Even when I quickly scanned to the end of the note and saw it was signed "Mary Jane" I still did not react, as my good friends were not averse to putting her name at the bottom of their notes. It was only when I recognised the hand-writing and saw no mention of homosexuality or male genitalia within the message that I realised it was, in fact, from my strawberry blonde neighbour, and former best friend. It read as follows:

Josh,
Thought you might like to know, we are now living with Mary next year.
Mary Jane

I read the note again just in case I had missed something, but the seventeen words still said the same on the second reading. I went up to Mark's room to show him. He was equally bemused.

Up until a few days ago we were all set to be living in a flat of five next year with myself, Mark, Faye, Mary Jane and the peanut-fearing Chip being the Fab Quintet. Everyone else, for better or worse, had also sorted out their flats, and so it was too late in the day for Mark and I to find someone else to live with, even though it would probably have been a good idea given current relations with my neighbour. Anyway, I really wanted to live with Faye, and I reasoned that Chip could be just the man to diffuse any lingering tension between Mary Jane and I. However, as we feared, Chip pulled out at the eleventh hour to live in a flat with Francesca and two other girls (good work Chip, I thought). He was clearly very sorry for letting us down, and I got at least four pints of lager out of his guilt. So, with the deadline for choosing flats just a few days away, Mark and I had simply assumed that we would be living in a flat of four. However, the note from Mary Jane suggested differently. I went to see Faye to get the full story, and, more importantly, to find out just who this Mary girl was.

Faye was sat in her chair, still in her red dressing gown, happily tapping her foot whilst listening to Coldplay, and eating a bowl of Weetabix with milk that I had strong suspicions had come from my bottle. After saying hello and getting one back, I decided to get straight to the point.

"Who the bloody hell is Mary?"

"You know, the girl who lives directly below me?"

I thought for a moment, but couldn't picture her.

"She's Polish and is going out with that mathmo, who looks a bit like an evil version of Mark."

I thought about it again.

"Oh yeah, and she was kind of seeing Duane for a bit, wasn't she?"

Not the best description I could have chosen, and Faye nodded quickly and returned to her Weetabix.

"So, how come we're living with her now?"

"Well, she's kind of become friendly with Mary Jane and me over the last couple of weeks, and she sort of asked Mary Jane if she could move into a flat with us. You see, she doesn't want to live with her boyfriend as she figures it would be too much, you know. Anyway, Mary Jane explained about the Chip situation, but once he pulled out, then she said Mary could move in."

"I don't think I've ever spoken to her."

"She's very nice," said Faye reassuringly, "and she says she's loves cooking. You don't mind, do you? I suppose we should have talked about it with you and Mark, but, well, you know how things are."

"Hey, if she can cook, she's more than welcome as far as I am concerned, and you could move a serial killer in with Mark and he wouldn't say anything."

"Oh good, that's our flat then?"

"Yep, that's our flat."

That was our flat. Me, Mark, Faye, Mary Jane and Mysterious Mary. I did a bit of investigative work to try and find out a few things about our new flatmate. She was indeed Polish, and her full name was Mary Jaczynska, pronounced "Ya-cheen-ska". She studied English, but didn't really like it, and had had a part in the Fresher Play. She had been seeing her boyfriend, who was now simply referred to as Evil Novak, for all of this term, and emphatically denied ever having gone out with Duane. Her room was on the first floor of M-block, sandwiched directly between Elizabeth on the bottom and Faye on the top. Elizabeth told me that Polish Mary had a tendency to play her guitar in the early hours of the morning, and then make grinding and groaning noises with her boyfriend for ages and ages, noises that kept poor posh, squeaky Elizabeth awake but that she was far too embarrassed to complain about. All in all nobody had a bad word to say about her, but then nobody seemed to know her very well at all.

None of the other flats had any dramatic last-minute changes. All had potential problems brewing up in them, some more obvious than others, but it was too late in the day to change. Caolan and Oisin were living in a flat of four with the quieter of the two Ents Reps (and not the one who was obsessed with Oisin) and The Girl Whose Room We Used To Hang Out In Who Didn't Really Like Me. Joe and Nick were with the Jewish economist Simon, and Caolan's Jewish neighbour, Fishel. Elizabeth was with Jude and two other medics. Francesca was with Chip and two other girls, both of whom had red hair, one natural, one dyed. The Movie Star Look-alike ended up living with three people she didn't know very well, but well enough to know she didn't like them. There was one "lads" flat of five that contained the likes of Adam "Sly" Sylvester and Jake Vincenzi, and one girls flat of five that would house Emma and four other Big Name women.

The random ballot was done in the bar on one rain-soaked afternoon by the Movie Star Look-alike and her penguin-loving colleague acting in their capacity as Welfare Officers. All thoughts that the ballot might be rigged were soon dismissed when the poor Movie Star Look-alike from Leeds' flat came out way down the bottom. She spent the last few days of term sulking, adopting the subtle slogan: shit location, shit flatmates. We fared little better, coming out second to last in the flats of five. None of the flats at Chads were really very much different from each other, but location was everything. We ended up in Flat 53, which was about as high up as you could go, and we could already foresee that whilst we might indeed get good TV reception, getting the TV and the rest of our stuff up and down at the beginning and end of each term would be a right royal pain in the arse. In our one pre-flat meeting, with an atmosphere similar to USA–USSR meetings at the height of the Cold War, I said I wanted Room A, and Mary Jane took Room D, thus putting us as far apart as space allowed us. Mark said he didn't really mind which room he got, and thus was given E, adjacent to

Mary Jane's room and thus making him a captured nation on her front, with Faye and Mary taking the neutral rooms of C and B respectively. All the rooms were supposed to be the same size and all had eight walls, but I was happy that mine looked bigger. Caolan's Flat came quite high up in the ballot, and they promptly snapped up Flat 20, a first-floor flat that had previously housed his Nanny, and was regarded as one of the best due to its central location. Caolan rigged the internal room ballot and secured himself Room B, whilst an unsuspecting Oisin seemed happy with Room C. Joe, Nick and the Jews landed another first-floor flat, number 26.

The lesson learnt in the previous term and to be re-enforced over and over again in the course of the next year was not to pick your flatmates until the last possible moment. With the benefit of hindsight I would have probably have chosen to live with Mark, Caolan and Oisin, and maybe chucked a stable girl like Francesca into the equation just to add that feminine touch. However, if Mary Jaczynska hadn't moved into our flat, and thus also into our lives, at the last minute, then my life at Cambridge wouldn't have been half as exciting and certainly wouldn't have left me with half as many stories to tell.

Chapter 44

There were just a couple of events to get out of the way before we could all return home for a much needed Easter break. The first of these was the Annual St. Catharine's College Economics and Land Economy Society Dinner.

Most of the subjects had their own annual dinner held in Hall towards the end of second term, apart from the smaller subjects such as Philosophy and SPS, which had to make do with a trip to Burger King, or something. They were all a Black Tie affair and all cost between twenty and thirty quid. Ours came in at an even twenty-six, which included, according to the ticket, five courses of the most sumptuous food, fine wine, port and sherry, and pre-dinner drinks. Mum had kindly given me money to buy a tuxedo as I would not only be needing it for tonight but also for the May Ball coming up at the end of next term (and any movie premières I might be invited to). Oisin and I had gone along to snap ourselves one up from town on the

Saturday before. The lady in the shop, who was wearing far too much perfume and far too much lipstick, convinced us that braces and a proper bow-tie were absolutely essential, but I drew the line at one of those funny cummerbund things. Needless to say, it took Oisin about seventeen hours to finally make a decision to buy one, and the look on his face as he handed the excessively decorated lady over £100 was enough to make the hardest of souls grimace with anguish. It was the first time I had ever worn a tuxedo, and I think that the last time I had worn braces was when I was three, and when I put them on in the shop it felt like I was doing an extremely well-dressed bungee jump. The bow-tie came with supposedly easy to follow instructions of how to tie it. Caolan, Mark, Oisin and I easily breezed passed Stage One where you had to hold the bow-tie out in front of you, but then we were lost, with Mark nearly choking himself with his final effort. Fortunately, a lad in our college who had gone to Eton, where apparently they had to wear bow-ties every single day, was on hand to help us out, as well as most people who were attending the dinner that night.

As always, pre-dinner drinks were held in Mr Stevens' room in C4. We arrived there early hoping to take advantage of the free champagne that was on offer, champagne that I was determined to keep drinking despite the fact that I didn't like it and it still made me sneeze. It was strange to see the people I saw every day all dressed up in tuxedos and dresses. Mr Stevens had taken his jacket off and now looked like a waiter as he poured us all glasses of the sparkling stuff dressed in his white shirt and black bow-tie. All the second and third year economists were present as well, along with the full cohort of Land Economists and, of course, their great leader, the Lord of the Landies, Brummie Dean, Dr Tinsley.

As we were happily drinking away, one of the Economic Society Presidents, a pretty Jewish female economist from the second year, came over to chat to Caolan. She often came over to chat to Caolan in various locations, and we had started a rumour that the Irishman had a thing for her. It was the kind of rumour that had absolutely no basis and we would have got easily bored of it had Caolan not got so worked up about the whole thing ("Look, I don't fancy her, alright? Jesus Christ, when are you lot going to grow up?"). Now, whenever he passed her in the street, we would wolf whistle or blow kisses until she turned around, leaving her wondering what was going on and Caolan smiling apologetically. Indeed, even as she chatted to him now, I was nudging him in the ribs trying to provoke a reaction. I didn't feel the slightest bit guilty as the Irishman would have done, and often did, the exact same thing to me. Tonight, however, their conversation was strictly business, not pleasure.

"What was that all about?" asked Oisin as soon as she had gone and Caolan had tried unsuccessfully to give me a dead-leg.

"She wants one of us to give a speech tonight after the dinner. Apparently it's tradition that one person from every year gets up and says a few words."

"And she wants you to do it?" asked Mark.

"Yeah, but I don't want to."

"Why not?" asked Mark again, suddenly sounding like he was hosting *Question Time*, or something.

"I don't like making speeches."

"So, who's going to do it?"

"Well, I kind of said that you would." He turned to face me.

"Why me?"

Caolan pause for a moment as if the words he was about to say were a real struggle to get out.

"Well, you're good at speeches, aren't you?"

The only time Caolan ever paid you a compliment was when he needed you to do something, or when he was being sarcastic.

"True, true," I smiled proudly, and Caolan made the International Gesture for a wanker. "But what do I have to say? I mean, I've had no time to prepare it or anything."

"You did a good one on your birthday," said Mark.

"Yeah, but I was pissed and I just slagged off the Landies. I doubt that will go down well tonight with good old Dr Tinsley and his troops around. I'll probably get taken out by a sniper."

"If they're a Landie sniper they'll miss anyway," chipped in the hockey-playing economist from our year. You were always guaranteed a laugh by poking fun at the Land Economists.

"Just give them a bit of chat. Talk your usual bollocks. You'll be fine," said the ever helpful Caolan, and that was all that was said about the matter. We moved from Mr Stevens' chambers to the small room adjacent to the Hall where Wednesday night formal hall's were held, my mind racing through all the things I definitely couldn't say.

A Tale of Friendship, Love and Economics

We were given designated seats with little name tags indicating the required parking spot for our behinds. The tables were arranged in an upside down "U" shape, with Mr Stevens, Dr Tinsley and the guest speaker in the middle of the top table. I found myself at the very end of the "U", with Mark on my right and our History supervisor who wore the short skirts on my left, and true to form she had opted for a particularly skimpy little number tonight. In a nice touch, all our supervisors had been invited along and were intermingled with the students at various points around the tables. I could see our Micro supervisor getting loud and animated about something, and our Politics supervisor captivating his surrounding audience with a story that I could only guess was about his mother-in-law. It was a bit strange chatting to them without a white board and a set of notes in front of you, but they all seemed pretty down to earth and remarkably capable at talking about things other than the wonderful world of economics. More so than us, maybe.

The meal was very nice with only one of the five courses containing fish, and only two having any funny sauce that I was compelled to scrape off as best I could with my knife. I had to run through the "Why I Don't Eat Fish" story yet again, followed by the complementary best-selling sequel "Why I Am Such a Fussy Eater", this time to my captivated female History supervisor. The kitchen staff, of which the football-playing contingent now referred to me as Big Josh, kept bringing around wine, a different one for each course, but not in sufficient quantities to get us drunk. Buzz also affectionately stuck his middle finger up at me as I caught him peering through the door. Needless to say, under the watchful eye of numerous supervisors, there was not much Pennying going on.

After the food had been eaten and the wine drunk, Dr Tinsley got to his feet and introduced the guest speaker who was to address the St. Catharine's Economics and Land Economy Society, raising the volume and slowing the speed for those two very important words. The guest speaker was an elderly Australian economist, with a slightly faded accent, who was about seventy and who was one of the world's leading experts on the great John Maynard Keynes. He was also really funny and appeared to be quite drunk. He entertained us with a few tales of his past meetings with other great economists and about how he had fallen in love with Cambridge having come over from Adelaide many years ago. His stories were littered with "bloodys" and "bastards" and the odd irrelevant comment about his preferred type of woman (Aussie blondes and English brunettes, but at his stage in his life, he explained, he would happily take anything he could get). He then went on to explain that he applied for the job of Master of St. Catharine's College, but the bastards wouldn't give it to him. He couldn't understand why.

After a stirring round of applause, Dr Tyler announced that it was time for the traditional speeches from each year. A third year lad from Bolton, who happened to be Trevor's Nanny and thus my Grand-Nanny, went first. He was, much to my despair, very, very funny. He had it all written down on a piece of paper and was flying out with jokes about lecturers and southerners that were being lapped up by his audience He had stolen my thunder with his northern accent and his anti-London-based material. He even got a bit political at the end making some point about equal access to the University and a critique of New Labour's current policies. Needless to say I hadn't factored a political element into the jumbled mess of words that were currently whizzing randomly around in my head. Thankfully, the speaker from the second year was woeful. It was the Jewish female Economic Society president. She was quite a shy, meek character, and looked terrified to be emitting sounds from her mouth. She thanked everyone for coming, instigated a few rounds of applause for Mr Stevens, Dr Tinsley, and the kitchen staff to fill in time, and then sat down. Next up was me.

I made my way slowly to the centre of the upside down "U" where everybody was making their speeches from. Caolan once again tried to trip me up but luckily this time I managed to connect quite solidly with his shin and I caught a glimpse of him grimacing with pain as I took my place and looked around at the audience. The faces staring back at me as I moved my eyes quickly around the room displayed more boredom than expectation; it had been a long night with not enough drink, and the bar was closing soon. I once more pointlessly and unconstructively cursed the fact that I didn't have any notes to follow, and then began.

The speech was the jumbled mess that it was always destined to be, but it did have a few underlying themes. I opened up by thanking the Land Economists for finding time in their incredibly busy schedules to be guests at our dinner. Dr Tinsley did not look amused. I had a little line about each one of our supervisors who were seated around the tables. I chose not to mention our History supervisor's short skirts and instead opted for a little dig at her for announcing in a lecture that the only county in Britain where literacy rates actually fell during the industrial revolution was good old Lancashire, home sweet home. Our Politics supervisor found himself on the receiving end of a line about the globalisation of his mother in-law, laughing away but not quite getting it. I took a big risk and brought up the strange vocabulary of our Micro supervisor, with his excessive use of "mega", "groovy", "fastiticomudo" and "Cowabunga". It was not risky in the sense that it might not get a laugh, it was risky because I was shit-scared of him. I saved my *pièce de résistance* for Dr Tinsley. He was already unhappy about the anti-Landie opening to the speech, but now found his ears open to this cocky first year with an awful haircut doing a woeful impression of him. I say woeful, because that's how people described it – I actually thought it was pretty good. For the next couple of minutes I banged on about the importance of the "package" and the "font", regardless of the content of our forthcoming Statistics project. I could and would have gone on for a while longer, for it was getting the laughs, had I not received a look from Mr Stevens that suggested it might be time to stop. I wrapped up the speech by calling Mr Stevens a legend, not because I was sucking up but because we all believed he was, and then explaining how pleased I was to have not been born a geographer.

Thankfully, the speech went down well, getting laughs in all the right places, and even earning the congratulations of my Bolton-born Grand-Nanny. In the bar afterwards, I had a couple of much-needed pints and, despite being pretty full up, I snapped up a packet of dry-roasted peanuts. The jukebox was playing a few classics and everyone seemed in a good mood. Even geographers Nick, Joe and Faye came in to join us for a drink, dressed less formally in jeans and jumpers. Also in the bar someone took a picture of a few of us, and for some reason whilst we were being lined up by the side of the pool table Caolan and I decided that it would be a good idea to drop our trousers and reveal our boxer shorts whilst Mark and Oisin stood at the side looking confused and disapproving respectively. That photo, in fact, marked the last time my long hair was captured on film. When I look back at the photo, proudly attached near the start of my "The Cambridge Years" photo album, it is like I am looking at a different person; some funny looking lad with a mop on his head and his trousers around his ankles, who didn't have a clue what misadventures lay along the road ahead.

It had been a good night, but then I supposed the coming together of so many economists was always going to be. I was pleased I had made the speech and that it had gone down well, but I was not looking forward to seeing the supervisors that I had mocked next term. In the case of my Micro supervisor, Mr Cowabunga himself, not only could I see my marks taking a vertical tumble, but also him pursuing the utility maximising strategy of murdering me.

Chapter 45

The second and final event of the term was the much-hyped Annual Football Dinner, and for once all the hype was entirely justified.

It had been a footballing term of extremes for me, with the disheartened 2nd XI relegated from Division 3, and the Mighty 3rd XI, kitchen staff and all, having already earned promotion and now pushing for the Division 5b title. It seemed that every weekend I would be on a roller-coaster ride of footballing emotions; pissed off on a Saturday after chasing the ball around the park all afternoon for the 2nds, in the end losing by at least six goals and usually knackering my leg in the process, and then over the moon on a Sunday when the 3rds destroyed some inferior opposition with a combination of Samba-style football and X-rated movie-style language from Buzz. Incredibly, the 3rds had also reached the semi-finals of the Shield, a cup competition open to all non-1st XI teams across the university, and a competition that our 2nds had embarrassingly crashed out of in round two. In the end we bowed out graciously after extra time to the best 2nd XI team in the university, and eventual winners, Queen's College, losing 5–4 in one the most exciting games I had ever played in (we were even winning 2–0 and 4–2 at various stages during the game). Such a contrast in forms had led to the Kitchen Staff calling for a swapping of teams, much to the disgust of the small, blonde 2nd XI captain and his ever-loyal companion, geographer Joe Porter.

The college 1st XI, of which Mr Joe Porter was a regular bench warmer, had had an even better season. They had been promoted to Division 1 last year, and this year had won the league title with a couple of games to spare. Moreover, they had also done the Double by winning the prestigious

A Tale of Friendship, Love and Economics

Cuppers tournament in a dramatic final against Girton College, a final watched by nearly all of Catz, girls and boys and Masters alike, creating one of the best atmospheres I had ever been witness to. Even football-hating Caolan came along, repeatedly shouting "Watch your house, Catz!" at the top of his voice, which we later deduced meant the same as "Man on!" Our hockey and rugby boys had also won their Cuppers events, making this an extremely good year for our sporty college, and making me feel even prouder to be a member.

With what had potential to be perfect timing, the final league match of the season for the Mighty 3rds was played on the day of the Annual Football Dinner. It was an away fixture against Christ's College 2nds. As the league table stood, any kind of win would give us the title, and anything less would put it in the hands of our academically minded, early-bar-shutting opposition.

Because of our very shaky start it had always seemed unlikely that we would be challenging for the honour of being crowned Division 5b Champions at the end of the season. Indeed, even with three games to go we were languishing in forth place with a dreadful goal difference. To put ourselves in a position to catch Christ's we had not only to win all our remaining games, but also somehow score sixteen goals. Incredibly, this unlikely feat was achieved in just one game with a 17–0 victory away against Peterhouse 1st XI.

Peterhouse was a college not exactly renowned for its footballing prowess, only having one team, a team that were struggling to hold their ground in our division full of 2nd and 3rd XIs. Peterhouse also had something of a reputation amongst Cambridge circles of being a college full of gays, a reputation not helped by the fact well-known Conservative MP Michael Portillo was an Old Boy. Indeed, before the game, Buzz told us in no uncertain terms to fucking make sure we kept one hand on our arse and the other on our dicks throughout the game. I wondered what he would have us do when we got a throw-in. I thought that they would be bad, but Peterhouse 1st XI were absolutely awful. Their goalkeeper started quivering whenever the ball was in his half, whilst their players fell over when they kicked the ball, congratulated you when you tackled them, and apologised profusely if they ever got the ball off you. 17–0 was a more than fair result, and set us up nicely for this final showdown with Christ's on a windy Wednesday afternoon right at the end of term.

The Cambridge Diaries

We had pretty much a full strength team out, and we were confident. We even had our largest crowd of the season as Jim the Barman had turned up with his dog, and an old lady stopped to have a look what was going on on her way back from the shops. Our goalkeeper was stuck in a supervision that he couldn't get out of, and so Mick the Cook dropped back into the nets, and young Nick MacLean was drafted in from the 2nds to join me at centre-back. After the warm-up, in which we all ran back and forth across the pitch, jumping and skipping, and generally looking like pricks, whilst the kitchen staff had a pre-match smoke, the captain gathered us around for the team talk. He was a quiet, well-spoken lad and, despite chucking in the odd worn-out cliché, always said things that made sense. Buzz, on the other hand, had a habit of inventing his own clichés. Whilst the captain calmly reminded us of the position we had earned for ourselves, and how well we had all played in our last few matches, Buzz explained that every last one of us had better work our fucking dicks off today. We had a group huddle and, with fire in our hearts, the Wheel on our chests, and excessively tight maroon and blue shirts wrapped around our bodies, we took up our positions ready for battle.

The game was a scrappy one with the wind seemingly having more of the ball than we did. We were clearly nervous and people just booted the ball away when they got it like they were playing pass the parcel or hot potato, instead of looking for the simple pass. Fortunately, Christ's were not fairing much better, and rarely looked like threatening to trouble the intimidating sixteen-stone-plus figure of Mick the Cook between the sticks. After about thirty minutes, a tall, skinny member of the kitchen staff headed home from a corner, and we went into half time 1–0 up. Early in the second half our captain latched onto a wind-assisted miss-kick from Faye's Duane in centre-midfield, and successfully rounded the keeper to double our advantage. It was then that Christ's piled on the pressure. They needed to score two goals to win the league and they were throwing everything at it. Our right-back fell on his arse for no apparent reason and at the worst possible time to gift them a goal (had he not been so bad throughout the season, there may have been talk of bungs). We now had twenty minutes to stop them scoring.

I always take sport a bit too seriously, and I am the world's worst loser. Whenever my best friend and I used to go and play pool at night, if I had lost I would always throw my chalk into the farmer's field on the way home. It got to the stage where my friend would bring along an old piece of chalk and just hand it to me without saying a word whenever we reached the point

A Tale of Friendship, Love and Economics

of release to save me from wasting another new one. I was also prone to smashing the ball into a nearby tree if ever tennis wasn't going my way, and had been known to tip the board at Scrabble. Basically, I was a delight to play games with. Today, I was knackered, my knee was sore and, I was cramping up, and I was determined that we were not going to lose this game. I started shouting and balling like I had Asperger's Syndrome, and bollocking poor Nick and the other two defenders to try and get them fired up. Thankfully, most others were feeling pretty similar, and everyone was working their dicks off as Buzz would have wanted. There were a few close shaves; a few corners that missed everyone's heads and a few frantic scrambles on the goal line, but in the end we held out. There was a big cheer when the final whistle went, and I fell to my knees like I had seen footballers do when they won the world cup. It was my proudest footballing moment – Champions of Division 5b. I gave Nick a big manly hug and shook the hands of our unlucky opposition who, to their credit, offered their congratulations with a grace and dignity that I knew I would not have been able to offer had I been in their losing shoes. We sang the *College Football Song* on the sidelines, a song usually reserved for 1st XI Cuppers victories or to bring a messy football outing to a close. A lot of the lads didn't know the words, but Nick and I had taken more than a few fines for forgetting them in the past and belted out the words that were fast becoming engraved upon our hearts and in our minds with pride. The song went as follows:

Ohhhhhhhhhhhhhhhhhhhhhhhh the lads.
(The ohhhhhhhhhhhhhh bit lasted for as long as the lung capacity of the louder "singers" allowed it)

>Should have seen us coming.
>Everyone maroon and blue
>Everyone was running.
>All the lads and lasses.
>All the smiling faces

(Whilst the majority were required to hold the "aces" part of "faces" for as long as possible in much the same way as the "ohh" of the opening line, some were given the job of repeating "smiling faces, smiling faces, smiling faces" over and over again, quickly, again for as long as was humanly possible)

> Walking up the Granchester Road.
> To see the Catz Three Aces.
> Whhhhhaaaaaeeeeeeeyyyyy!

I don't know the original author, or if the song had been changed over the years, but it was a beautiful little number and always brought about one of those shivers across my body normally reserved for moving speeches and the corny lines in films, teen drama series and songs that most other people laughed at.

I was in a great mood for the rest of the day. I was definitely in pain, there was no doubt about that, and walking was not proving straightforward, but it was a nice kind of pain, the kind of pain that you feel you've earned and was worthwhile, not like when you crack your big toe on the side of a door because you were not looking. I had a long shower to wash all the mud and sweat away, and then treated myself to a cup of tea whilst sat alone in my room, dressed only in boxer shorts, listening to the Rolling Stones, and reading the gossip pages on Teletext, where, astonishingly, the story of our epic victory was not to be found.

Fortunately, I didn't have too much stuff to do before I could go to Football Dinner that night. You see, a couple of weeks ago the 3rd XI captain asked me if I would like to take over his role next year. Being in a particularly power-hungry mood that day I readily accepted. I liked the idea of being 3rd XI captain. Whilst it was by no means the most prestigious sporting position on the college, it carried far less stresses than running the 1sts or the 2nds, and it was a good opportunity to get to know the new bunch of Freshers, and maybe to pass on a bit of my priceless expertise and experience to a younger generation who could then follow in my footsteps to greatness. However, it did also mean trying to control Buzz, Mick the Cook, and the rest of the kitchen staff week after week. I was to be officially made captain that night, and Joe Porter had been given the same role for the 2nds, having made it perfectly clear that his job was infinitely more important than mine. It was traditional that the new captains should buy their predecessor a gift to be presented at the Football Dinner and also make a little bit of a speech. After pestering him for a week, Joe finally

A Tale of Friendship, Love and Economics

decided he had an hour spare in his busy geographic life to come shopping with me for presents. We found a joke shop, and after half an hour of looking for better gifts, resigned ourselves to buying two plastic penises. With the present out of the way, all that was left to do was choose a suitably bad shirt-tie combo for the Dinner, and think about what I was going to say in my speech, the latter of which I decided could wait until nearer the time.

Whilst I was concerned that my friends and family thought I did no work at university, at the same time I was also conscious that they might well think every time I had a good time it was because I was drunk. In much the same way as a riveting tale about a day in the library was not going to win the Booker Prize, a sober night in with my friends just having a laugh would not have sounded funny to anyone else. Drunken tales were often eventful and out of the ordinary purely because people behaved differently as inhibitions were lost, thus more often than not making them better stories. So, whenever my Dad said for the 3000th time, "You lot do no work and you're out drunk all time", he was only getting half a story. We had great times when sober and great times when drunk, it was just that the latter were the tales most often repeated. It was like Dad was watching the highlights of a match of football, seeing all the best bits but missing observing the nitty gritty that told the proper story of the game, the bits that some connoisseurs enjoyed the most. The only reason I am making this long, drawn out, and ultimately pointless point is because Football Dinner provided the setting for yet another drunken story.

Football Dinner was always going to be a drunken affair. After all, every football outing was drunken and this was by far the biggest of the lot. The second and third years smiled whenever we asked them about the Dinner, a smile that suggested they knew something that we didn't.

Nick MacLean, Joe Porter and I arrived in the 1st XI captain's room, dressed from head to toe in awful clothes, just before the designated time of 6.30 pm. We were experienced enough by now to know that lateness brought with it punishments. The captain lived in a ground-floor, two-person set along the edge of Main Court called A1. It had two small bedrooms, a tiny storage room and a large living-room area that housed a TV, a few comfy chairs, a couple of desks, and just for tonight, a dangerously large quantity of alcohol. We were received warmly by the second and third years that were already there, and presented with a round of smiles and a plastic cup containing a brown liquid that emitted a pungent aroma, which my inherent survival instincts told me smelt of danger. I don't know exactly what was in the cocktail, or if it had a name ("Death in a Cup" or "This Won't Be the Last Time You See Me Tonight" would have been appropriate) but it tasted like shit. There was definitely whisky in there, and probably gin, and I was also picking up the taste of vodka and maybe a dash of rum. It was painful to drink, and even worse when you saw another drink being prepared for you whilst this one was still making its way slowly from the cup to its temporary residence in your stomach.

There was little doubt that the Football Dinner was designed to give maximum pleasure to second and third years, and maximum pain to the Freshers. Each Fresher was assigned to someone who would personally "look after" them for the evening, kind of like an evil Nanny, or something. Basically, that person was in charge of making sure his Fresher drank more than was humanly possible, mixing up disgusting concoction after disgusting concoction, being like a guinea pig in an experiment that the RSPCA would definitely have banned. The problem was the whole event was stuck in a vicious circle, with last year's Freshers having suffered so badly that they now elected to make this year's cohort suffer even worse. They knew no limits because no-one had imposed limits for them, and they had no sympathy because no-one had had any sympathy for them. They had the smiles and the eyes of their persecutors of year's gone by, and carried out their duties and inflicted pain with the efficiency of an army that the world was supposed to have gotten ridden of sixty years ago. It was nothing personal, it was just the way things worked.

By the time pre-dinner drinks were over, we were already written off. At some stage we had had our hair painted in the college colours of red and blue (maroon was sadly not available) and streaks now ran down our faces like coloured tears. Tonight's chosen restaurant was regarded as one of the city's best. We made our way there as a group, singing songs as we walked the streets of Cambridge, the coldness of the night more than offset by the drink-induced numbness. The restaurant was called Don Pasquale's, and was located on one of the corners of Market Square. It was expensive enough, nearly thirty quid a head, but for that we got a three-course meal, a bottle of house wine each and a separate room upstairs. Again, the faces of the staff dropped to the floor when we walked in, a tribe dressed from an era that never happened, and every third person looking green and being carried.

A Tale of Friendship, Love and Economics

Each Fresher was seated opposite their guardian. Mine was the 3rd XI goalkeeper who I liked a lot but who had turned into a bastard tonight. Joe Porter and Nick MacLean were on other tables, but we often made eye-contact with each other out of mutual sympathy and a desire to not be the first to drop. Duane was on my table, slurring his words and asking to go to the toilet. My would-have-been-flatmate Chip was on the far table, dressed in a purple shirt that was far too tasteful, and complaining of a migraine that had incredibly emerged just that very morning thus rendering the lad unable to drink. We were not happy that he was avoiding the pain that we were currently suffering, but we did not join in the thankfully unsuccessful movement to punish him by means of a peanut.

The first course was onion soup, a tasty dish usually, only tonight mine had the added ingredient of half a bottle of red wine. I knew I was going to be sick, it was just a question of when and where. After that delicious first course it was time for the speeches, starting with our 3rd XI captain. For some reason he was as pissed out of his head as us Freshers were. He had his speech written down, but couldn't read it. He was clearly very proud as we had won the league that day, but couldn't remember any specific matches, scores, goal scorers, or even players' names to add flesh to his comprehensive review of the season. He decided just to slag off a few colleges (Trinity and John's were always safe bets) and then presented his prizes. Every captain was supposed to buy a prize for each member of his team, a prize that was cleverly thought out to be appropriate to the individual, in much the same way as Joe and I had carefully selected a pair of plastic penises. I was given a hooter because I was loud on the pitch, and Duane was given a piece of Indian (as in Cowboys and Indians) headgear for no apparent reason. Next came the announcement of next year's captain and Player of the Year. Now next year's captain was decided solely by the present skipper, and I already knew this was coming my way, but Player of the Year was voted for by the players, and I really wanted this award. I had even tactically voted for a lad who didn't have a snowflake in hell's chance of winning just so my vote wouldn't help the challenge of a rival. Although it took a while for it to sink in as my attention was concentrated on keeping le soup d'onion et du vin from making a second appearance, it turned out that I did win the Player of the Year award, and got a nice little trophy for it. The captain described me as a rock at the heart of the defence, and I assumed that he meant I was solid, hard and reliable, and not that I didn't move during games. I was helped out of my chair to make my speech. I don't really know quite what I said, but I have been told that the previous night's Brummie accent was wheeled out yet again, and that I gave my penis present to the outgoing captain by trying to shove it in his ear.

I didn't bother returning to my seat, instead opting for the direct route to the toilet, where I stayed for the rest of the night. In an incident that I can only be thankful I was too drunk to properly remember, one lad who was desperate to use the toilet that I was in reasoned, wrongly as it turned out, that the bowl was easily big enough for my head and his flowing urine. Whilst I was trying to stay alive in the toilets and getting an unusual shower, the action was still going on in the main room. New captain Joe Porter, who had also been sick, had won the prize for 2nd XI Player of the Year but had stayed slumped in his chair for his acceptance speech. He was not too drunk, however, to point out that this accolade was infinitely better than mine. Young Nick MacLean, staring at the main course that I never got to see, reportedly apologised calmly and considerately to his table and then threw up onto his plate and into his wine glass. I think it was at this stage that we were asked to leave.

Back in college I somehow found my way to the bar and was promptly taken to my bed by a concerned and tutting Faye ("Ooh no, Josh, ooh no"). The geographers Joe and Nick remarkably managed to complete the traditional Main Court Run (one, very speedy, lap around Main Court, naked) and then Joe managed to go one further and make it to Cindies.

In the morning I stumbled straight into the shower and feared for my life as I witnessed what I thought was blood flowing in large quantities from my head down the plug hole. After two shampoos the hair spray came off. After three days I started to feel better again.

Chapter 46

I was more than ready to go home at Easter; ready for a break from work and a break from drinking, ready to see my oven-cooked friends and my long suffering mother, ready to watch ridiculous teen dramas on the TV instead of living them.

A Tale of Friendship, Love and Economics

Against my better wishes, I didn't stay home for long. It wasn't as if it was one of those things that seemed a good idea at the time, it was one of bad ideas that I was never going to do in a month of Sundays but where agreeing was far easier than saying no. I assumed that I would be able to pull out at a later date, be labelled a let-down and a kill-joy from afar, safely out of the range of my ears, and so too did Faye. However, no sooner had we got ourselves reacquainted with the beautiful North, breathing in its clean air and getting soaked by its friendly springtime rain, than we found ourselves sat on a train heading down to London. We had agreed to go down and watch the Oxford-Cambridge Boat Race; the pinnacle of the university's sporting calendar, the clash of the educated titans, light blue against dark blue, us versus the Other Lot, it was even on the BBC. Nick MacLean had kindly said that we could stay at his house after I had offered up our lack of accommodation as an excuse for our abstention. Mark Novak, a fellow Londoner living not more than five minutes away from Nick in a town called East Sheen, was going to be there, as was my M-block late-night cereal eating companion Barnet-based Jude, and the notorious Croydon Boy, Adam "Sly" Sylvester.

I had brought a book to read with me on the train, a riveting tale about the macroeconomics of the interwar years by an economic historian and Cambridge lecturer named Solomos Solomou. Needless to say the three hour journey to Euston seemed to last a lifetime. Reading this book was part of the revision programme I had drawn up for myself over the Easter break. It was a light programme, never more than two hours a day, but it was already proving difficult to stick to, hence the necessity of the boring book on the train. Faye, on the other hand, had boarded the train armed with a tabloid and a walkman, probably reasoning quite rightly that she could work some of what she learnt from these two items into next term's geography exams.

Nick kindly offered to pick us up from Euston in his car, and then rather unkindly charged us for petrol money, much to Faye's disgust. We arrived on the Friday evening with the big race being the next day. Faye and I were starving and I had texted Mark to tell him to get the tea on. Needless to say he hadn't and so we dined out in style at East Sheen's best chip shop where I tried for the first time, and quite enjoyed, a battered sausage. The Scottish one and I were fairly knackered after the trip, and so we declined the offer of a few drinks and headed off to our beds well before Friday became

Saturday. I'm a great believer in equality of the sexes, equal rights and all that, and so I had no qualms at all about pushing Faye out of the way whilst I secured the comfy mattress leaving her with just a sleeping bag on Nick's hard bedroom floor. I fell asleep almost immediately, my ears filled with the sweet, soothing highland sounds of: "Piss off, Josh, will you, enough is bloody enough, I'm a *lady* for Christ's sake".

Nick didn't have any Weetabix, and so I had to make do with dry toast. Nick was one of the most organised people I had ever met, and he had a schedule drawn up that we had already fallen behind due to Faye stubbornly locking herself in to her sleeping bag cocoon, desperately trying to clutch a few more minutes in dream land. Nick moved us through breakfast with military efficiency, stopping only shout at me for singing and not eating at the breakfast table, and no sooner had the toast been acquainted with the acid of my stomach, we were on a bus bound for Hammersmith.

The day was a good one. We met up with the rest of the gang in a pub called The Ship. Adam Sylvester was there, as were Jude and Elizabeth, thankfully all awkwardness seemingly under the bridge. Whilst it was good to see the crowd in unfamiliar surroundings it was certainly not good to pay just under three quid a pint. Faye soon decided that she could go without drink for one day. Nick, who'd implicitly taken command of proceedings, suggested that the best place to watch the race was by the side of Hammersmith Bridge, the second time post, and so, with plenty of time to spare, off we trotted. Unsurprisingly the streets, river banks, bridges and nearby pubs were jammed-packed with people of all ages. Some enterprising individuals were selling commemorative T-shirts on the river bank to mark the occasion, T-shirts that looked like they'd be done the night before by a three-year-old armed with a pack of felt-tips and in possession of zero artistic potential. We bustled and barged our way through the crowds, Adam Sylvester being an expert at this, until we settled upon a river-side spot just a row behind the specially erected fence. There we waited. The BBC's large screen was just in view and we could see interviews and profiles of the two crews as part of the build-up. We didn't know any of our light-blue lot, presumably because a lot of the rowers of both crews were overseas "students" brought to the university solely to row, and maybe do a degree in paper-folding or coffee-making in their spare time. The second boat of each university, Goldie for us and Isis for them, race before the Main Event, but the TV cameras don't cover this. Hence, when two boats and sixteen frantically swishing oars flew past us, we were both surprised and completely confused as to what was going on and who to cheer for. We cheered anyway, and only after the main race was over did we find out that the Goldie crew, complete with one member from our beloved St. Catharine's, had in fact won.

We were more prepared for the big race, having used the big screen to figure out which side of the river our lot were on. As the two crews lined up down the river at Putney Bridge, our attention was focused more on events a little closer to home. The mighty River Thames seemed to be rising, and rising fast. It was now less than a metre away from the row in front of us, a row predominately made up of old people whose chances of enjoying or even surviving a quick dip I didn't fancy. A few of them moved as soon as they discovered their failing eyes weren't deceiving them. A few, however, presumably the stubborn that exist in all age brackets, refused to be moved by something as insignificant as a bit of water (after all they'd probably fought in the war for this water). One elderly couple, but a few minutes ago, had been proudly sitting on their portable chairs, pouring themselves a couple of cups of steaming coffee from a brown plastic flask, and smiling contentedly about the how comfy they were, what a good view they were going to have, and how a bit of forward planning could make life a whole lot more enjoyable. Now, the solid ground underneath their seats and that their illusions were built upon was giving way. As the water scurried around their chair legs the old lady gathered together their things, a handbag, a couple of carrier bags, the flask and a wooden walking stick, and got to her feet. The old man, however, refused to concede defeat to the elements. He stayed seated almost to the point where his chair was launched into the river, only to be finally helped away by two concerned stewards. With the front row evacuated and the river finally showing signs of setting up camp at the level it had reached, we now became the front row, and enjoyed a cracking view of the race as it went by.

Due to the watery excitement happening right in front of our eyes we only found out later that there had been a restart after the oars of the two crews clashed. When the race eventually did get underway, and despite our front-row view, I found it tricky to figure out exactly what was going on and who was winning. I suppose it must be like horse racing, although I have never been. There was so much action over such a short period of time, that my brain gave up and begged my eyes to return to the simplicity and slow pace of the big screen, but at least I could say I had seen it. In the end we won by two and a half lengths, which is apparently a lot in rowing terms, leading to some half-hearted inter-university banter. Personally I felt no strong allegiance to Cambridge, at least nothing like what I felt for my college, and probably would have had just as good a day had we lost.

If the day was good, the evening was even better. Nick, Mark, Jude, Sly, Faye and I headed off for a night out in Covent Garden, in what was to be mine and Faye's first taste of the London nightlife. It was the week after the boy members of the goodie-goodie band S Club 7 had allegedly been caught smoking dope outside in a pub in the area, so we knew it must be cool. We wandered around for a while, absorbing the almost carnival atmosphere taking place on the streets. There were performers of all sorts; jugglers, singers, magicians, knife throwers, human statues and people that bent into positions that shouldn't have been possible, all being ignored or observed by people of all sorts; Chinese, European, American and various mixtures somewhere in between, either tourists or permanent residents of the ever-widening culture of London. I enjoyed soaking it all up. I never thought London was for me, and maybe it still wasn't, but it was certainly a spectacle that I was pleased to be a part of. Eventually we stumbled upon a bar that took everyone's fancy, or at least was not met by any serious objections, and sat down at a round wooden table in the corner.

I seemed to have been hanging around with Adam "Sly" Sylvester, the dark destroyer of my first night in Cambridge, far more in recent weeks. He just always seemed to be there, whether it was with Jude or Elizabeth, or through the friendship that was beginning to develop between him and Nick MacLean. I still did not particularly like the fellow, or trust him one little bit, but if I was not exactly warming to him slightly, I was certainly growing less cold towards him. To give him his due, he was entertaining, and he certainly didn't mince his words. Whenever there was silence in a conversation it would inevitably be broken by: "I'll tell you what, so-and-so is a right cock", and so-and-so would be seemingly chosen at random from a list that could include just about anybody. You had to be careful around Sly as he had a tendency to play mind games, tricking you into saying something about somebody that he would then inevitably use against you at a later date. He was the kind of person that whenever he was being nice to you, you found yourself asking why, and whenever he ignored you for no apparent reason, you were not in the least bit surprised. However, I had grown to tolerate him, and even enjoy his company on occasion. I figured this was necessary as it was clear the troublesome historian of Sri Lankan origin would not be leaving my life any time soon.

It was quite clear that our student budgets were not going to allow us to get drunk, with this particular bar turning out to be relatively expensive for Covent Garden, and Covent Garden itself being expensive compared with the rest of already expensive London. We got a few rounds in anyway, and pretty soon the inevitable happened and the drinking games started. Drinking games had really caught on that term amongst our group, and would be regularly played before nights out, either sat in the bar or in someone's room. They were a good way to get the reluctant drinking, and very handy when over familiarity had left us with nothing much to talk to each other about.

There were several drinking games that we played. By far the most popular was the "Celebrity Name Game". This game employed the "drink while you think" principle, and basically the game progressed clockwise around the group with the first person saying the name of a celebrity (e.g. Tom Cruise), and the next person having to come up with a celebrity whose first name began with the first letter of the latter's surname (e.g. Chris Evans). There were other rules such as if the celebrity's first name and surname began with the same letter (e.g. Roland Rat), then the order of play was reversed, you were not allowed to use celebrities that had already been said in the game, you had to keep drinking until you came up with an answer or finished your drink (hence, "drink while you think"), and if more than half the people hadn't heard of your celebrity, you had to finish whatever was left in your glass. Mark Novak was woeful at all drinking games, but especially bad at the Celebrity one. After a while, whenever his turn came around, he would resign himself to defeat, like some depressed dogs that kept getting electrocuted in a famous study that we had learnt about in A-level psychology, and just see away his drink without even thinking.

There was also "Pass the Buck". This game started with one person saying a word (e.g. hockey) and then the person next to him or her saying a related word (e.g. gay). This game also employed "drink while you think", as well as challenges if your word was not associated closely enough, and yes old Novak was terrible at it. Adam Sylvester was a fan of a variant on the theme known as "Pass the Buck: Snog Web" where any old words were replaced by the names of people in college, and when your go came around you had to come up with someone who the last name mentioned had pulled. Sly liked this game as it was a chance to stir up some trouble if a girl he knew you fancied had pulled someone, and also an opportunity to list for the 17,000th time all the poor souls in college that he had pulled.

Another classic was "The Spelling Game". In this one a person said a letter (e.g. "t") and then the person next to him had to say another letter that was on its way to spelling a word without actually completing one (e.g. "r" would be good as you could spell "train", "o" would be useless as you had just spelt "to", and "x" was not looking good either as if challenged you had to come up with a legitimate word that started "tx"). This game always caused a lot of controversy and a lot of laughs with countless dodgy spellings and equally dodgy words produced. Mark Novak, whenever it was his turn to start a round off, often opened up with "a" or "I", and found himself finishing his drink from the very start.

My personal favourite didn't really have a name, but it required at least six people to be effective. Someone signalled the round had started and then anyone could stand up and say "one", and then another person stand up and say "two" and so on right up until six, or however many were playing. If two people stood up for the same number, they had to drink, and then the game started all over again. The harshest of all fines was reserved for the cautious soles who kept their backsides on their seats hoping the game would end without them having to get up and risk drinking. If it got all the way to them, with everyone having stood up and said a number, they had to down a full glass.

"Thumb Master", "Boomerang Master" and "Shoe Master" were also played in the background whilst another more full-on drinking game was in progress. The rugby team had games like "Twenty-One" and "International Drinking Rules", the former involving a lot of complicated tapping and the latter banning pointing and drinking with the wrong hand, that I never really understood, and we rarely played.

Tonight, in Covent Garden, we mainly played the "Celebrity Name Game", but were forced to chuck in a few rounds of "Pass the Buck: Snog Web" to keep Sly happy. Mark Novak was, predictably, loosing badly, but seeing as his wallet couldn't keep up with his misfortunes, it was decided that he should do another kind of forfeit. After much discussion we decided that the skinny economist from East Sheen should go up to the barman and ask him if he served cocktails. Whenever the barman replied that he didn't, as we knew he would given that the place didn't do cocktails, young Mark had to then ask: "So I can't have a Deep Long Hard Screw Up Against The Wall then?" Needless to say, Mark was a wee bit reluctant, but amazingly he did it, much to our initial amusement and then longer-term embarrassment and regret as we realised that it was now probably best to leave the pub and take Mark with us. Mark was always the quiet, studious one, but on occasion would do mad things like that, maybe just to remind us not to attach such general labels.

Anyway, despite our premature exit, the night had been a good laugh. We bid farewell to Jude and Sly as they made their way back to Sly's house in Croydon, and the four of us caught the tube and bus back to East Sheen. After a surprisingly good night's sleep, having finally conceded the comfy mattress to my ever moaning, high-maintenance Scottish companion, we caught the 12.23 Euston to Glasgow train, thankfully calling at Preston, all the way back home. In the end, I was glad I went.

Chapter 47

The only other significant even of the Easter holidays was that I finally decided enough was enough, and went along to have my hair cut. It was just getting too long. I couldn't remember what my ears looked like, and the back of my neck would itch all the time. Whenever something went missing in the house, Mum would always check in my hair first, which was funny the first time she did it, but got a little annoying on the forty-fifth. Worst of all, whenever it rained or I had a shower, my hair would take ages to dry, and if I went outside with it wet I would get cold.

"Either use my hair-dryer or get the thing cut off," had been Mum's unasked-for advice.

There was no way I was blow drying my hair. A lad at school had tried that technique once and his hair looked like blonde candy-floss, so fluffy, light and bouncy. So, after weighing up my options, I concluded that the hair had to go, and with it my cool student look.

I had not been to the hairdresser's for over six months now, and I was very nervous. I went to the local guy who had been cutting my hair for the last seven years or so, and charging me just £3.50 a time for the privilege.

He had seen me through wedges and undercuts, centre-partings and side-partings, the Spiky Gel Days and the Do What You Want To It Days. He'd never seen it like this though.
"Bloody hell, is that you Josh?"
"Yep. I've kind of let my hair grow a bit."
"Bloody students. You send them away to university, and they come back looking like *that* I don't know."
He was talking to the old man in the adjacent chair who was nodding along approvingly whilst flicking through *FHM* magazine. I was sure he only came to the hairdresser's so that he could read it, or look at the pictures anyway, without his wife finding out.
"So, anyway, what do you want doing with it. I've got some shears and a lawn-mower out the back."
"You might need them. I want it all off, back to the way it used to be."
"Number two on the back and sides, and choppy on the top?"
"Yep, reckon you can do it?"
"I'll try my best."
And off he went. Clumps of hair fell like leaves from a tree as the scissors and the clippers worked their way through the jungle on top of my head. I cringed when the first bit came off, but then relaxed knowing that there was no going back now. My hairdresser thought he was a funny man, and once again he decided to try and prove it today. Having cut all but the back of my head, he announced that he had finished. He got the mirror out which revealed to me a lovely curly mullet flowing elegantly down the back of my neck. I looked a right prick, like someone a pop-star from the 1980s or a stereotypical Austrian. The old man laughed and then returned to an "article" on Jennifer Aniston. Finally, he clippered the mullet off and did a bit of tidying up. I had a new haircut, and I even gave him a 50p tip. For the next few days I felt the chill of every gust of wind that blew past the side of my now unprotected head, and I missed twiddling around with the curly bits whilst watching the telly, but I was glad I had it done. My mum approved, even describing me as looking sophisticated.
The rest of the holiday I spent seeing my friends and family, and doing a fair bit of revision. Time seemed to fly by, and no sooner had my Easter egg reached the bottom of the hill, than I was back in John's car, this time Mum coming along too, armed with a new haircut, heading down south, via

A Tale of Friendship, Love and Economics

Stoke, for the third and final term of first year; a term promising exams and May Balls, and hopefully the prospect of a bit of romance.

Third Term – April 2001

They decided to have breakfast outside. It was a clear day with only the slightest of breezes. She had toast with butter and a strong black coffee, he had toast with jam and a glass of tap water. They placed their things down on a wooden table that overlooked the garden and the neighbours' fields. They ate for a while, listening to the sound and songs of God's things. It was inevitable that on their last day together they would talk about the past. She carefully rested her cup of half-drunk coffee on the saucer and asked him if he regretted anything. He asked her if they had to have a bloody deep and meaningful, or could he just enjoy his toast and jam. She pressed him for an answer, as she always did. In the end he gave in, as he always did. He thought about it for a moment and took a sip from his water. A bird flew over his head and settled on the branch of a tree. He told her he only regretted things that he couldn't have changed anyway. The bird moved to another branch. They both knew what he meant, and they both had another bite of toast. It was too early in the day to get into that. It was too late as well.

Chapter 48

Mum was quite impressed with how tidy my room looked, and even said she'd treat me to a meal tonight because of it. I was shocked and thought I had walked through the wrong door.

There was no way this was the same M14 that I had left behind but a month ago. My room was immaculate, and it looked twice as big as I remembered it. I smiled and thanked her, and tried to give a look that said: my dear mother, there is no need to reward me in any way, for nineteen years you have brought me up to be a clean, tidy boy, and here before you lie the fruits of your labour. I decided to keep quiet about the fact that it was only tidy because the bedders had clearly been working overtime and cleaned out all my crap for the benefit of the various conference guests and overseas students that had been staying in the M-block rooms over Easter. Indeed, my room was an absolute disgrace all throughout the term, but especially towards the end. It was like the stereotypical student hovel; a cliché before

A Tale of Friendship, Love and Economics

the eyes. There were crisp packets and sweet wrappings competing for floor space with beer cans, wine bottles, empty Pot Noodle cartons, biscuit crumbs, old hardened tea bags, my tissues, other people's tissues, various items of sticky cutlery, odd socks, boxer shorts that could have been clean but probably weren't, and various items of girl's clothing, mostly Faye's and Mary Jane's, which I liked to keep on display in the hope that people would assume women frequently removed their clothes in my room. In fact, the cleanest part of the room was probably the bin, which lay untouched in the far corner. With so many people coming round all the time for Kerplunk or *Neighbours*, the mess just got out of control, and after initial frantic clean-up sprees, I soon became resigned to defeat. It wasn't my mess after all, but it was my room. Eventually I learnt to tolerate a messy M14, regarding it as the common room it had fast become. Now, however, I saw I had a chance to make a fresh start. My room was clean, and I was determined it was going to stay that way.

We unpacked all my stuff in a new personal best time and headed out for something to eat. I guiltily accepted Mum's kind offer of a meal because I was starving after the Burger King-free drive down, however my annoying conscience, consistently the source of my problems, wouldn't allow me to lead them into an expensive restaurant, and so as the hour reached three John, Mum and I found ourselves sat in the largest pub in England, Wetherspoons. Mum was always one for a bargain, and thus was mightily impressed by the Beer-Burger meal deal, although given the time of the day we all opted for a coke.

"Remember to ask for no ice, Josh, they give you more coke then."
"What if I want ice?"
"Then get ice."
"Yes, Mum."

We ate our food, went to buy a light bulb for the upstairs bedroom, whose purchase apparently couldn't wait until John and Mum got home, and then returned to college.

I had come back early from the Easter holidays a full week before we had to be back, in fact. However, I wasn't going to be staying in Cambridge all that time. My tiny, posh, squeaky friend Elizabeth had kindly invited me to come and stay at her house for a few days before the start of term, and then get a lift back to Cambridge with her and her father. A few people, including Jude, had already been to stay, and it seemed my turn had come around. I had heard rumours that she had a massive house, and thus was very keen to go. Mum was also very much in favour of me making the trip presumably hoping I would eventually marry Elizabeth – she hadn't met her of course – and then she could live in this big house that neither of us had seen as well. And so, with Mum and John bidding me a thankfully tearless farewell, I packed up my rucksack with boxer shorts, socks, toothbrush and a couple of T-shirts, and began the long walk to the train station, a walk that, in fact, took me past Wetherspoons, suggesting that a bit of forward planning might have saved my poor legs.

Knowing that I had zero common sense and that I was a virgin when it came to travelling around London on my own, Elizabeth had emailed me a Josh-proof set of instructions that would get me from Cambridge to her station in Weybridge, Surrey. Needless to say, I still managed to mess up. King's Cross station was just so big, well, bigger than Preston station anyway. I couldn't find Platform 14, and by the time an unhelpful fat man had vaguely pointed me in the right direction I wasn't sure that the train standing there was my one, and by the time I decided that it probably was, it had pulled away. In the end, I made it to Weybridge just two hours behind schedule, and was met by a relieved Elizabeth, and a Dad who was clearly thinking: what kind of idiot can't catch a train. As I shook his hand, Elizabeth introduced him to one.

Chapter 49

Apparently everyone knew Weybridge was posh, everyone apart from me that is. I had never heard of the place, and only knew Surrey as the county that kept beating Lancashire at cricket. I thought it was just another part of London, and thus was bound to be full of red buses, pigeons, litter, cockneys and tube lines. In fact it was a lovely area. It even had grass and trees, presumably imported from the north. And the houses were massive, every single one of them. All were detached, with huge front gardens undoubtedly maintained by a professional, drives containing about six cars, and gate posts that rivalled our very own St. Catharine's. I felt like a kid going to Disneyland as I sat in the back of her Dad's car, my head staring out of the window, eyes wide open, bedazzled by the sights that were streaming past my eyes.

    Elizabeth's house was amazing. I lost count trying to keep track of how many rooms there were. Some of the rooms had names like The Drawing Room and The Games Room, and even one of the bathrooms had been bestowed with the title of Master. My favourite bit of the house was the circular gap on the first floor that allowed you to look down on the floor below. It made the house more expansive, and also meant that you could drop things on unsuspecting people's heads as they walked past oblivious. Elizabeth said such a move might not exactly go down a treat on her mother. They had a pool table and a grand piano, a wide-screen TV and a log fire. They even had a canal that ran along the back of the house, complete, of course, with their very own barge. My only criticisms were that they had a dog, and their huge garden had been ruined by tasteful rock features and flowers, whereas a large, flat piece of green, with a couple of goal posts at either end would have been far more preferable. I made a mental note to bring this matter up over dinner. I felt a little intimidated by the whole thing, but also realised that my Mum's plan for marriage might not be the worst one in the world.

    Elizabeth had warned me that her family were a bit crazy, especially her Mum. She told me not to take offence at anything she said, and advised me that it would probably be best not to say the word "nob" in front of her. I asked if "dick" was any better or should I just stick to "cock", and as Elizabeth thought about it for a moment, her eyes trying to keep up with the thoughts that were flying around in her head, I smiled to let her know I was only joking.

    I was nervous as I always was before meeting parents, but doubly nervous this time because of Elizabeth's warnings and the lavish settings. I started twitching around and even whistling, and as her Mum came into the kitchen, I took a deep breath to prepare myself for the big meeting.

    "Mummy, this is Josh."

    Elizabeth always referred to her Mum and Dad as "Mummy and Daddy", as if she was doing everything possible to fit into the role of My Posh Friend. Luckily, this was not the first time I had heard her say this, and hence I had practiced not laughing.

    "Hello, Josh."

"Hello, Mrs Braithwaite. Nice to meet you." Again I opted for the handshake over the kiss. By this stage I had just about perfected the amount of pressure and grip required for a female handshake, and thus was pleased of any opportunity to try it out.

"What a strange accent."

"Mummy!" It was the high-pitched squeal that signalled anger. I had to smile.

"I know. I'm from Preston, in Lancashire. We all speak funny up there."

"Lancashire, you say? Never been myself."

"Oh, it's really good, you know? We've got Blackpool, with its Illuminations and Pleasure Beach, and we've got loads of fields and cows and things, and I suppose we've kind of got Manchester with *Coronation Street* and Oasis, and Liverpool with The Beatles and *Brookside*, and the Lake District with water and hills, although they're not technically Lancashire, and although it rains a lot and it's freezing most of the time..." I was rambling like an idiot. Elizabeth's Mum had long since stopped listening and had now turned away. I finished my "Come to Lancashire It's Great!" spiel under my breath, and turned to Elizabeth to be rescued. She smiled sympathetically and led me upstairs to my room.

It was one of those houses where a map would have come in handy. It was something like three left turns and a couple of right ones to get from the kitchen to my room, a route which I made no great effort to remember, quite fancying the idea of getting lost inside a house. Needless to say, my room contained an *en suite* and a double bed, even though it wasn't even the premier guest room, and needless to say I swore when I saw it.

There was little doubt that Elizabeth's family were loaded. her Dad was a partner of a major law firm, and those that knew about these things told me that he was on big money, very big money indeed. It was the level of richness that I had expected, and feared, more people would be on at Cambridge, but so far she was the first I had seen. But Elizabeth was very down to earth. Her Dad only gave her a certain amount of money for university, and she was always running out, forcing her to scrounge Sainsbury's Economy Ham Slices from our fridge at least once a week. She seemed to have been brought up to know the value of money, which couldn't have been easy with so much of it around. Indeed, she was far more down to earth than some people I knew at university, who were not half as rich as Elizabeth, but paraded around the wealth they had for the

A Tale of Friendship, Love and Economics

world to see. her Dad was also surprisingly normal. He too had been to Catz, where he did a law degree, and was a Blue at rugby, and now had the ears to prove it. He was very easy to talk to, and whilst it was quite clear that he was very intelligent, he never forced it upon you. Her Mum was more of a handful, but once you relaxed and didn't take literally everything she said, she turned out to be lovely as well.

The few days I spent down at Elizabeth's house were really good fun. I awoke the first morning with an unexplained dry throat in desperate need of water. I successfully navigated my way down to the kitchen on my sixth attempt, wearing only my skimpy boxer shorts and an old T-shirt. As I reached for a glass I was accosted by Elizabeth's mother, wearing a pair of ridiculously large yellow gloves, black wellies and a lop-sided hat, who proceeded, without a word, to put the glass back in the cupboard and fill my now empty hands with a shovel and spade. I looked at her disbelievingly.

"Gardening time, my boy, gardening time."

I smiled back, and kept smiling in a confused fashion as I was led hand on spade outside and presented with a rather sizeable hole to dig. I don't know if she mistook me for the gardener, or if this was the regular induction process for her daughter's friends, but Mrs Braithwaite was not certainly joking when she said she wanted me to dig a hole, and stood by watching me until I had done it. Only then was I allowed the glass of water, and God did I need it. Elizabeth was clearly embarrassed and apologised profusely when I told her about what happened, explaining that Mummy was a bit funny like that some times and that I should take no notice. I made her promise to accompany me down to breakfast on subsequent mornings.

During the afternoon I went out on the family barge with Elizabeth, her little sister, and her big sister's boyfriend. I had met Elizabeth's big sister and her boyfriend once before when they came down to Cambridge. She had seemed very nice, and not half as posh as her younger, squeakier sibling. Her boyfriend seemed a bit of an eccentric. He was originally from Scotland, but his current accent was a blended mixture of about seventeen different regions. He wore kilts and said thinks like, "Jolly good lad" and "Right-o my boy, spiffing." He had also been too drunk at the time to remember me now, so I introduced myself again. This was the first time I had met Elizabeth's little sister, who was fourteen, and already showing signs of the very attractive woman she would one day become (the football team referred to such girls with potential as "fledgling fitties", and these girls were often on the end of a few wolf-whistles, much to their mothers' disapproval). The little sister was posh beyond belief, making her sister sound common as muck. She was a right little drama queen and prima-donna, with every story she told starting with: "Oh, the most frightful thing happened to me today..." and every request with "Oh, be a darling won't you and pass me the..." Elizabeth said that she had only become like that in the last couple of years and blamed her school friends. Even if she was pretty, I could only handle her in small doses, and I had to work hard to escape her on the confines of a barge. The barge trip was really good fun. I managed to mess up any role I was given in getting the boat through the numerous locks, whether it be throwing the rope and missing, or opening the wrong lock gate. We stopped to have a picnic and urinate in a bush, and made it home, quite exhausted, before nightfall.

The next morning was happily gardening free, and I spent a relaxing time with Elizabeth in front of the telly, and playing the odd game of pool which I happily won, largely because poor little Elizabeth couldn't reach 70 per cent of the shots. She explained that she would have to spend most of the day packing to go back to uni tomorrow, so I could either stay and help, or take her little sister to the cinema. I could foresee me being more of a hindrance than a help, so I said that as long as Elizabeth could bare to be without me, I would happily take her younger sibling to the cinema.

"You won't try to nob her, will you?"

I loved the way Elizabeth said "nob". I found it such a funny word, and even funnier when it came from her squeaky posh voice. It stood out like a baby saying a single word amidst an inaudible assortment of sounds. Much as she said it was a frightfully filthy expression, I think Elizabeth liked it too.

"I'll try my best," I said with a wink.

And so, from gardener to chaperone, I headed off to the local cinema to see the recently released *Bridget Jones's Diary*. I assumed it was going to be one of those girly films that I hated, but in fact it was quite good. Elizabeth informed me that I was the first boy to take her sister out to the cinema, and I felt quite proud to be chosen for this milestone in the young girl's life. After chatting to her when the previews were on, and also when I had missed the bit in the film that said who this new girl was, I found out that she too was quite down to earth and had a good sense of humour. We got on really well despite the five-year age gap, largely because she was quite mature and I was very immature. At one stage during the film, just as

A Tale of Friendship, Love and Economics

Bridget is about to catch Hugh Grant with another woman, Elizabeth's little sister got up to go to the toilet and "accidentally" brushed her hand across my thigh. I got the feeling I wasn't the first boy that little Ms Innocent had done that to. I sat nervously eating my popcorn in silence for the rest of the film.

In the morning, bright and early, Elizabeth, her Dad and I began our journey in the fully loaded car from Weybridge to Cambridge. I bid farewell to the family and told them to call in anytime they were bombing around Lancashire. Her Mum smiled and nodded but looked a bit confused and disgusted. I phoned my Mum to tell her all about it and that I was now working on the right time for my marriage proposal, so she should probably start to think about what hat she would wear to the wedding. I had survived and had a lovely time. It wasn't quite *How the Other Half Lives*, but it was certainly an eye-opener, and a pleasant one at that. I guess it taught me that money didn't define who people were, that there were as many rich pricks as poor ones, but more importantly, that one day I just had to be rich enough to afford my own pool table. It was a good, relaxing way to start a term that would undoubtedly contain some of the hardest weeks of my life so far.

Chapter 50

"You've had your hair cut. Looks good," said Mark.
"Hey, baldy-sclady," said Oisin.
"Well, hello there, and what have you done with my long-haired neighbour?" said Faye.
"Aw, I liked your long hair... but you still look alright," said Francesca.
"You still look gay," said Caolan.

With hair-talk taking up twenty minutes of my first conversations with people upon our return after the Easter break, talk tended to move swiftly on to the dreaded subject of exams. I was happy with the amount of revision I had done over the holidays. I hadn't exactly worked my arse off, but I had done enough not to feel guilty. As with anything, however, it was not the absolute amount that mattered, but the relative.

"No-one's done any revision or anything stupid like that, have they?" asked Caolan, as we sat in his room the day the two Irish landed.

"Nah, I can't work at home. There are too many distractions, or whatever," replied Oisin.

"You'd get distracted in solitary confinement," I replied. "No, I've just done a bit, you know, just gone through the tricky bits of Micro and done that essay for Stevo, that one on the gold standard."

"Yeah, I've done a bit too, pretty much the same as Josh."

Both Mark and I sounded as if we were confessing to a serious crime when admitting that we had done work over the holidays. It was always the way at school, but I didn't expect it to be like that at Cambridge.

"The exams aren't for another, what, six or seven weeks?" I said as means of an apology.

"Aye, something like that, thank fuck," replied Caolan.

"We'll still be able to go out and stuff, won't we?" I asked, more to reassure myself than as a direct question.

"Aye, of course we will. No exams are stopping me having a good time, and anyway, like you say, they're not for ages. Bags of time," said an animated Caolan.

"Bags of time," I repeated.

Whilst the Irish boy-band look-alike may have done no work over the Easter holidays, he had seemingly picked up a new hobby. Stuck up on the wall of his *en suite* Gostlin room lay a yellow A3 sheet of paper upon which were written words such as: heteronym, dvandva, palimpsest and sibilate.

"What the hell is that?" I enquired as the piece of paper caught my eye just before leaving the room.

"I've decided to expand my vocabulary." Caolan replied both proudly and patronisingly. I looked confused, and so the Irishman carried on.

"You see, every time I come across I word I don't understand, I look up its meaning in the dictionary and then write the word down on this piece of paper. I then give myself a little test each day to see if I can remember them."

"Are you being serious?"

"I am merely aspiring to even more greatness, Bailey, I wouldn't expect you to understand."

Now this was typical Caolan. He would do something like this, something that if someone else did it he would call them gay or a dick or something equally flattering, but because it was him, it was suddenly a perfectly reasonable thing to do. Doing a bit of work over the holidays was gay, but consciously teaching yourself new words every day was absolutely sound; Football was gay, but polo was fine; double vodka lime and lemon was gay, but always insisting on diet coke with his vodka was completely different; I was attention-seeking when I did *Millionaero*, he wasn't when he stood for First Year Rep; being quiet when sober was a really bad character trait, whereas being abusive to your friends when drunk was funny; going to the gym was gay, but spending an hour pruning yourself in front of the mirror was fine; wearing football shirts was gay, but strutting around in a particularly expensive long, white coat and naming it Penelope was possibly the most normal behaviour imaginable. I knew he was only joking, I knew it was just his sense of humour, but it annoyed me all the same.

There wasn't much time for revising in the first few weeks of term even if we had possessed great desires to do so. For a start we hadn't yet finished being taught the course, with lectures and supervisions continuing until the end of week four, and secondly, we had the small matter of an EQEM exam and a Statistics project to do.

It was fair to say that most of us had forgotten all about EQEM; not just the forthcoming exam taking place a couple of weeks into term, but the course itself. You see, the whole point of the course was to make sure we were all at or above a certain level of mathematical proficiency. Being the good boys that we were in first term, we had toddled along to the first few lectures of the course, and couldn't believe what we were hearing. A young academic from Germany spent lecture one telling us what numbers were, lecture two telling us how to add up, lecture three telling how to subtract, and lecture four reviewing what we had learnt so far. Pretty soon we decided to bin the EQEM lecture series, after all we had all done Maths and Further Maths A-levels; this was an insult to our intelligence. The problem was the course got a little bit harder. With two weeks to go before our exam, failure at which could potentially get us thrown off the economics course, we decided it might be wise to print out a couple of past papers, just to see what stage of adding and subtracting the course had got to (maybe three – or even four-digit numbers?). Our smug smiles were soon well and truly wiped off our cocky faces when our eyes fell upon the kind of questions we were going to be asked. Matrices, consumption functions, national income accounting and not even a hint of a three plus three. Bloody hell, I thought.

And so, with the use of a textbook, we set about teaching ourselves the EQEM course. To be fair, a lot of it was Maths A-level stuff sneakily dressed up in an economics costume, and after a bit of practice it all came flooding back. Indeed, I realised I had missed a bit of good old differentiation and substitution, solving that tricky quadratic and then seeing what happens when x tends to infinity. In the week before the exam, Caolan, Oisin, Mark and I did a past paper each morning and then went through the answers together. We only needed 40 per cent to pass and, though we didn't want to start counting any chickens, we were all pretty confident of getting though it.

Nerves were inevitably present on the day of the exam. After all, this was our first exam in Cambridge. I had bought myself a new biro to mark the occasion, sharpened up my pencils, broke in my rubber and made sure my calculator was giving all the right answers. Just like at school you weren't allowed to take pencil cases in unless they were see-through, and just like at school, I opted for a plastic wallet to transport the necessary stationery. Mum sent me a packet of wine gums to keep me going, and Faye stuck a note on my door wishing me good luck. I met the faithful trio of Caolan, Oisin and Mark outside the Plodge at 8.15am, and we walked down to the exam together. It was a day of unremarkable weather.

Normally economic exams were held up at the Sidgwick Site, however today's little EQEM number was to be held on a foreign site on the way to Wetherspoons. This made no difference to us as we'd never sat an exam anywhere in Cambridge before. Our one girl economist, the curly haired Bulgarian, Leila, caught us up as we crossed Silver Street. Leila often panicked before supervisions and even occasionally before the odd important lecture, and had duly upped the stress levels to an all-time high degree for today's exam.

"Guys, guys, I'm going to fail. I just know I'm going to fail," she wailed.

"You'll be fine, Leila," said Oisin

"Well, I don't know. It wouldn't surprise me if you failed," replied Caolan, much to Leila's disgust. I covered my smile with my hand.

With Leila now giving the cold shoulder to the impressively sideburned Irishman, the feisty Bulgarian now explained to Mark, Oisin and myself that she knew a shortcut to the exam. We were not pushing it for time at all and I failed to see the point in taking an unnecessary risk, but I had quickly learnt that the only way to an easy life was just to go along with whatever

Leila said. And so, following our fearless leader, we found ourselves taking a left turning down an unknown alley. Ten minutes later we were walking, a mite bit brisker than before, back up the alley and back along our original path, with Leila cursing and stressing, Caolan laughing, and the rest of us keeping quiet fearing that anything we said would inevitably be the wrong thing.

We still arrived in plenty of time for the exam. The other seven Catz economists – "The Magnificent Seven" as I thought at the time and duly kept to myself – were clearly visibly amongst the masses, huddled together as they were by a pillar.

"I'm going to fail, guys, I know I'm going to fail," cried Leila again to her new audience.

"Oh shut up, Leila," replied any number of people.

Apart from Leila, the mood was generally quite relaxed. Oisin was complaining of stomach pains, but apart from that everyone seemed well and happy, and just about ready to try and earn ourselves an Economics Qualifying Examination in Elementary Mathematics.

We were led in to a large draughty hall, littered with rows of single desks, by a plump, bearded invigilator and told to find our seats which were arranged in Candidate Number order. Sat at my desk, I laid out my pens, pencils, rubber, ruler and calculator (I kept my compass and protractor in the plastic wallet – they were only there for an emergency), adjusted my chair, arranged the closed exam paper that lay in front of me so that it could be quickly opened, and then took a look around me. The room was full of familiar faces, with familiar nicknames. The Egg, many people's choice for most attractive girl in lectures, was sat a couple of rows behind me, armed with a warehouse full of stationery, with a collection of pens that spanned the entire colour spectrum. The Russian, my choice for hottest girl, was sat three rows in front of me and a couple of seats to the left wearing a very nice green top. Cock Head was complaining that his desk was wonky, and currently had the plump, bearded invigilator on his knees tucking several pieces of folded paper under the offending short leg. Westbrook was clearly panicking, and was clicking her heels together like she was Dorothy (there's no place like home, there's no place like home). Stare was staring at me. I tried to get Mark Novak's attention but he was all eyes down ready to go. I gave Caolan the finger and promptly received one back, and I couldn't see Oisin.

The exam itself was fairly uneventful. The invigilator ran through the set of rules ("Read through the instructions carefully, do not turn over the exam paper until instructed, all mobile phones should be turned off and handed in to me, blah, blah, blah") and when the clock struck nine he uttered those three dreaded words: "You may begin". I could do most of the questions, and only really messed up one of the big money-maker Section B questions – I just couldn't get that last x to cancel out. I finished the exam in plenty of time, and in an act that would have made my high-school teachers proud, I checked my answers thoroughly. I was a bit annoyed at myself for needing the toilet twice in the two-hour-fifteen-minute exam, and made a mental note to get my bodily functions under better control for the big ones in six weeks. All in all I was very happy. I had survived my first Cambridge exam.

And so too were most others. Mark said it went alright, which we took to mean he got 95 per cent. Caolan explained that for Question 6 he just put down seven as the answer for no other reason than it was his lucky number, but apart from that it went fine. Oisin said it went grand, or whatever, but had to go to the toilet four times to see to those mysterious stomach pains. The Cypriot ex-sergeant, never one to beat around the bush, said it was simple, and even Leila had to confess that in all likelihood she probably had passed.

Our EQEM results came back to us via Mr Stevens a week or so later. Thankfully all of us had surpassed the necessary 40 per cent mark, which meant, for better or worse, we were all still economics students and members of St. Catharine's College. Mark had got 86 per cent, which Mr Stevens said was in the top decile of marks in the year, and I got 82 per cent, which, regardless of what decile it was in, meant that the bastard had beaten me by 4 per cent. Oisin got somewhere in the seventies, and Caolan didn't want to know what mark he got, explaining that he was just happy to have passed (I was equally happy to assume that I had beaten him). All eleven Catz economists went to the bar for a few drinks to celebrate, but any wild blow-out was put on hold because in the next few days we were set to receive our next bundle of fun, the Statistics Project.

The Statistics project was worth 40 per cent of our total statistic mark, making it 8 per cent of our overall Part I mark – a small portion of the pie but certainly not one to be sniffed at. We had been in training for the project all of last term under the guidance of the Leader of the Landies and

A Tale of Friendship, Love and Economics

College Dean, the Brummie Dr Tinsley. The main lesson we had drawn from these supervisions was that as long as we used a good computer package and a good font, we would be flying. We were sceptical. We received the project after our ten o'clock lecture on Friday from the Faculty Office. Some of the economists sprinted from Lady Mitchell Hall to the Faculty to get their project a whole minute before everyone else. Our complementary instruction sheet informed us that the project had to be handed in by 3 pm on the following Tuesday, and answers could not exceed 1,500 words, which could include up to eight tables and eight graphs.

We didn't have any more lectures until the twelve o'clock one on "The Third Way," so Caolan, Oisin, Mark and I found a table outside the Buttery and had a look at the paper. Littered all over the Sidgwick Site were Part I economists doing just the same as us, some with a coffee and a smile, some with shaking hands and terrified eyes. Our very own Leila was sprinting around from group to group like a crazed escapee from an asylum, frantically shaking her head and babbling words that no-one appeared to understand. We kept our heads down as her seemingly random path brought her over in our direction. A few keen economists had tried to beat the crowd and were now stumbling out of the Marshall Library, their faces obscured by a mountain of books. In the comfortable and relaxed vacuum we had created on the bench, we took a deep breath and studied the choice of questions.

1. "A country's current account balance improves immediately following a devaluation." Examine this hypothesis using international data relating to the exchange rate crisis of the European Monetary System in September 1992.

2. Assess the relationship between stock market performance and interest rates using data available to you.

3. Empirically examine the hypothesis that the growth rate of labour productivity depends on the growth rate of the capital/output ratio.

4. Using data available to you examine the relationship between changes in consumption and changes in income.

It was decided long before seeing the paper that it would be best if we could all do the same question. Of course, copying was strictly prohibited, and you had to sign a piece of paper declaring the work you were handing in was your own. However, if we could pool resources and work together on the data collection part of the project and the analysis bit, we could then go off and do the write-up all on our own. Mark Novak was the least keen for this approach, but was forced to admit that there could be benefits. Such talk would be academic, however, if we could not decide on a question. We began the process with the tried and tested technique of ruling out.

I was not keen for Question 1, being notoriously shit at anything to do with the balance of payments. No-one else seemed terribly keen for it, so it was provisionally ruled out. Question 2 was also declared a goner – none of us, not even the great Mark Novak, were any good at stocks and shares, at least not compared to the brain-boxes we would invariably be competing against if we took on this question. You see, that was another consideration when weighing up what questions to attempt in exams. If you thought you could do an alright answer to a given question, but you knew that there were a whole bunch of people who could do an ace answer, your answer would stand out as being rubbish when it came to the marking (this was particularly the case in maths-based questions, where unless you were going to get the answer completely right, it was best not to take it on at all). Question 3 could not be ruled out, but was hardly a classic, and good data for labour productivity and the capital/output ratio would probably be tricky to get. Question 4 was a nice question. It stood out like a bright light in a room of darkness. We had studied the relationship between income and consumption in some detail in our Macro course, and data would be easy to come by. The only other consideration was that it was immediately clear, without talking to anyone else, that every Tom, Dick, and Harry would be taking on this question. It would thus be hard to make your answer stand out from the crowd and get a really good mark, however such a scenario was far more appealing than talking rubbish about the stock market and subsequently standing out for being shit. It didn't take long for us to decide that Question 4 was the way to go. The remaining seven Catz economists had independently reasoned the same.

For the whole of the weekend the two computer rooms of college were taken over, both night and day, by Part I Catz economists. Casual emailers were told in no uncertain terms to piss off. Each workspace contained a wall of textbooks and files, together with loose pieces of A4 paper containing the odd scrawled insight or wonky diagram. We trawled through textbooks for the theory and the internet for the statistics. Apart from Leila's daily manic outburst about failure ("Guys, guys, I'm going to fail, I just know it") or rumours she'd heard from a friend of a friend of a friend ("Guys, apparently the examiners will deduct marks unless you write in size 12 font"), it was a pretty relaxed atmosphere. We even had some music on the Saturday night.

In the end we all survived and came up with pretty much the same stuff: Keynes' Consumption Function, Friedman's Permanent Income Hypothesis and Modigliani's Life Cycle Hypothesis to be compared and contrasted for the Theory Section; used the same figures from the Office of National Statistics Website for the Data Section; explained that the data suggests no theory could account for all the trends, although for such a simple theory Keynes' is pretty good; discussed the weakness of our approach; and, finally, outlined possible extensions. We added our own "Catz Twist", recalled from a previous supervision given by Mr Stevens, that consumption is different from expenditure, and is virtually impossible to measure (e.g. when you pay £10,000 for a car, that is £10,000 expenditure, but you consume a certain portion of its value each time you use it). Seeing as we could only get data on expenditure, and the question was about consumption, this needed pointing out.

"There's no way those retards from Trinity will come up with that one" explained Caolan.

Although most of us finished the bulk of the project with a couple of days to spare, we were all still stuck in the computer rooms until late Monday night, changing sentences that were perfectly fine in the first place, and making our diagrams look prettier. Oisin did an "all-nighter" on the Monday after a few too many wee breaks over the weekend, and had a wee lie down for the next three days whilst he recovered. I was fairly happy with how my project had turned out, although we wouldn't find out our mark until the summer holidays. All eleven economists gathered on Sherlock Court on the Tuesday afternoon just before we handed our projects in and paused for a photo. It was a lovely sunny day, and we took the rest of it off to celebrate. With 8 per cent of our Part I now in the bag, Wetherspoons' Beer-Burger tasted even better.

With the Stats project out of the way, we still had the usual time-consuming array of supervisions and lectures to attend. In this final term our Director of Studies, Mr Stevens, had arranged a weekly series of lectures for Part I students like ourselves across the university. The topic of the series of lectures was "The Third Way," which was directly relevant to the Politics component of our course, so we were repeatedly told. Each lecture was held on a Friday at twelve o'clock, and was given by a distinguished outside speaker. More importantly, as far as we were concerned, after each lecture, good old Mr Stevens would put on a free lunch for us back in college in his room, C4.

Most of the speakers during the series were excellent, and the air in Lady Mitchell Hall was filled each week with their passions and insights on a topic that they were clearly very knowledgeable about. Will Hutton, author of the book *The State We're In*, a book that every economics interviewee claims to have read and enjoyed, drew in a particularly big crowd. However, as I sat there, week after week, listening to the relative merits of social democracy, the durability of the stance of the current Labour government, and whether the Conservative Party required and could credibly sustain a leftward shift, my mind became filled with thoughts of chilli con carne and baked potatoes. I tried to concentrate, but I couldn't. I wanted to make a leftward shift out of the lecture theatre and I didn't care whether I took the first, second, or third way back to college. It was Friday afternoon, I had had a hard week and I was starving.

After the lecture, Mr Stevens would invite the speaker back to C4 along with prominent members of the Economics Faculty. The invitation was also open to all who attended the lecture, but most undergraduates, unaware of the culinary delights that Mr Stevens had to offer, skulked off back to hall in their own colleges. Caolan, Mark, Oisin and I would always be first into our Director of Studies' room, ready to take up our positions by the door that led to the food. With our prime location secured, we would help ourselves to some of the finest apple juice my taste buds have had the pleasure to encounter, and wait patiently for our signal. Some weeks we were unlucky and would reluctantly get drawn into a long conversation about the merits of the euro or the lack of tangible evidence of productivity in the New Economy by some over-keen Fellow. Caolan and I would nod and explain that Mark had some particularly interesting views on the topic. Some weeks Mr Stevens would beat us back and would set up camp himself by the gateway to heaven. Some weeks, however, everything went just right. The four of us would huddle together, keeping ourselves to ourselves, happily sipping our apple juices and then, when Mr Stevens deemed it was time, be told to help ourselves to the food that lay waiting beyond the door.

Food in hall was pretty poor in those days, especially at lunch time. You knew things were not good whenever you had to ask the kitchen staff what each dish was even though you had the menu in front of you, and then you still weren't so sure once you'd tasted it. However, when a Fellow put in a special order for some food, the standard increased immeasurably. And so it was for Mr Stevens' Friday afternoon get-togethers, funded by his economics budget. The catering staff excelled themselves. There were bread rolls, salads, baked potatoes, spaghetti, rice, all complemented by either curry or chilli con carne. Simple food that tasted great. I had never had either dish before that epic series of "Third Way" lectures, but I soon grew to love them, especially chilli con carne. I would have several helpings. At first I did this in secret and much to the disapproval of Oisin, who would chastise me for being a greedy wee egit, but later I ate and ate with the full encouragement of Mr Stevens, who I think respected my healthy appetite, and even started ordering extra for me. Hard as it was, I always tried to save room for desert, for it was fresh fruit salad with the most delicious cream known to man. Mark Novak was such a fan of this cream that he used to by-pass the fruit entirely, and just pour himself a bowl of white liquid, before lapping it up like a sweet-toothed cat.

Those Friday afternoon lecture-lunch combos became an essential way to start a weekend that would often be full of work.

Chapter 51

Cometh the hour, cometh the Catz Bop. With exams far enough in the future to be ignored, the two small weird Ents Reps got their act together and organised another couple of events. Not surprisingly, these nights out were not billed as: "From the people that brought you *Who Wants to be a Millionaero?...*"

The first of these was a regular Friday night Catz Bop, with the theme: Childhood Heroes. Most of us were still young and enthusiastic enough to go to great lengths to dress up for these Bops, and seeing as we hadn't been able to do so for the last couple because of formal halls, the group consensus was that we should make an effort for this one. This consensus didn't include Caolan and Oisin, however. In what was already becoming a bit of a pattern, Caolan decided dressing up was gay, and Oisin had an essay to finish and so would only be able to make the Bop later on. Mark Novak was reluctant to dress up, but was easily persuaded with a bit of peer pressure. None of us really knew what we were going to dress up as, and we agreed to meet at 3 pm that day in my room to figure something out.

It was a Friday morning, a time of the week usually spent stuck in three lectures and then looking forward to lunch at Mr Stevens. However, on this particular Friday thoughts of "The Third Way" and my third dish of chilli con carne were banished due to prior engagements. Today I was going to the Master's Lunch.

The Master of St. Catharine's College was a nice guy. He had only been appointed at the start of the year, and as such was as new to St. Catharine's as the rest of us. Apparently he was extremely distinguished in the field of gardening, or "horticulture" as the other Fellows and various college publications preferred to call it, but I had never heard of him. He didn't really strike me as one of those celebrity gardener types like Alan Titchmarsh or Charlie Dimmock. However, he always smiled and said hello when he passed you around college, and was always at the big college sporting events (sadly, he appeared to have been too busy to attend the glorious game that brought the Mighty Thirds the Division 5b title last term). Trinity College seemed to have a thing about getting Nobel Prize-winning Masters, and at that time had the great economist Amartya Sen. However, I preferred our one, and anyway, at least our gardens were always kept in good shape. Once a year the Master invited each student to come to lunch with him and his wife in the Master's Lodge, which was a large detached building standing next to college along Queens Lane. Mr Master and Mrs Master invited students in groups of about fifteen, and in our first year these groups were determined by your surname's position in the alphabet. Hence, I found myself in the group with three As, seven Bs, four Cs and a D. The only person I knew well in my group was posh, squeaky Elizabeth Braithwaite, and so I made her promise to save me a seat next to her.

I was running late for the Masters Lunch as I had somehow got roped into playing tennis for the college second team in the morning. Before coming to university I had considered myself quite the tennis player, but all illusions were promptly shattered with a 6–0 stuffing on our very own grass tennis courts by a scrawny lad from Churchill College. Hence, I arrived at the Master's Lodge not only in a bit of a bad mood, but also in shorts and a T-shirt. The invitation had just said "Dress: Casual", but as soon as I walked in the door, I realised that "Do not come in shorts and a T-shirt and holding a tennis racket" was taken as a given by everyone else. A roomful of shirts, trousers, ties and dresses greeted me as I entered. I smiled an embarrassed smile and offered a nod at a few familiar faces, before covering my face with my racket as if it were a really bad mask at a masked ball, and trying to find Elizabeth. I discovered her by the drinks table, dressed in a very pretty yellow dress and sipping a glass of white wine. I told her she looked nice, but she did not return the compliment.

"What on earth are you wearing?" she squeaked.

"I had to play tennis this morning."

"Couldn't you have gone home and got changed?"

"I was already running late as it was. Anyway, this is about as casual as you can get, and I think I saw the Master's wife admiring my legs."

Elizabeth chose not to reply, and instead shook her head in disbelief, causing her blonde hair to dance around on her head.

The Master announced, without the means of the gong that I had expected, that dinner was served. I followed Elizabeth in and promptly sat down right beside her before she could go back on her earlier promise. She was still not happy, and appeared more than a little flustered.

"Hey, Elizabeth, will you just pass my tennis racket down to the Master and ask him to chuck it in the cloakroom?"

For a few seconds, Elizabeth Braithwaite was lost for words. Eventually she regained the ability to speak, but at an octave higher than normal and with a little beetroot red race.

"For God sake! Keep that bloody thing under the table. Honestly, Josh, honestly!"

Elizabeth was one of the easiest people in the world to wind up. Being little Ms Prim and Proper, the worst thing you could do was to threaten to show her up in a formal setting. There were certain ways one did things and, if one wanted to be associated with Elizabeth Braithwaite in such a formal setting, one would conform to her high standards. Hence, one did not pick one's nose, say the word nob, or dress oneself in sporting attire complete with sporting equipment. Such behaviour would provoke an even stronger reaction from my fellow M-blocker when our Master was involved. You see, being an Old Boy of the college, and having sponsored various things like college boats, as well as having given talks to the Law Society, Elizabeth's Dad knew a lot of the Fellows, and had already been acquainted with the new Master. Shame would thus be brought upon the Braithwaite family if Elizabeth were to be shown up in front of the college figurehead. Of course, I had absolutely no intention of showing her up, but it was hard to resist pretending you were about to.

The meal passed without further incident. The food was a creamy rice dish, which was nice, but certainly not up to Mr Stevens' Friday Club standards, and my taste buds couldn't help pining after whatever the economists were enjoying up in C4 at this very moment. I introduced myself to the Master and apologised politely for my unsuitable attire, nudging Elizabeth as I spoke. The Master said it was no problem at all, and that he enjoyed the odd game of tennis himself. I said that he probably would have fared better than me this morning and he laughed. I was fitting in like a glove.

After the meal, we again convened in the hall, and I got chatting to a few of the As, Bs and Cs that I didn't know too well (the lone D had to rush off to a supervision). The obvious topic of conversation was what people were dressing up as for tonight's Bop.

"So, what are people thinking of coming as?" I offered as an opener.

"Are you coming as Tim Henman?" asked a male C, who was an engineer. I couldn't think of a funny reply so I just gave an appreciative giggle.

"I might go as Tina Turner," said a female B, and received a universal nod of approval.

"I might go as Lawrence Llewellyn-Bowen," said the guy who had gone as Lawrence Llewellyn-Bowen to the Famous People Bop, and who I was beginning to suspect had a bit of a thing for the flamboyant interior designer.

"I'm not sure what to go as," I explained, "but I am quite keen for the Terminator."

There was a pause whilst everyone considered my suggestion.

"Bit of a strange choice for a childhood hero, isn't it?" said Mr Bowen in one of the worst cases of the pot calling the kettle black that I had ever heard.

"I think it would be quite cool," said the future Tina Turner.

"Thank you, and strange as it may sound, I was a big fan of him when I was little, 'I'll be back' and all that," I replied.

In the next few minutes I switched off from the conversation, my mind now occupied with thoughts of the Terminator. I said "I'll be back", "*Hasta la vista*, baby" and "Are you Sarah Connor?" under my breath seventeen times each, with each repetition convincing me more and more that I was born for the role. And so, there and then, stood in the Master's Lodge in a pair of shorts and a T-shirt, and holding a tennis racket, I decided that tonight I was going to be the Terminator.

I contentedly sat through the three o'clock meeting whilst the rest of the gang decided what childhood hero they were going to transform themselves into. There was under five hours until the Bop, and little progress was being made.

"Who was your hero as a child, Faye?" enquired Elizabeth, hoping that some kind of structure might stimulate the much-needed ideas.

"Oooh, I liked James Bond. Sean Connery, now there was a real Scottish man."

"You don't look much like James Bond," pointed out Elizabeth.

"Odd-Job, maybe," I said, and received a cushion in the face for my troubles. "Look, is there no group of people you could go as, then you only need to come up with one idea instead of five?" I replied, constructively trying to atone for my comment to Faye.

"Why thank you, Mr Schwarzenegger," said Jude.

"Alright, groups, groups, groups?" said Elizabeth, who was desperately trying to get things moving, "What about The Beatles?"

"No."

"Abba?"

"No."

"The Jackson 5."

"You're the spitting image of Wacko Jacko, Elizabeth."

"Alright, someone else suggest something then," Elizabeth said with a short, sharp, angry squeak. Jude took this as his queue to have a go.

"What about comic-book characters, you know, like X-Men, or Power Rangers, or…"

"Or Beano characters!" squealed Faye. "Ooh, I love the Beano, please can we go as the Beano, please, please, please!"

"That's not actually a bad idea," said Jude, and I stuck my lips out like Mick Jagger and nodded my approval.

"Okay, but who's going to be who?" asked Elizabeth.

"Well, I think Jude should be Dennis the Menace, we'll both be wee Mini the Minxes, and Mark can be Gnasher. What does everyone think?"

"Yep."

"Yep."

"There's no way I'm being a dog."

"Why not, Mark?"

"'Cos I'll look stupid."

"It's a Bop, everyone looks stupid, that's how you save 50p."

"Still, I don't want to be a dog."

"That's Okay" said Elizabeth, I'm sure my medic friend Lionel will be Gnasher if Mark doesn't want to. He's thinking of coming as Mother Teresa otherwise."

"Last chance, mate."

"No, I'm alright. Thanks anyway."

"So, who the hell are you going as?" I asked.

"Don't know, probably won't bother," replied Mark in the same defeatist way as he downed his drink without trying when his go came around at the "Celebrity Name Game".

"Come on, there must be someone you could be. Has anyone ever said you look like anyone?"

"He kind of looks like Tin Tin," pointed out Jude, still grinning at the prospect of being Dennis the Menace.

"Yeah, you do a bit, actually."

"Yeah, you do."

"Aye, a wee bit, maybe."

He didn't really, but all sensed that something was better than nothing, and universal encouragement was a necessary ingredient for success.

"We could just give you a quiff at the front of your hair, find you a little white Snowy, and you'll be flying."

"Oisin would make a good Snowy. With his hair he looks like a dog."

"Aye, put the wee laddy on a leash."

"From what I hear it wouldn't be the first time."

"Oh behave Josh, Oisin isn't into kinky sex."

A Tale of Friendship, Love and Economics

"Elizabeth! Stop lowering the tone. Deary me." Elizabeth went bright red and tried to squeak out her protests, but I continued. "Anyway, Oisin's working tonight, remember. Right Mark, what's say me and you head off into town and try and find you a Snowy?"

Mark reluctantly agreed, and so whilst the remaining three went to round up Lionel the medic and set the wheels in motion to make the Beano idea a reality, Mark and I walked along Silver Street and across Market Square in search of little white dogs. Apparently Mark had ruled out nicking the one out of the blind man's hands as he sat on a bench eating a pie, and instead suggested we try the Disney Store. Low and behold, lying in the middle of all the stacks of over-priced junk was an over-priced little white dog, apparently from the film sequel *102 Dalmatians*. Mark, clearly desperate to put an end to the search and also to commit himself to the idea before he changed his mind for good, handed over £30, yes *£30*, for the tiny little fluffy mutt.

"Maybe you could take it back and get a refund tomorrow," I suggested as we sauntered back to college, Mark carrying the dog under his arm like a parcel.

"Oh yeah, 'cos no damage at all could possible happen to it at a Catz Bop," he replied dryly. Fair point.

After a particularly unpleasant dining experience in hall, we all went our separate ways and agreed to reconvene in Elizabeth's room at 7.30 pm, fully dressed and ready to go. My costume didn't take much preparation. I wore black shoes, black jeans, a black T-shirt, Jude's black leather jacket, a pair of slick black sunglasses, and gelled my hair back. I also found the plastic gun that Nick MacLean had left in my room, the same gun Mr MacLean had bought for the Freshers' Play in his role as Props Manager, even though such semi-automatic weapons were not really called upon in the 1925 script. I looked well hard. I looked at myself in the mirror, said "I'll be back", went away for a minute, and then reappeared saying "I told you". It was a bloody good job I was on my own and the door was shut.

I decided to go up and see how Mark Novak was getting on transforming himself into Tin Tin. I took the gun with me just in case, and walked up the stairs of M-block with slow and heavy paces. I thumped three times on the door.

"Are you Mark Novak?" I said in the worst Austrian accent ever produced.

"What are you doing?"
"Are you Mark Novak?"
"Yes."
"I need your clothes, your boots and your motorcycle."
"You can have this stupid dog for a fiver if you want."
"How's the costume coming along," I had now dropped the accent, and was now emitting the sweet sound of the Red Rose county.
"Not so good. What does Tin Tin wear anyway?"
"Oh, you know, he'd be keen for trousers, a shirt and a jumper over the top"
"Yeah?"
"Oh God, yeah," I didn't have a clue.

Mark told me to wait outside a moment whilst he changed, and reappeared in the doorway looking like a nineteen-year-old economist wearing trousers, a shirt and a jumper over the top.

"Spot on," I said.

We quiffed up Mark's hair at the front, and with his ever-faithful, bank-breaking Snowy in hand we marched down the stairs of M-block, Tin Tin and the Terminator side by side, to see how the others were getting on.

To be fair, Team Beano looked really good. They all had red T-shirts on, and had wrapped strips of black tape around them to give the obligatory stripy effect. Elizabeth and Faye had makeshift freckles dotted on their faces with permanent marker, and pig-tails in their hair. Jude, who luckily had not gotten around to having his hair cut for some time, was able to spike his dark mop up like a hedgehog just as "D the M" had it. To top it all off, Lionel the medic, who had a reputation for being sleazy, had managed to steal a real-life bone from the lab, which he was now gripping between his teeth.

We exchanged compliments, got a small girl with dreadlocks to take a few pictures of us, and headed off to the Bop. Thankfully, most other people had got dressed up as well. Adam "Sly" Sylvester had come as the Silver Surfer, and was getting increasingly annoyed as no-one knew who the Silver Surfer was. Rachael, Contestant Number 1 in *Millionaero*, had come as Batman, and was looking in the boys toilets for Robin. Poor Duane, who had been told there weren't enough places in the Beano clan for him, had turned up dressed in a stripy T-shirt and stripy shorts, and explained to a confused Elizabeth and I that he was, in fact, Mr Stripy from the Mr Men.

A Tale of Friendship, Love and Economics

Charles, the giant special needs child who had stolen Cassandra from me, had come as the Cookie Monster, and was running around the Bop tickling everybody. The only thing that was different from his usual behaviour was that tonight he had a blue face and a tub of biscuits. Nick MacLean had to go home for the weekend to play in a tennis tournament with his Dad, and fellow geographer Joe Porter, like Caolan, had decided not to bother dressing up. Bops were never English student Francesca's thing, and she had decided instead to drink a bottle of wine round in Julie's room, no doubt talking about books using big words, but promised she'd pop down for the last half-hour or so. Oisin arrived late in the day, essay not quite finished but on a wee break, again able to pass himself off as any 1970s icon he should choose. Mary Jane had come as Pippi Long-Stocking, who I had never heard of, but told her she looked good in the interest of future flat relations. Also present in the sweat-pit of a room was Paul Gascoigne, Kylie, James Bond, Hulk Hogan, Einstein (only in Cambridge), Tina Turner, Winston Churchill, Karate Kid and, of course, everyone's childhood hero, Laurence Llewellyn-Bowen.

It was hard for me in the early stages of the Bop. Apart from a few people mistaking me for Neo from *The Matrix*, my costume was going down quite well. However, I was roasting hot in Jude's leather jacket, and the mechanical personality of my chosen childhood hero prevented my face from breaking out into a smile at any stage. This did have one advantage, however. I posed for a photo with overgrown baby Charles, and whilst he was all smiles with his blue face and his biscuit tin, I was able to remain stone-faced and serious whilst pointing my plastic gun to the side of his head. I was well over Cassandra at this stage, but it was still nice to be so close to Charles with a gun in my hand.

That Bop was one of the best I ever went to. The music was no different to any other one, and the quantities of drink taken on board were no more or no less than usual. It was just that everyone seemed in a really good mood. Perhaps people were getting it out of their system before revision kicked in, or perhaps the theme just struck the right chord. Anyway, I allowed Mr Terminator to break out into a nice big smile as I looked around the room towards the end of the night, amidst the dancing and drunken swaying, and saw Winston Churchill kissing Kylie, a randy Einstein pinching the backside of Tina Turner and trying to pass the blame onto a confused

Laurence Llewellyn-Bowen and, happily, Mini the Minx (the Scottish one) holding hands and dancing with her Mr Stripy.

The second Bop, just a few days later, was good but not as good. It was arranged for a Wednesday night, and for once it was held out of Catz in the club Po Na Na's. Now Po Na Na's was a place that I had never been to before, nor had any great desire to, as every night was either Hip-Hop (increasingly referred to by us as Shit-Hop), R'n'B, Garage, or something equally as painful. Tonight, however, we were promised cheese, and the two weird Ents Officers had booked the place out just for our lovely college.

The theme of the Bop was "Porn Stars", and pretty early on we decided not to dress up for it. Others, however, had. Dale was a medic in our year, a good friend of Elizabeth's, and had held the honourable position of Statistics Co-ordinator in our crazy Kerplunking days of last term. He was also a bit dodgy to say the least. Some said he was gay, some said he was bi-sexual, some said he was just a bit camp. What was certain, though, was that Dale was a sailor, and that was all a lot of people needed to know.

Dale came round to my crowded room before we all set off to the Bop. The conversation was happily flowing along, with Caolan explaining to a sceptical audience that his new T-shirt was not a white one that had been put in the wash with a red sock, it was supposed to be pink, and it was very fashionable. All fell silent however when Dale walked in.

"Well hello there boys," he announced like he was in a Carry On movie, although certainly not one that I'd ever want to see.

"Holy fuck," said Caolan.

The Irishman had said what the rest of us were thinking. Dale was dressed from head to toe in what can only be described as black leather bondage gear. His skin-tight revealing outfit was completed by a leather hat, a false moustache, and of course, a whip that could be attached to his belt. There was something unnatural bulging around his groin area, but I tried not to look. Where he had acquired this outfit from, I dreaded to think, but from the way he was strutting around the room, I guessed it was not the first time he had had it on. Not for the first time, silence filled M14. Pairs of eyes were either staring right at Dale or anywhere but. Faye's jaw had to be scooped up off the floor by Elizabeth and put back in its place. When I had regained the ability to speak I broke the silence,

"Dale, you do realise the theme's been changed to Nursery Rhyme Characters?"

A Tale of Friendship, Love and Economics

And so, when everyone had recovered, we made the ten-minute journey out of college to Po Na Na's. Anywhere else in the world, the sight of eight people dressed normally walking along with Mr Bondage 2001 would have raised a few eyebrows at least. However, this was the city where every other person seemed to be wearing a gown, and where most nights out had a theme requiring some form of dressing up. As we sheepishly made our way along Cambridge's streets, people just carried on regardless. The passing public had seen worse, and passing students had worn worse. Even the tramps still asked him for money.

The Bop wasn't a great one. Quite a few people had dressed up, none to quite the degree of Dale. Many of the girls' outfits were hardly the most flattering, with rolls of flabby skin bouncing up and down trying to squeeze their way out of their leather constraints. At first it was funny, but then it became quite disturbing. And whilst all the usual faces were there, and all the usual music was being played, it just wasn't the same. Towards the end of the night we even found ourselves sat down quietly on a large table in the corner. Catz Bops needed to be held in Catz.

There were, however, two notable incidents. Firstly, this was the night that the Movie Star Look-alike first pulled her soon-to-be boyfriend, Mr Enforcer, much to the displeasure of poor Nick MacLean. To cheer him up we pointed out a rather large girl who had gone on record as saying Nick had the second best pair of legs in Cambridge, but she looked bad at the best of times and even worse tonight. Nick said he'd rather pull Dale. Secondly, Jude had a couple of his mates from Barnet staying with him. Both had come along to the Bop and both, along with Jude, had got absolutely smashed. Jude explained that events were a little hazy to say the least, having no memory of getting back to college or going to bed, but when he opened his door in the morning, he was greeted by the sight and the smell of a rather large puddle of sick. And the smell was awful, truly awful. It hit me as soon as I left my room, even though there was a wooden door separating Jude's part of the M-block corridor from my own. Jude went to Sainsbury's to buy some Fabreeze, but, if anything, emptying the contents of the little green bottle onto the offending carpet tiles made the smell even worse. No, Fabreeze wasn't enough; more drastic action was required. Under the cover of darkness, and dressed in black more out of desire than necessity, Jude and I removed the offending carpet tiles and transported them across Main Court and into Bull. There we climbed several flights of stairs and laid them, purely by chance, outside overgrown baby Charles' room. We then smuggled his sweet smelling carpet tiles back over to M-block, replaced them outside Jude's room, and no-one was any the wiser. We had a cup of tea and a couple of bowls of cereals to celebrate.

Chapter 52

I hadn't seen Imogene yet this term, but I had thought about her a lot. I regretted not having asked for her mobile number at the time, and now didn't fancy the prospect of asking Lauren Broad for it over a lecture about the Great Depression. Luckily, with Lauren and Caolan still seemingly getting on like the proverbial burning residential property, a second chance presented itself.

Whenever a group of boys invited a group of girls to a formal hall, implicit in the agreement was that you would get an invite back. After all, this was only fair as the hosts were out of pocket by a good few quid, obliged as they were to buy two tickets each. In my experience, rarely was this adhered to, with the girls taking their free feeding and then chasing after another bunch of suckers. Of course, if the girls in question were a bunch of mingers, this was by no means a bad thing. Fortunately, however, in the case of New Hall, Lauren Broad did invite the Catz boys back up the hill, her motives no doubt revolving around getting a certain Irishman on home turf rather than fulfilling any social obligation.

This certainly suited me, and indeed the rest of the boys, who were always keen for a cheap feed and to have a formal hall in another college, but it did not suit Caolan. Apparently the impressively sideburned Irishman had gone off Lovely Lauren from London. I don't know why it happened, or what was said between them and, of course, Caolan wasn't going to divulge anything, so once again I was left to speculate. Maybe he could see things getting serious in the future, so decided to put a stop to things there and then. Maybe he saw their kiss as just a random pull, and that was all he wanted. Maybe he liked someone else, although who I had no idea. Then again, maybe he was only seeing her for her economic ability, and when he discovered she was not that hot, decided to bin her. It seemed that the more I got to know Caolan, the less I understood him.

A Tale of Friendship, Love and Economics

Whatever the reason, the bottom line was that as eight suited St. Catharine's boys marched our way along Kings Parade, then Trinity Street, then over Magdalene Bridge, then up the big hill, armed with two bottles of cheap, and no doubt disgusting, wine each to trade for tickets, Caolan was not with us. He instructed us to apologise for his absence and explain that he had a JCR Committee meeting that he had to attend. Indeed, the Irishman did have a Committee meeting, but he had missed them in the past for less good reason. Hence, in his absence, I assumed control of the group. There was always something of an implicit power struggle whenever both Caolan and I were around, nothing major, but enough for me to notice the difference when he was absent. I felt more relaxed, I felt I didn't have to watch what I said. Jude was signed up as the eighth member of our team for this away fixture, and on the way I reminded him of the rules: he could try to pull any of the girls except Imogene, oh, and except the girl with the unusually large mouth who had a boyfriend but had recently pulled one of our economists, the guy who always dined in Gardi's, and clearly fancied him. Jude nodded his understanding.

I was quite calm and collected walking for most of the journey, in fact right up until the point where we entered through New Hall's glass doors and walked past the Porter's Lodge. Suddenly all blissful ignorance fell away and I realised I didn't know how to act around Imogene. What if she knew I fancied her? After all, according to most people I'm not so good at hiding it, and I did give her the gift of my lovely pink hat, a sure sign of true love if ever there was one. If she didn't like me, then she might be cold towards me, and I would come across as a love-sick idiot. But, if she did like me, then how would I make the first move? After all, I only had one pulling technique, and I would be surprised if *Billy Jean* came on during the formal hall. But then again what if she didn't know I fancied her? After all, I had only met her once and I had not made any attempt to get in contact with her since. In that case she might have assumed I was not interested, and gone and got herself another boy (probably from Fitzwilliam College – their location also on top of the hill gave them strategic advantage when it came to picking up New Hall girls). Oh God, I wished I had a JCR Committee meeting to go to. And whilst my thoughts were making me dizzy doing circles in my head, I saw her, standing at the end of the corridor with the rest of the New Hall clan, ready to greet us. She looked as lovely as I remembered; her blonde hair tied back tonight, and her pretty eyes blinking away, as if they were offering their own greeting, as she talked. Our troop of boys moved forward down the corridor of the all-girls college like an army marching into battle, and I quickly abused my self-appointed role as our fearless leader to take up a position at the back. Somebody had turned the bass up on my heart, and my face began to go red. We got closer and closer, and I got redder and redder. And then, as we reached the group of girls who would eventually become a part of all of our lives in way that we couldn't have foreseen at this stage, I did what I always did in these situations, a reflex action that is inexplicable and infuriating, both to me and to others: I pretended not to see Imogene. I avoided looking in her direction, keeping my head down, and allowing myself to be immersed in a pointless conversation with one of her friends. I then hovered at the back of the group of sixteen when we were led up the stairs and into hall after ten painful minutes.

"Which one's Imogene?" whispered Jude.

"The one I just ignored," I replied.

New Hall's hall was far more modern than ours and, although I am unashamedly biased, nowhere near as nice. It didn't have the traditional feel, lacking the wood, the dim lighting, and the paintings of past Masters that struck you straight away in St. Catharine's. It was too open, too light, looking more like a school cafeteria. Moreover, they even charged you 50p to open up your wine and then handed you a corkscrew to do it yourself. However, formal hall at New Hall did have a feature that was, if not redeeming, certainly memorable. When everyone was seated, a bell sounded, kitchen staff shuffled out of the way, our ears bore witness to a mechanical concerto of clattering and grinding, and through the floor in the centre of the hall, like a monster out of the sea, emerged the kitchen. Two white-hatted chefs appeared along with the kitchen brandishing carving knives in what looked like the spectacular climax of a culinary-themed magic show. We gasped with amazement and prepared to applaud, whilst the girls cut into their bread rolls, the effect for them seemingly eroded by over-exposure.

Due to my entry position at the back of the group, I had to take whatever seat was left. As a result I found myself sat on the end of the table, with Lauren Broad on my left, and Jude opposite me. A glance down the table revealed that Oisin was sat next to Imogene, and by the sounds of it had already fired up his pneumatic drill of laughter. Give the poor girl a hard hat and a pair of ear guards, I thought bitterly to myself.

The formal hall was not a great one for any of the three stuck at the end of the table. Lauren Broad was clearly only there to see Caolan and in his absence was turning every topic of conversation into one about the Irishman, her links getting less relevant and more annoying as the night went one. I had one ear open to her incessant ramblings, and the other open to the conversation between Oisin and Imogene, but all I could make out of that was a lot of drilling and a lot of "or whatever"s. Jude wasn't happy because he was hungry and his vegetarian option appeared to be no more than a burnt pepper. To top it all off, when the meal had finished, most of the girls, Imogene included, announced that they had a load of work to do for the morning, and so couldn't come out anywhere with us tonight. I hadn't spoken a single word to her all night. I waved a half-hearted goodbye in her direction and promptly looked around for someone to take my frustration out on. The fact that I was more than a little bit drunk made this course of action seem an even better option.

"They're a lovely bunch of girls, don't you think?" remarked Oisin to no-one in particular as we walked out of the door.

"Nothing special," I replied, as cold as the wind that was blowing against the side of our faces.

"Didn't you have a good time?" he was now talking just to me as the rest of the group walked on.

"Not as good as you by the looks of things."

"What do you mean by that?"

"Nothing."

"Is this about Imogene, or whatever?"

"What are you on about?"

"Well, you're obviously pissed off at something, or whatever."

"I'm fine, alright?"

"Jeepers Josh, I know you like her…"

I shrugged my shoulders, and the Irishman continued,

"… and I would never try anything on with girl a mate liked."

I shrugged again.

"I'm not like that, Josh. I would have hoped you'd have known that by now, or whatever."

Oisin was annoyingly hard to fall out with, probably because he never did anything wrong. After thirty seconds of silence, during which I tried to kick a stone into a bush and missed the stone completely, my conscience got the better of me and I apologised. Oisin said it was no bother, but I felt bad nevertheless. I explained to my shaggy-haired friend that I was just pissed off because I hadn't talked to her all night, and I knew that the only one to blame was my own stupid, immature self. Oisin listened as he always did. He said that Imogene had kept talking about me during the meal, but I was pretty sure he was just saying that to make me feel better.

A change of subject was clearly needed, and so for the rest of the walk home, utilising the fact that Oisin and I had broken off from the rest of the group whilst I temporarily turned into an idiot, we started discussing the highly amusing situation about to happen. You see, the eight that had started the journey up the hill a few hours and a few bottles of wine ago, had now become nine going down it. During the meal, Lauren Broad had correctly identified Mark Novak as the most easily persuadable drunk amongst us. Indeed, with a bottle of wine in him, Mark would uncharacteristically do just about anything, well, apart from miss a lecture, of course. Tonight, all Ms Broad wanted him to do was invite her back to Catz, and young Mark, glad of her structural support on the long walk home, duly obliged. She was a ruthless, determined woman, and nothing was going to stand in her way.

"Caolan is not going to be happy," said Oisin.

"Not one bit," I replied.

Still in our suits, we went into Catz bar where I had previously agreed to meet Caolan. It was about 9.30 pm, and his meeting had finished a good twenty minutes ago. He was leaning against the bar, supping a pint, and talking to an Australian medic from our year when we walked in. He'll need more than a pint to deal with this, I thought. His face lit up when he saw us, and was promptly extinguished when he caught sight of Lauren Broad, who was holding onto Mark like he was a hostage to negotiate with. All thoughts of Imogene had temporarily been banished from my mind, and now I winked at Caolan.

"Hey Caolan, mate, look, Lauren's come back with us."

"Oh, great," said his mouth. "Oh, shit," said his eyes.

Caolan came across and timidly greeted us. With Ms Broad clearly happy with the terms of the agreement, Mark was released, and fled with me to the

A Tale of Friendship, Love and Economics

bar to get a drink. From the safety of a table in the corner, the eight of us, increasingly thankful we were not the object of Lovely Lauren's affections, sat and watched events unfold.

Caolan's body language clearly said he was not keen. This was in stark contrast to that of the commander and chief of the New Hall drinking society, who had managed to hoist the Irishman's arm up and around her hefty shoulders, and was now backing him towards the wall. If it had have been anyone else I would have launched a rescue attempt, but we all knew full well that Caolan would have gladly sat and watched us suffer, and anyway, he'd kissed her before, now he'd have to deal with the consequences. But Caolan didn't seem to be doing a very good job of dealing with it. He appeared overcome by the considerable brute strength and determination of Lauren Broad. The next thing we knew, Caolan was leading her out of the bar, or, as was far more likely the case, she was leading him.

"Poor bastard. She's an animal," said Jude.

"I hope he's got his rape alarm with him," chipped in one of the economists.

"Hey, who's keen for following him?" I said, realising that since Kerplunk appeared to have died a death this term, my evenings were often crying out to be filled.

"You can't frickin' follow him, or whatever," said Oisin, at once taking the moral high ground.

"Nah, leave him alone," said Mark Novak.

"Hey, I'm only concerned for his safety. Nick, Jude, you're concerned for Caolan's safety too, aren't you?"

"I'm concerned that if we don't hurry up we'll miss it when she pushes him in a bush and tries to have her wicked way with him. Let's go."

And with that, myself, Jude Richards and Nick MacLean quickly finished our drinks and set off into the windy night, three nineteen-year-old students of Cambridge University, chasing their friend through the city streets for the simple reason that he was with a girl and we weren't.

We immediately decided that Caolan, if he had any sense, wouldn't have dared take Lovely Lauren from London to his room in Gostlin; once she found out where that was he was finished. Hence, it was a matter of turning right or left out of college. New Hall was to the left and the Marshall Library of Economics was to the right. If we had been chasing Mark Novak we would have taken a right, but unanimously we went for left. We sprinted up Kings

Parade stopping to reassess and catch our breath just outside the main gates of King's College. In the distance, just approaching the Senate House, we saw what looked like two figures walking side by side. It was only when they passed under a street-lamp that we identified them as Caolan and Lauren. They were about 100 metres in front of us. After the "Puke on the Mat Incident", Jude and I considered ourselves experts in the art of covert operations. We agreed that the best course of action was to cross the road and dash from building to building, stopping to hide ourselves in the shadows of each shop doorway to ensure we were not spotted. Safely concealed in the doorway of a shop that sold official Cambridge memorabilia, we silently observed the two targets taking a left past the Senate House, down a small lane that led to Trinity Hall College.

"Where's the god-damn son-of-a-bitch going now?" asked Jude. Seemingly inspired by the thrill of the chase we had subconsciously adopted dodgy American accents and our conversation had become the script of a low-budget action movie.

"God-damn-it, I just don't know. But I'm sure as hell gonna find out" I replied, screwing up my face for emphasis.

"Boys, this could be dangerous," Nick sounded more like Julian Clary than Bruce Willis.

"Fuck the danger. This is our friend, and this is our god-damn job."

And when the coast was clear we scurried across the road and stopped at the entrance to the lane, hiding this time behind the walls of Caius College. We saw the figures in the distance approaching the end of the lane. From where I was stood I was sure they were holding hands. This observation was confirmed by Jude and Nick, the latter proudly explaining that before he needed glasses he had twenty-twenty vision. We gave the apparently happy couple a minute or so to clear the end of the lane, and then sprinted off after them. We poked our heads around the corner but saw nothing.

"Right, they've either gone into Tit Hall, right round and back onto Trinity Lane, or over the bridge," said a characteristically clear-thinking Nick MacLean.

"They would have no reason to go into Tit Hall, and it would seem a pointless detour to take just to get back on Trinity Lane," said Jude.

There was a pause.

"I reckon they've taken the bridge," I said.

"God Josh, what would we do without you?"

A Tale of Friendship, Love and Economics

We sprinted past Tit Hall and slammed to a halt just before the lane that led to the nice little bridge. Again, we peered round the corner, and again we saw nothing. We sprinted down to the bridge, and stopping on the top we looked down the deserted winding lane that lay before us, the only sign of life being a bird looking for scraps of food in the dim glow of a distant street-lamp.

"Looks like we've lost them."
"God-damn-it."
"Cup of tea?"
"Yeah."

We never found out exactly what happened that night, or where they ended up. Caolan's story, for what it's worth, went along the lines of: "yeah, I just walked her back to New Hall and then came straight back". He emphatically denied ever walking hand in hand with her, and claimed he knew we were following him all along. He added that we were a bunch of gays. After that night, however, Caolan no longer sat next to Lovely Lauren from London in lectures, and there were no more formal halls organised between our two colleges that year. However, this was no means the end of the Catz – New Hall saga; after all, the Imogene situation lay unresolved, and there was still a few more twists to be had in the tale of Mr Caolan O'Donnell and the lovely Ms Lauren Broad.

Chapter 53

There was little doubt that exams were getting close now. Ours were less than four weeks away and, seeing as the economics ones were traditionally the last to start and finish, other people's exams were even closer. We had certainly been working hard this term, but the fact that we were still going out at night and still drinking often meant that we were not operating on full capacity, with hazy mornings being the price of crazy nights. We were faced with the sad reality that soon we would have to knuckle down to some real work. With this in mind we decided that a Saturday in early May would be our last big blow-out before exams. And what a blow-out it proved to be.

The sun seemed to have heard that we needed one last good day and had appeared in its best yellow suit bright and early. We took ourselves off into town for breakfast to a place called Café Carrington – a frequent destination of Oisin Kerrigan whenever he was on a wee break, or whatever. There we ate an over-priced and under-cooked full English breakfast happy in the knowledge that the sun was shining, we were reasonably healthy, for once we had no work at all to do that day, and more importantly, in an act of scheduling that can only have been commissioned by the gods, it was the day of both the FA Cup final and the *Eurovision Song Contest.*

Everyone had signed up for the Big Day Off. Geographers Joe and Nick, having been doing at least two hours work each day for the last week, were advised by the college nurse to take a break. The History exams that Jude and Sly were set to take shortly were Prelims, which meant they only had to get 40 per cent to pass, and thus they were quite relaxed about the whole thing. Oisin Kerrigan was far from relaxed about the exams and was only supposed to be coming to Café Carrington for a wee break before embarking upon a full day of work; however, as often was the case, his wee break ran a little over schedule. Mark Novak had run out of A4 paper, and so was forced to stop. Even Caolan, who hated football with a passion, signed up for the day, not wishing to miss out on anything ("You dicks would only miss me if I wasn't here"). Girls were allowed to come, but only if they treated the FA Cup final with the respect it deserved.

The game kicked off at 3 pm, but with nothing else to do we gathered round in my room when we came back from our late breakfast just before one o'clock. On the way back from breakfast, inspired by the unusual heat of this May afternoon, historians Jude Richards and Adam Sylvester had nipped into Argos and purchased two top-of-the-range Super-Soakers. Immediately you could see Sly's eyes light up and feel the rumble of trouble brewing as he clutched the plastic gun menacingly in his hand, his mind working overtime thinking of all the things he could do with it. Back in my room, whilst we sat round watching the build up and Caolan once again stated his case that football was gay, Adam Sylvester stood ominously looking out of my opened window. An evil light bulb illuminated in his head, and he immediately reached for the Super-Soaker and filled it up using my tap. For the next two hours he indiscriminately soaked passers-by; young, old, male, female, black, white, humans, animals, in cars, on bikes and especially in the tourist buses. Yes, all were equal in the eyes of Sly, but tourists buses were his favourite. The combination of sun and Saturday had brought the tourists flocking to Cambridge, and the open-top level of the double-decker bus, a level that passed no more than three metres under my window, was jam-packed full. As the recorded message invited tourists to look to their left to see the accommodation of St. Catharine's College, a college opened in 1473, they were given something of an interactive experience as Sly unleashed his weapon. The passengers screamed, using handbags, arms and small children for cover, causing them to miss the story about Catharine of Alexandria and her wheel. Sniper Sly ducked for cover behind the curtain and chuckled away to himself, before eyeing up his next target. I tried to show a distinct lack of interest in his childish, irresponsible and potentially dangerous pursuits, but it was so funny to see people wondering which part of the clear, blue sky this sudden burst of rain had come from.

It took a while for everyone to settle down after Sly's bout of watery assignations, but the sight of the players running out onto the Cardiff pitch soon brought about a bit of order. Arsenal were playing Liverpool, and the room was clearly divided in terms of support. Mark Novak and Jude Richards were dedicated Spurs supporters, and so were naturally going for Liverpool today. Sly and Oisin (because London is so close to Derry, of course) were loyal Arsenal fans, and thus were gunning for the Gunners. I didn't have a great preference, but went for the reds on grounds of proximity to my house, and using the same logic, and because it gave him another opportunity to disagree with me, Joe Porter went for Arsenal. Caolan said he didn't give three shits who won and just wanted the game to be over. We each put a quid in and had a guess at the final score.

The game wasn't a bad one as far as FA Cup finals go, and there was enough vocal interest in the room to see us painlessly through the dull bits. Sly tried to get a song going about Michael Owen's Mum, but none of us could remember the words, and he didn't know all of them himself. Mark Novak, usually quiet and reserved unless pissed, revealed that football also acted as a stimulant. It was f-in' this and f-in' that the whole game, and he flew excitedly out of his chair and straight into the wardrobe door whenever Liverpool scored. In the end the game finished 2-1 to Arsenal, with Sly winning the score sweep-stake and Caolan asleep in the corner. Seeing as his team won, Sly announced that he was donating his winnings to tonight's drink fund, which got a round of appreciative nods, but not the standing ovation he was no doubt anticipating.

With a great afternoon already under our belts, we set off to Wetherspoons for a round of Beer-Burger meals to work out a plan for the *Eurovision Song Contest*. The *Eurovision Song Contest* was one of those things that I had really looked forward to each year as a kid, even though it got a bit boring after a couple of songs, until the Germans preformed their regular woeful number, and then when the bi-lingual scoring kicked in. Seeing as we were planning to drink a lot, and hence things were likely to get messy, it was decided that tonight's event would be held in the JCR Common Room instead of my precious M14. It was also decided that to keep things interesting, and to make sure everyone drank their fair share (all eyes instinctively fell upon a certain shaggy-haired Irishman, who had even tried to order a coke with his meal), we would have a few rules. These were written on the back of a beer-mat during consumption of the Beer-Burger meal, and then transferred onto paper and put in the protective covering of a plastic wallet when we got back to college. The rules for watching tonight's *Eurovision Song Contest* were decided by the self-appointed Eurovision Song Contest Committee as follows:

1. Each person shall be given a country by means of a random draw. By the use of BBC subtitles, each person is requested to sing along in English to his country's entry, and consume one beer by the time the next entry begins.
2. All persons drink two fingers each time host Terry Wogan makes a joke that dies on its arse.
3. All persons drink two fingers each time host Terry Wogan makes a comment that could be perceived as racist.
4. Any use of numbers must be spoken in French.
5. All persons drink two fingers each time a song lyric rhymes "love" with "above", "cry" with "eye", "heart" with "apart" or "tear" with "near".

With both the rules and our food settled we headed back to college. There we picked up Elizabeth and her two medic friends, sleazy Lionel and dodgy Dale, and headed down to OddBins to get some beer. Now seeing as May Week was coming up, we figured that it was probably best to save the pennies at every opportunity. Thus, Stella, Kronenburg, and Carlsberg, were binned in favour of a new beer called Meteor. It cost 27p a bottle, contained a badly drawn meteor on its label, and was three weeks past its sell-by date. The man behind the counter said it was just about drinkable, and thus we promptly snapped up every last bottle.

Armed with a couple of cases of Meteor we arrived in the JCR Common Room early to reserve our seats. A group of lads were watching *The Simpsons*, but promised they would turn it over as soon as our show started. And so, at seven o'clock on a Saturday evening, smack bang in the middle of our third term at St. Catharine's College, Cambridge, my good friends and I, clutching our bottles of Meteor, sat back, relaxed and watched the global phenomenon that was the *Eurovision Song Contest*.

It didn't take long for Wogan to unleash his first woeful joke upon the nation, something about Brussels Sprouts, and the Meteor began to flow. It tasted every bit the 27p bottle of piss that it was always going to be, and I doubted that the three weeks that had transpired since its sell-by date had anything to do with it. Still, after three or four bottles, it started to slip down a bit more easily. Thankfully, there were not too many other people in the JCR that night, and hence only our ears bore witness as young Nick MacLean sang along passionately to the Swedish entry. By the time Mr Wogan had cracked his ninetieth bad joke of the evening and simultaneously announced that we were halfway through the competition, we were all pissed.

A few Meteors later, Jude and Sly produced from under their chairs the two fully loaded Super-Soakers that they had purchased earlier in the day. At first they were used only as a threat to try and make Oisin sing along to the Bosnia-Herzegovina entry, but as soon as a squirt of water landed in the shaggy-haired Irishman's ear, first blood was spilt, and all hell broke loose. Suddenly the previously serene JCR became a war zone and with their Meteor in hand, everyone ducked for cover. Sly was once again ruthless and indiscriminate with who he squirted, and by the time Wogan made his twenty-eighth howler, a howler observed by an astute Mark Novak from his hiding place behind an overturned chair, we were all well and truly super-pissed and super-soaked.

During the carnage, Joe Porter and I somehow managed to commandeer the two offending weapons, and scurried off the toilets to fill them up and form a plan. The plan, from two of next season's football captains, wasn't the most tactically sophisticated I have ever heard, but we carried it out to the T. It involved super-soaking as many people as possible, paying particular attention Jude and Sly for wetting us, and Oisin Kerrigan for no real reason at all. We returned to the JCR all guns blazing. Unfortunately, in our absence, the room had become filled by a few other people, people who had popped into the JCR on their way to bed to catch the result of the Contest that we had lost track of, people who had not had a Meteor between them, people who were not that keen to get super-soaked. Still, Joe and I were not to know that, and super-soaked them all the same.

One particular girl got an almighty soaking from my gun. She was standing by the door as I walked in, and was drenched from head to toe at point-blank range. She did not look happy. I recognised her from college, although I had never spoken but a word to her. She was that French girl who wrote the "Serious News" page in our college magazine, *Catz Eyes*. I tried to think of her name; something foreign, French I presumed; like Carrio, or Carrette, or Carine. Yes, Carine, that was it. Oh God, I thought, I've soaked a French girl that I have never spoken to in my life and who writes the "Serious Articles" page. If I were selecting the characteristics of people who might see the funny side of receiving such a soaking, those two wouldn't be top of my list. Like many throughout history, she was but an unfortunate casualty in a war that she had nothing to do with. I smiled as means of an apology and pointed, as means of an explanation, towards Joe Porter who was shooting at the crotch area of a giggling Nick MacLean. But as the water dripped down from her dark-brown hair, Carine's face was unmoving, and without a word she turned and walked out of the door. Bloody hell, I thought, and went after Adam Sylvester.

The battle raged on for at least half an hour and, fortunately, I managed to keep hold of the Super-Soaker. Anyone who had popped into the JCR to see the result had been shot and had since fled, and all that remained were the original gang and a few bottles of Meteor. We were wet, drunk and happy, and we didn't have the slightest notion who had won the *Eurovision Song Contest*.

"We'll assume it was Ireland" said Caolan, cracking open his final bottle.

It was then that I went to the toilet. Having carried the Super-Soaker around for most of the battle I had avoided a good deal of the soaking, and was actually quite dry. Even though the soldiers were currently subdued, I took the gun with me just in case any watery trouble flared up again. Just as I was heading into the toilet, and getting quite desperate to relieve my body of the large quantity of Meteor currently swishing around down below, I was confronted by a familiar face.

"You wet me and I don't even know you."

"Erm... I'm Josh."

"Well, Josh" she said my name with a venom that I had never heard before. She had quite a distinctive French accent, tonight making her sound like a deadly female Bond villain. "I'm Carine. Pleased to meet you"

"Oh, pleased to meet y..."

And before the words had left my mouth I was hit full in the face by a high-velocity pint of water. It went up my nose and in my eyes, in my trouser pockets and down the front of my shirt. I was stunned. Carine was smiling. I forgot all about my need for the toilet, took hold of my Super-Soaker, and opened fire. Carine fled, screaming. I chased her out past the library, along Main Court and into Sherlock Court. I finally caught up with her by the side of a wall. I held the gun to her head and tried to think of a good line.

"Like I said, I'm Josh, nice to meet you"

And then I soaked her from head to toe. She screamed and screamed, but through her shrieks and occasional rather rude derogatory remarks, some in French, some in English, I sensed laughter, and so I kept going. I was only stopped by the night-porter, who duly called me immature and pathetic, confiscated Adam Sylvester's Super-Soaker, and sent me on my way to bed.

"Well, *au revoir*, Carine. *Peut être*, I'll see you again." I bet she didn't know I was virtually fluent.

"*Peut être, peut être.* Sweet dreams, Josh."

I returned to my room, took off my wet clothes, and rubbed a towel through my hair. I pulled my mobile out of my pocket to text Mark, but my mobile was too wet to text, too wet to even turn on. I wrapped it in a dry T-shirt and put it on my radiator to dry. In three days' time my mobile would come out of its coma, but it would never ring again; a silent reminder of that water-soaked night, and the water-soaked girl.

As I lay in bed I smiled at the memory of the day just gone by; with its over-priced breakfast, watery snipering, frantic football, beautiful Beer-Burger and meteoric finale. It was one of the few days that we built up to be big and then it actually surpassed expectations. I thought about the mysterious Carine; the French girl who took herself too seriously in her articles about the Middle East and asylum-seekers, the French girl who I had spoken to for the first time tonight, the French girl who I had wet for the first time tonight, the French girl who had thrown a pint of water over me and in the process broken my mobile phone, the French girl who I had chased through college whilst wielding a pump-action Super-Soaker, the French girl who had wished me sweet dreams, the French girl who would one day, for better or worse, become the biggest part of my life.

The following day I saw her again. I was walking down the stairs and out of M-block when I passed her about to make her way up. She was holding hands with her boyfriend, whilst my hand was taken up affectionately clutching an overdue library book. It wasn't a remarkable scene in any way, and I only recalled it from the back draws of my memory at a much later date. It was like a seemingly insignificant bit in a movie that leaves you wondering why the director put it in, and it is only when you watch the film for the second time that it all falls into place. I was feeling a little embarrassed about my actions last night, in particular the super-soaking of a girl I had not spoken to before, and a French one at that. I spotted them immediately as they stood at the bottom of the stairs that I was descending. I thought about pretending I hadn't seen them, but realised that our proximity wouldn't support my case. I sheepishly looked in their direction. Her boyfriend turned away from me, but she smiled. It was a smile that I will never forget, because it was a smile I saw so many times. In that brief moment, before her boyfriend whisked her away, it showed me not only that I was forgiven for my immature, inappropriate watery behaviour, but also the warmth of a connection. I smiled back and scurried out of the door.

Chapter 54

After that eventful Saturday, and the obligatory relaxing Sunday morning comedown, the four economists – or the Fab Four as nobody called us – settled down to do just under four weeks of solid work.

And it was an intense, rigorous, demanding programme we set ourselves. Up at 8.30am, down at the Law Faculty for nine. Start work as soon as we had climbed the steep staircase, found a seat and caught our breath. Work right through until lunch at 12.30 pm. Grab a quick baguette from Nadia's canteen on the bottom floor, and start work again at one. Work through until four, then take a half-hour break in the Law Faculty, or outside on the grass if the weather was nice, maybe having a chocolate bar and a hot drink.

A Tale of Friendship, Love and Economics

Back to work at 4.30 pm sharp until 6.30 pm when we returned to college for dinner in hall. Work a few more hours in the evening, watch the news to remind ourselves that there was in fact, a world outside of the Cambridge bubble, and then get an early night. Of course, there wasn't one day when we stuck to the programme.

It was strange how the Law Faculty became the place we spent so many hours revising; after all, none of us were lawyers. Caolan was the first to venture into it, the first to break the pattern of either going to Catz library or our very own Marshall Library of Economics. Caolan loved the fact that he was the first to try it and loved the way we all seemed to follow him ("Sheep following the shepherd, you're just sheep following the shepherd").

The Law Faculty Building was located on the Sidgwick Site, the same place that housed the Marshal Library, and where we had all our lectures. It was a huge building, including two storeys below ground as well as four storeys above, housing not only the library with all its books, desks and computers, but also five auditoriums, as well as numerous seminar rooms and offices. It was designed in 1995 by the famous architect Sir Norman Foster, the same guy who knocked up plans for the New German Parliament at the Reichstag in Berlin, as well as Stansted Airport and the white-knuckle ride that was the London Millennium Bridge. It was a funny-looking thing. From some angles it looked like a spaceship, and from others like a giant greenhouse. The north wall was curved, and entirely glazed, thus letting in a good amount of light, whereas the other walls stood up straight like walls are supposed to and were only partially glazed, apparently for energy efficiency purposes. As a special feature, the glass was apparently designed so that the people inside couldn't hear the rain. I only wish the glass also blocked out the ever-irritating noises of people sniffing and fidgeting. All in all, the Law Faculty Building was a good place to revise. Due to its immense size, you could always find space to work, especially if you were prepared to venture right up to the top, which could not be said for the often congested Marshall. The first underground floor contained a Nadia's outlet, where sandwiches and cakes could be snapped up and consumed, as well as a couple of vending machines, and a hot-drinks maker that produced things called "Creamy Chocs", consistently the best 35p I spent each day. As a general rule, female lawyers tended to be above average on the attractiveness scale, which gave you something pleasant to look at whilst you whittled away the hours studying, and yet another reason to frequent the Law Faculty.

Inevitably, in the way news of a good thing always spreads, the Fab Four were soon joined in the great glass Law Faculty Building by other people. Geographers Nick MacLean and Joe Porter were the first to jump aboard the economists' band-wagon, soon followed by Elizabeth and a couple of the medics. Sly and Jude paid us the odd visit but spent most of their time in the Sealey History Library, the Law Faculty's next-door neighbour. After a couple of weeks, the top floor of the Law Faculty was at least 20 per cent Catz. Faye never quite made the journey down ("It's too bloody far") and Francesca preferred to study the essential details of the great English language in the peace and tranquillity of her room.

Although we were all from the same college, our revision techniques differed immensely. Even within the Fab Four, universalism was not the order of the day. Caolan and I tended to hit the Law Faculty each day full of high spirits and good intention, work through solidly until lunch, sticking to our programme to the T. It was in the afternoon session that things started to go wrong, taking the odd five-minute break here, the odd ten-minute break there, and rarely working in the evenings. However, looking back, we always got a good bit of work done each day. I suppose we were both a good influence and a bad one upon each other; if one was working, the other would feel guilty and work too, but if one was talking a break, the other reasoned that he might as well also. Mark Novak was a loner. He always stuck to the programme, or at least always tried to, working quietly, with his head down for hour upon end, only stopping, and then with great reluctance, for essential food and liquid, and the odd toilet break. However, with a bit of persuasion Mark would eventually concede to taking that extra five minutes ("Remember, five minutes now will mean you can keep going for an extra hour later, Mark"), or having just one more cup of coffee ("Remember, it'll give you the energy you need to keep going, Mark"). We had his best interests at heart. Oisin would tell the whole world he was talking absolutely no frickin' wee breaks today, or whatever, and even moved from the top floor down to the second floor to get away from all the frickin' distractions. However, whenever we were bored, Caolan and I would pop our heads over the side and just observe the shaggy-haired Irishman on his big frickin' day of work. He would look at the page for a couple of seconds, think about picking up his pen, then he would spot something on the ceiling and look at that for ten minutes or so, then he would rub his eyes and clean his glasses, maybe scratch his head and blow his nose, then, just as he was about to pick up his pen again, he would spot something that needed looking at on the floor. We would always call down for Oisin on our way for a break, and he would always reply: "I've no time for a frickin' wee break. Big day of work."

The geographers were a different breed altogether. I had observed Faye's working practices first hand during the last three terms, and they basically involved getting her books out on the desk, putting Radio One on, lying on her bed and falling asleep. Nick MacLean was far more motivated, extremely conscientious and well organised. However, he would only work one hour at a time and then take a half-hour break (after all, too much colouring in can hurt your wrist). Joe Porter was the worst. The man who liked to claim he looked like Charlie Sheen would perpetually talk and moan about how much work he had to do and how little time he had to do it. He would then explain at length, to an audience who had heard it countless times before, how he was definitely going to do eighteen hours tomorrow, definitely. Then, when tomorrow came, Joe would do about twenty minutes, go for a walk to clear his head, decide it was too late to do any proper work now, rule out the rest of the day, and talk about starting a fresh tomorrow, where he now planned to do twenty-nine hours. It was a little down-heartening and frustrating to see the geographers continually on breaks whilst we worked on, but we were comforted in the knowledge that at least we were doing a proper degree.

Chapter 55

In those dark days, imprisoned on the top floor of the great glass Law Faculty, my mind inevitably started to wander. My eyes still read the words in front of them, but my thoughts were elsewhere, either lost in the promised land of May Week, dreaming of lies-in and lazy days, wondering what my Mum was up to, or thinking about Imogene. Indeed, it had now been three weeks since I had seen Imogene, but never more than three minutes since I had thought about her last.

I didn't know what to do about the Imogene situation, and the longer I left it the worst it got. I had rolled the situation around in my head time and time again, but reached no solution. I was pretty sure I had blown something, but just not sure what, and I certainly had no clue what I should do next. The frosty relations that continued to endure between the two superpowers of Lauren Broad and Caolan O'Donnell had reduced further the likelihood of me getting Imogene's mobile number off her friend. Email was always an option, but then I always thought it was a bit impersonal, and anyway, what would I say? "Hey Imogene, sorry for being a dick at the formal hall"? Then I would inevitably have to explain why I was a dick, which would mean I would have to say that I fancied her, and then even that wouldn't explain why I didn't talk to her that night. No, I had ruled out sending an email. A letter was better than an email, more personal anyway, but I would still have to think of something to say in it, and as for a poem… But then even if I could find the perfect way to contact her and find the perfect words to say, they were words I should have said three weeks ago. Basically, apart from inventing a time machine and then sending her a telepathic message, there was not a lot else I could think of, and Keynes' explanation of the Liquidity Trap that my empty eyes currently perused was proving most uninspiring.

Just when I thought all was lost, a most unexpected opportunity presented itself. During a much-needed revision break, I decided to check my emails. There was one from Mr Stevens to inform us about a revision session he was organising on Macro, one from the Senior Tutor about not getting too stressed during the revision period, and one from the Chaplin reminding us that both he and God were always there for us. Then there was one from an "I. J. Head." I laughed at the name, and opened the email fully expecting some crappy porn thing sent around by either Nick or Jude. What I didn't expect was a message from Imogene.

Hey Josh,

Long time no hear! I hope all is well in Catz and you are not working too hard. Lauren says she sees you lot in the library all day everyday. She hasn't done any work yet, you know, but she doesn't seem too bothered. My exams start in two days. I know they don't really count for anything but I'm still stressed.

A Tale of Friendship, Love and Economics

Anyway, I was just wondering if you guys were planning to go to Robinson May Ball. We're all going, and it would be great if you were too. Right, best be off and change the habit of a lifetime and do some work.

Don't work too hard!

Imogene xxx

Bloody hell, I thought, Imogene has emailed me and her surname is "Head". I was so excited about the email that I told Caolan, Oisin and Mark as we sat around in the Law Faculty drinking Creamy Chocs and eating crisps on our pre-dinner break.

"She seems keen, you know, with the invite to the Ball and the kisses, or whatever," said Oisin.

Mark nodded in silent agreement.

"I can't believe your going after someone with a surname 'Head,'" chipped in a smirking Caolan, his mind already running through a list of potential blow job-related one-liners.

"And how is the lovely Ms Broad, Caolan?" I replied.

Although I always liked to think the worst when it comes to my chances with women – a pessimist will never be disappointed – I had to, in the safety of my own thoughts at least, agree with Oisin; Imogene did sound keen. Thankfully it was not hard to convince the gang to sign up for Robinson College May Ball. It was the cheapest of all the May Balls, and had a reputation for being a real good laugh. It was taking place on the first Friday of May Week, the day us economists finished our exams, and so was seen as both a good way to celebrate the coming of that longed for day, and a good way to warm up for the main event of Trinity May Ball on the following Monday. Tickets were easy to come by, merely involving the filling out of a form and then sending off of a cheque, and pretty soon the Fab Four, geographers Nick, Joe and Faye, Elizabeth and the medics, historians Jude, Sly and Duane, English students Francesca and Julie, Movie Star Look-alike, and a load of others duly found tickets for Robinson May Ball waiting in their pigeon hole one chilly Thursday morning.

Having sent off our cheques I emailed Imogene to tell her the news. It took me a mere seventy-eight minutes to write it:

Hi Imogene,

Thanks for your email, it was a nice surprise. Spoke to the gang, and they were well keen for Robinson, and now we've all sent off our cheques (us economists don't mess around – efficiency is everything!).

Bit sick of revision, but we have enough breaks to keep us going, and anyway, not long to go now. Can't wait for May Week. Your exams must be nearly over now, I know Jude's are (he was the guy with the floppy black hair at the formal, and he does history too). I hope they are going well.

Hey, if you want to join me on a revision break one afternoon, just let me know. My mobile number is: 07776 588220.

Best of luck with the rest of the exams

Love Josh

Brilliant. Worth every minute. Anyway, the following day I received a text message from an unknown number wondering if I was free for a break at quarter-past three at the bottom of the Law Faculty. I made Caolan promise that he hadn't borrowed someone else's phone, and he looked annoyed with himself for not having thought of that. I spent the afternoon work session with one eye on my Micro text-book and the other on my watch, which today was attached to an especially shaky hand. I couldn't believe I was nervous about meeting up for a Creamy Choc. I guess it was just because I hadn't seen her for so long.

At nine minutes past three I made my way down the stairs. Oisin and Mark wished me good luck and Caolan explained that if I got an erection, then *The Daily Telegraph* was as good a newspaper as any to cover it up.

Imogene was early. I saw her as I made my way down the final set of stairs. She had just bought herself what looked like a cup of tea, thus immediately ruling out the most obvious gentlemanly gesture. Maybe I could buy her a Kit Kat Chunky. I pretended not to notice her as I walked down the stairs. I placed one hand in my pocket and started whistling a made up tune. God, I was cool. When I sensed she was close enough I looked up and acted surprised (if only the directors of the Freshers' Play could have seen this performance).

"Imogene!"

"Oh, hi Josh."

A Tale of Friendship, Love and Economics

There was a temporary awkward silence whilst I considered whether it was appropriate or not to shake hands (I wish there was a book on this thing), but in the end I decided not to and carried on talking.

"How are you?"

"Good. How are you?"

"Good."

Right, that was the standard stuff over with. Now I needed to come up with some magical conversation to sweep her off her feet. I thought about it for a moment.

"So, how's revision?"

"Not bad. You?"

"Not bad."

Okay. Not the greatest of starts. I needed a break, a chance to gather my thoughts.

"Hey, I'm going to get a Creamy Choc, can I get you anything?"

"No, I've got my tea, but thank you anyway. What's a Creamy Choc?"

"You've not had one?"

"No."

"Oh, Imogene, they are by far the finest hot drink available in the whole of the Sidgwick Site. Five pence more than a cup of tea, but worth every penny, and more."

"Are you on commission or something?"

"No, just a big Creamy Choc fan."

"Well, you make them sound too good to refuse. Looks like I'll have to get one."

Imogene reached into her bag and pulled out her purse.

"Hey, my treat. Anyway, there is the slightest chance that you are one of those strange breed of people who don't like Creamy Choc."

"God, I hope not. Thank you, Josh."

And she smiled that smile. Give praise to the Lord for His gift of Creamy Choc.

Imogene did indeed enjoy her chocolatey drink experience, finishing the whole lot and licking her lips. We sat down on one of the circular tables by the notice board. We talked non-stop for just over half an hour. It turned out that Imogene's exams were going alright, but she wished she had done more work for them. After her three years at uni, Imogene planned to do a Law conversion course and then get a "Big Job" in London. Either that or she was going to marry someone rich and go shopping every day. Imogene wasn't a great fan of animals but was a fan of most types of music (except "that techno rubbish"). Imogene ate fish, but could fully appreciate my point about their eyes, adding that fish fingers definitely didn't have eyes. Imogene often thought about going to the gym, but then she often thought about giving up chocolate. Imogene didn't mind watching sport, didn't like playing it, and couldn't ride a bike. No, honestly, she couldn't. Imogene was still as pretty as ever.

The time flew by, and it was only a text message from Caolan ("hey dicko, has Blow-Job made her excuses & left yet?") that alerted me of the lateness of the hour.

"I suppose we best go and get some work done?" said Imogene, taking the opportunity to look at the clock whilst I promptly deleted the Irishman's message.

"I really can't be arsed, you know?"

"Not long to go now, as a wise man once said to me in an email."

"Yeah, yeah."

"Well, I've had a really nice time, Josh."

"Yeah, Imogene, so have I, so have I."

The first awkward pause in the last thirty minutes.

"Hey, listen, do you want to do this again sometime?" I said, trying not to sound too desperate.

"That would be lovely." She smiled sweetly as she spoke. "Well, we've both got each other's numbers, so I'm sure we'll sort something out."

"I'm sure we will."

"Right, back to the history library I go."

"And I'm off up all those bloody stairs."

"Healthy body, healthy mind."

"Not if it kills me first."

"See you soon, Josh."

"Yeah, see you soon, Imogene."

And as I climbed the stairs I watched her walk out of the door.

We met for several cups of Creamy Chocs on the ground floor of the Law Faculty over the next few weeks. Imogene finished her exams, which she said could have been better but could have been a lot worse, but still had essays to write, and thus was still working away in the Sealey History Library most days. Each meeting was as fun and as easy as the first, and continued to brighten up those otherwise dark days. There was little doubt that Imogene was a lovely person, and little doubt that I had fallen for her. I wasn't sure if she liked me in that way though. Again, I remained a natural pessimist, not wanting to build up anything that could so easily be knocked down. However, the rest of the gang said I was definitely onto a winner, and even Caolan had to admit that things looked good. I decided to make my move, whatever that was going to be, at Robinson May Ball.

Chapter 56

It was hard to know exactly how to revise for those bloody exams GCSEs, and A-levels to a lesser extent, had all been about remembering large chunks of information and then just slapping it all down in the exam. Now, however, there was far too much stuff to remember, but also too much stuff to learn and understand. Us poor little economists had five papers to get through, each paper containing at least six separate topics, and each topic having at least thirty chapters from various books written about it. I soon realised that a system was required.

Not wishing to blow my own trumpet, although certainly nobody else ever did, I was good at revising. I may not have had much in the way of so called "common sense" when it came to changing fuses, ironing shirts, or finding my way around town, but when it came down to work, I was good at using my time efficiently and effectively. I wrote down a list of all the topics we had to do across all papers and compared this to a realistic, perhaps even pessimistic, evaluation of how much time I would spent revising, with breaks and bad days fully accounted for. I then ordered the topics in their relative chance of coming up in the exams, both by their occurrence in previous years and the emphasis lectures had put on them this year, and in their relative difficulty. I then allocated a time slot for each topic, leaving myself at the end of it all a day each to go over each paper one last time. I also decided just how I would approach each topic. I had a four-stage plan. First I would go through lectures and supervision notes (if it was a topic that we had binned in lectures, then this process was more accurately described as "vision" as opposed to "revision", which at least kept things fresh and interesting). Stage two involved doing a bit of extra reading and note-making on the topic from the lectures series reading list or the supervision reading list. I considered stage two very important. Basically, everyone in the year had the lecture notes and everyone had done a supervision on the topic, so everyone had the same basic knowledge and information. Hence, doing a bit of wider reading gave you that edge or that twist that would make you stand out from the crowd, hopefully in a good way. Stage three involved collecting all my information on the topic together, condensing it, and grouping it into sub-topics. This was a scary stage as it meant you had done all the reading, written down all your information, and so what you didn't know now you would never know. Finally, stage four involved making essay plans (just bullet points about what would go in each paragraph) from all past paper questions on the topic and even a few made-up questions. Then, in the day I had allocated for going over a paper, I would just flick through my pile of essay plans and hopefully it would all come together.

This was my system, and, although it was sometimes boring and monotonous, I knew it was the best way for me to revise. Caolan said my system was gay, and promptly introduced a similar one a couple of days later. Mark had his own system, and was equally happy with it. As well as the standard stages, he had a "brainstorming" stage where he allowed his mind to pour out onto a piece of A4 paper. Mr Novak was also a fan of writing timed essays under exam conditions, which I personally found a waste of time. I don't know if Oisin had a system; it was hard to tell. If he did it seemed to involve putting in hours of work and not getting much done. The shaggy-haired Irishman from Derry would spent all day making the most comprehensive notes imaginable on what was in reality a small and insignificant part of the course. We could all see that he wasn't using his time effectively, and that if he kept it up he wouldn't cover half of the course, but what were we supposed to say: "Look Oisin, I know you're nineteen, and I know you got straight As at A-level, and I know you're at Cambridge, and I know that we're equally inexperienced at university exams, but I don't think you're revising properly"? Caolan, Mark and I talked it over, but apart from continually asking Mr Kerrigan if he was alright, to which he would reply "Aye, I'm grand", we reasoned that it was not our place to say any more. Who were we to know better?

As the exams got closer increasingly the discussions in our revision breaks, discussions that had previously been about football or the pair of sideburns that Joe Porter was clearly trying to grow, were almost entirely

A Tale of Friendship, Love and Economics

dominated by economics. Caolan, Mark and I (Oisin took less and less official breaks these days and more and more "hey, what's that on the ceiling, or whatever" breaks) would discuss bits of the course that we didn't understand. It was boring as hell for geographers Joe and Nick, who promptly starting taking their breaks at other times, but really useful for us three. Even Caolan displayed a previously unseen level of maturity by not taking the piss when one of us didn't quite get something that he did. Indeed, Caolan specialised at Macro, I was more of a Micro man, and Mark was generally good at everything, and especially Statistics. Breaks soon became almost as beneficial as time spent up in the top floor of the library. Mr Stevens had said right from the start that we would all benefit from discussing work with each other, even those who knew most of it. It was very much like the theory of Comparative Advantage, which proves, with a few restrictive assumptions of course, that even a country that is more productive at producing two items will benefit from trading with a country that is worse at producing both items. During those breaks we were trading ideas and explanations, and all benefiting from it. When I pointed this out to the other two one afternoon, and they found themselves nodding in agreement, we all realised that perhaps we had done enough economics for one day.

Indeed, it was certainly possible to do too much revision. It's an overused cliché in exam times, but success, and even staying sane, is all about striking the right balance between work and play. Some people in Cambridge clearly had not struck the right balance. With exams fast approaching, the college library had become many people's first place of residence. There was not a desk free at any time of day or night. Moreover, people had brought in pictures of their family, cuddly toys, ornaments, pillows, blankets, kettles, and many more things to keep them motivated and allow them to become self-sufficient in the library. People would work all day at their desks and then just allow their head to drop whenever they had done their fourteen hours, or whatever, and this was not one of geographer Joe Porter's fourteen hours, these hours actually did happen. It seemed to be the girls who went the craziest. Apparently Mary Jane was on Pro-Plus, Memory Tea, and some imported herbal Japanese stuff, all washed down by about nineteen cups of straight, black coffee a day. Even the calm, laid back, Francesca was staying up until the early hours doing whatever it was English students did. Faye was a refreshing exception explaining, as she crawled into bed at nine o'clock: "I'm too bloody tired to work, and anyway, they're only bloody exams."

Faye was right, they were only exams and, happily, none of our lot went as exam crazy. Oisin started working more and more, and Mark often tried to, but both had to concede that breaks were necessary and beneficial. And so, each day, we tried to do something fun, something to look forward to that would give us the incentive and the will needed to get through yet another day of revision.

At least twice a week we tried to organise a game of football on the local park. Geographers Nick MacLean and Joe Porter, along with my good self, would march around college, dressed in shorts and a sweatshirt, affectionately clutching the ball as if it was a new born baby, knocking on people's doors to see if anyone wanted to kick our baby around. Faye's Duane, Jewish Simon, peanut-fearing Chip, wee break Oisin, workaholic Mark, cool dude Jude, Mr Sly, and a bunch of random NatScis were all on our twice-weekly route. We even extended it to include girls, as long as they could kick and they weren't better than us. On good days we got sixteen people or more, giving us a really good game, on bad days it was just us three (and poor Mark, who was not allowed to say no). Often people had too much work on, which was kind of understandable, and often they would only play if we got a certain number, which was the most infuriating response in the world because if everyone adopted that attitude there would never be any games. We would play in the early evenings, and maybe call into Wetherspoons for a Beer-Burger (coke standing in for beer in those days) if we were all still talking.

Indeed, whilst the whole idea of the kick-around was to relax us after a hard day's revision, often the game was more stressful than the fast-approaching exams. Joe and I had a strong competitive rivalry (started entirely by him, of course), and if we were picked on different teams, there was always trouble.

"These teams okay, Joe?"

"Well, if your definition of okay is 'completely unfair', then I guess they are."

"What's your problem now?"

"Well, look at your bloody team, and then look at mine."

Poor Mark Novak was on Joe's team and seemed to take his captain's comment personally.

"Right, Joe, what do you want to do about it?"
"I'll swap you Rachael for Nick."
"Piss off... No offence Rachael."
"Jesus, stop taking things so seriously. It's only a game, Josh. Just a kick-around, that's all."
"Oh, is that why you started moaning first and your wearing footy boots and shin pads whilst we're all happily unprotected and in our trainers?"
"Piss off, Josh."
"Piss off, Joe."
"Right, let's play."

Moreover, young Nick MacLean was hardly the least competitive individual I had ever come across, often flying in with the late sliding tackles, once causing a tennis ball-sized lump to appear on my right calf (needless to say, I milked this injury for a good couple of weeks, getting poor Elizabeth and Faye to make their invalid friend cups of tea, and Nick to go into town and get old hop-along a burger and chips). The normally quiet, reserved, Oisin Kerrigan was also a terrier on the football field, happily letting his elbow finds its way into people's ribs. Only Mark Novak played like a man who didn't really care what was going on, his feet moving where they were told whilst his mind longed to be in the comfort of the Marshall Library of Economics. Basically, there were always arguments, always injuries, and always grudges held. Cathartic, some would call it. It was just what we needed to take our minds off work.

As well as football, there was the odd venture out on a punt. Now, if you were looking for a stereotypical picture-postcard of the city of Cambridge, then it would more than likely feature a punt. Some people called Cambridge the Amsterdam of East Anglia, but then these same people said the Blackpool Tower was just as good as its Paris equivalent. Basically, punting was good for two types of people. Firstly there were the tourists. They would more than likely hire out a chauffeur driven punt, float happily along the Backs, allowing the River Cam to gently rock them into relaxation, their feet stretched out in front of them, under the guidance of a well-informed young man or woman dressed in a waistcoat and a straw hat and expertly handling a large wooden pole, their open ears being filled with anecdote after anecdote, some true some utter bollocks, about the various colleges passed along the way, including the Big Three of Queen's, King's and Trinity. Then there were the students. We had heard all the stories, and anyway we couldn't afford a chauffeur. We opted for the cheaper self-hire option, and took the open seas under our own steam. We often took out a couple of punts and had races to see who could get the furthest down the Backs. Punting ability was certainly mixed amongst the group. At the bottom end were the girls and me. The girls at least had the excuses of size and lack of strength. I was just shit. I could never work out which way to angle the pole to steer the boat ("Oy, malco. It's just like a bloody rudder on a boat" yelled Captain Caolan), and the pole itself often got stuck in the mud that lined the bottom of the River Cam. Caolan was annoyingly good, so too were Oisin and Nick, and even Mark, who could normally be relied upon to make you feel better in most non-work situations, was not too bad.

Punting quietly up and down the Backs, from The Anchor to Magdalene Bridge, was never going to be enough to satisfy a bunch of stressed-out students, lacking a socially acceptable channel to release their pent-up aggression and energy. We often spiced up the trip by playing "Chicken" with other, mostly unsuspecting, punts, or even swapping boats in death-defying stunt sequences at our usual turning point just short of Magdalene Bridge. However, on one particular night a little bit more was required. It had been an especially boring day of revision, and an especially nice day weather-wise. No-one was that keen for football (I was still limping from Nick's vicious late challenge) but many were very pro-punting. Indeed, even the normally reserved English students Francesca and Julie signed up on the naive presumption, backed up by my convincing assurance, that we were merely off for a quiet, pleasant, early evening punt – the perfect way to end the day.

There were ten of us in total that night, a number immediately lending itself to an even five in each punt. Francesca first began to suspect something was amiss when we picked sides to see who would go in which punt, and each team was issued with a Super-Soaker. Due to a lack of willing volunteers, and through a seemingly perpetual need to simultaneously lead and oppose each other in the process, Joe and I stepped forward as captains. I managed to secure the services of Caolan (a solid punter, and someone, like me, who hated losing), Jude (useful punter, and someone who added a chilled-out vibe to the vessel), Mark (expendable) and Francesca (last pick). Our opponents were a motley crew led by fearless Joe Porter, with subordinates Oisin, Sly, Nick and a petrified Julie. Armed with

A Tale of Friendship, Love and Economics

our Super-Soakers, and on the receiving end of a dirty look from the punt shop employee, we set sail. No rules were ever laid down, and the term "water-fight" was never used once, but everybody knew what was going to happen. As we passed under the first bridge that took us into the grounds of Queen's College, the first shots were fired – Mark Novak was hit in his left ear by a long-range effort from Sly. Whilst Francesca screamed and I saw to my injured comrade, our Gunman Jude promptly fired back, and Chief Punter Caolan skilfully steered us into optimal firing range.

It didn't take long for the sea battle to get out of control. Super-Soakers were not enough, and soon I had transformed my water bottle from a mere rehydrating device into a nuclear weapon. Joe, despite the reverent protests of Julie, retaliated by some good old-fashioned hand splashing action. Francesca was screaming uncontrollably at this stage and whining on about her hair, or something. I filled up my water bottle again for another assault, and as shells of water dropped all around us, I grabbed the dark-haired English student from Sheffield and employed her as a human shield ("It's for the good of the boat, Francesca, for the good of the boat"). Sly tried the same thing with Julie but received a slap for his troubles.

It didn't look like the watery carnage would ever end. There was not a dry eye, ear, nose, hair, top or trousers in either punt, and people seemingly had nothing left to lose. Then, however, I had one of my few strokes of genius, and a rather evil one at that. Young Nick MacLean was doing a fine job as Chief Punter for our enemies, but I knew he had one weakness. I whispered instructions to Gunman Jude, who with a nod of comprehension, promptly carried them out with the cold-hearted efficiency required to win such wars. He fired his Super-Soaker straight into the eyes of the camp geographer. Almost immediately the pole was dropped and Nick slumped back into his boat complaining about his contact lenses having fallen out. As their punt careered head on into the banks of the mighty Trinity College, victory was ours. As we sailed home, shivering as the sun went down, with our wet clothes clinging to us like leeches, we were left to ask ourselves what the point in all that was. Francesca said she would never trust me again, Julie said she would never speak to me again, Nick said he would probably never see again, Oisin said it was a dirty frickin' trick, Joe said it was typical, just typical, and Caolan and I said it was all Mark's idea.

Not all revision breaks were as eventful as the punting trip, or as stressful as a kick-around in the park. Most nights, if we had nothing special on, we would convene in my room and watch TV. Whilst such quiet nights would have seemed perfect to launch the Second Kerplunk World Championships, or even have a few friendly games, none of us ever desired it or suggested it. It seemed that finally, the moment had passed and the revolution was over. Thankfully the second series of *Big Brother* had just started, and better still it contained a homosexual Irishman who bore the slightest of resemblances to Caolan, but more than enough from him to get annoyed about it.

"Day 6 in the *Big Brother* house, and Caolan is again trying to kiss men."
"Piss off."
"Hey, you've got a tight pink T-shirt like that, haven't you?"
"Yeah, so?"

Indeed, *Big Brother* was just the show we needed; on every night, easy to follow, good to discuss, perfect to take the piss out of Caolan to.

Also, on many of our nights if front of the telly, young Nick MacLean would whip us all up some flavoured teas. He had received a box set for his birthday off an auntie who assumed her nephew had a taste for tea, and Nick had kindly agreed to share them with us. We tried a new flavour every night, with most tasting pretty much the same, but some especially disgusting. After an initial sip I tended to add milk and sugar with mine to try and extract that Typhoo taste from the lemon and coriander, or whatever tonight's delicacy was.

Finally, during those dark days of revision, Sunday mornings were always kept shining. We would treat ourselves to a lie-in (although rumours were rife with reported sightings of a hooded Mark Novak up in the library at the crack of dawn), all gather in my room for another classic episode of *Dawson's Creek*, and then go and have Sunday lunch in hall (the one meal that they actually did a really good job with). I had always been a huge fan of *Dawson's Creek*, having probably seen every single episode of the American teen drama, but was yet to find another male who felt the same.

"What a load of shit," the sideburned Irishman would say with fresh enthusiasm after each episode.

"No-one's forcing you to watch it, Caolan, and anyway, if you give it a chance, it might just teach you something about life."

"Teach me something about life? The only thing it teaches me about life, Josh, is that you don't have one."

Chapter 57

Every year the Part I economists (that would be us) were the last to finish their exams. Like most things, there were two ways of looking at this fact. You could argue that we were the lucky ones as we had more time to revise, and thus were under less pressure. Alternatively you could quit fooling yourself and realise that whilst you were still stuck in the library after a month of revising most hours of the day, bored out of your arse, knowing by heart every bit of graffiti on your desk and the catalogue number and title of every library book within a three-shelf radius, everyone else was finishing their exams and starting partying. Revision period was hard throughout, but that last week was absolutely awful.

Like every week in Cambridge, May Week officially started on a Thursday. Our last exam, Statistics as it happened, was on the Friday morning, one day into May Week, and the same day as Robinson May Ball. Most subjects had wrapped up their exams early on in that final week. The geographers finished on Tuesday, the medics on Monday, the English lot on the previous Friday, and the Landies a week or so before that (typical). However, it was History that finished the earliest, getting their results back before we had even started our exams, and it was this fact that gave rise to a night that no-one in college would ever forget.

Adam Sylvester was a bright lad. There was no getting away from this. He was one of those people who was annoyingly bright, quick-thinking, always able to use the right words and win every argument. He was also more than a little bit crazy. He had started seeing this girl at the beginning of term, and she was crazy also (she was Landie, after all). We couldn't decide whether it was a match made in heaven or a match made in hell. Likewise, if they were going to mate, would it be a good idea for them to mate together, combining their DNA to produce a few super-crazy kids, or spread their genes around to get twice as many semi-crazy offspring? Anyway, the relationship was by no means a conventional one. She would regularly throw tennis balls and other objects at his head, and he would regularly tell her to piss/fuck/anything else off. Moreover, there were rumours flying around that Sly had instructed her to go and see a therapist because she didn't want to sleep with him, hence implying that she clearly had a problem, and the stupid girl had reportedly gone along. Like I say, they were crazy. Anyway, the relationship had recently come to an end and Sly had taken it pretty badly.

And so, on the Thursday night before our exams begun, the History results came in. Jude and Duane had got 2:1s and were very pleased. Adam Sylvester had got a first, and appeared to be over the moon. Some subjects dished out firsts like they were going out of fashion, but by all accounts they were difficult to get in History, and anyway, only geeks with glasses and twitches were supposed to get firsts, not psychos from Croydon. Caolan, Oisin, Mark and I were crossing Main Court on the way to the college library (variety is the spice of life, and another minute in that bloody Law Faculty would have killed us) when Sly told us the news from his favourite position flung out on a bench. We passed on our congratulations via the medium of a handshake.

"Well done, mate. What are you going to do to celebrate?"

"Just have a couple of drinks, you know. Care to join me?"

"We wish. Only four days until the bloody things start, so best not fall off the wagon now."

"Fair enough."

"You have yourself a good time, though."

"Will do."

And with that we skulked off once more to the stuffy library, slowly becoming less and less inhabited as the days went on and more and more people finished, once again cursing the fact that we were economists.

Seeing as exams were so close, we had taken to doing quite a few hours in the library in the evening as well (still stopping to watch *Big Brother* with a flavoured tea, of course). On this particular Thursday night it was just past nine o'clock when we decided to call it a day, and a very long, boring day at that. I put the finishing touches to an essay plan about the role of tariffs in the interwar period (Mr Stevens thought they were a good idea, the rest of the world disagreed), gathered up my files and headed for the door. Mark said he'd just be another five minutes (that meant at least forty), and Oisin and Caolan had left early to phone home. I was whistling a weary tune as I made my way towards the archway that led into Main Court when I was brought to a halt by a sound coming from behind me.

"Joshua Bailey, you are a wanker."

As I turned around my eyes fell upon a figure sitting on the bench by the side of the library door, glass of something in one hand, mobile phone in

A Tale of Friendship, Love and Economics

the other. The light wasn't great, but I could clearly make it the familiar bulky frame and the jacket with the number sixty-nine on it. It was Adam Sylvester.

"What was that, Sly?" I didn't think I had misheard him, I just wanted to hear it again.

"I believe I said, Joshua Bailey, you are a wanker."

He was clearly pissed, and I was absolutely knackered. I weighed up all available options, and lying on my bed, watching *Big Brother* and sipping a flavoured tea won hands down.

"Okay. Have a good night."

And I turned and walked back to my room, my night just about over, Adam Sylvester's only just begun.

I saw Jude in the morning as I was nipping back to my room to get another file, and he was just getting up. He did not look too good.

"How are you?" I asked.

"Not great, mate."

"Must have been a good night then?"

"Not really."

"*Porquoi?*"

"Sly."

Using Jude Richard's testimony, given under oath using the *Kerplunk Bible*, as well as those of several other key eye-witnesses, I was able to paint what I considered to be a fairly reliable picture of the night gone by.

Adam Sylvester had hit the college bar, along with the other celebrating historians, with the intention of having a few drinks and then maybe going on to a club. A few drinks had soon become a few too many drinks, and the combination of alcohol, delight at his excellent exam result, despair over his failed relationship, and the fact that he was crazy in the first place resulted in a lethal cocktail of behaviour that few were spared from. Calling me a wanker was simply one of many insults that flew from Sly's mouth that night. Again, regardless of age or gender, the rampaging historian had an insult with your name on it. He ruthlessly barged into people on his way to the bar, and barged passed them some more on his way back. With a countless number of drinks on board, Adam Sylvester then (allegedly) went on a tour of college in search of his now ex-girlfriend. When Jude went after him, Sly (allegedly) pushed him to he ground and threw a barrage of names his way that made me cringe when I heard them second-hand over a cup of tea and a custard cream. He then (very allegedly) punched a girl who got in the way of his quest, leaving a roomful of screams and tears in his wake, before finally running out of energy and bad things to do, and returning to bed.

Of course, much of this report was bound to have been hyped and exaggerated by many of those involved, especially the girls, who publicly despised the historian of Sri Lankan origin. However, it was the way Jude spoke that convinced me that Sly had done something quite out of the ordinary that night.

"I've had enough of him, Josh, I really have. That's it."

This was Adam's closest friend, and his cold, passionless voice said more than a thousand accounts of gossiping females.

In the weeks to come, Jude would forgive Adam for his outburst, but their friendship would never be the same. Moreover, Mr Sylvester was blacklisted throughout the whole college, making a new set of enemies overnight, and those that despised him before could not begin to describe their feelings now. It was a night of behaviour that could not be passed off as drunken stupidity; it revealed a darkness hidden at the heart of his character. For me, it made me even more wary of him. For Caolan, he was simply a bad man.

Regardless of the severity or the validity of the allegations against Mr Sylvester, it was all very entertaining for us, who were close to breaking point after over a month of solid revision. The dawn of Friday brought with it the cold, hard fact that we had just three more days to go before exams started; a fact that was met with both relief and fear. The evening of Friday brought with it a universal desire for a break amongst the Fab Four. Even Mark Novak had had enough of indifference curves and marginal rates of substitution for one day. We decided to go for a relaxing punt, just the four of us; no teams, no Super-Soakers, no Adam Sylvester.

Instead of going along the Backs, we decided to head up towards Granchester; a route that was cheaper because there was less to see, but also quieter. It was just after we had eaten in hall when we set off, giving us about two hours of light left. The punting itself was uneventful, with us each taking turns, mine unanimously regarded as the least successful. Throughout the punt, Oisin Kerrigan complained of stomach pains; the same pains he had felt during the EQEM exam earlier in the term.

"Just puke in the Cam. I doubt the swans will tell anyone."

A Tale of Friendship, Love and Economics

"Nah, I'll be grand. I'll have a wee lie down when I get back to college, or whatever."

Back in college, the shaggy-haired Irishman went to his room, and me and the other two went to mine for a cup of tea and to discuss this stupid Micro diagram that none of us could understand. About half an hour later, with the tea finished but the diagram not ("It'll never come up in the exam anyway"), we decided to check on our friend before going to bed ourselves. As soon as we knocked on his door it was clear something was not right. Instead of the usual "Jeepers, come in!", our ears were greeted by a series of moans and groans.

"Maybe he's got a girl in there."

"Maybe he's just having a little fun on his own, you know, relieving all that built up exam stress."

"Oisin, what you up to in there?"

With a stumbling and a shuffling, the Derry man opened the door. His face was a white as a sheet and he was bent over clutching is stomach with both hands like someone had stuck a knife in it.

"Call me an ambulance," he moaned.

It's always amazed me how people change in an emergency. The quiet become loud, the immature become leaders, the jokers become serious. Without a word, Mark and I rushed to Oisin's side whilst Caolan went to the Plodge to call an ambulance. We helped our friend down the stairs of M-bock, across Sherlock Court and into the Porter's Lodge. Throughout the short journey, our friend grew weaker and heavier, slower and quieter. Loud words of pain had been replaced by a worryingly low murmuring sound, and even that was faltering. It sounds so melodramatic now, but as we stood with him in the Plodge, his arms slumped around all three of us, with his knees buckled and his head hung low, his shaggy hair only adding to the image of the crucifixion of Jesus, I honestly thought Oisin was going to die.

"It's going to be alright, mate," was all that any of us could say, with the conviction behind our words was non-existent. "The ambulance will be here soon, mate, just hang on a bit longer".

Thankfully, the ambulance came quickly, and three men in green coats helped the Irishman into the back. One of them came out to speak to us. We told him all that we knew, which was not a lot. Oisin was having pains in his stomach. He'd had them before but never this bad. He wasn't on drugs and he hadn't had an alcoholic drink for about a month. We didn't know whether it was a heart attack, a stomach ulcer, a reaction to something, or what. We were economists.

We called a cab and followed the ambulance to Addenbrooke's hospital. We didn't talk much on the way there. There wasn't a lot to say.

"I hope we're back for *Big Brother*," I said, but it wasn't the time or the place.

I hate hospitals. I hate the smell the most. The air always seems heavier than outside as it enters through your nose and mouth, as if you can feel the weight of the viruses and bacteria that are being carried around in it. Friday nights had the added bonus of drunken fight victims, with accompanying police officers and tearful girlfriends. I tried not to make eye-contact with anyone as I walked through the front doors. The lady at reception got a young nurse to show us to our friend's bed.

As she drew back the curtain I prepared myself for the sight of an unconscious, shaggy-haired Irishman, with tubes coming from every part of his body, a monograph relaying the ominous beat of his vital signs, and an upside-down accordion helping him to breathe. What I found instead was a rosy-cheeked Oisin Kerrigan sat up in bed reading a magazine.

"How you doin'?" he asked, chirpy as a happy bird.

For a moment there was silence whilst all three of us sought to confirm what our eyes were seeing. Finally, Caolan spoke.

"How are *we* doing? How are you doing, you dick? We thought you'd be dead."

"Nah, I'm grand."

"Grand? What's up with you?"

"They don't know. They're going to run some tests, or whatever."

"But you're alright, yeah?" It was about time I spoke.

"Aye, grand, just grand. As soon as I got in the ambulance I felt right as rain."

"But you were so... bad," said a concerned, disbelieving Mark Novak.

"Aye, I know. And then I just felt fine."

"You're a freak, Kerrigan," said Caolan and I at exactly the same time, before looking at each other strangely, and then dismissing it.

"So," said Caolan, on his own this time, "are you coming back with us tonight?"

"Nah, they're doing these tests in the morning, or whatever."

"Might be the only tests you pass in the next few days."

"Aye, I know."

And for the next half hour, or so, we stayed and chatted to our bed-stricken shaggy-haired friend. We talked about how he was a drain on scarce NHS resources, and tenuously linked this into our Micro course on adverse selection and moral hazard in the market for health insurance. All the talk of economics seemed to trigger a coughing fit in Oisin (and a reaction of an altogether different kind in Mark's trousers), so we quickly changed the subject. After Caolan and I started messing around with the oxygen mask and the plastic potty (using the latter as a helmet for an unsuspecting Mark Novak), Oisin said he'd be fine now, and we could leave. We passed on our best wishes, and ordered up another taxi, which Mark had to pay for as we had no money left (or at least no change, anyway).

The tests found nothing wrong with the shaggy-haired Irishman. He was a medical curiosity. He returned to college on the Saturday morning, and after having a wee lie down until the early afternoon, he put in a full six hours of work and wee breaks. For a short time the whole experience made us realise that no exam was worth risking our health for. However, the rest of us weren't feeling too bad. The bottom line was that we all had a hell of a lot of work to do that weekend, and a few sniffles and sneezes, aching heads, and pairs of weary eyes weren't going to stop us. We couldn't afford to let them stop us.

Chapter 58

The day before exams, a Sunday painted with a bright blue sky, our Director of Studies, Mr Stevens, called us up to C4 for some last-minute advice. He ran through the usual selection of snippets that we'd all heard a hundred times before; read the question properly, make sure you actually answer the question, don't just throw down everything you know about the topic, plan your answers, leave yourself enough time for each question, write clearly and concisely. We all nodded obediently.

"I know you've probably heard all this a hundred times before, but you'd be amazed how many people forget these simple things."

We nodded again; we'd heard that before as well.

Mr Stevens then started going on about how the examiners' minds worked. He explained that they were looking for a normal distribution in the marks for each question, with the majority getting a low 2:1 (a 62 or a 63), and then a few at either extreme (a few firsts, together with a few 2:2s and thirds). It was our job, apparently, to get to the higher end of the distribution, and we could only do this by making our answers stand out from the crowd. Writing about unicycles instead of business cycles or sex change instead of the stock exchange would no doubt make our answers stand out, but perhaps not in the way Mr Stevens had in mind. He ended the meeting by telling us that we'd worked hard all year, and so we'd all be just fine. We weren't convinced.

Sunday night was spent running through my completed batch of Micro essay plans, supposedly covering anything and everything that could possibly come up, and double checking anything I wasn't sure of in the textbook. I made sure I was in bed for ten, although I knew, rightly as it turned out, that I wouldn't get to sleep until some time after twelve. I lay in bed with my eyes shut but my mind completely open and alert. I embarked upon tried and tested methods of getting to sleep (used in the past on the eve of both exams and Christmas). I tried new lying positions, took my T-shirt off and put it back on again, put my socks on and took them off again, ran through song lyric after song lyric, tried to come up with film titles that began with each letter of the alphabet, and even banged out ten sit-ups and a token press-up. The more frustrated I got, and the more tired I told myself I was, the further away sleep felt. I don't think I was particularly nervous, just excited in a funny kind of way. Trying hard to drift off eventually tired me out and sleep and the light of morning finally arrived.

Chapter 59

Our first exam, Micro, was in the afternoon, kicking off at 1.30 pm. This annoyed me for two reasons. Firstly, I felt at my sharpest in the mornings and knackered after lunch, and secondly I didn't really know what to do with myself. God knows how many times I had read through those same stupid revision plans, and the thought of another couple of run throughs didn't exactly get my heart racing. I had already bought my pens and pencils, Mum had mailed in some wine gum reinforcements, and everything (water bottle, sweets, calculator, exam sheet, plastic wallet for stationery) was laid out on my desk ready to go. I had already had a shower and cleaned my teeth (twice, in fact), and I had already replied to my "good luck" text message from Imogene. There was nothing else I needed to do. I went to see Caolan and Mark, and they were feeling pretty much the same. We decided to force ourselves to do a couple more hours and then stop at twelve for lunch. Oisin had been up all night, and his eyes told the story of every hour, but even he called it a day as the clock struck noon.

Lunch time in hall was a pretty relaxed affair. The four of us were the only economists in there, with the rest either carrying on cramming, or opting for a baguette from Smilies (I never ate these due to the mayonnaise factor). We didn't talk about the wonderful world of economics, a rare treat for Nick and Joe who had joined us, for fear of adding to the confusion that already existed in sufficiently large quantities in our heads. We just ate our lunch (a baked potato in my case, fish for the others) and listen to Nick MacLean's latest batch of bad jokes.

After lunch we returned to our rooms to pick up our stuff and agreed to a rendezvous in the Plodge in T-minus five minutes. This was sufficient time for me to slap on Jude's *Rocky* Soundtrack tape (thankfully back as our number one gym choice over *I've Been Dumped*) to shadow box the necessary confidence into my head. I had an image of Caolan doing the same to Ronan's *When You Say Nothing At All*.

On the short walk to the Sidgwick Site, economics inevitable snuck up on us and ambushed our conversation.

"We've covered most topics, haven't we?" said Caolan.

"Oh yeah," I replied, "we'll be fine."

The four of us smiled and nodded unconvincingly.

"Hey, what question would you have to be the most desperate to take on, you know, like the kind of question that the mere fact you are considering it is a sure sign you are in trouble?" I asked, partly because I couldn't think of anything else to say, and partly because I was a big fan of these hypothetical questions.

"Anything with maths in it," suggested Mark, "those Chinese guys at the front will cane us on anything like that."

Oisin and I nodded, and I again nostalgically let my thoughts drift back to those halcyon days not so long ago when I was good at maths.

"Hey, what about something on inequality?" said Caolan. "We went to one out of eight lectures, didn't pick up the hand-out, and we haven't even had a supervision on it. No, you know you're fucked if you start banging out an answer to an inequality question."

"Fair point." I said, "Yep, the answer to today's 'You Know You're Desperate If...'" is definitely inequality."

The notice boards in the Sidgwick Site were surrounded by Part I economists, some of whom we had never seen in lectures ("Should at least beat them" said Caolan). We looked on the notice boards to see which rooms we were in. I was in Lecture Room 6, the same room as Mark, and the other two were in Lecture Room 4. We were also reassured by the notice board that it was actually Micro today and that it started at half-past one and not nine. Our lot were gathered by a wall, and Leila, four open files in her hands, looked like she was going off on one again.

"Guys, guys, what does it mean if there's a cross price elasticity of one, and where does that dead weight loss triangle go, and..."

"Oh, please shut up Leila, will you?" said the hockey-playing economist, who looked a bit nervous himself.

"But I'm going to fail, I'm going to fail."

"You'll be fine, okay?" said the Cypriot ex-sergeant, and no-one ever argued with him.

I was quite happy to chat away before the exams. It was a bit annoying that so many people were saying they were going to do rubbish and that they hadn't done enough work when it was obvious that they were really clever and had virtually lived in the library for the last month. Caolan and I asked Leila if she'd revised sub-game perfect outcomes in game theory, because we'd heard it was definitely coming up, and only told her we were joking when the first signs of tears emerged. Mark stood quietly with the others, and only talked when he was spoken to. Oisin preferred to be on his own and went and stood by a tree.

Eventually the doors were opened and we were led up the stairs. The exam room was the same place we had had Politics lectures in the second term. The only thing different about it today was the presence of the stern-looking, gowned invigilator, and the large white clock that was attached to the front of the raised stage. Instead of the separate desks that we had enjoyed for our EQEM exam earlier in the term, we were now seated on benches, with three or four candidates to each bench. I was placed on the

A Tale of Friendship, Love and Economics

isle, which had the advantage that I could stretch out my legs, but also meant that I had to get up every time someone wanted to get out to go to the toilet. Just before I settled down I gave a thumbs up to Mark and mouthed the words "Good Luck," to which he smiled and reciprocated.

The invigilator, a lady this time, ran through all the usual warnings and instructions, and then, at 1.30pm, with a red wine gum in my mouth, we were told to begin.

I immediately scanned through all the questions on the paper, and quickly decided that it could have been better but it could also have been a lot worse. The paper was divided up into two sections. Section A contained short-answer questions, and you had to do six from a choice of ten. They often contained a statement that seemed true, but that you had to prove was wrong by means of an economic example, usually backed up by a diagram. If you couldn't find the twist, you would not get too many marks. Section B contained the essay-based questions, and you had to do two out of five. Both sections carried equal marks, and dividing the three hour time limit up accordingly, meant that you were supposed to spend fifteen minutes on each Section A question, and forty-five on each of the Section Bs. I had decided that my technique would involve doing four Section A questions at the start, then the two essay ones from Section B, and finishing off with the last two Section A ones. My logic was that I was needed to get into the flow of the exam before I took on a long essay, I might be able to buy myself some extra essay time if I could do the four short questions quick enough, and finally, if I was pushing it for time at the end of the exam, it was better to do a sketchy answer to a Section A question than to rush the conclusion of an essay. I had explained my technique to Caolan, and he said it was gay.

I was fairly happy with my answers to the four Section A questions. Question 8: "Short-run cost curves lie entirely above their long-run counterparts. Comment." was one of the ones Mark and I had discussed once over a Creamy Choc during a break in the Law Faculty. We had found the twist when the short-run and long-run cost curves actually touch each other thus proving the statement wrong, and we had the 'envelope' diagram to illustrate it. I knew Mark would be taking this one on as well. I had to think for a while about Question 6: "Equilibrium outcomes are not necessarily efficient. Comment, using an economic example." We had tackled a similar question in supervisions, but I could not remember whether it was a question about trade or game theory. I preferred the latter, and so I threw down a few definitions, set up a standard Prisoner's Dilemma game, and showed that the equilibrium outcome was Pareto inefficient as at least one party could be made better off without making another worse off. I imagined my supervisor reading through my answer, and I couldn't decide whether he would be yelling "Cowabunga" or "Wrong".

All in all I approached Section B seven minutes ahead of schedule, and feeling pretty content. I had two wine gums to celebrate. Section B was far harder, and the answers needed planning. I also needed to find two answers that I could do. Question 11 was a maths one that had five parts to it and I couldn't do any; Question 14 required you to specify a production function for potatoes; Question 12 was about inequality (and you knew you were fucked if you contemplated taking that one on); and 16 looked a bit dodgy. In the end I opted for Question 13: "How useful is the first fundamental theorem of welfare economics as a basis for identifying public interventions to improve outcomes in a market economy?" which we had a supervision on (not directly related to the question), and involved a few space and time-filling diagrams, and Question 15: "The scheduled departure times of the daily flights operated by major airlines from London to San Francisco are closely clustered. Give an economic account of this phenomenon." which I gambled was all about an application of Hotelling's Location Model, although we'd only been taught it with respect to the position of ice-cream vans along a beach on a hot summer's day.

I spent a bit longer on the two essays than I should have done, and was forced to speed through the last couple of Section A questions. This worked out well in the end as I didn't really have a lot to say for either of them, and I finished with five minutes to spare. I was desperate for the toilet, having drunk far too much water, but decided to tie a knot in it and hold on until we were dismissed. I checked through my answers, tidied up my diagrams and made a few of my words a bit less illegible. I handed in my paper with a satisfied smile. One down, four to go.

Outside the exam hall it was time to gauge people's reactions. Mark said it went okay, Oisin said it didn't. The Cypriot ex-sergeant said it was easy, Leila said she'd definitely failed. Caolan was laughing as he came down the stairs of the Lecture Block to join us.

"How did it go?" I asked.

"Not brilliant, but alright, you know. You?"

"Pretty much the same."

"Hey, guess which pissing question I ended up taking on?"
"Which?"
"Bloody inequality. God, I churned out some shite."
"Maybe you'll get marks for originality."
"I bloody deserve them, I tell you."

We decided to have a break from revision until after hall, and went for a walk to clear our minds of the exam gone by. We returned to college to "enjoy" a meal of beef something with some kind of potatoes, and then hit the books. I called my Mum to let her know I was getting on okay, and she told me that she had decided to paint the lounge again. Thankfully I found it far easier to get to sleep that night, and after a few last flicks through my essay plans, and a couple of self-imposed date tests, I drifted off into a deep sleep.

Chapter 60

I rolled out of bed at eight-thirty ready to take on a History exam. Once again, this one was in the afternoon, which left me at a bit of a loose end. I did the same three hours work and then headed to lunch with Caolan, Mark and Oisin. On our way to the Sidgwick Site we ran into the geographers who had just finished all their exams Full of high spirits, they were on their way to the pub, then planning to go for a punt on this gorgeous June afternoon. We passed on our congratulations and then stuck our fingers up at them as they walked away.

History was a subject that I wasn't very good at. This was probably because I didn't enjoy it and I hadn't put a lot of work into it during the last two terms. I quite enjoyed the interwar stuff we had been doing with Mr Stevens in that third term as this was more modern and had plenty of economics in it, but the stuff about the farmers rotating their crops and enclosing their fields, and the importance of soft water for cotton and fast water for mills did nothing for me. Moreover, the various articles that we were set to read for our essays and supervisions annoyed me further. One historian would use one data set to support his argument, and then another used a completely different one that supported his argument. In his follow-up article, the first historian would explain all the things that were wrong with the second's data set, and the latter would duly reciprocate in his sequel, thus sparking off a few more rounds of nit-picking. It all seemed a bit of a waste of time to me. Caolan loved it, and our short-skirted supervisor loved him. Nevertheless, I had revised hard for history, and I had a comprehensive set of essay plans that I was pretty confident would see me through, with a bit of luck.

Again I was in Lecture Room 6 for the exam, again Oisin had been up most of the night revising, again Leila was panicking, and again Caolan and I temporarily convinced the crazy Bulgarian that a bizarre topic was coming up (this time the role of Uruguay in the textile industry).

As I sat down by at my desk I started stretching the fingers and the wrist of my right hand and double-checked that my fountain pen was fully loaded. There was going to be a lot of writing today. Like yesterday, this was a three-hour paper, but this time there were no short-answer questions or diagrams to break things up. History was just four forty-five minute essays, meaning 180 minutes of solid writing. With the permission of the bearded invigilator (a man), we all turned over our papers and began.

I quickly found three questions that I could do, and decided to worry about finding the forth one nearer the time. Question 9: "Tariffs and devaluation during the 1930s formed an inconsistent policy regime." Do you agree? If so, what policies would have been better?" was a particularly nice one for us St. Catharine's students. Our Director of Studies was proud to be one of the only people in the world who thought the introduction of tariffs was a positive policy move in the interwar period. All the textbooks took an anti-tariff line, saying stuff like they stifled competition and kept inefficient businesses going, but we were armed to the teeth with arguments to take them down. This was the twist that would hopefully make our answers stand out in a good way.

I also banged out answers to questions on the persistent effects of the 1920–1 depression, and the lack of innovation in the Victorian era. With just under forty minutes to spare (I had gotten a bit carried away with the depression), I assessed my options and eventually went for Question 3: "What role, if any, did agriculture play in British industrialisation?" I wanted to avoid agriculture at all costs for fear that my lack of interest would find its way into my answer, but it was either that or start banging on about the Edwardian period, which I didn't even know when it was, or if we'd studied it.

Once again I left the exam room feeling fairly content. Thankfully, so too did everyone else. Oisin explained that he hadn't had enough time to finish the last question, but it went frickin' better than yesterday, or whatever. We again took a break until after hall to give ourselves time to recover, and then hit the books. Tomorrow's Macro exam was a morning one, but fortunately I'd done a bit of Macro revision the previous evening having seen this sneaky bit of time-tabling coming. Again I called my Mum, and again I slept well.

Chapter 61

We decided to meet for breakfast in hall at eight o'clock. It was a wrench to get out of bed, but fortunately adrenaline kicked in and helped me into the shower. Oisin again had been up most of the night and was not looking good ("I'll have a wash and a wee shave when I've got time, or whatever"). Even though the sausage and bacon that was on offer looked and smelt really good, I didn't want to risk changing anything and opted for Weetabix (42p for two!). Buzz came out to see how my exams were going, and also to tell me that he had scored three goals for his local team last night, one of them a fucking blinder from forty fucking yards, apparently.

Macro was the exam that I was most worried about. In Micro you could focus in on a specific element; it was more precise, more technical, and more often than not there were wrong answers and right answers. You knew where you were with Micro. With Macro, on the other hand, you often didn't have a clue where you were. What was causing high unemployment? Well, maybe a lack of growth? Yeah, but maybe it was the other way around and high unemployment was, in fact, causing a lack of growth? And what about the exchange rate, and what about inflation, and what about gross capital formation, and what about productivity, and what about outsourcing, and what about the oil price shock, and what about trade unions, and what about America? There was too much going on for my liking, too much to take into account, too many questions and not enough answers. But still, I really enjoyed Macro, and I tried hard to be good at it. After all, it was proper economics.

The format of the exam itself was identical to Micro, requiring you to do six short answer Section A questions and two Section B essays. I opened the paper with a slightly quivering hand, and scanned the multitude of questions with twitching eyes. I popped in a wine gum before I made any big decisions. There were a few Sections As that I could definitely do. Question 8: "A sticky nominal wage implies that the real wage is counter-cyclical. Comment." had been tackled in a Novak, Bailey, O'Donnell Revision Forum, and the Keynesian and real business cycle explanations were pretty straightforward and easy enough to compare and contrast. Question 6: "Describe the effects of a recession on the job-finding rate, the separation rate and the natural rate of unemployment." seemed straightforward enough, we had had a supervision on it with Mr Stevens, and the question itself gave you a tidy three-part structure to the answer.

That was about it, though. I knew some serious amount of bullshitting would be needed to survive this paper. I banged out another couple of Section A questions, one on the slope and location of the aggregate supply curve and the other on the quantity theory of money — both questions that I knew the general answer to but struggled on the specifics — and quickly moved onto Section B, where I crossed my fingers hoping for better fortune.

We had all been banking on an easy real business cycle question and an easy growth question. Neither were there. The growth question I was hoping for went something along the lines of: "Chat for a while, without going into too much detail, about growth." What I found myself answering instead was: "Suppose a country wants to increase its long-run growth rate of income per capita. It considers (a) a boost to domestic savings or (b) an opening up of its capital markets to international investors. Discuss the effects on the levels and growth rates of income per person of the two policies along the adjustment path and in steady state." Whether they liked it or not, they pretty much got the answer to the question I was hoping came up.

In the absence of anything resembling a question on real business cycles, which surely should have been a Section B question given that it was such a big part of this year's course, I found myself taking on the following: "European Monetary Union is much more ambitious in its aims and institutions than the international monetary system created at Bretton Woods in 1944. Discuss." I was quite happy with my answer, despite the fact that we

A Tale of Friendship, Love and Economics

had not been lectured on EMU and I was not too sure exactly what this Bretton Woods thing was.

I returned to finish Section A with just under half an hour to go. Motivated and inspired by my flowing imagination, I took on questions about the multiplier and the effects of population growth with an authority that would suggest as I was one of the globe's leading experts.

All in all I was not too happy with the way Macro had turned out, although once more I had to admit that it could have gone a lot worse. Mark Novak was the most pissed off I had ever seen him because having, like all of us, banked on a real business cycles question, he had been forced into making up forty-five minutes of rubbish about the relationship between interest rates and exchange rates. Oisin was also not too happy, Leila had now definitely failed and was making plans to repeat the year, and Caolan said it went a bit shit. Still, at least there were now just two to go.

It was whilst I was revising for the following day's Politics exam that I got really fed up. It was seven o'clock and I was sat outside on a bench in Sherlock Court. I had just had a very unpleasant meal in hall, and someone (it had to be Faye) had taken my last bit of milk, thus rendering me cup-of-tea-less. Every single person in college had now finished their exams and they seemed to have chosen that particular moment to walk past me merrily on their way to the bar. I smiled at them and tried not to swear. I knew that someone had to finish their exams last, but why did it have to be us? I reminded myself that there was not long to go, and continued reading about Thatcher's economic policies.

Chapter 62

Politics was another subject that I was not too hot at (I was beginning to think that maybe I was doing the wrong degree). Our supervisor, who all year seemed to be banking on a question about mother-in-laws coming up, had been giving me 2:2s for my essays for most of the past three terms, essays which I thought were pretty good. Still, I had done a fair bit of work on my politics over the last few weeks, and now had a batch of essay plans that I was very proud of. Moreover, if I was able to talk rubbish in Macro and

Micro exams whenever I was stuck, I was bound to be able to in a Politics exam. I was feeling fairly confident.

Politics was another morning exam, the first morning of May Week in fact, and after another over-priced bowl of Weetabix, as well as a banana to give me that extra energy boost, I felt wide awake and ready for action. The format of the exam was the same hand-aching one as for History, with four big essays to write in three hours.

I opened the paper, read through the questions, and had a wine gum (I was getting more than a bit sick of them by this stage). Surprisingly the paper contained no questions about mother-in-laws, or our supervisor's lawn-mower, but the questions on the whole didn't look too daunting. I circled the four I fancied taking on, and started to write. I took on Question 3: "Does 'The Third Way' constitute a coherent political philosophy or an incoherent fudge?" Because I liked the use of the word "fudge" and just to show that I had gotten more out of Mr Steven's recent lecture series than simply a belly full of jacket potatoes and fruit salad, and: "Far from being an unprincipled and incoherent compromise, the post-war consensus possessed a coherent intellectual underpinning. Discuss." Because I had had a long chat about a very similar question with Jewish Simon, and he had a lot of good ideas that were just crying out to be passed off as my own.

I was scraping the barrel a wee bit for the other two, but I was used to this by now. In the end I churned out three pages each on the concept of globalisation and the future of the Conservative Party. Again I left the exam not over the moon, but reasonably happy.

As we sat in a deserted hall (anyone who had finished exams was treating themselves to nice food) we constantly reminded ourselves of the fact that, given that we'd already handed in the Stats project, we were now 88 per cent of the way through our Part I, and more importantly, tomorrow night, in just over twenty-four hours time in fact, we were off to Robinson May Ball. One more to go, just one more to go.

Now Stats was the one part of maths that I had hated at A-level. It was just so boring. I hated all those stupid tables, stupid distributions and stupid Greek letters. Moreover, Caolan and I, and Oisin on the sly, had spent most of the year copying Mark. During revision time, however, remembering the advice of my old maths teacher who said the only way to get good at maths was to practice, I had made sure I did at least one hour of answering Stats problems each day. Sure, there were large parts of the course that I didn't have a hope of being able to do, but I was confident I had enough tools in the shed to get me through.

That night, ten economists (Oisin preferred to work/take wee breaks alone) piled into our deserted college library for one last revision session. The library had actually been locked yesterday evening by the porters who assumed everyone had finished; after all, we were in May Week now. It's a bad state of affairs when nineteen-year-olds find themselves begging to be let into a library. Anyway, just as I was getting ready to call it a night, Leila burst in with news of a question that was definitely, definitely coming up. The friend of a friend of a friend had apparently come up with the goods again. The only problem was none of us, not even the Cypriot ex-sergeant, had a clue how to do it. Not a problem, said Leila. The provider of this information had also provided a foolproof method for answering any such question. And so, whilst the rest of the college began the process of getting drunk and having a good time, ten Part I economists began the process of teaching ourselves an eight-lecture course in two hours. By the end, tiredness convinced us that we had nailed it, and we left for bed with yet another string attached to our healthily-stringed Statistics bow.

Chapter 63

I entered the Stats exam buzzing. It was only a two-hour exam which, given that we were used to three-hour epics, I reckoned was bound to fly by once I cracked open the calculator and began a bit of number crunching. Hence, the start of our long-awaited May Week, the week we had spoken and dreamt about for months, was almost here. I grinned at the prospect, popped a wine gum, had a sip of water, and opened the paper. Shit.

I closed the paper and checked the front to see if I had the right one. As I looked around the room I saw I was not the only one doing this. Many had their heads in their hands and one girl had even started to cry. This was not like any of the past papers I had seen. There was no sign of any of the usual hypothesis testing, normal distributions, poison distributions, two-tailed tests, rolling dice, type-one errors, or red and white balls in a bag. In fact, there we very few numbers at all. As my eyes scanned down the questions I realised I couldn't do any of them. A voice in my head told me not to panic, and then another one asked what the hell else I was supposed to do.

You had to do six questions from Section A and two from Section B, both sections carrying equal marks, thus giving you ten minutes for each Section A and half and hour for each of the big money Section Bs. I could have written all the information I knew that appeared to be relevant to that particular paper in four minutes. Not knowing what else to do, I started writing. I decided to take on Question 4:

You are asked to perform a hypothesis test about a population mean, μ, with known variance σ^2. Which of the following assumptions are needed to use x, the mean of the data?
       I   the data represent a random sample from a population;
       II the population distribution is normal;
       III the sample size is large.
a). I, II and III
b). I and either II or III
c). II and III
d). only II

largely because it was multiple choice, although I was guessing they were after a bit more than just a one letter answer. Moreover, I was fairly sure that the answer was I and III, but unfortunately that wasn't an option. After sticking down b), and writing down an explanation that I had to smile at (it was either that or cry), I moved onto the next little beauty, Question 8:

Consider the following output from a regression equation:
    • = $-4009.55 + 5.43\ x^1 + 2824.61\ x^2 + 17105.17\ x^3 + 7634.90\ x^4$
where • is the forecasted sale price, x^1 = total lot size, x^2 = number of bedrooms, x^3 = number of bathrooms, and x^4 = number of floors.
A first year student from the University of Oxford comments that, "*An extra square foot of lot size will add another £5.43 onto the price of the house.*" What is wrong with this interpretation of these results?

I picked this one because it enabled me to call a student from Oxford stupid (even though I thought his interpretation was quite a good one, and far better than anything I would have come up with). Apart from the fact that I didn't know the answer, the other thing concerning me about this question was the significance of the dot at the start of the equation – normally S or P would be chosen to stand for sales price, not funny little dots. I thought about pointing this out in my answer, but decided it might not be quite what the examiner was looking for.

I didn't even know where to begin with any of the other Section A questions, so I moved onto Section B in desperate need of marks. Things didn't get much better there. I took on Question 13:

> Each week the owners of a hamburger chain must decide how much money should be spent on advertising and the price specials to be introduced. To this end an economic model of the form:
>
> $$r = \beta^1 + \beta^2 p + \beta^3 a$$
>
> where r = total revenue (£1000 units), p = price (£), and a is advertising (£1000 units) is constructed. Application of ordinary least squares to 52 weeks of data provides the following results:
>
> $\beta^1 = 104.79$ (6.483)
> $\beta^2 = -6.642$ (3.191) $R^2 = 0.867$
> $\beta^3 = 2.984$ (0.167)
>
> where (.) denotes standard errors.
>
> a) Interpret these results. Are they consistent with your prior expectations? What is the predicted total revenue for a price of £2 and advertising expenditure of £10,000?
>
> b) Construct a 95% confidence interval for β^2 and β^3, and comment on your findings.
>
> c) β^3 measures the response of total revenue to a change in advertising. Based upon standard economic theory, we would expect diminishing returns to continued advertising expenditure. Discuss how you might incorporate this feature into the model.

and prayed that the last part wasn't worth any marks (just a bit of fun put in by the humourous examiners), because I didn't have a clue what it was on about. I lied my way through another Section B one, this time on a dispute between a coffee company and Trading Standards – needless to say it was a dispute the I was wholly unable to resolve – before returning to Section A for more punishment.

I can honestly say it was by far the worst exam I had ever taken. I was not confident that I had even gotten close to the right answer on any question.

I was writing sentences that I knew just weren't true, putting down answers that were in no way correct, reasoning that writing anything was better than writing nothing.

Eventually the examiner sensed we could suffer no longer and brought the exam, and with it Part I of the Cambridge Economics Tripos, to a close. I had thought that the feeling of putting my pen down for the final time would be more momentous, maybe produce a tingling in my bones and make the hairs on the back of my neck stand to attention. However, all I felt was anger; anger that we had been given such a shit paper that was nothing to do with what we had been taught, and anger that I wasted hours and hours revising stuff that never came up. As I walked out of the exam there was a reassuring shaking of the head and displeased murmuring from most of my fellow economists.

Outside everyone was fuming.

"What the fuck was all that about?" enquired Caolan, with no hint of a smile.

"Frickin' stupid," said Oisin.

"That was shit," said Mark

"The examiner, he is crazy," said the Cypriot ex-sergeant.

"I fell asleep in it," said the Malaysian lad.

"I've failed, guys, I've failed," said Leila.

"We've all failed," said everyone in subdued unison.

There was a moment's silence whilst we ran through in our minds exactly what we would like to do with the dick who set the paper. This was not how it was meant to happen. Where were the fireworks, and the hugs? Where was the champagne and the tears of joy? It wasn't so much an anti-climax as the worst we'd felt all week. Then I finally spoke.

"Hey, come on. There's nothing we can do about it. We've finished our exams, we've no work to do for four months, and we've got May Week coming right up." I tried to sound enthusiastic to convince myself if no-one else.

"Josh is right," said Caolan, using three words that he had never put together in that order before, "I know it's taken the shine off finishing, but everyone else will have fucked it up, especially New Hall."

"Yeah" said the hockey-playing economist, "they'll have to bump everyone's mark up, otherwise they'll have no-one to take Prelims next year."

"We'll probably end up getting firsts," said the small, chubby lad who liked to sleep a lot and eat in Gardi's.

"Come on, let's get out of here," I said.

And so, we turned our backs on the Sidgwick Site, on a year of lectures, libraries and exams Our May Week had finally begun.

Chapter 64

Caolan, Mark, and most of the other economists went straight off to the pub to get some lunch and to reacquaint their mouths with the long-lost taste of alcohol. I would have loved to have joined them, but I had obligations of a sporting kind. Today, as well as being the day of the Robinson May Ball, was also the day of the annual St. Catharine's College Five-a-side Tournament, and we had entered a team.

The rules stated that only two regular 1st XI players were allowed in each team. Nick MacLean, Jewish Simon and myself had only reached the dizzy heights of 2nd XI football this season, although Simon was easily good enough for the firsts, and Oisin Kerrigan had been too lazy to play anything other than the odd game of park football. With us four on board there was room for two "seeded" players. We were kind of obligated to have Joe Porter (it was his idea in the first place), and we also managed to snap up the services of another Irishman, a second year mathmo, going by the name of 'Headlock'. Headlock was so called as he was prone to putting people, both men and women, in headlocks when drunk. He was also a bit of a psycho on the football field, often injuring his fellow midfielders in a variety of ways. We were glad he was on our team. Hence, our squad of six, with the woeful team name of "Future Champions" (nothing to do with me) consisted of a healthy quota of 50 per cent economists, a worrying high quota of 33 per cent geographers and 17 per cent Irish psychos. And so, with a full set of five exams freshly under our belts, and in what sounded like the start of a bad racist joke, an Englishman, an Irishman and a Jew jumped on our bikes and cycled back to college as quick as we could.

We were supposed to be down at Catz sports grounds for 11.30am, but seeing as our exam had finished just after eleven, we were always going to be pushing it. Regardless of the time factor, complemented and reinforced by Nick MacLean's unrelenting cries of "hurry up, will you?", going without food was not an option. Four Weetabix and six wine gums were never going to be enough to get me through a footy tournament, and so I prepared myself a stack of cheese and ham sandwiches (Elizabeth had introduced me to the delights of ham slices, and I had been stealing hers ever since). In the time it took me to construct, eat and enjoy three such sandwiches, have a pint of economy orange juice, find my shin pads (in my boxer short draw. Obviously) get changed, text my Mum ("hi Mum. exam was rubbish. glad they're over. playing footy now. speak soon. xJ") and listen to the first three songs on *Definitely Maybe*, Oisin Kerrigan had managed to achieve the feet of getting into his room. Not only was the shaggy-haired Irishman the world's worst drinker, a bit on the tight side, a bit on the "take a wee break, or whatever" side, he was also always late, and never for any good reason. Nick MacLean was clearly not happy. I couldn't help but smile.

"How can you possibly not be ready?" he asked disbelievingly.

"There's no rush, or whatever" Oisin replied, as he began considering whether or not to have an apple.

"No rush? *No rush?*"

Joe, Simon and I kept out of it. It was always best to when Nick was in one of these kinds of moods.

Eventually, the five of us were ready to roll. Headlock was already at the grounds, or so his text message told us. The only colour T-shirt that we all had was white, and so that was the chosen strip of the Future Champions. Unfortunately, it was also the only colour T-shirt that everyone else had, and hence a combination of bibs and skins had to come into play. We arrived at the college sports grounds half an hour late, but were still some of the first there.

"See, no rush," said Oisin.

Nick's response was inaudible and probably unrepeatable.

The tournament consisted of two groups, one with four teams in it, and ours with five teams. Each team played each of their fellow group members once, and the top two teams in each group after all the games had been played went through to the semi-finals, and then onto the final or the third place play-off depending on their successes. As well as the main tournament, there was also a girls' tournament and a barbecue.

Any time that wasn't spent eating, playing, or laughing at how rubbish the girls were, Simon, Oisin and I spent sprawled out on the grass asleep.

The toils, troubles and stresses of the week had finally caught up with us. Oisin mentioned something about the need for sun-cream, but his words floated along and got lost in my hazy dreams. Anyway, this was England; nobody gut sunburnt in England.

Incredibly, we got through to the final. I say *we* but it was more like Jewish Simon got to the final and the rest of Joe Porter's Future Champions just hitched a ride. His skills were unbelievable and opposition players were just falling on the floor as he danced around them just like they did in really bad football movies. Simon either scored or set up each goal. Proud geographer, and next year's 2nd XI captain, Joe Porter also played really well, taking his aggression out on the opposition instead of me for a change. Headlock was as dangerous as ever, and at one stage booted Oisin in the thigh by mistake. The shaggy-haired Irishman, after getting high as a kite on his inhaler before each game, never stopped running, and never stopped saying "For frick's sake" or "Jesus Christ" any time he lost the ball. Nick MacLean stayed in goal most of the time – he was less of a liability in there – and was only let out when the game was well and truly won. He turned out to be actually quite a good goalkeeper, suggesting that maybe we weren't the first team to insist that he stayed between the sticks. I didn't play too badly, but the sun had drained my already low energy reserves to next to nothing. I promptly employed my oft-used tactic of switching to a continental, non-running style, and even managed to score a goal with a misdirected pass ("Yes Joe, of course I meant it").

By the time we reached the final, we had most of the crowd on our side. You see, our opposition had ever so slightly bent the rules. The rules stated, amongst other things, that no more than two 1St. XI players could be on the pitch at any one time. To be fair, our opposition only had two such players in their team. However, they also had two university players and a bloody Australian five-a-side international. Buzz, who's kitchen staff lot had been knocked out by them in the semis, described them as a bunch of cheating bastards, and his advice to us before the game was to break their fucking legs.

After a gallant performance, we were eventually defeated 1–0. We consoled ourselves with the fact that we were only little first years and moreover we were the only legitimate team in the final, and hence in most people's eyes – well, ours at least – we were the real winners.

I returned from the football battered, bruised and sunburnt. It was only when I looked in the mirror and saw a beetroot looking back at me that I realised the extent of the problem. To save my ears from any more pain, I decided not to tell my Mum. ("You're so irresponsible, Josh. How many times have you gotten yourself burnt now? How many? And still you moan at me, and still you never learn. I don't know Josh, I really don't.") Anyway, I had a couple of hours before we had to set off for the rougeness ("It's *rouge*, Faye, not red, alright?") to fade, and on top of that it would be dark at Robinson May Ball; Imogene would never notice.

Chapter 65

I had a much-needed snooze for an hour, leaving myself just under sixty minutes to get ready. Plenty of time. Faye had already had her shower (girls need time for Balls), and Mary Jane wasn't going. Jude and I played scissors-paper-stone to see who would go in first and, with my paper well and truly wrapped around his rock, in I went. I sang a few classic tunes and washed all memory of the exams away. I came out of the shower feeling fresh and revitalised, like one of those girls on the shampoo adverts, gave an unsuspecting Jude a high-five, and disappeared into my room.

Apart from the rouge/red face, everything was going well. I put a bit of gel in my hair, and for once it didn't look too shit. Those of us with proper bow ties managed to track down our regular "bow-tie tier", the mathmo from Eton, and by seven-thirty, a mere forty-five minutes behind schedule, we were all assembled on the grass of Sherlock Court for photos. The girls looked amazing. Faye, Elizabeth, Francesca, Julie, and Movie Star Lookalike all scrubbed up well and turned into princesses. After the obligatory but heartfelt exchange of compliments, we grabbed a guy who looked like he was up to nothing in particular, and loaded him up with fourteen cameras.

Robinson May Ball opened its doors to the world (as long as they had tickets) at nine o'clock. Mr Organisation, Nick MacLean, wanted us there in the queue before eight. He had factored in the time it takes girls to get ready, but not the time it takes shaggy-haired Irishmen. Oisin was the last onto Sherlock Court, then he forgot his camera, then, just as we were finally leaving, he turned into Columbo and said "Just one more thing". Eventually we embarked upon the best-dressed walk to Robinson College ever, and arrived at the back of an extremely large, and equally well-dressed, queue at half-past eight. As we made our way to our place at the back, I thought I spotted Imogene in the crowd. I was pretty sure it was her but I didn't want to say anything in case the rest of the lads, especially the usual suspects of Sly and Caolan, made some kind of scene that made me look a prick. I put my head down and kept walking.

The queue was about as fun as queues can be. The theme of the Ball was "Misbehavin'", hence transporting you back to 1920s New York, a time were gangsters ruled all and life and death could be bought and sold like fruit and veg. The May Ball Committee had hired the services of the university's thespians, and they were out in force to try and keep you entertained as you waited patiently for entry. It would have been easy to take the piss out of them, but we thought it best to try and get in the spirit. One weird-looking lad dressed as a policeman, complete with truncheon, whistle and notepad, excitedly asked us if we'd seen any funny-looking people around who might be murderers (we tried to get him to arrest Sly, but he was not keen), then a chubby gangster came and told Oisin to watch his back, and then two golden girls came and gave us lollipops (I put mine behind my ear thinking I looked cool). We were in the queue for the best (or worst) part of an hour, and though the performers tried their hardest to keep us all entertained, all everybody wanted to do was get inside. Eventually we edged our way to the front, handed in our tickets in exchange for wristbands, and were led into the Ball.

It was hard to know what to do first, well after taking a couple of glasses of free white wine, of course (throughout the night I referred to anything and everything we got – food, drink and rides – as free, and was promptly reminded by those around me that it was not free but included in the ticket price. Still, if you forgot about the small matter of £70, it was free in my book). Robinson is not a particularly attractive college, with its late 1970s red-brick walls resembling an inner-city block of flats, but it had been done up well tonight. The stalls were covered in glitz and gold, and the actors and actresses continued to mingle amongst the crowds, offering both cigars and warnings about an imminent murder from the notorious Bugsy Malone.

We decided that it would be pointless all trying to stay together, and thus Caolan, Nick, Oisin, Mark and I set off on our own, vaguely agreeing to meet up with people later on. We were like five excited school children let loose on a school trip. For no particular reason we took a right, and walked passed a "bucking bronco", a room containing a string quartet and ballroom dancing, a candy-floss stall (we grabbed some – after all it was free), a jazz band, an ice-cream stall (we grabbed some), a stall offering a drink called Burn (we grabbed some, impressed by the cool black can complete with double flame, but promptly discarded it when we discovered to our horror that not only was it non-alcoholic, it was also rank), a stall offering pints of Carlsberg (we grabbed two each, and even Oisin dipped in), until finally we came out into the open air. On the grassy grounds at the back of the college was where the real action was. There were fairground rides, tents for dancing, crêpe stalls, burger stalls, more drink stalls, all in all a real feast for the eyes and the rest of the senses.

Unfortunately, being the start of the Ball, and after a lot of queuing, most people were hungry, and hence their first port of call was at a food stall, or more accurately, a long queue for a food stall. Indeed, undoubtedly one feature of May Balls and May Week in general was the queuing, but at least there was always something worthwhile at the end. Our candy-floss was never going to fill us and so, after a bit of deliberation, and seeing as there was not much to choose for between the stalls in terms of queue length, Nick and I wedged ourselves in a hefty queue for burgers and sausages, a stall run by a company called Pig Out Catering. The rest went off in search of crêpes.

Then I saw her. I was trying to keep both my balance and my place, and not doing a very good job of either. She was stood near to the front of the stall, trying desperately to make eye contact with the sausage man, who looked like he'd had more than a few Pig Out Catering products in his time. I couldn't see much of her, but that brief glimpse was enough to render my eyes incapable of looking at anything else. I was by no means an expert, but she had definitely done something to her hair. It was wavy and hanging free, and it looked good. I didn't want her to see me. Not yet. Not in the queue for a sausage.

I don't know how I planned to ask her out, even though I had thought of little else (non economical) lately. I had one idea, but it was a bit corny to say the least, and for that reason I kept it well and truly to myself. It was a scene inspired by a dozen movies and a hundred love songs. There would be a room, a special room, some kind of dancing hall maybe, full of people

A Tale of Friendship, Love and Economics

but not too crowded, with the lights dimmed and shadows dancing across the floor. There would be music playing, a tune with no words, and a melody that filled your head with memories of happy times. I would be stood in the corner with my friends, maybe having a drink and sharing a joke, and she would be stood with hers, a large group of them, giggling and gossiping about all the handsome men in the room tonight. As one song gave way to another, I would catch her eye, and give her a smile just before she turned away in embarrassment. I would wait a while before returning my gaze, only to catch her looking my way again. This time she would leave it a little longer before she turned away, just long enough to return the sweetest smile I had ever seen. My friends would ask me if I wanted to go somewhere else, maybe go and get some food, and hers would tell her they were going to stand closer to a bunch of good-looking guys on the far side of the room and asked her if she wanted to come to. We would both say no. We would be left standing alone, two people waiting for something to happen. I would look like I was thinking about something important, she would search in her handbag for nothing in particular. Eventually our eyes and smiles would meet again, neither of us in any hurry to turn away this time. I would take a sip of my drink and go over to her. I would ask her how she was, if she was having a good night, tell her how beautiful she looked and how glad I was to see her. I would ask her to dance, and she would say that would be lovely. A slow song would be playing and we would dance hand in hand in a space that had opened up towards the middle of the dance-floor. Neither of us would notice anybody else. We would dance in perfect time and be lost in the moment and the music. She would move closer, pressing herself against me, until her head was resting on my shoulder. I would be able to smell her hair and the perfume she was wearing. We would dance a little slower, until we were almost still. Then she would raise her head up. I would look into her eyes and realise just how beautiful she was. We would hold our gaze until the moment was right, until that something that we had both been waiting for finally happened, and then we would kiss. A simple kiss. A kiss that would light a fire in my heart. A kiss that would be the start of the sweetest journey that I had ever known. Alternatively I'd have been happy enough to stick my tongue down her throat behind the back of the burger van. Either way, you know.

Whilst I had been lost in my thoughts, the world carried on around me. Nick and I had been painfully bundled closer to the front, and Imogene had disappeared into the night armed with two sausages. We eventually managed to get a burger and two sausages each, and ate them by the side of the bouncy castle whilst we waited for the others. I spotted Oisin, Caolan and Mark in the crêpe queue, with the shaggy-haired Irishman locked in conversation with a girl I recognised from the formal hall with New Hall. A few bites later, the three lads, crêpes in hand, came over to join us.

"How are the crêpes?" I asked.

"Not bad," replied Mark, who had somehow managed to get sauce on his left cheek, "and your meat?"

"Aye, beautiful. Just what I needed, just what I needed."

I noticed Oisin wasn't looking his chirpy self. He was nibbling at his crêpe and shuffling his right foot around nervously.

"Hey, you okay mate? You're not still thinking about that shitty Stats exam are you?"

"Nah," he replied, before pausing.

"They can stick their hypothesis tests up there arse, mate. We're here to have a good time."

"It's not that."

Nick and I looked at Oisin expectantly, whilst the other two looked at the floor. I wondered what we were missing out on, maybe some secret that only crêpe eaters were allowed to know. Eventually he spoke. "Josh, about Imogene..."

And then my world fell apart. The music stopped in the fictional ballroom, the lights came on, and everyone went home, and I was left standing there wondering what went wrong. Imogene, the Irishman explained as painlessly as he could, just four days ago, had started going out with a lad from Fitzwilliam College. They had been friends for a while, and Imogene didn't think there was any more to it until the lad, Pete was his name, had asked her out. Her friend, the one who Oisin was talking to in the crêpe queue, had explained to the Irishman that Imogene still wasn't so sure about the whole thing, but had decided to give it a go. Oisin said I was four days too late. When I was writing about the role of agriculture in Britain's industrialisation, someone was doing something I should have done a long time ago.

"You alright, Josh?" asked Mark

I nodded.

"That's a shit one, mate," said Caolan.

"Yeah, but shit happens," I said with an attempted indifference that fooled nobody. "Hey, look I'm just going to go for a walk. I'll catch you guys in bit, okay?"

"Sure," said Oisin, "do you want anyone to come with you, or whatever?"

"Nah. Cheers anyway. I'll come and find you in a while."

And then I started walking. Nowhere in particular, but away from people I knew, people who couldn't say anything to help, and whose sympathy only made me feel guilty. I lost myself and the others for an hour. I wandered around looking for somewhere to go, passed stalls and attractions, through fairgrounds and casinos, graciously accepting any delicacies on offer, and politely declining the request to help a fictional police officer in his ongoing and equally fictional investigation. I decided that a May Ball was perhaps the worst place in the world to be when you felt like this. There was so much pressure to have a good time, so much fun shoved in front of your face that you could see nothing else.

But I hated myself when I was like this, and I hated other people when they were like this too. I mean, it was so pathetic. So what, I had fallen for a girl who apparently didn't feel the same? It was hardly the first time it had happened, and none of them had killed me. For God's sake I was here, in Cambridge, at a May Ball, with all my friends, with nothing to worry about apart from tomorrow morning's hangover. And it was not as if I loved Imogene, or anything. God, I hardly even knew her. This was not the behaviour of the hero of a film; more like that of the irritating whiney character, the one who probably wears glasses and has an annoying voice, the one who no-one gives two shits what happens to. I told myself to snap out of it, at least for tonight. I could be sad all I wanted, if that was necessary, tomorrow, when I was all on my own in my room. I quickly downed a few "green" cocktails, gave myself a symbolic, but not too hard, slap on the face, and went off to find my friends.

And for the rest of the night I tried hard to have a really good time, and partly succeeded. They were all having the time of their lives, especially Oisin, who couldn't get over the fact that you could just take whatever you wanted, and I fed off that. I knew that I would regret it if I didn't at least try, and as long as I kept myself busy, and I didn't catch the sounds of any romantic songs, or see any couple walking hand in hand, I was able to put her out of my mind.

We had even been joined by the hockey-playing economist who had successfully crashed the Ball. May Ball crashing was hobby of a lot of people at this time of the year, and involved a great deal of planning if you were to be successful. Every May Ball had security guards at all potential external access points, and within the Ball itself wristband checks were regular occurrences. For obvious reasons, the colour of the wristband remained a closely guarded secret until the actual night of the Ball, and it was not uncommon to see would-be crashers wandering around outside the glamourous events with their wrists covered with bands of all the colours of the rainbow, flashing them at their mates like dodgy watch salesmen. Few crashes were successful, and bouncers could often be seen marching the grinning daredevils out of the Ball when their dastardly deed was detected. However, our fellow economist had not scaled walls, swum across rivers, hidden inside dustbins, or paraglided himself in. Oh no, he had simply wandered through the front gate, past three security guards, pretending to talk on his mobile phone. And now, here he was, doing all the things we were doing, having saved himself £70. We congratulated him, the more the merrier and all that, but secretly wanted the bastard to be caught.

A particular highlight of the night was a visit to the hypnotist show. We had been bouncing, dancing and bumping around for a good couple of hours, and the thought of a comfy seat, a cocktail and a crêpe would have been appealing regardless of the presence of the Amazing Johno. I was inherently sceptical about most things (apart from the power of economics to save the world, of course) but especially so when it came to hypnosis and stage hypnotists. In my A-level psychology course we had dabbled in a bit of hypnotism, and the explanation that seemed to have gained the most scientific support over the years was that hypnotism was a simply a state of increased suggestiveness. In other words, the people apparently "hypnotised" were fully conscious of what they were doing, they were just more willing to do it. And so, as we shuffled our way into some spare seats in the little theatre that showed movies in non-Ball times, and the dramatic music started, I had little faith in the Amazing Johno's ability to "take over our minds and guide us places we would never normally venture", and even less faith that his jet-black hair was naturally that colour.

With his red and gold cape flowing behind him like part of a bad Superman costume, Mr Amazing asked for volunteers. Without thinking (maybe I was already under his amazing powers) up went my hand. So too did Sly's. As I squeezed passed Caolan on my way to the stage, I prepared myself for the inevitable call of "attention-seeker", often disguised as a cough in such public situations, and the accompanying trailing leg designed to trip me up. However, none came. Maybe this was a rare act of conscience after what had happened earlier in the night, but far more likely it was due to the fact that the Irishman seemed a good deal drunker than the rest of us, and as a result didn't really know where he was, who the idiot in the cape was, or who was squeezing past him saying excuse me mate in a northern accent. People always said it was impossible to get drunk at a May Ball due to the huge amount of food soaking up the excess alcohol and the numerous fun activities that temporarily stopping you drinking. Moreover, due to the length of time you were at the Balls, you did not feel the same need to throw as much drink into the system as quickly as possible as you might at a Bop. Whilst there was a certain amount of truth in all of this, the bottom line was it was still very easy to get very pissed very quickly, especially if, like Caolan, this was your first night of drinking for over a month, and you had consumed a quantity that can only be described as a shit-load.

Sly and I made our way to the stage along with about a dozen others, one of whom was the Lovely Lauren Broad, and another was the Great One himself, the Stalking Philosophising Preacher from Bradford. If the Amazing Johno could hypnotise the latter into being not such a dick my scepticism would have been dissolved.

As it happened, the Amazing Johno only wanted six people for the main part of his show, and so embarked upon a selection procedure. This was very clever of old Johno. He made us all close our eyes, put our hands together and imagine that they had become superglued, and we now couldn't pull them apart. Really imagine they have, he repeated in a voice that he had to be putting on. We were then asked to try and pull them apart. Those that could were either people who weren't prepared to put on an act, or troublemakers out to prove that hypnotism was a load of bollocks and thus look good in front of their friends. Johno promptly dismissed the owners of any hands that were separated, thus leaving people who would give him the best show. I could very easily have separated my hands, but I wanted to stay up there, and so they remained superglued together.

Even the greatest hypnotists could not have instigated a hypnotic trance that would have blocked out the next incident. Just as Johno was calling for a round of applause as the unsuccessful, unsusceptible and uncontrollable were returned to their seats, a familiar Irish voice filled the hall.

"Sly, you are a wanker!"

In case anyone missed it, Caolan promptly repeated his statement several times at increasing volume. This was followed by a noise that could only have meant one thing, and the surrounding seats promptly cleared as the sideburned Irishman projected vomit all over the theatre and all over himself. A partly digested piece of crêpe also attached itself to Mark Novak's right shoe, and remained undetected as it toured the Ball with him for most of the night. Caolan was promptly removed first from the theatre, and then, after taking a few tumbles which slightly dented the credibility of his "Oh it's just an upset stomach" story, from the Ball itself by three unimpressed Ball staff. Oisin later told me that the sideburned one had assured all concerned that he would be just fine going back to college on his own, but was later seen leaving with his arms flung around a mystery girl. Lovely Lauren Broad was still hypnotised with me as we listened to the events unfold, so unless she could also clone herself, he was with someone else. It would be a while before the full details of Mr O'Donnell's drunken May Ball debut and its eventful aftermath emerged.

With Caolan sent packing, the Ball and the hypnotist show could continue. Sly had been returned to his seat having separated his hands instinctively upon hearing his name. The Stalking Philosophising Preacher from Bradford, Lovely Lauren from London, and my good self were still up there. As the show continued we willing participated in increasingly stupid set pieces. At one stage we were rowing a boat, next we were falling in love with our chairs, then we were touching ourselves provocatively at the mention of farmyard animals. All the time I was aware what I was doing, and I am pretty sure everyone else was, but the crowd were loving it, and it was good to be part of the show. Afterwards I told my friends I couldn't really remember what I had done, but I had a vague recollection of a seeing a rather attractive sheep. I didn't want to shatter their illusions.

After the hypnotist, we tried to do absolutely everything that was on offer in the Ball. We drove around on the dodgems for a bit, generally targeting Oisin for driving too cautiously. Nick and I, thinking we were James Bond with our tuxedos and vodka martinis, quickly lost a fortune in plastic chips in the casino ("You do not need to shout 'snap', sir, this is poker"). We jumped around on bouncy castles, cheered as fireworks crashed and banged above our heads, danced and heckled along to the sounds of a Robbie Williams tribute act (he was one of those that actually thought he was Robbie: "Ladies and gentlemen, but especially the ladies, will you *Let Me Entertain You* tonight?" "No, piss off you big dick"), giggled away at some comedy, and got booed off-stage as Nick, Jude, Sly and I tried to unleash upon the Ball an impromptu strip act. Above all we ate and drank more than we had ever done in our lives.

Before we knew it, morning had arrived, and with it a cooked breakfast and a Survivor's Photo. Survivor's Photos happen at the very end of all Balls, and I often had sympathy for the poor photographer assigned with the task. He would be perched perilously high up on some building, armed with a megaphone that only made his voice more inaudible and a single credibility-deficient threat of not taking the photo unless we all behaved (because, of course, his employers would completely understand when he told them that the reason he had not taken the photo, the photo that would make the company a small fortune as Ball-goer after Ball-goer forked out for a lasting memory of a special night, was because a bunch of big, clever kids were being naughty boys and girls). Because it was the end of the Ball, 6 am in the case of Robinson, everyone was shattered, drunk, and in no mood to take orders from a man they could hardly see. Moreover – everyone, and this was close to a 1,000 – wanted to get near the front row, or on somebody's shoulders so that they could be seen. Thus, calls from the air for the girl in the black dress to move to the left a bit, and for the lad in the tuxedo to let the girl behind him be seen were met with boos, grunts and little else.

I had successfully avoided Imogene all night, the sight of her large entourage of New Hall vixens acting as a reliable warning that she was close by, but as Sly dragged and barged us all towards the front of the photo, I inadvertently, and painfully, bumped into her.

"Hi Josh!" she exclaimed. She was at that tired, drunken stage, where if she didn't have any support, she'd be on the floor. "Oh, this is Pete." Luckily, she had Pete for support. Pete the new boyfriend. Good, old Pete.

"Hi Pete, nice to meet you," I shook his hand and squeezed tight. 1–0 to me.

"Hey Josh, I can't believe I haven't seen you tonight. Have you been avoiding me?" Luckily she laughed as she spoke.

"No, no, no," I replied, a little too quickly, "I've been erm... I've just been around, you know."

"Lauren said you were hypnotised. I wish I had seen that."

"I think I might have made a prick out of myself."

"Knowing you, you will have done," she smiled and gently nudged me in the sides just to make sure I knew she was joking.

"Oh, sorry, you look nice."

"Why thank you. You've got all the lines, although I'm looking a bit rough now. Oh, and so do you... not look rough, but look nice, if you know what I mean. Sorry, I'm a bit... you know."

I smiled, and tried to think of something else to say. I wanted to be beamed out of there. Luckily, she spoke next.

"How did the exam go today?"

At first I didn't know what she meant. The exams seemed such a long time ago.

"Not bad," this was my automatic response, which I quickly changed as soon as I remembered that bloody Stats exam. "No, pretty shit actually."

"Still, at least they're over, and I bet you've done fine."

"Yeah," I said, feeling I was obliged to give some sort of reply.

"I'm so tired. I can't wait to get into bed," she added after a few moments of silence, during which Sly had told a girl in a purple dress to get the fuck down because she was blocking his view.

"Me too, me too." It was the first thing I had said and really meant in the whole conversation.

Indeed, the conversation was going nowhere. I didn't really want to talk to her, and she was fading fast due to fatigue and alcohol. Fortunately, we were saved by the photographer who, after twenty minutes, finally announced, to cheers of relief, that he was now ready to take the photo that would bring this eventful evening to an end.

I hugged Imogene good night, told Pete it was very nice to meet him, and departed the Ball with Jude, Oisin and a few of the others. As we left Robinson College almost eleven hours after first arriving we were given the morning papers to read, but my eyes were too tired and my mind too disinterested. Back in college I chatted to Jude for ten minutes or so, sat on the steps outside my room, then de-robed and climbed into bed. I was too tired to sleep, and the light and sounds of morning traffic streaming in through my window didn't help, but eventually my overloaded system shut itself down.

Chapter 66

I awoke at eleven the following morning; far earlier and much less tired than I had anticipated. I didn't feel like seeing anyone just yet, and it was with relief that I opened the door of M14 to an empty corridor. I prepared myself four Weetabix and binned the usual orange juice in favour of a cup of tea. It was going to be one of those days. I returned to my room and shut the door. I thought about last night; not about the dodgems or the hypnotist, the bouncy castle or the casino, not about how lucky I was to have finished my exams or how lucky I was to be alive and healthy, but about Imogene. To tell you the truth, I still couldn't believe it. For once I had been so sure. For once I was seeing all the signs in a positive light. For once, all the upsets and misadventures of the last year seemed to serve a purpose. For once things seemed to be happening the way they did in the movies; the happy ending coming just before the credits came down. But I had been wrong. And now it hurt so much.

I thought about the week in prospect, about lazy days in the sun, about the carnage of Suicide Sunday, about the guaranteed delights of Trinity May Ball, but none of it brought a smile to my face. I had allowed myself to imagine spending those days with her, allowing images to form in my mind, perfect paintings of us walking home, hand in hand, on a starlit night. And now I didn't want to go through them. Now I wanted to go home. I crawled under the covers of my bed and shut my eyes.

But did things have to end like this? I sat up in bed to enable this new line of thought to be processed more effectively. I mean, she had only just started going out with this guy, and he was quite short for a boy his age, and Oisin said that if I'd asked her earlier it could have been me. Maybe he was right. Maybe it still could. Maybe she was only going out with what's-his-face because she thought I didn't feel the same way. After all, I had every opportunity to ask her out, and took none of them. Maybe it wasn't too late.

I took out a pen and paper. I was both amazed and thankful that my hand was able to write non-economic things. I didn't stop to think what I was doing, I just poured out the thoughts in my head.

Dear Imogene,

I really don't know if I should be writing this letter, and I am so sorry if it hurts you in any way.

Getting to know you has been the best part of my term. You have made me laugh and smile so much. You are the only one who puts up with my crappy stories that go on and on about not very much, and laughs at my rubbish jokes. The thought of a Creamy Choc with you was the one thing getting me through those long, boring days of revision. I am pretty useless at saying what I am trying to say, but you are one of the most wonderful people I have ever met. I know it sounds really, really corny, but you are funny, kind and clever. You are also very beautiful.

Nothing in the world would make me happier than to go out with you. However, I realise that I am a little late. Please believe me that I am not writing this letter to mess up things between you and your boyfriend. I am writing this just to let you know how I feel, and to let you know how happy you've made me. Whether I have a right to tell you this now, I just don't know.

I realise there is a very good chance that you do not feel the same way. Your friendship is by far the most important thing in all of this. I hope we can still stay friends, but I completely understand if you don't think it would be a good idea.

Once again, Imogene, I am so sorry if what I have said upsets you in any way, and I hope you can forgive me for writing this letter.

Josh

I read and re-read the letter. I wasn't at all happy with it; the way it flowed, the way its words and sentences made me cringe, the way it laid the path for rejection. But then I knew I wouldn't be happy however it was written. I folded up the paper and sealed it in inside an envelope that Mum had sent me to encourage me to write a letter to her. I wrote the word "Imogene" on the front and propped it up against my TV. I sat and stared at it for a while, the little white object that was bound to change so much, whatever happened. As much as I pretended, Imogene and I could never be friends in the same way after this. I changed my mind seven times in my room, twice on the way out of college, and thirteen on the long walk up the hill to New Hall. In the end, and for reasons that I was too tired to evaluate, I put the letter in her pigeon hole, guiltily smiling at the sight of "Head, I." and returned home. I treated myself to a chunky chocolate muffin from Nadia's, but it didn't taste as good as it should.

I told Mark, Caolan and Oisin what I'd done. None of them thought it was a good idea, but all, even Caolan, could understand why I had done it. I obediently listened to their advice about not letting it ruin my May Week.

We spent that Saturday night in my room watching a video. People were still shattered from the extravagances of the previous evening and early morning, and we had enough events in the pipeline for us not to feel we were wasting our hard-earned time. The movie was called *Orgazmo*, and sadly was not a mindless porno. Caolan described it as the biggest pile of shite he had ever had the misfortune to see, with Oisin chipping in that it was frickin' painful. I didn't say much during the film, and my silence was enough to tell my friends that I wanted to be left alone once it had finished.

I was tired but not sleepy, angry but not upset. I was angry at myself for falling for yet another girl, and angry for not doing anything about it sooner. I was angry that she had found somebody else, and that he had just been a friend like me. I was angry that I couldn't think any bad thoughts about her that would have made this process easier. I was angry that I couldn't keep my feelings hidden from my friends. I was angry that I didn't have the carefree attitude of Caolan, or the apparent lack of desires of Mark and Oisin. I was angry that I kept making the same mistakes over and over again, and never learnt anything from them.

Chapter 67

I knew there would be a letter waiting for me in my pigeon hole that Sunday morning, and I knew what it would say. I picked it up, went to get a sausage sandwich and a coffee from Smilies, and brought it back to my room. My hand was shaking slightly as I opened it. I sat down on my bed and began to read.

Dear Josh,

Thank you so much for your letter. Please don't be sorry for writing it – honesty is underrated. Now I get to the really awkward part, because I really don't want this to turn into a "Dear John" – type thing. I don't know how to reply to such a sweet and, I hate to admit it, very flattering letter, but here it goes. It came as such a shock to me. I think I must be bad at reading those kind of signs – either that or you are very cunning!

That we have such fun doesn't really have anything to do with me. I've never laughed so much in conversations about *Dawson's Creek* and board game societies. I really wish I could see you in the way you hope, but you're too much of a friend – God that's such a cliché but I can't think how best to express it.

The last thing I want is for you to regret telling me because in all this the one thing I want is not to hurt you. Of course I'd love it if we could stay good friends. Please just tell me how you want it to be, I mean, would it be better for me to become bitchy so you can just get bitter, or something? It's not at all what I want but if taking a step back is the best thing then just let me know. If you want to have a chat or anything, just ring/email/write.

Please don't feel embarrassed, or anything, and definitely don't apologise for telling me. I'd much rather know, and you haven't messed anything up. I'm really truly sorry if I'd led you on or hurt you. I think I'm filling out the bitch role without even trying.

Take care, Josh.

Love,
Imogene.

I cried when I read it; the first tears since I broke my wrist trying to kick a flat football on an icy day in primary school. I didn't even cry at my grandad's funeral, although I tried to. But I wasn't crying because Imogene had said no, or because I felt sorry for myself, or because I regretted not doing anything sooner, or because I regretted doing anything at all. Anger had dealt with these feelings last night, and I didn't have the energy to be angry any more. I was crying because the letter confirmed what I already knew – Imogene was an amazing person.

I put the letter in my special box, the same place that held her note about my pink hat.

I didn't want to talk about it with anyone. There was not a lot anyone could say and it was not fair to expect them to share my problem. I told the

A Tale of Friendship, Love and Economics

other three that Imogene had written back, but left it at that. They looked relieved.

"I tell you, they're bloody crazy up in New Hall," Caolan said eventually. "Even the ones who seem normal are bloody crazy. Their bloody surnames should have been a clue. I'm sure it's a mental hospital pretending to be a Cambridge College. We'll stay well clear of that place in the future." I smiled back. He was a good man, although he tried his best to hide it.

"Right," I said, decisively drawing a line under that topic of conversation, "I suppose we best be setting off soon."

Just before we embarked upon on our big Sunday afternoon adventures, under the guise of needing the toilet, I nipped into the computer room to send one quick email.

Dear Imogene,

Thank you for your lovely letter, and thank you for being so understanding. Believe me, you have absolutely nothing to be sorry for. Everything that has happened is my fault entirely. You did not lead me on in any way, it was just me trying to see something that was never there in the first place. Also, I don't reckon the bitch act would be the best policy. Firstly, I don't reckon you could pull it off, and secondly, nothing would make me happier than to stay good friends with you.

I have now officially given up on women, and am turning gay (I'm sure Caolan would be keen). If going gay doesn't work, then celibacy and a career as a monk beckons (so long as they'll let me play Kerplunk in the monastery).

Thanks again for your letter. You really are a special person, Imogene, and I really do wish you all the happiness in the world. Have a fantastic May Week.

Take care,
Josh

I had to put in the gay bit as being serious for such a length of time was killing me. I still didn't feel right ending the email with love, however. I logged off, walked out of the computer room and back into M-block.

I took a deep breath as if to make sure all of these mixed up feelings were sucked up and hidden away inside. I looked at myself in the mirror and practised smiling. In the safety of my room I openly blamed *Dawson's*

Creek for all my problems and called myself a stupid prick three times. I then went to pick up Mark and Oisin.

I hate it when you know you are supposed to be having fun, but you just don't feel like it. I knew that in the weeks and months to come I would look back on wasted days like these with great regret. After all, these were the days I had worked so hard for. I forced myself to go along with the rest of the gang, and to try and smile as much as possible. I knew that it would be really shitty for them to have me moping around all day, and to tell you the truth, the experience of Caolan being nice was starting to freak me out a bit. I ended up having quite a good time, but I couldn't help allowing my mind to wander into the forbidden land of what might have been.

Today was Suicide Sunday, and this was not my name for it. Traditionally this was the day that a lot of exam results came out for finalists, and the subsequent origins of the name are not hard to fathom. Indeed, Cambridge is very big on stopping its students taking the so-called easy way out. During revision and exam period, each college bedder must go in every room to make sure the occupant is still breathing (during the rest of the term, if you left your bin outside your room it was a sign that you didn't want the bedder to come in) and, moreover, the high tower of St. John's College is closed during the revision and result period to stop any ropeless bungee jumpers. On a brighter note, Suicide Sunday was now more known for good times in the sun and excessive drinks binges. Everyone went to at least one garden party that day, most went to two or three, and all the best ones started early.

There were a lot of options open to us as the Fab Four stood by the Plodge in the obligatory garden party dress of a shirt and a tie. However, we had promised Caolan's Jewish neighbour, as well as our very own Jewish economist, Simon (Joe and Nick's flatmates next year) that we would go along to the Jewish Society Garden Party. Tickets were only £5, and we were assured of plenty of food and drink.

Caolan's neighbour was called Fishel. He had a first name, but nobody used it. Very few used his surname either, and he was soon Fishy to all. Despite the fact that Simon and Fishel we both of the same religious persuasion, the contrast between them couldn't have been starker. Simon was a Jew, whereas Fishel was more Jew-*ish*. Simon was very devout and very orthodox. He would always wear the circular piece of cloth on his head (called a "couple", I was informed), and never ate anything that wasn't kosher. He would go to Jewish Society meetings every Friday night without

A Tale of Friendship, Love and Economics

fail, and his Sabbath started strictly when the sun set on a Friday. Fishel was also devout, but not quite as orthodox. He would go to Friday night meetings unless there was a Catz Bop on (poor Simon never got to see a proper Catz Bop), he would only dig out his couple for special occasions (or fancy dress parties) and would tuck into any old food if he was hungry enough. Fishel was the bad Jew of the family. In time I would get to know him better, but I already liked him.

I am ashamed to admit that I was more than a bit wary as we walked into the big white marquee that had been erected especially for the J-Soc (that's what those in the know called it) garden party. Simon was the first Jew I had ever met, and Fishel was the second. My school in Blackburn was very much mixed race, but not mixed enough to contain any Jewish students. The only previous experience I had had was in depressing films, the tragic writings of history books and the punch-lines of racist jokes. I thought all Jewish people were accountants, with beards and big noses, supported Spurs and were tight with their money. I wasn't even sure what language they spoke, or whether they had Jesus and God like we did.

I was ashamed of this ignorance, and embarrassed by all the questions I had asked Simon over the last few terms. He repeatedly assured me he didn't mind, so I continued. I was fascinated by what he told me, fascinated by his dedication and discipline, and absolutely convinced that I couldn't do the same. I was also relieved that both he and Fishel liked to joke about it all, laughing both at my ignorance and their practices. This was a good job because I don't really know any other way of dealing with things that I don't understand.

The marquee was full of people with those funny little hats. Caolan asked Fishel if we should perhaps put a serviette on our heads to help us fit in, and Fishel told him to keep his bloody voice down. It was clear that today Fishy was putting on his good Jew act. He smiled and nodded his coupled head as he greeted the parents of his Jewish friends. We decided to keep a low profile in case we said something wrong. We poured ourselves a glass of Pims each (every garden party in Cambridge had to have it) and scurried off into a corner along with geographers Nick and Joe and a couple of medics. Seeing as Nick MacLean was half Jewish (and had had the snip) we directed our questions to him. How could you tell if someone was a rabbi? Did women also wear couples? How old did you have to be before you could

The Cambridge Diaries

wear one? If you were only half a Jew, did you wear a single? He had no answers. Eventually Fishel came over to see how we were getting on.

"Fishy, can we tuck into this food yet?" asked Caolan. It was lunch time and our bodies needed feeding.

"Help yourselves. It'll soon be gone once some of these lot get started." We followed his eyes in the direction of a plump, red-faced man.

"Hey Fishy, what's on offer? Any chance of some sausage rolls?" I asked, the thought of food finally overriding anything else.

"Of course, 'cos we're well keen on eating pigs, aren't we?"

"Oh yeah. What else have you got?"

"Loads of lovely smoked salmon."

"Rank."

"Cheese?"

"Cheddar?"

"Kosher."

"Anything else?"

"Cakes?"

"Anything funny about them?"

"Yeah, they tell you a joke just before you eat them."

"I mean, any funny stuff in them."

"No, Josh, they're just normal cakes. Even Catholics can eat them."

"Nice one. I'll have some of those then."

Armed with food and more fruity drink, we returned to the safety of our corner. It didn't seem like the kind of gathering where mingling was a viable option. It was more of a family thing, and we felt a bit out of place.

"Hey, should we play some drinking games?" I asked, the food having perked me up, and my mind as far away from Imogene as it had been all day.

"We can't play frickin' drinking games with family around, or whatever," said Oisin sharply, taking a token sip out of his first cup of Pims. Once again it was evaporating faster than he was drinking it. I gave a knowing look in Caolan's direction.

"Okay, what about another game, like... song titles that you can put the word 'Jew' in."

"Bloody hell, Josh, a bit on the racist side, isn't it?" announced Joe Porter disapprovingly.

"No Joe," replied Caolan before I could get a chance, "real racists are those that think things but don't say them."

There was an awkward silence following the Irishman's comment. Joe often had digs at people, Caolan in particular, for making what he called "racist comments." Caolan said them more and more these days just to wind Mr Do-I-Look-Like-Charlie-Sheen up.

"Jew Know What I Mean, by Oasis," I said, after weighing up whether it was a good idea to persist with the game.

"Jew To Me Are Everything," offered Nick straight after with a mischievous grin.

"Come on, Mark, you're normally good at these kinds of games" I said sarcastically.

"I Only Want To Be With Jew" said Nick again, followed by "Jew Are The Wind Beneath My Wings". Joe tutted his disapproval, but failed to hide a smile.

I could see Caolan running through Westlife's greatest hits, the only songs he knew, trying to find one that worked. Oisin, it seemed, had done all his thinking for these exams and just stood there not drinking. Mark Novak thought for a while, looked like he had an answer, then looked like he didn't, then finally, and reluctantly, let it out, "Love Me Jew, you know, by The Beatles?"

We spent the rest of the J-Soc garden party drinking and eating the remains of the food. All the good stuff had gone, but there were still the odd cake and piece of fruit dotted around. Just as Fishel had finished telling us every Jewish joke he knew, making sure Simon's parents were well out of earshot, of course, a tall, thin guy stood on a box and called the room to attention. Fishel said he was a bit of a prick. He looked like someone who would grow up to be a physics teacher.

"I'd like to thank you all for coming today, especially the families and guests (Fishel gave us a sarcastic whisper of thanks). Now, we have a little treat to bring the 2001 J-Soc Garden Party to an end ("Watch they don't try and charge you for it," whispered Fishel). If you'd all like to gather around here, we will have some music."

We were shepherded into position, and found ourselves worryingly on the front row. I say worryingly, because this resembled a situation where Caolan and I would inevitably start laughing and need to be hidden. A choir of six stepped forward and on the count of four, and to the beat of a lone tambourine, burst into song. The tune was *Don't Worry Be Happy*, but the chorus had been changed to "Don't Worry, It's A Shabbats". I felt the giggles coming on and turned to see how my Irish friend was getting on. He had turned to a tent post for support. Thankfully, it was a light-hearted, fun song, and after people had picked up the tune and a few words, they started joining in. Not wanting to seem unenthusiastic or disrespectful, we sang along with the rest of the marquee, not having a clue what we were singing about. Simon told us later that the Shabbats that we were not worrying about is, in fact, the Hebrew term for the Jewish Sabbath.

After a few more songs to which we knew no words but sang along anyway, we were ushered outside for the photo. Unbelievably, and much to the annoyance of many prominent J-Soc members, we managed to secure of spot on the second row, right behind a couple of rabbis. We smiled, said kosher, and went home.

It had been a good start to the day, and I was glad I made myself go. Back in college we had just about enough time to dump our ties, clean our teeth, and have a quick look at ourselves in the mirror (a forty-minute process for Oisin) before we were off on our next outing.

When we were planning out our May Week during the frequent revision breaks in the library, quite a large group of us had decided to go to the St. John's College Ent that was happening tonight. Faye, Elizabeth, Movie Star Look-alike and the louder of the two Ents Reps came along to add a much-needed female presence to our testosterone-fuelled crew, with the promise of more Catz girls coming along later. We set off at about four o'clock in search of tickets.

Someone had heard off someone else, who had heard off the second cousin of someone else that tickets were available for John's Ent at five o'clock, but to get there early as they were bound to be in high demand. Someone was wrong. We arrived at the designated point, an outhouse by the side of a white wall, and waited. And waited. By half-five no-one had arrived. People got out their mobiles and started looking through their list of names for a contact in John's. I got out my phone as well and starting flicking through purposefully, knowing full well I didn't know a sole from the college. Eventually, it transpired that tickets were only available on the door when the Ent opened at 7.30 pm. The chain of communication had become so complicated that we couldn't work out who to blame, and instead went for a few pints in a nearby pub.

A Tale of Friendship, Love and Economics

At seven o'clock, and getting increasingly hungry, we returned to John's only to find queue of about one hundred people in front of us.

"It is better to be at the back of a queue containing people, than at the front of a queue containing no-one," I announced, employing a deep voice and bold hand movements.

"What?" said Oisin.

"Very deep," said Mark.

"You don't half talk some shite, Bailey," said Caolan.

As we joined the back we were spotted by an incredibly drunk Adam Sylvester, who grabbed Elizabeth's wrist and hoisted her up the queue to his position. We followed, as much for her safety as to increase our chances of getting in. Sly had been out drinking on Jesus Green with the rugby lads since ten this morning. His eyes were looking everywhere but in the right place, and he was swaying around as if the music had already started. He seemed happy to see us, but then blamed us for the rest of the queue.

The order the four economists entered John's Ent that night was the order we entered most things. Caolan and I would subtly jostle to get in first, neither of us wanting to be seen trying too hard to get ahead of the other in case we failed. Oisin and Mark would jostle in a similar way for who went in last, often resulting in numerous people passing them as the "after you" "no, after you" reached Round Seven. And so it was that whilst Caolan and I had flown through the gates, the other two were being told by a burly bouncer with head-gear that looked like it belonged to a cheap walkman, that the Ent was full and that they'd have to go home.

"Every bloody time," said Caolan, and I nodded in agreement, as we turned around to see what was going on.

The sideburned Irishman specialised in talking shite, especially when he was a bit drunk, and he promptly tapped the bouncer on the shoulder and began his case. Fifty per cent of the time this technique works, and fifty per cent of the time it results in us all being sent home. Tonight, however, he was able to find the right words, and the other two were let in.

"How ace am I?" he asked no-one in particular, and got no reply.

The Ent itself was expensive and a bit shit. I didn't mind paying the twenty-odd quid to get in, but then to have to buy drinks and food inside, especially as we were all so hungry, was a bit too much. And as for the music... Well, the phrase "absolutely awful" doesn't even come close. I was reliably informed by the hockey-playing economist and his Gardi's-loving friend that the awful racket that was making me cringe was, in fact, a banging Hip-Hop tune, whereas the other tents had some garage, techno and the mis-titled happy hardcore going on. I felt like an old man. I just wanted S Club 7.

I bought another sausage and went in search of Nick MacLean and Mark Novak. I found them together sat on a wall. Both were clearly drunk; Nick was camp and Mark was floppy.

"Shite music, hey?" I opened up with, before polishing off the remainder of my sausage in one.

"Some people like it," replied Nick

"It's shit," said Mark, who didn't usually swear, unless drunk or economically annoyed.

"Any action with any ladies?" I asked, trying to wipe all reminisces of tomato sauce off my hands.

"Nah."

"Nah, you?"

"Nah."

And I joined my two good friends on the wall, all three of us staring at nothing in particular, only finding our way out of our own maze of thoughts to comment on the next song that leaked out from the tent behind us.

"Shit."

"Yep."

Finally, with just one hour of the Ent. to go we were saved. It was like a mirage for the ears, an audial illusion, that caught us all by surprise and had us poking our finger about in our ears to check they were working alright. Thankfully the opening beats of *Club Tropicana* continued. We shot up from the wall and followed the sounds like hungry dogs. We barged our way through the spaced-out masses and found our paradise. The room that had previously housed R'n'B had been taken over. We flew straight onto the empty dance-floor and began boogying. Before the end of the song we were joined by most of Catz. People I didn't even know where at the Ent came running to the sound. If the university ever wants to wipe out St. Catharine's College, they simply have to get a Pied Piper to play something like Wham or S Club 7, and we would all scurry along after him up into the mountains (no doubt doing the actions as well). For the next hour the Catz Circle dominated the dance floor, and the DJ received a mighty boo when the end

A Tale of Friendship, Love and Economics

of *Bohemian Rhapsody* signalled that enough was enough. It was like Catz Bop on tour, and it made the previous painful hours seem worthwhile. We walked home with smiles on our faces, and our hands in our pockets to hide them from the cold. Rumours were circulating that Caolan had pulled fellow First Year Rep and object of Joe Porter's affections, Emma, in a bush of all places. However, both parties denied the charge, and the case was dropped due to lack of evidence. I had a missed call from Francesca on my mobile, but I figured it was too late to call her back now.

I got back to college more tired than drunk. It had been a long day, and it had finally caught up with me. I bid my fellow M-blockers, Mark, Elizabeth, Oisin and Faye goodnight, and trundled up the stairs. Before I opened my door, I had a change of heart and went down to the computer rooms in I-block to see if Imogene had replied. She had.

Hey Josh,

Thank you for being so sweet about everything, but please don't blame yourself. I wish you had told me the gay thing earlier. Pete has just had his gay friend to stay with him for a couple of days and I could have done some matchmaking! But I think it would be a loss to womankind for you to do so. Just because I'm not the one doesn't mean somebody else isn't. I don't really know if this will help but over the past couple of months I have had a number of spinster crises, thinking that nobody truly liked me, and I wouldn't have a relationship that would work. I'm by no means sorted now, but I think we just have to kind of muddle through and things definitely work out in the end, and so you might as well have as much fun as possible along the way. I'm sorry, I'm starting to sound like a greetings card, or something, but do you see what I mean? Endless optimism has to be the way forward, and I expect you to give me the same advice when you find the girl of your dreams and I'm living in my bed-sit, because what else can you do with a history degree?

Speak to you soon

Love,
Imogene xx

I read it a few times, and both smiled and felt sad the same way on each run through. I decided against replying tonight, reasoning that I was in neither the physical or the emotional state to concoct a reasonable response, and no doubt something stupid like a poem would find its way in there. I wrote one back the following day smattered with a few more apologies, a few more "thank you"s and a few more bad jokes. As the chain of replies continued, the emails got more and more light-hearted, and brought many a smile to my face in those last few days. I knew that I definitely wanted to stay friends with her – I hadn't just put that bit in out of obligation or to sound nice but I didn't really want to see her before the holidays.

Once more, I guess things could have worked out a lot worse, but then again they certainly could have gone a bit better. The only way to know if you truly like someone is by the pain you feel when it all goes wrong. This one hurt for a long time.

Chapter 68

Monday was time for forgetting about Imogene; a time for forgetting about the ultimately insignificant problems in life that had tended to dominate in recent weeks. Monday was all about one thing – Trinity May Ball.

Once again, for at least the 1,000th time in my short life, I was thankful that I was not born a girl. On top of periods, pregnancies and the unreliability of orgasms, lay the amount of time, effort and money required to go to a May Ball. For boys it was simple. We made sure our tuxedo was reasonably clean, and made sure we had someone to tie our bow-tie. We then had a shower, did a bit of something with our hair, maybe give the old teeth a quick brush, and that was that. Twenty minutes if you were pushing it, forty if you took you time. Even Oisin could complete the process in under an hour. For the females of our college it was a different matter entirely. They had to buy a dress (and God forbid, it couldn't be the same one they wore to Robinson May Ball, and it couldn't be in anyway similar to anyone else's). Then they had to get matching shoes and matching jewellery. Then they had to have their hair done; an appointment that had to be booked weeks in advance. Then they had to carefully apply the full range of the make-up; foundation, concealer, mascara, moisturiser, lip-stick, lip-gloss, you name it – if Boots sold it, on the face it went. After all the planning and the shopping, the whole getting ready bit took the best part of six hours, and involved unprecedented levels of stress. Me and the boys kept our distance.

Given that later in the day we would be enjoying some of the finest delicacies that man could produce, we decided to take ourselves off to Wetherspoons and tuck into a good old Beer-Burger meal just to balance things up. You could tell everyone was excited, and although we tried desperately not to build it up in our minds, it was obvious that everyone had. Just for that feeling of anticipation the queuing in the snow had been worth it. Mark, Caolan and I had had a haircut especially, and Oisin had put an extra coat of shampoo on his flowing wings.

To be fair, even us boys spent a wee bit longer getting ready for Trinity than we had for Robinson, although ultimately we still looked the same. I contemplated doing something different with my hair, but bottled out of it at the last minute. With our suits on and our bow-ties tied, we congregated on the grass of Sherlock Court to wait for the girls. Unsurprisingly, they were late, later than Oisin as it transpired, but when they emerged from their rooms and joined us on the grass on this pleasantly warm Monday evening, they looked beautiful. We once again secured the services of a willing sole to take pictures, and were even snapped by our friends who hadn't been lucky enough to get tickets, making me feel a bit like a celebrity posing for a centre-page spread in *Hello* magazine. We had a few whole group pictures taken, which with over twenty of our cameras queuing up for a go, resulted in several severe cases of jaw-ache as we tried to sustain those smiles, and a few spells of temporary blindness as the bright lights of the flashes lit up the early evening. We then gathered for a few select group photos, with us four economists posing for one, before the geographers and the historians jumped on the band-wagon (again) and set up their own subject-based photo. A few months ago I would happily have bet £100 that I would be rushing to pose with my two neighbours, Faye and Mary Jane, for a photo that we could maybe frame and put up in the flat next year, but times had changed. After a while, Nick MacLean signalled that it was about time we were off, and after checking we all had our tickets and partners (I had been unable to trade Nick for a female model), we departed through the Porter's Lodge and made our way up Kings Parade, our excitement growing with every step we took.

Trinity's grounds are simply amazing. The courtyard that greets the eye as you enter through the Great Gate is breathtaking. Those that know about these things say that it is built in a Tudor-Gothic style, and it is the largest court in either Oxford or Cambridge, with an area of about two acres. The grass is pretty much perfect, simply crying out for someone to play cricket or tennis on it, with only the numerous "Please keep off the grass signs" and the beady eyes of the porters and their cameras stopping students making the most of it. At the centre of the court stands a giant stone fountain, a popular feature for hoards of tourists to get their photo taken beside. There is also a grand eighteenth-century clock at the far side of the court that Mr William Wordsworth described in his *Prelude* as the clock with a male and female voice, because it dongs each hour not once but twice, with a low note immediately followed by a high one. Would you believe it, there are yet more interesting clock facts? There is apparently a tradition, although I never saw it, that when the clock hits midnight or midday, students have to dash around the perimeter of the court before all of the twenty-four bells have sounded. This means the keen student must cover a distance of 347.5 metres (or 380 yards, if you prefer it that way) in just forty-three seconds. Not an easy task. This very run was featured in *Chariots of Fire*, but, like most movie things, it was not filmed on location but in a boring studio. Anyway, the bottom line is that Trinity College, from the moment you set eyes on it, simply oozes extravagance, riches and a colourful history.

Not even the great Trinity May Ball could avoid a lengthy queue to get in. As we entered the Great Court, our eyes fell upon a sizeable line of suits and dresses decorating the lower part of the surrounding buildings. We said our farewells to Caolan as he went to join the non-dining riff-raff, whilst we wandered to the other side of the Court to join the thankfully shorter dining queue. Whilst standing there both willing the minutes to fly by so that we could be let in and at the same time wanting this feeling of anticipation to last forever, we were entertained by a succession of jugglers, fire-eaters, and magicians. Indeed, the magician was my favourite, not only because at one stage it looked like he was going to make Adam Sylvester disappear, but just as he finished his otherwise woeful act he said,"Right, I know I'm crap, but cheer loudly so that the next group along think I'm brilliant."

We duly obliged.

As promised we were admitted though the gate and adorned with wristbands a full hour before the non-diners, and led into Trinity's Great Hall for our banquet. To be fair, the Great Hall wasn't all that great. It was nicely lit by candles, and had a refined but relaxed atmosphere to it, but then so too did Catz Hall. We were serenaded by the college choir as we took our seats, which was a pleasant touch even though they weren't doing any songs we'd heard of. I took my seat between Joe Porter and Mark Novak, and opposite Elizabeth (who had once again told us in her posh squeaky voice to behave ourselves). I knew that the chance of me consuming over 50 per cent of whatever fine meal was laid down in front of me was minimal. I was not to be disappointed. The starter was not exactly my cup of tea: prawns and scampi in caviar sauce. If it had been served with a side-order of mayonnaise, it might just have been my worst meal ever. I swapped mine for Nick's bread roll, and out of sympathy Elizabeth gave me her mango sorbet, which was delicious, but I still maintained that it was more suited to being a desert. The main course was venison, which Nick explained to me was deer ("I hope so after what we paid for the ticket," I replied, and had to repeat it several times before anyone laughed, and then it was only to shut me up). I ate quite a bit of the venison, but I found it a bit tough, also I wasn't too keen on the idea of eating Bambi. Seemingly everyone else had no such qualms, and a table full of empty plates signalled their approval. Throughout the meal, various wines were brought around, and we gratefully accepted and saw off each glass. Most people were too full to take on the summer fruits pudding, so I helped myself to three portions, being careful to remove as many of the sultanas as possible. Cheese and port were next on the menu, but by that stage Joe Porter and I had decided that enough was enough. We hadn't paid over £100 to have a formal hall. Dinner was just our means of getting into the Ball. We announced our departure, downed our glass of port, and headed out into what was officially, apparently anyway, the world's second greatest party.

"Let's see how much of this two-million quid we can consume," I said to the footballing geographer as we made our way into the night. We giggled excitedly, and gave each other a high-five, my first since I was seven, just because it felt like the right thing to do.

It was a good job the order of the May Balls was as it was. Don't get me wrong, I had a great time at Robinson, but if things were the other way around and had we gone to it on the Monday having attended Trinity on the previous Friday, it would certainly have paled into insignificance. It would have been like seeing the awesome main act, and then being forced to listen to the support act afterwards. It was perhaps unfair to make comparisons, but as Robinson was our only previous experience of May Balls, we were left with little choice. Trinity May Ball was simply on another planet; both living up to and surpassing all our expectations, and truly making our ticket price seem like the bargain of the century.

The setting was perfect, both in size and beauty. Whereas Robinson tried desperately to cover up its 1970s red-brick walls, Trinity had the gorgeous Neville's Court open to the world as the focal point of the Ball, refined and classically illuminated, and surrounded on all sides by exquisite stalls. A bridge led you over the river to a village of marquees that constituted the bulk of the rest of the ball, complemented by the luminous orb which magically hovered above the river-side marquees to aid navigation between them – it seemed that even providing the moon on a stick was not too much trouble for Trinity May Ball. Indeed, it was simply a delight to walk around and take everything in. The choice of drink and food was simply incredible. Where Robinson had white wine Trinity had champagne, the finest French champagne apparently, and it didn't run out all night, and it didn't even make me sneeze. Trinity also had on offer every other drink imaginable, with the usual beers and cocktails as well as an unbelievable range of spirits, from kahlúa to amaretto to three single malt whiskies. I hated whisky, but it seemed rude not to try it. Where Robinson had burgers and sausages, Trinity had oysters (3000 as legend has it; one of them somehow finding its way into my hand, and then promptly being thrown onto the floor together with a girly squeal) and caviar, Mexican food and Chinese food, stalls containing mountains of fresh fruit and the finest French and Italian cheeses. Nor were the quantity and variety the only attraction; as Elizabeth squeakily pointed out there was also a suitable level of decadence to the Trinity cuisine, from the wild rocket in the ciabatta to the tropical papaya and star fruit in the Thai food tent. This was all well and good for the food connoisseurs amongst the group, but to be honest I was more interested in plain and simple meat, and even then I was not to be disappointed. Trinity had also secured the services of Pig Out Catering (us economists concluded they must be operating a monopoly as providers of May Ball meat), but tonight there was more meat on offer – lamb, chicken, steak, very few queues, and even the serving staff were better-looking. And there were yet more differences. Whereas Robinson made do with no more than the existing college toilets, Trinity shipped in a batch of luxury toilets, with hand towels and gold-plated taps. Indeed, Oisin spent forty minutes in them at one stage, and then returned a few more times later in the night, describing the experience as frickin' brilliant. Trinity's fireworks were the best I had ever seen, and Robinson may as well have handed us all out a sparkler and left it at that for all we remembered of their show. Where Robinson had dodgems, Trinity had chauffeur-driven punts. Where Robinson had a bouncy castle, Trinity had an ice-rink and hot-air balloon rides. Robinson's theme was "Misbehavin'", Trinity officially didn't have one, but if it did it would certainly have been "Money". You simply walked around, eyes and mouth wide open, feeling like a king. There was just no comparison.

But it was the musical entertainment that was the most obvious difference. Robinson had given us a Robbie Williams tribute act, whereas Trinity were providing the popular indie band Ash and, which actually got us far more excited, none other than former *Neighbours* star, Mr Jason Donovan. The musical acts performed in the Main Tent which was located in the middle of Neville's Court. I was not a huge Ash fan, none of us were, but I knew a few of their songs *Burn Baby Burn, Girl From Mars,* and all that – enough anyway for me to be happy that they were playing, and pencil in a trip to the Main Tent in plenty of time to hear what they had to offer. Jason was a different matter. Jason Donovan was one of those people who had I not found out he was playing tonight probably would never have thought about again in my life; however, as soon as I heard he would be strutting his stuff, I couldn't think of anyone else I would rather see. I had been a huge fan of his when I was a little kid, and had gone to see him in *Joseph and his Amazing Technicoloured Dream Coat* with my Mum for a birthday treat. Moreover, he was (apart from Kylie) the biggest thing to come out of my beloved *Neighbours*. No, forget U2, Oasis, the Chilli's and Jacko (well, maybe not Jacko), there was nobody on the planet I would rather see in concert than Mr Donovan.

And everyone else was just as excited as me. We were positioned in the front row, our pockets stuffed with expensive snacks and delicious fruit smoothies, a full half-hour before the Aussie legend was due to hit the stage. The crowd was buzzing. People wanted to know what he would look like after all these years, would he be fat and bald, would he do some drugs on stage, would he bring Kylie along? A rumour was circulating around that Ash had cost six times the amount paid to poor Jason, and judging by his performance and the pleasure it gave the crowd, the May Ball Committee had got an absolute bargain. He wandered onto the stage wearing a large yellow fisherman's jacket and the Main Tent erupted. He was looking good. His trademark blonde hair had receded somewhat, but he was still the same fresh-faced Jason that we all had known and loved. If the girls' ball gowns weren't quite so complicated around the bottom half I'm sure he would have been bombarded by a deluge of knickers (and probably a few boxer shorts as well). My only remaining concern was that he might have some crappy new material out, but I needn't have worried. In a thirty-minute set that left us all begging for more, Jason ran through all the old classics: *Any Dream Will Do*, *Sealed With A Kiss*, *Everyday*, *Too Many Broken Hearts*, and as he sang the audience were transported back a childhood full of primary school discos and singing along in front of *Top Of The Pops*. Judging by the noise, most remembered every single word.

At one stage there were a few chants of "Kylie, Kylie" which the great man passed off with a smile and a rather cheeky "Fuck Kylie". As he moved through his set the yellow jacket was removed to reveal a tight white T-shirt and a hint of a beer belly. He even treated us to a bit of dancing, and moved near the front row of the audience to allow us to touch him. Elizabeth, being hoisted up by her medic friend, managed to grab his hand and it didn't look like the Aussie superstar was ever going to be let go, and after a long period of stretching, I managed to stick my hand up his armpit. I have not washed it since. Jason didn't have any band or backing singers and, in fact, it was just like karaoke down at the local pub. But it was so special. We begged for more, but Jason apologetically shrugged that he didn't have any more and, anyway, he only had the one CD with him. He left to a universal chorus of cheers from an audience that were sweating and in awe. Jason truly was a living legend.

It was impossible for Ash to live up to what had gone before, but they did a pretty good job trying. We moved back from the front row to catch our breath and allow a few overly keen die-hard fans to get up close. They played the songs that most of the audience knew, and even threw in a few cover versions, such as a cheeky version of Abba's *Mamma Mia*, and a rousing rendition of The Undertones' classic anthem, *Teenage Kicks* that got the whole tent bouncing along. Indeed, during the latter a girl was dancing rather provocatively next to me, but I was pretty sure I didn't want to hold her, tight or otherwise. We danced, jumped and sang along for the best part of an hour. It was kind of strange being at a gig in a tuxedo, but then this

A Tale of Friendship, Love and Economics

was Cambridge. We left the tent dripping with sweat, absolutely knackered, but over the moon. If the night had just been about the music I would have been more than happy with what I got.

As the hours ticked away like minutes, we tried to do as much as we could. Joe and I were sure we'd already eaten at least £200-worth of food, and probably drank even more, thus putting us well in profit for the night before we accounted for the music, the ice-skating, the hot-air balloon and the casino. Being Trinity May Ball, there was one final surprise left for us. As we were posing for the Survivors' Photo, just about to say cheese, exhausted and praying we would remember every moment of the wonderful night forever, the Red Devils flew by overhead and caused jaws to drop to the floor for the umpteenth time that night. A fitting way to end a night that was simply without compare.

By seven-thirty we were sat on a bench in our very own Main Court, perusing our complementary newspaper ("That's another 20p," pointed out Nick), and recalling magic moments from the night gone by in a way that made it sound like we were telling each other our dreams. The bedders and maintenance men walked past us at the start of their day and asked us if we'd had a good night, and even the morning porters were in high spirits, only intervening when Sly, for some unknown reason, tried to get a relay race going around the perimeter of he court. All seemed happy. All except for Oisin.

The start of May Week was the time the big romance was due to officially commence between the shaggy-haired Irishman and the loud one out of the two weird Ents Reps. However, nothing much seemed to change between them. Indeed, if anything, they saw each other less now that they were going out than they did in the three-month transition period. No more cups of tea in his room, no more searching for ties together in his cupboard. Oisin didn't see that there was any problem.

"Aye, it's no bother. We're both busy, or whatever."

"But you are going out with her, yeah?"

"Aye, I think so."

However, as the sun moved its way up into the sky early on this Tuesday morning, it was clear that there was a problem. The Loud One had also been at Trinity May Ball, but had spent the whole night with Jude and hardly a second with Oisin. Moreover, the uninformed onlooker, as well as those who thought they knew what was going on, would definitely have assumed Jude and her were going out from the way they were carrying on. Now I knew that Jude would never dream of doing anything with a girl who was going out with one of his mates, and he seemed equally confused by the situation, choosing to avoid talking to Oisin or being seen with the Loud One when the Irishman was around. Her behaviour at the Ball had clearly upset Oisin Kerrigan. As far as he was concerned, there was a way people were meant to act, and she was failing miserably, although he would never say anything to her or to anyone else. He didn't seem to know what was going on, and we thought it best not to press the issue. However, Caolan and I were pretty sure we knew what the deal was.

History had shown that the Loud One went through phases of liking and, more often than not, getting obsessed with men. Oisin was an obvious choice to get obsessed with. He was a good-looking lad, and the nicest guy in the world. Moreover, he was one of the few that never embarked upon random pulls, and hence was regarded as untouchable. For the Loud One, the fun was in the thrill of the chase, and once she snared her shaggy-haired prey, she didn't want anything to do with him. Oisin probably realised that this was a possibility when he signed the buy now, pay later, contract with her at the end of second term, but it still upset him as much when it finally happened.

It seemed, for the time being at least, that none of us were destined to have any success with the ladies of Cambridge.

Chapter 69

The days were fast running out on both May Week and our first year at St. Catharine's College, Cambridge. Tuesday was spent mostly sleeping and trying to convey to those that asked just how good Trinity May Ball was.

By Tuesday night, however, we were refreshed and ready for adventure. We could have gone to Cindies, but we wanted to do something different with our Tuesday night, seeing as it was still May Week. After ruling out a big game of hide and seek, we took to the waters and set sail down the Backs in a punt, for tonight was the night of St. John's May Ball, an event that stood side by side with Trinity right at the top of the May Ball league table. None of us had tickets, and none of us could be arsed trying to crash it, but we were all quite keen on the idea of punting down the river to see the Ball close up and catch a best-seat-in-the-house view of the fireworks. Unfortunately, about a hundred other people had a similar idea, resulting in gridlock along most of the River Cam.

"Perhaps they should introduce a congestion charge," suggested Mark with an uncharacteristically cheeky smile.

"How would they work out the marginal congestion cost, so they would know what to charge each punt?" I enquired, making sure geographer Joe Porter overheard.

"A good question, Mr Bailey," replied Caolan in his posh English accent that sounded neither posh nor English, "perhaps they could keep a tally of the number of punts on the river, and then charge accordingly. So, for example, if there were just three boaters on the river, the next punter might only pay a couple of pounds sterling, but if there were fifty, then he would have to pay something like forty pounds sterling. It would be a crude method, but no doubt better than just charging a flat fee whatever the conditions on the river."

"Economics to the rescue again, hey?" I added, twisting the knife in a little more. Joe had been grinding his teeth through our little play so far, but finally he took the bait,

"I've a better idea, perhaps you economists could just shut up. Jesus Christ, it's May Week for God's sake. Get me out of this punt," replied geographer Joe Porter sharply, looking around the punt for support but finding none.

"Don't criticise what you can't understand," I replied, knowing that the use of Bob Dylan would infuriate Joe even more.

We had taken two punts out that night. Joe was stuck with us three economists, whilst Oisin, Nick MacLean, Jude and Sly were the motley crew of the other craft. We bumped, barged and bundled our way through the wall of punts that had congregated to take in the atmosphere of Queen's College May Ball, which was also taking place on this Tuesday evening, and steamed on down the river. We sailed past Trinity, with its May Ball Committee members busily trying to remove all signs of the previous night's extravagances like little children hurrying to tidy their room before mummy and daddy got home, and pressed on towards John's.

John's May Ball had been in progress for about an hour by the time we got there. Suits and dresses walked hand in hand across the bridge, and mean-looking security guards patrolled the banks of the river. Apart from witnessing some spectacular fireworks, we were also in prime location to observe some of the most elaborate Ball-crashing attempts that I had ever seen.

There was little doubt that Trinity and John's were the hardest May Balls to crash. Legend had it that Trinity spent as much on security as our college's Ball spent in total, and it was a fair assumption that John's was at a similar level. As well as the numerous security guards, all armed with muscles and walkie-talkies, there were also fences, walls, locked doors and regular wrist-band checks to contend with. Something told me that the hockey-playing economist's technique with the mobile phone would not have proved quite so successful tonight.

As the fireworks roared above our heads, making the sky look like the splattered black canvas of an eccentric painter, an attempted crash was taking place very close to us. To our left lay a punt containing two lads in tuxedos, two girls in dresses, and one lad in jeans and a jumper.

"I bet he's the driver," I said.

"No shit, Sherlock," replied Caolan.

As the well-dressed crew looked around, assessing the best course of action, we gave them a thumbs up to signal our approval. It was then that we became accessories to their forthcoming crime. One of the lads in a tuxedo beckoned us over. We opted for the oar instead of the pole and paddled slowly over to their boat.

"Hey, fellas," began the tuxedoed one. He was skinny with spiky hair, and definitely from the cockney part of London, "do you fancy lending us a hand for a couple of minutes?"

The fireworks had reached their climax, and apart from pointing out and whistling at the attractive women as they walked across the bridge, begging Ball-goers to throw us a burger, or tenuously linking economics into another aspect of the night to infuriate Joe further, there was little else for us to do.

"Sure, mate," I said, speaking on behalf of my ship-mates, "what do you want us to do?"

The spiky Londoner, who was a third year computer scientist from Queen's College, was a man with a plan. We were going to sandwich his punt between our two, thus hiding the suspicious attire of his crew from the eagle eyes of the security guards, and slowly make our way downstream to

A Tale of Friendship, Love and Economics

the far side of John's College. Once there, the three punts were to form a path to an otherwise unreachable part of the college. Then, our job would be done, and the foursome would attempt to scale a decent-sized wall, which would apparently lead them to an unguarded part of the ball. They then planned to stick it out as long as possible before their un-banded wrists eventually gave them away.

We nodded in agreement and beckoned over Nick and Sly's boat to fill them in on the plan. It was carried out to perfection. The ever-friendly Oisin even confidently asked the security guard if he was having a good night, or whatever, as he eyed us sailing under the bridge. We constructed the wooden path with out three punts and gave the two girls a hand getting out. They thanked us for out help and we wished them good luck. I felt like I was part of some crack commando unit, maybe like the A-Team. If there was a Ball, we could get you in it.

Not satisfied with helping one group, we scoured the river for other crashers to offer our services to. One lad, also dressed in a tuxedo, had opted to moor his punt up on the banks of the college, and simply make a run for it. By the time he had scrambled up the bank he had a big mud-stain down the front of his white shirt, and three security guards were waiting for him at the top.

"Amateur," said Caolan disapprovingly as he was promptly escorted to the exit.

Much as we tried, no-one else seemed to want to hire us. We asked one of the Committee still cleaning up the Trinity mess if they were thinking about crashing John's, and they replied that they'd had enough of May Balls to last them a life-time. We eventually found one potential crasher; a puny-looking chap wearing a tuxedo but no bow-tie, who was standing on the bank of the Cam on the outskirts of John's College, staring up at a twelve-foot wall. We looked over in his direction, and he shouted out to us, "Where's Shaffrey?"

"Who?" we replied.

"Shaffrey. Have you guys seen Shaffrey?"

"Who the fuck is Shaffrey?" whispered Caolan and, after two boatfuls of confused shrugs, the Irishman repeated the question out loud, leaving out the naughty word.

"You know? Shaffrey" came the reply.

Caolan turned away to face us.

"What's this dick on about?" he asked.
"He wants to know where Shaffrey is," I replied.
Caolan shook his head in disgust, and then turned back to face to our new friend.
"Did you say *Shaffrey*?" he asked.
"Yes," came the reply again, "have you seen him?"
"Oh yeah, we've seen Shaffrey alright. He said he'd be along to meet you in ten minutes."
Caolan nudged me as he spoke.
"Yeah," I added, "he's running a bit late. You know what he's like."
"Tell me about it," he replied with a chuckle and a shake of the head.
"See you later, mate, and good luck," shouted Caolan, as he revved up the pole for our getaway.
"And say hello to Shaffrey for us," I added.
The guy gave us a friendly wave and then turned back to look at the wall. It was still as tall as he remembered.
"Mentalist," said Caolan when we were out of earshot.
"You two are well lousy," tutted Oisin, from the safety of his own punt.
"Piss off," we replied in Anglo-Irish unison.
The river was beginning to clear and, apart from an old lady with a dog, there was no-one who looked like they might be persuaded to embark upon a potentially fatal mission to crash St. John's College May Ball. Resigned to retirement, we made our way back towards college, had a cup of tea and went to bed.

Chapter 70

The mornings of May Week were often spent happily dozing in bed, drifting in and out of consciousness, not giving a second though to what the rest of the world was up to. I wished I could temporarily impose the pain of a full day's revision in a stuffy library and its complementary desire for nothing other than to be in bed with not a single thing that needed doing, so that I could really appreciate a luxury that I was already, after less than a week, beginning to take for granted.

A Tale of Friendship, Love and Economics

On that particular Wednesday afternoon, apart from having a cup of tea with Francesca and kicking a footy about in the park with the gang, my hectic schedule also involved a garden party, and signing the exeat form with our Tutor, the lesbian spy Dr Harris. As usual, Dr Harris had very little to say, and nervously wished us a happy holiday. We were in and out in under two minutes.

The garden party was officially billed as the Economics and Land Economy Garden Party, and as such was co-hosted by our Director of Studies, Mr Stevens, and the Lord of the Landies, the Brummie Dean, Dr Tinsley. The garden party was conveniently held on Sherlock Court, literally a stone's throw away from my home in M-block, and kicked off at three o'clock. All the usual suspects were present, and Mr Stevens had put on (well, placed the order with the kitchen staff at least) a spread of delicious fruit salad, salted peanuts, wine and apple juice. With May Week already beginning to catch up on me, I consumed everything but the wine, and was promptly called gay by Caolan because of it.

Half an hour into the pleasantly relaxed event, Mr Stevens came over to talk to our group. As ever he was dressed smartly, this time opting for a nice pair of cream trousers, and a long-sleeve blue shirt, complemented as always by a pair of shiny silver cufflinks, that suited today's moderately warm weather conditions. He had been stuck talking to Dr Tinsley and a few of his troops for the last thirty minutes and looked like he needed a break, although he was far too professional to have ever admitted it. We had been talking about how much weight one of the female Land Economists had put on this past year when our esteemed DOS joined us, and we promptly altered the course of the conversation onto the likely success of the euro. We didn't have much to say on the matter, and luckily Mr Stevens intervened. After a few minutes of answering questions about what I would be doing over the summer, and what paper options I was thinking about taking next year, I realised that the rest of the group had deserted me and I was left talking alone with my DOS. I smiled awkwardly and immediately ran out of things to say. I took a prolonged sip of the lovely apple juice to fill the void. Thankfully, Mr Stevens took the initiative.

"So, Josh, how do you think everyone has done in the exams?"

"Erm," I replied, as I tried to decide in my head whether I should answer this question truthfully. Something about Mr Stevens made me trust him. I told him that Jewish Simon and the Cypriot ex-sergeant would definitely get firsts. Mr Stevens nodded in agreement, but reminded me that nothing was a certainty in exams. I nodded back whilst I tried to remember who else I had been studying economics with for the past year.

"Yeah, and I reckon Mark will get one. He probably deserves it more than anybody. He works so hard, you know, and he always helps us out when we don't have a clue, which is quite a lot as you can imagine."

Mr Stevens smiled.

"And the rest of them?"

"I don't know. I mean, if you believe half the things Leila says then she's definitely coming bottom of the year."

Mr Stevens raised his eyebrows, and if he were a cartoon character he would have had a thought bubble coming out of his head that said: "Bloody women".

"Caolan should get a 2:1 hopefully. He certainly deserves it, the amount of work he did."

Mr Stevens again nodded. As I poured out my honest thoughts, he was not giving anything away.

"I hope Oisin gets a 2:1. I mean, he worked so hard. Too hard sometimes. It's just he said the exams didn't go too well, and I'm not too sure how good his revision technique is, but then who am I to say?"

"We'll see how the results go and then maybe I'll have a word with him next year."

"I'm sure you know best."

"I'm sure I don't. And the others?"

"Deary me, Mr Stevens, I feel like a mole. You'll get me shot, you know. Can you imagine if Leila found out I was talking about her behind her back?"

"This won't go any further, I can promise you that."

"Okay. Well, there's no reason why the rest shouldn't get 2:1s. I mean, I know you don't believe us, but we do all work quite hard, you know."

"Like when you're dancing away, or whatever else you lot get up to in that Life place."

"We need the odd break, Mr Stevens. All work and no play, and all that. Maybe you and Dr Tinsley could join us one night, have a few Aftershocks, do a few moves on the dance-floor, you know."

A Tale of Friendship, Love and Economics

"After-whats? No, thank you. I think I'll leave the nightclubs to you youngsters. And I'm only joking, I know you all... well, most of you... work hard, and I'm proud of you for it."

"Cheers, Mr Stevens."

"And tell me, Josh, how do you think *you* did in the exams?"

"Erm... I don't know. I mean, they were going alright until Stats, which was a right nightmare, but then everybody found it bad. I honestly don't know. I'll be a bit upset if I don't get a 2:1, but I'll survive."

"I think you'll be alright, Josh."

"Fingers crossed. And how are you, Mr Stevens? Any big dramas in your life at the moment?"

"No, not really. I'm trying to write a paper about the importance of protecting our manufacturing industry, and I'm worried my five-year-old son is going to be a capitalist. Apart from that, everything is going along nice and quiet."

"Surely the fact that our manufacturing industry is in rapid decline isn't that big a problem?"

Mr Stevens smiled and just about refused to take the bait.

"And what did your son do?"

"Oh, he lent me 40p, and then told me he wanted 50p back."

"You'd better keep an eye on him. Next he'll be telling you trade tariffs are a bad thing for the economy."

"I'd like to see him try. Right, I think it's about time we all moved on. The Music Society, or something like that, have booked Sherlock Court after us, and I don't fancy falling out with any more Fellows."

"See you soon, Mr Stevens"

"Goodbye, Josh."

There was no doubt that Mr Stevens was a good man. I would have liked to have asked him out for a drink with us all, and he probably would have liked it too and had a really good time, but it just wouldn't have been right. He was our Director of Studies and we were his students. I still found it a bit strange when he signed his name as Jonathon at the end of his emails to us, and for all my life I don't think I would refer to him by anything other than Mr Stevens. He had gained our respect by striking the right balance, and whilst we would have gone off him had he gone all high and mighty on us like some of the other Fellows, we also would have if he had tried to be one of us.

That Wednesday night Mr Stevens would have been pleased to know that we binned the last Life of the year in favour of an all-night punt. During the summer term the punting company ran a promotional offer whereby you could hire a punt out all night (it had to be back at 10 am the following morning) for just £10 and the deposit of a credit card. "All-Night Punting" was one of those things that seemed a great idea at the time, just the thing to do on a Wednesday night in May Week, but turned out to be a disaster. When young Nick MacLean proposed the idea, everyone was well keen.

"Oh yeah, it'll be ace. I mean, all night in a punt. Great idea."
"We could take a radio."
"And loads of food and drink."
"We could get pissed."
"It will be like a May Ball on a punt."
"We could take a tent and set up camp until the morning."
"Maybe we could finally use that barbecue"
"Must remember a torch, or whatever."
"And some blankets."
"And a heater."
"A heater?"
"Alright, maybe not a heater."
"This is going to be ace."
"Definitely."

The Fab Four economists, as well as geographer Nick MacLean, historian and general troublemaker Adam Sylvester, Movie Star Look-alike, and the wee Scot Faye signed up to the event that just had to be good. We acquired the punt from the office just after nine o'clock (Caolan and I "forgot" our credit cards, Oisin claimed he didn't have one, so Mark reluctantly put it on his) and were launched into the River Cam. All-night punts could only be used following the river on the quiet route up towards the village of Granchester, as it was not deemed sensible to have punts flying up and down the Backs at all hours. The punting company's regulations stated that only six people could fit in any one punt, and so Nick and Sly sneaked along the path and hopped aboard when we were out of sight. With all eight of us contained in our wooden vessel, conditions were a little cosy to say the least.

At night the route to Granchester resembled the Vietnam portrayed in all the movies. Trees overhung the river, thick clusters of reeds protruded sporadically from the water, and we sailed along to the tune of invisible insects. Never one to shy away from a *risqué* comment, Nick promptly warned us to look out for any "nips".

At first the trip was fun. It was a new experience to be punting in the dark, and the relaxed mood and tranquil rippling of passing water was very pleasant. Pretty soon, however, the novelty wore off. We had forgotten the radio and blankets, decided against taking the barbecue, and the only food and drink we possessed between us was Oisin's half-drunk bottle of water, and Faye's two custard creams that she had made very clear she wasn't prepared to share with anyone. It was freezing cold, and there was no room to move. Everyone was clearly uncomfortable, but some were making it more obvious than others.

"I'm bloody uncomfortable," exclaimed Faye.

"Me too," moaned the Movie Star Look-alike, "Josh, is there any chance I could put my legs here?"

A quick demonstration revealed where the Land Economist from Leeds wanted to put her legs.

"Can you bollocks," I replied.

As the minutes ticked away slowly, and Caolan managed to steer us into the bank for the seventh time, Sly decided to boost his ship-mates' flagging morale.

"Right, anyone keen for a game?"

"Which one?" I asked, as if I needed to.

"What about... Pass the Buck: Snog Web?"

"Here we go" whispered Caolan.

"Right," began Sly, who seemed to have been given a new lease of life, "I'll start, and we'll move down the boat, so Mark's next, then Josh. Okay?"

"Yes, Mr Sylvester, sir," replied the Movie Star Look-alike sarcastically.

Everyone knew the rules as Sly had made us play the game a hundred times before. As the go moved down the boat, you had to name a person who the previous person mentioned had pulled. We also knew that the chances were Sly was planning to cause some trouble with the game.

"Caolan O'Donnell" he began.

"Piss off, Sly," said the sideburned Irishman.

"It's your go, Novak," pointed out Sly, ignoring Caolan's comments as if they were merely the sound of passing wind.

"Erm" began Mark, which was how all his answers to questions in such games began, "Lauren Broad."

There was a few giggles around the boat. It was my go.

"Most males in Cambridge," I replied.

"Except you," replied Caolan once the second bout of laughter had died down and he had given himself adequate time to come up with a reply, "you probably wrote her a poem or a letter and she told you to piss off."

"Dickhead," I replied.

"Dickhead," came the echo, only in an Irish accent.

Mark and Oisin looked at each other but didn't speak.

"Right, next go," said Sly in a satisfied voice, "I'll start..."

After a few more rounds of "Pass the Buck: Snog Web," no-one in the punt was talking to each other. We sat there, cramped up like grumpy sardines in a tin, and shivering away in silence. Just when it seemed things couldn't get much worse, Oisin was attached by a killer swan.

"Jesus Christ," he yelled. "What the frickin' hell was that?"

It turned out Caolan had a phobia of swans, which brought a smile to my face and a look of terror to his. He cowered away in the far corner of the punt, nearly capsizing the craft on his travels.

We carried on going in silence for another ten minutes or so. It was clear that everyone was thinking the same thing, and finally Oisin said it,

"Hey, should we call it a night, or whatever?"

"Yes," was the unanimous response.

Nick skilfully turned the punt around, and we began the long journey back home, still in silence, but now more because of the cold than any lingering bad feelings. We secured our wooden punt with the padlock we had been provided with and headed back to college. We went straight to the bar to get some much-needed food, drink and warmth. There was little doubt our all-night punting adventure had been a failure. It was half-past ten.

Chapter 71

Dad was picking me up early the next morning, so most of Thursday daytime was spent packing up all my stuff. Under normal circumstances I would have certainly left it all until the morning, but I wanted to make sure I had time to say goodbye to everyone before I left. There was no way in the world it was all going to fit in the car, even accounting for the things I was leaving in the storeroom, such as the sacred Kerplunk set and the unused barbecue and complementary 5 kg bag of equally unused charcoal. I could here my Dad's voice as his eyes fell upon the ever-growing stack of belongings piled up in the corner of my room ready for departure: "Bloody hell, Josh, did you think I was coming in a lorry or something?" I started practising my polite smile.

Having "folded" my clothes (Mum was going to kill me) and rammed them into the suitcases, I began the task of taking down my posters and photos from the wall. I soon realised why the college were so against the use of Blu-Tack, as the departure of my photos left in its wake a white wall-face with hundreds of blue freckles. I flicked through the photos of my uni friends before I tucked them away in the sleeve, and saw snapshots of happy times; captured moments of days out, evenings in, Bops and May Balls, starring everyone from Dennis the Menace to Laurence Llewellyn-Bowen. I got the same shivery feeling that I often got when remembering times gone by, feeling both happy at the memory and sad because the moment was gone forever. But these were memories that would stay with me long after the pain of a broken heart had crumbled away. I paused for a moment, lost in thought, and then quickly kicked my football around in my room to remind me that I was not a girl. Satisfied that my masculinity had returned, I carefully rolled up Messrs Lennon and King, finally allowing them to take their eyes off each other after nine months and have a bit of time to themselves, and wondered whether they would have a place in my new room in Chads.

I started my packing to the sound of The Beatles, and finished it off, a couple of hours later, to Bob Dylan. Then, just as I was wondering what to do next, Mark came around to talk about the holiday.

We had been chatting about the possibility of going on holiday together all term, but in the last few weeks, realising that time was against us and we thus needed to get our arses into gear, it had become a reality. I was long past going on holiday with my Mum, and I had missed out on all the arrangements with my mates back home, where no doubt another two-week drink and sex fest to Tenerife, Shaga-luff or Vala-cacky was the order of the day. And so, as well as the fact that I quite liked the idea of going on holiday with my uni friends, it was also imperative that I did, or else I would be stuck alone in sunny Preston for three months.

Before we could do anything, there were two major questions that needed answering: where were we going to go; and who was going to come? The first was far easier than the second. As soon as Caolan said, whilst tucking into a bacon-double cheeseburger, that he had always wanted to go inter-railing around Europe, everyone suddenly remembered that they had as well. It was the kind of holiday that university students were supposed to go on, and a refreshing change from the Club 18–30 scene that I had tasted enough times. That was that sorted, but who were we going to take with us? The general consensus was that girls tended to fuck up holidays, especially holidays that were likely to involve sleeping rough and having to be ready for certain times, so that ruled out half of the world's population. Seeing as Caolan, Mark, Oisin and myself were there in Burger King when the idea was conceived, we were automatic choices. We all agreed that geographers Joe Porter and Nick MacLean would be good holiday-mates, along with cool historian Jude. Nick signed up straight away, Joe, knowing that his grand plans for working all summer and earning a fortune would no doubt amount to nothing, said he couldn't afford it, and Jude told us he'd think about it but to go ahead and book without him.

We didn't know anyone else well enough to ask them on their own, and if more than a couple more people signed up to the trip, things could get awkward when it came to getting accommodation and stuff. No, having thought about it, we decided that five was a fine and dandy number for travelling.

It was looking like Jude wasn't going to come after all, so the five of us took the initiative and grabbed a few brochures from the travel agents, perusing them on a fairly bright Sunday afternoon slap bang in the middle of our dark days of revision. The cheapest option seemed to be to buy one rail pass that allowed you to go on any train instead of buying individual tickets. We decided that two months at home would be sufficient time to earn enough money to go, and hence pencilled in three weeks in September as our prospective dates. We got out a biro and drew a rough route around a map of Europe, starting in Germany, going through Italy, and then a quick circuit around Eastern Europe. Nick reckoned that this route would nicely fill our three weeks, giving us sufficient time to spend in the good places, but making sure we didn't dilly-dally anywhere. We nodded in agreement. Being the only geographer, Nick felt obliged to say these kinds of things. Such a route required the purchase of a three zone inter-rail ticket, coming in at a hefty £199. To make sure that all this talk and planning actually amounted to something, and to give ourselves something else to look forward to if we got through the coming exams, we promptly booked five cheap return flights over the internet from London Stanstead to Frankfurt Haan, flying with Ryan-air. We even applied to the college travel grant fund and, having claimed the trip would be of great educational value because we could see how the Eastern European economies were getting along in their bid to join the EU, were rewarded with a cheque each for £175 – the first positive monetary returns to our Cambridge degree. Team Europe was born. Sorted. Apart from one small thing.

It was not that we'd forgotten about Sly, it was just no-one wanted to be the one to bring his name up. I was certain that I didn't want him on the trip; I didn't like the guy and trouble tended to follow him around wherever he went. I was pretty sure the others, apart from maybe Nick, felt the same, however no-one ever said anything. I knew that as soon as his name was thrown into the equation, we would no doubt feel obliged to invite him as everyone kept their true feelings well hidden. We had decided not to talk about the trip in front of people in case anyone was offended that we hadn't asked them along, and this policy was implicitly extended towards Sly. Whenever he walked into the room, all talk of holidays and trains was promptly brought to an end. With just one day to go before we went home for the summer, it was looking like this policy had proved successful.

Mark had come around to give me my copy of our flight details, to have a chat about how safe I reckoned Slovakia was ("Is that in Europe?"), and to tell me that the two Irish were talking about going to Bella Pasta tonight for a kind of "farewell to first year" meal. I told him to sign me up.

I had never eaten in Bella Pasta, nor felt any strong inclination to. My policy had always been not to order pasta in a restaurant, even though it was one of my favourite foods, because I knew it cost about 20p to make. Caolan reminded me that such behaviour was economically irrational, and I reminded him that he didn't have a clue what that phrase meant. Moreover, the fact that it had "pasta" in its name suggested to me that this particular restaurant chain didn't specialise in pizza, which I was a huge fan of. Nevertheless, everyone else seemed keen and I always tried to avoid judging a book by its cover. Anyway, I don't think it would have been fitting, or perhaps it would have been *too* fitting, for our last meal of our first year together to be spent in Wetherspoons with the inevitable Beer-Burger delicacy.

Joe and Nick had a geography drinks party to go to, so it was just the Fab Four that walked into Bella Pasta on that Thursday night. Oh, and Adam Sylvester as well, who was at a lose end when Oisin had bumped into him around Main Court. We were shown to a table in the corner of the restaurant by an overly friendly waitress, who was surely too old for the pig-tails that were happily dancing on the back of her head. She left us with five menus and one cheesy smile. I decided to go crazy and opt for a mushroom pizza, and Caolan offered to go halves on some dough-balls for starters. Sly announced that he could easily consume a plateful of dough-balls all on his own, and promptly ordered them up along with a Filetto di Salmone. Mark and Oisin declined a starter and after much deliberation, several mind-changes, and several "For God's sake, will you hurry up, I'm starving"s, they went for Penne Marco Polo and Gnocchi alla Romana respective. Caolan's choice of main course was the same as Mark's, although the sideburned Irishman was quick to point out that he chose it first. Our wallets, light and worn out after a busy and pricey May Week, couldn't stretch to a bottle of wine each, so we got two bottles for the table. When he saw the prices, Oisin announced that he was sticking to water; *tap* water, he reminded the smiley waitress several times. As our food was delivered and we were once more left alone by Ms Piggy, we began to chat.

"Looks quite good, doesn't it?" I said, immediately swallowing as my mouth filled up with saliva.

"All food looks good when you're starving," replied Caolan.

I didn't bother responding, opting for a few mouthfuls of pizza instead.

"So, this is the Last Supper," I said, as my ravenous appetite began to be satisfied.

"What?" said Sly, not looking up from his food.

"Well, it's the last meal we'll have together as first years."

"Hopefully the last meal we'll have together full-stop," said Caolan.

He was beginning to annoy me, so I happily took the last dough-ball whilst he was pre-occupied chasing an elusive bit of penne around his plate.

"It's been a funny old year, or whatever, hasn't it?" said Oisin, serviette in one hand, knife in the other.

"Mmm," replied Mark in agreement.

"Will you pass us the salt please?"
"Josh, you've got a pizza. Why do you need salt?"
"I always put salt on my pizza. That's how the Italians do it."
"God, you talk some shite."
"Yeah, yeah. Hey, whilst we're all here, let's go through everyone's favourite bits of the year," I suggested excitedly.
"Oh here we go," said Caolan, with a flick of his head.
"Here we go, what?"
"Well, you always do this, don't you?"
"Do what?"
"You know, favourite bits of this, worst bits of that, top ten of this, bottom five of that, all those gay games you like playing."
"Well, I apologise for trying to make conversation. I take it Caolan doesn't want to play, does anybody else?"
As happened so often, Mark saved me.
"Well, May Week as a whole was brilliant, but if I had to pick one single thing, then it would probably have to be Trinity May Ball"
"Good call."
"Yep."
"I mean, all that food and drink, and it was quality stuff as well. And then you had the ice-rink and hot-air balloon, then the music was awesome, and then the Red Devils pop up at the end. What a night."
"Aye."
"It certainly was."
"Well, thanks for that, Mr Novak. Oisin, do you have one?"
"Jeepers, I don't know."
He began ruffling his hair, which seemed to be a necessary part of the Irishman's thinking process, as if he was hoping the answer was lost somewhere in his shaggy main and would just fall out onto the table with enough ruffling.
"It'll be the end of third year and we'll have graduated before he comes up with an answer."
"I'll tell you what, I'll come back to you, Okay?"
The shaggy-haired Irishman nodded.
"Sly?"
"Well... It's got to be the overnight punt. Classic."
"Oh yeah, that was just brilliant."

"Shite."
"Whose crappy idea was that anyway?"
"Not mine."
"Well it wasn't bloody mine."
"We'll assume it was Nick's seeing as he isn't here to defend himself."
"Anyway, go on Sly."
"Alright, my favourite moment was probably either the boat race or Eurovision night."
"Well, which one are you going to choose?"
"What?"
"Well, you can't pick two."
"Why not?"
"You just can't, alright? It's against the rules."
"Bloody hell. Alright, then I guess I'll go for the boat race. Getting Novak to ask that barman if he could have a deep, long hard screw up against the wall, or whatever it was, was a classic."
"Yep."
"You are a dick, Mark."
"Yep."
"Right, Oisin, any chance you are ready to share your best moment?"
"Aye, I think so."
"We're all ears."
"Well, there are so many, and it's so hard to chose, or whatever, and I don't really know, and…"
"You must have so many splinters in your arse the amount of time you spend on the fence."
"Come on, Oisin, get on with it."
"Okay, well I guess it would have to be Trinity May Ball."
"Mark's already had that one."
"We wait all this time and you come up with one that's already been said."
"Well, I'm sorry, but it was my favourite moment, or whatever."
"And why, Oisin? On second thoughts, if this is going to take another half-hour and then you are just going to say what Mark said, then forget it."
"Do you want to hear, or not?"
"Yes, go on."

A Tale of Friendship, Love and Economics

"Well, it was just frickin' amazing, or whatever. As much champagne as you could drink, oysters, caviar, hot-air balloons, Ash, Jason, Red Devils. Amazing, just frickin' amazing."

"That's pretty much what Mark said, but with a few frickin's and a few or whatevers thrown in."

"I don't know why I bother sometimes."

"Neither do we."

"Right, Josh, your turn."

"What about my go?"

"I thought you weren't playing. I thought it was a gay game."

"Yeah, well, I've changed my mind."

I smiled at him, and Caolan chose to ignore it.

"Right, well, my favourite moment of this year was…"

"Tucking into Lauren Broad?" interrupted Sly.

"No, Mr Sylvester, it was probably hearing all the stories of what you got up to that night you went mad. Is she out of hospital yet?"

"Allegedly."

"Yes Josh, you're right, allegedly"

"Piss off, you two."

"Come on, Caolan."

"Right, I think I'm going to go for Freshers' Week. It was good meeting a load of different people, and just getting pissed all the time. Unfortunately, I had to meet you lot as well, but then you can't have everything, can you?"

"It's a miracle you've managed to put up with us for a year."

"It's not been easy"

"We are truly grateful, Caolan."

"I hope so. Right, Bailey, I'm pretty sure the whole object of this game was for you to tell us all your best moment. Let me guess, was it falling in love and making a dick out of yourself for the seventh time, or did you prefer the eighth?"

"You are piss funny, Caolan O'Donnell, you really are."

"Tell me something I don't know."

"Right, unless nob-head over there has any objections, I'll tell you my best moment."

"I wouldn't dream of interrupting you, Joshua."

"Okay. Well, I'm not to sure what my favourite moment was. Stupid question whoever asked it. It really has been such a good year. I mean, Freshers' Week was brilliant, and May Week was, and I quote, 'frickin' amazing,' and the boat race was ace, and the Kerplunk days were great..."

"Gay."

"...and the Bops were always a good laugh, especially that Granny one in first term, and I loved the formal halls, especially birthday ones and the Christmas one, and just taking it easy watching *Neighbours* and the Creek was good, and footy on the park and Beer-Burgers in Spoons, and..."

"Jesus Christ, Josh, we're not asking you to write a book on it, just give us one moment for God's sake, so we can end this shitty game of yours."

"I do apologise, Caolan. Right, well, I'd probably go for Eurovision night. It was our last big session before hardcore revision really kicked in, and right from breakfast in the morning until the water battle at night, it was just a great day."

"Good choice, Josh."

"Why thank you, Mr Kerrigan."

"Right, that killed about five minutes, any other great games for us?"

"Well, what about what's everyone getting up to over summer?"

Shit. Not the greatest idea I've ever had. As long as no-one mentions the holiday, that'll be just fine.

"Erm," said Mark, and then another couple of erms, and then, "I'll be working at the Bank of England for a couple of months, trying to earn some cash."

"Bank of bloody England, have you heard him?"

"Big job."

"Barclays, or any other high-street branch just isn't enough for our Novak."

"Central Bank or no bank."

"Don't get pissed and start messing around with interest rates."

"God, if you've been on the vodka the previous night, the economy won't know what's hit it in the morning."

"The Novak Boom."

"When asked why he cut interest rates by a record 7 per cent, Governor of the Bank of England, Mark Novak, simply shrugged his shoulders and proceeded to be sick on the pavement."

"Could be just what we need."

"Give it a rest, economists."

"I'll probably do the same," said Oisin, when he was sure Caolan and I had run out of material about Mark's job, "although not at the Bank of England."

"And not with the vodka either."

"Where will you work, Oisin?"

"Oh, probably just in an accountant's in Derry. It's crappy money, or whatever, but it's easy work."

Answers seemed to be moving around the table in an anti-clockwise direction, which meant next up was Sly.

"I don't know what I'll be doing," he began, keeping his eyes fixed on his food. "I mean, I'm working as a security guard for July and August, but I wouldn't mind going on holiday in September, you know."

Then there was silence. Painful, fork-fiddling, feet-shuffling, desert-menu-staring silence. Caolan spoke next, and I just prayed he was going to launch into his plans for the summer, probably involving doing no work and going out at night.

"Erm... why... why don't you come on holiday with us?"

I kicked the Irishman on the shin, but the words were already out there.

"Well, nobody invited me."

"Nobody was invited it just sort of happened" continued the Irishman. "Come along, you'd be more than welcome."

"Haven't you lot sorted everything out though? Isn't it too late?"

Yes, yes, yes.

"Not really," I said.

"All we've done is book a cheap return flight to Frankfurt. I bet if you do it tomorrow you could even get on the same flight as us, or whatever," said Oisin.

"Yeah," added Mark, feeling obliged to sound as positive as the rest of them.

"Sweet," said Sly.

And that was that. At 11 am the following day I received a text from Adam Sylvester saying he was all booked up and ready for action. Team Europe was now six, and I was positively dreading it.

Chapter 72

Predictably, Dad was early, and I wasn't ready. I ignored his first two calls, rolling over happy to assume they were part of my dream, but felt obliged to answer the third.

"Hi Dad... yeah, sorry about that... no I was not sleeping... I was, erm, returning some books to the library... no I won't still be in my bed clothes when you come up. Deary me, Dad, you really do need to learn to have a bit more faith in me." Bollocks. As Dad rattled the door, I slipped on a pair of jeans, and a pair of odd socks. At least I had packed.

Whilst Dad loaded up the car, I tried to catch as many people as I could before I setoff back home. The two Irish had caught the 7 am flight back to Derry that morning (as a gesture of the strength of our friendship I told Oisin to knock at my door as he was leaving, knowing full well there wasn't a chance in hell that I would wake up and that he was too nice to knock anyway), and I had said goodbye to Mark, geographers Joe and Nick, and good riddance to Sly in the bar last night. Happily, I even managed to fit in one last sentimental late-night bowl of cereals sitting, as so many times before, on the steps outside my room with my good friend Jude (using the still unseen Kip's milk, of course). I reckoned there were only three people I really needed to say goodbye to this morning.

I descended the stairs of M-block, and knocked on her door. There was no squeaky, posh answer from inside. Fortunately, she was one of the few people who had a piece of paper pinned to the outside of her door, together with a biro held in place by some Blu-Tack. I detached the pen, leaning against the door, and started to write, stopping after every few words to shake the ink back into the right place.

Dear Elizabeth,

I don't know what you could be doing on a Friday morning that is more important than sitting in your room and waiting for me to knock. Anyway, I just popped around to say goodbye and to wish you a very happy summer. Say hello to your Mum for me, and tell her that Josh Bailey Gardening Services will be operating throughout the months of July and August. I hope your little sister has finally come to terms with my departure (it usually takes most women three to four months), and that she has perfected that accidental hand on the thigh trick.

Take good care of yourself, and if you happen to be passing by the Grim North, be sure to pay us a visit.

Loads of love,
Josh xxx

I looked with satisfaction at the illegible scrawl I had created, and continued on my journey out of M-block.

Next up was a trip across Main Court and up the windy, narrow staircases of Bull. Happily, no note was needed this time.

"Oh, hi Josh."

"Hi Francesca. Have I come at a bad time?"

"No, not at all. Come in."

"Cheers."

"Sorry, the room's a bit of a mess"

"No probs, you should have seen mine yesterday."

"And sorry, I look a bit of a mess."

"You look beautiful as ever, Francesca."

"I know, the 'just got out of bed, still in my pyjamas, not brushed my hair, or put on any make-up' look is really sexy. And to what do I owe this visit?"

"After all this time, do I need a reason to visit you?"

"I'm all out of custard creams."

"That's fine. No, I just came to say goodbye."

"You're off today?"

"Certainly am. Dad's loading the car up as we speak."

"Do you not have to help?"

"Told him I'd be along in two minutes, and that was twenty minutes ago. When are you off?"

"Dad's coming tomorrow morning, so that's why the room's a mess now. The last thing I feel like doing right now is packing, but I know I won't get up at six tomorrow to do it."

"Just slap on a few tunes, sing along, and the time'll fly by."

"I might just do that, Josh, I might just do that. Oh, I'll miss you over the holidays."

"I'll miss you too."

"It's gonna be weird not seeing people for three months after living on top of each other for a year, isn't it?"

"I know. Be glad to see that back of some, though."

"Surely not. You like everyone, Josh."
"With a few exceptions, one of whom is coming on holiday with me."
"I'm sure it'll be fine, and if not, at least you'll have a few stories to tell."
"Hopefully none of them involving a murder. Anyway, I best get going. Look, Francesca, I just wanted to say, and I'm really shit at saying stuff like this, but thanks for always being there for me this year. I know I've taken up way too much of your time with my shitty problems, and I'm sorry for that, and I hope you know that I really appreciate everything you do for me."
"Don't go getting all emotional and corny on me Joshua Bailey, you'll make me cry."
"I'm sorry. I just wanted to say thanks, that's all."
"Well, there's absolutely no need. For a start, if I wasn't listening to you, all I would be doing was wasting my time watching some crappy soap opera, and your life is far more entertaining than that, and, secondly, you always cheer me up."
"I suppose I am pretty hilarious."
"Well, I wouldn't go that far, but you are quite funny."
"And listen, you know I'll always be there if you need to talk about anything. I do have some big insights occasionally."
"I know, and thank you."
"Right, well give us a hug and I'll be off."
"Okay, and you will ring me over the holidays, won't you?"
"I'll see if I get a chance. I might not get a spare moment in these next three months, especially in crazy, happening Preston."
"You better had do."
"Take care of yourself, Francesca."
"You too, Josh."
"See you soon."
"Bye, and have a safe trip home."

I walked down the stairs of Bull, and across Main Court for the last time as a first year. I waved across the grass to Buzz and Mick the Cook as they wheeled an empty metal food trolley into hall.

"You off home, you northern monkey?"
"I am indeed. Can't wait to mix with people who talk proper again."
"It's Yorkshire you're from, innit?"

I chose not to answer that one.

A Tale of Friendship, Love and Economics

"Hey listen, you two better get into shape over summer if you want to get into my 3rd XI next year."

"My body is a temple, Josh."

"A temple full of shit," replied Mick.

"Shut up, you fat bastard."

"You shut up."

"See you later, lads," I shouted, sensing my contribution to the conversation was over, and bid them farewell with a wave.

I ventured through the stone archway, across Sherlock Court, and back up the stairs of M-block. Two down, one to go.

"Well, hello there Mr Bailey."

"Hi, Faye."

"You off on your wee way home now, I presume."

"Nothing gets past you, does it?"

"It certainly doesn't. I saw your Dad lugging all your stuff down the stairs. I asked him if he needed a hand, but he said that if you weren't helping, he could hardly bloody well ask me to. He looked like he was struggling."

"He'll be fine, he needs the exercise."

"I have to catch the bloody train home tomorrow, as my Dad won't get off his lazy arse and drive down."

"It's a long way from Glasgow, I suppose."

"Too bloody right, it is, and now I have to spend it all on my own on a bloody train."

"Have you no colouring in you can to do get ready for next year's geography course?"

"Very funny."

"I try my best. And how have you been these last couple of days?"

"Oh, you know, fine."

"Have you done anything exciting?"

"Had a wee bit too much wine the other night, and I felt a bit poorly in the morning. Duane made me a wee cup of tea, and soon I felt better."

"And how is Duane?"

"Oh, he's fine as well."

"You two going to meet up over the holidays?"

"Aye, probably, although he's too scared to come to Scotland since I told him that my Dad hates all Englishmen, especially the posh southern ones."

"The poor lad. So, things are still going alright between you two?"

"Aye, things are going fine, you know."
"Good."
"And you, Josh, tell me has that wee Imogene girl come to her senses yet?"
"Nah, we're just going to be friends, I think. Probably best that way, you know."
"That's a shame. Anyway, blondes are stupid, especially ones from New Hall."
"You're probably right."
"And have you your eyes on any more ladies?"
"No, I'm taking a break from women for a while."
"Not for too long, I hope."
"I don't think I am capable of lasting too long anyway."
"I'm sure you'll be beating them off with a stick next year. I'll bring a wee broom with me, and we can shoo them all out of the flat."
"Sounds good to me. Hey, has Mary Jane gone home yet?"
"Nah, she's off tomorrow as well. She's in her room now, I think."
"Oh."
"You gonna pop round and say goodbye?"
"Don't think so."
"Oh Josh, what happened to you two?"
"I don't know, Faye, I really don't know. Should make next year pretty interesting, though."
"Aye, it certainly will. Poor Polish Mary doesn't know what she's letting herself in for, asking to live with us."
"We don't know what we're letting ourselves in for letting her live with us."
"True, but I'm sure she'll make an interesting flatmate whatever happens."
"I'm sure she will. Well, Faye, I think that's my Dad I hear stomping up the stairs, so I best be off."
"Okay, Josh, you have a safe trip home, and a lovely summer."
"Farewell, Faye McLaughlin."
"Farewell, Joshua Bailey."

I hesitated as I passed Mary Jane's room, but kept on walking. Now wasn't the time.

Dad was not impressed that I hadn't helped him carry my stuff to the car.

"Just like you're bloody mother," he said, in between heavy breaths, and whilst wiping the sweat off his reddened forehead with an old green handkerchief.
"Have you got everything?"
"Yes, Dad."
"Keys?"
"Yes, Dad."
"Wallet?"
"Yes Dad."
"Mobile?"
"Yes, Dad."
"Are you sure?"
"Yes, Dad now do you fancy going home at some stage?"
"We'd probably be home now if you'd helped me carry your stuff instead of gallivanting around college looking for girls".

I send Dad to wait and recover in the car whilst I had one last check in my room. M14, the room that had held the inaugural Kerplunk World Championship and the religiously attended *Neighbours* and *Dawson's Creek* sessions, the room where I had written over thirty essays, one letter and two poems, the room where I had sat in silence when a cloud came over me on that first Sunday some nine months ago, and where I had more recently shed my first tear in over ten years, the room where we had squirted the open-top tour bus as the late springtime sun poured in through the windows, the room where the Stalking, Philosophising Preacher from Bradford had warned me to stay away from the Movie Star Look-alike, the room that used to be visited by a strawberry blond neighbour every night what now seemed like so long ago, the room that had been frequented at some stage by most people in my year, the room where I had turned nineteen and supposedly grown up in the process, the room where more often than not I had been reminded just what really mattered and just how stupid I could be, now looked bare and empty, stripped of all possessions, but filled forever with a thousand memories. I picked up my keys and locked the door.

I handed in my keys and signed out for the final time at the Plodge, wishing the Porter with the bowler hat a happy summer, and getting a friendly grunt in return. I climbed into Dad's car and turned on the radio. Robbie was singing about the price of fame whilst the midday sun secured its spot in the sky for the afternoon. I texted my best friend back home to find out if anyone was going out over the weekend, and called my Mum to let her know I was on my way home. Sitting there, as the world went by my window, I could not have known what next year was going to bring. A French Connection, a stint in a boy band, a taste of stardom on primetime TV and the most bizarre love triangle imaginable may as well have been far-fetched plot-lines in a soap opera for all the relevance they had to my life on that Saturday afternoon in the June of 2001. All that I knew for certain was that there was a long way yet to go in this little tale. To borrow the sentiments of a great war-time leader; this was not the end, it was not even the beginning of the end, but it was, perhaps, the end of the beginning.